FATE OF EXCALIBUR

THE ABDUCTION CYCLES

JOHN ELIJAH CRESSMAN

ISBN: 978-1-954524-13-2 (Paperback)
ISBN: 978-1-954524-14-9 (Hardcover)
ISBN: 978-1-954524-12-5 (Amazon Kindle)
ISBN: 978-1-954524-15-6 (Audiobook)
Any references to historical events, real people, or real places are used fictitiously. Names, characters, and places are products of the author's twisted imagination.

Front cover image by Christina Myrvold
Editing By Celestial Rince.

Printed by Maverick-Gage Publishing in conjunction with IngramSpark, in the United States of America.
First printing edition 2021.
Maverick-Gage Publishing
Allentown, PA

info@maverick-gage.com
www.maverick-gage.com
John Elijah Cressman
www.johnecressman.com

Dedicated to my first grand-niece, Lacie

PROLOGUE

Ethan looked out over the ocean as the twin suns were setting on the horizon. Between the two suns was the black hole that, along with the suns, reminded him that he wasn't in Kansas anymore. He wasn't anywhere on Earth. He was on another planet.

The smell of salt and the slight fishy odor was reminiscent of oceans of Earth but that's where the similarities stopped. Water spouts, hundreds of feet tall, rose and fell all over the ocean in a beautiful, if terrifying, dance.

He wasn't sure exactly what caused the spouts and had no real way of finding out. The moon he was on, and he was certain it was a moon, rotated around a huge, ringed gas giant that reminded him of Saturn. His prevailing theory was that the gravity from the planet was somehow causing the spouts, but he had no way to prove that.

"Are you coming back to the fire?" Nia asked from behind him.

Ethan turned and gave his wife a smile. "I'll just be another minute."

Nia nodded, spun and walked back to the fire, her hips swaying hypnotically. The swaying of her hips caused her fox tail to sway back and forth. Yes, she had a long, puffy fox tail and matching fox ears but the rest of her was all too human.

Like him, she had been abducted by aliens too and dropped onto this strange world with no explanation. Unlike him, she wasn't human. Nia was a foxling. She had the athletic body of a 20-year-old human dancer or ballerina, but her body was covered in a very short, soft fur. And, of course, there were the fox ears poking through her long, curly auburn hair to remind him that she wasn't human.

And the foxgirl wasn't the only alien. When he first arrived, he'd met an elf named Yuliana, and a dwarf named Ainslee. He didn't think they were an actual elf and dwarf, from Earth mythology. Rather, they were aliens who appeared similar to the folklore of his homeworld.

Now, both of them were gone. Ainslee, who had been their dwarven tank, had never wanted to adventure and had decided in Camelot that she wanted to return to the village of Hawkshead and start a smithy.

Ainslee had been gruff and sometimes more than a little annoying, but she had been a steadfast companion who had done her best. It had only been a day since she left, but he was already missing her coarse banter.

Then there was Yuliana, the elven druid. She had decided to stay back at Camelot and help the tree lords, or what she called the caretakers. On her world, she had tended a grove where the caretakers had lived, so once she found out there were caretakers on this world, there had been no stopping her.

Yuliana had been a druid and had been able to do healing magic. But she hadn't been the only one who could do magic. Ethan could do magic as well. He was a wizard.

Ethan still had no idea exactly how the magic worked or why it worked. Perhaps there was some strange effect of the nearby black hole. He could be in an entirely different universe where the laws of the universe, as he knew them, were different.

Together, his group of alien friends had stopped the village of Hawkshead from being destroyed by a tribe of kobolds who wanted to burn it down. It had been a tough fight, but they'd saved the village and Ethan had been made the mayor.

After that, he and his original companions had sought out an ancient library that was actually a trap that transported them to another planet. Ethan had managed to figure out a way to open a portal back to this planet, but they'd been ambushed by a rogue warlock.

They'd returned to Hawkshead, only to find that some sound from the nearby mine was scaring away all the game and the people of the village were starving. Ethan and his group had found a trapped tomb in the mine and after investigating it, discovered it held the remains of King Arthur - yes, the real King Arthur.

They'd also discovered the Holy Grail, a magical cup that could cure nearly any wound once a day per person.

Almost as valuable as the Grail was the magic pool that Arthur was buried near. The Fountain of Youth.

The group found that the Holy Grail had been disturbed by a nest of giant alien spiders, including a gigantic queen. They'd defeated the spiders, but Ethan had almost died and only the Grail had been able to restore him.

Once the spiders were dead, Ethan and his friends had drunk from the pool and had received immortality. They would never grow old, but would stay the age they were now. They could still be killed by other means; they just wouldn't age.

After returning the Grail to King Arthur's tomb, Ethan had discovered the location of Camelot and a library that was a treasure trove of magical knowledge. He'd convinced his friends to come with him to Camelot to investigate but it had been a trap.

Mordred, the son of King Arthur and Guinevere, had transformed into a demon and had manipulated Ethan the entire time. When they found Camelot, it was in ruins and there was no library. Only Mordred, who was now a squid-headed demon, and his mother, Guinevere, waited to capture and transform them into demons.

Ethan had killed Mordred and freed Guinevere from her son's mind control. The former queen had decided to come with them to find Excalibur, Arthur's magical sword, but Ethan still wasn't sure about her or her motivations.

She was one of his new companions. While Nia, Yuliana and Ainslee had been his original companions, he'd met new friends too. The first had been Par'karr, a kobold. Kobolds were small lizard men, about three feet tall and scaled, with long lizard tails.

Par'karr was a summoner, a type of mage who could summon a specific type of creature from another dimension. In the kobold's case, they were rabbits - demon rabbits. At least, that's how Ethan thought of them. They had long unicorn-like horns and glowing red eyes. But Par'karr loved them and they seemed to like him.

The next friend he'd met was Michalus. Michalus was an elf, like Yuliana. Unlike the female elf, he was a native to this world. He was a wizard and capable of all sorts of magic. He was also an experienced enchanter and had created a number of interesting items - even an invisible shed.

Then there was his most recent new friend, Guinevere. Like he and his friends, she was immortal and still looked like a college-aged young woman. The ex-queen of Camelot looked like a beauty pageant winner, with a slim, athletic body, blue eyes and long golden blonde hair.

And yet, despite her appearance, she was over a thousand years old and an amazing warrior. He had also learned that she was Merlin's daughter. Yet, despite her magical lineage, she seemed to have no magical ability of her own.

He wanted to trust the woman, but he barely knew her. Add that to the fact that she'd been under Mordred's mental control for hundreds of years, and Ethan still wasn't completely sure he could, or should, trust her.

Still, she had agreed to help them find the magical sword, Excalibur. Ethan knew the legends of Excalibur, but he had no idea what actual abilities it had. Nor did he even know whether or not it still existed. He just knew Arthur had used it to kill the Doemenagg queen.

Ethan frowned as he thought of the Doemenagg. They were a race of giant, praying mantis-type creatures and he was pretty sure they were the ones responsible for killing wizards and sucking out their brains.

In Camelot, two of them had attacked their group and they'd barely managed to fight them off. During his fight with one of them, he'd used a form of Mental magic to enter the creature's mind. There he'd found some sort of mental link to another, much more powerful mind. It was the Queen, he was sure of it.

He was also sure the Queen knew about him. If so, that meant he and Michalus were in even more danger. Now, the Doemenaggs knew who to look for. All he could do was continue to hone his magic skills and hope they were enough when he met them again. And he would meet them again. He was sure of it.

"Ethan," Nia said. "The food is ready. Come and eat!"

Turning away from the ocean, and his own thoughts, Ethan walked over to the fire and took the offered food. He may as well enjoy this brief moment of peace. Who knew what the journey ahead had in store for them.

A fishman, or Akugyo, lunged at Ethan with a trident, trying to skewer him through the chest on its wickedly barbed tip. A second fishman tried to circle around him while the first kept him distracted. It didn't work.

Even with rain in his eyes, Ethan saw the fishman's movement. Channeling *Mana* through the Chymera crystal in his own trident, he summoned *Air*. Willing the tendrils of *Air*, Ethan grabbed the Akugyo trying to flank him. He dragged the startled fishman into the path of his friend's trident. The trident impaled the fishman causing its eyes to bug out.

Ethan thrust the creature back against the trident with more *Air*, causing the spikes of the trident to burst from the back of the unfortunate Akugyo. The creature opened its mouth in a silent scream, before collapsing to the ground with the weapon buried deep within it.

> ***Reef Clan Raider dies.***
> ***You gain 30 experience. Experience to next level 11,380.***

An Akugyo's body flopped to the ground as Guinevere sliced off its head in a huge spray of pungent blood. A moment later, the head dropped to the ground, next to the twitching carcass.

Another fishman stammered, three demon rabbit horns buried in its chest. The creature looked down, seeming not to understand what was happening. One of its arms rose as if to paw at the embedded rabbits as they thrashed and squirmed. After a moment, the thing's eyes glazed over and it dropped to the ground.

Nia danced between two others, slicing the legs of one while deflecting the trident of the other. At the same time, a blast of fire from Michalus turned another of the Akugyo into a charred corpse that toppled to the ground.

The foxgirl, in constant motion, sliced one of her scimitars across its neck, a deep gash in the neck of the first fishman. The creature dropped its trident and grabbed at its neck before dropping to its knees and then collapsing.

Continuing her motion, she whipped the scimitar low and when the other Akugyo blocked low, she spun in towards it, slamming her other scimitar into its chest. The stunned fishman's eyes went wide as it looked down at the blade sticking in its chest before the trident slipped from its lifeless fingers and it joined its friend on the ground.

That left one last fishman. The one near Ethan. Pointing his trident at the remaining enemy, he channeled his magic. With a blast of *Air*, he slammed the last Reef Clan Raider backwards, just as Par'karr's demon rabbits launched themselves into the air. Their momentum, combined with the fishman's momentum, caused their horns to imbed themselves deep into the creature's back. The Akugyo stiffened and it collapsed face first into the dirt.

Reef Clan Raider dies.
    You gain 25 experience. Experience to next level 11,355.

"That's the last of them," Guinevere growled. The warrior looked around at the ten fishman bodies that now littered what had been their camp. "Why in the Nine Realms do the Akugyo keep attacking us?"

"A better question is: how do they even know we're here?" Michalus said as he tried to wipe some fishman blood from his own clothes. "The dune almost completely obscures us."

Par'karr frowned and pointed up. "Rain too."

"It does seem coincidental that they keep showing up during the rain," Ethan agreed. It was true. With the exception of the first attack, before Camelot, all of the attacks had taken place at night and all during rain. "Could they be causing the weather?"

Michalus shook his head. "I don't know of any wizard capable of controlling weather."

Ethan frowned and sent his globe of light around in a wide circle around the camp, making sure there were no more fishmen lurking around. Satisfied there were none, he brought the light orbs back to hover over his head and wiped the rain out of his face. "So it's just a coincidence? Or are they more easily able to survive on land during the rain?"

Most of the group shrugged but Ethan hadn't really expected anyone to know the answer. He glanced from Michalus to Guinevere. They both brought up good points earlier.

This was the fourth such attack since they'd portaled from Camelot, back to the shore. They'd been traveling south for only two weeks and in that time, they'd fought off three other attacks from the fishmen. Why were the fishmen attacking them and how did they know where to find them?

The first time the Akugyo attacked them, before they'd found Camelot, there had been a wizard who led some sort of hunting party against them. Ethan and his friends had killed the fishmen and they hadn't seen any more until they had returned to the shore. In fact, Ethan still carried the trident from the fishman wizard they'd killed because of the Chymera crystal it had.

None of the new attacks had involved a wizard or a magic user of any sort, just Akugyo rangers. And like Michalus, Ethan wondered how the fishmen even knew they were here. Was it magic? Some sort of scent ability? Coincidence?

Nia looked up from wiping her scimitars on one of the fishman bodies. "Perhaps they are patrols. This may be their territory and they could be defending it."

Michalus rubbed his chin. "That's an interesting hypothesis."

"I do not remember the Akugyo aggressively patrolling the shores," Guinevere told them. She looked up and down the road. "In fact, there were very few actual reports of seeing them. And back then, there was significantly more foot traffic along the coastal highways."

"Par'karr not see any travelers," his kobold friend pointed out.

"That's true, we've seen no travelers, and then there was that burned-out village we passed." Ethan nodded. A week ago, they'd come across a small village of less than a dozen buildings that had been burned. "Is it possible the fish guys are responsible?"

"I do not understand their motivation," Nia confessed. She prodded the neck of one of the dead fishmen with her scimitar, pointing out the gills. "These are water-breathing creatures, like fish. Why would they make war with creatures on land?"

Ethan snorted. "It's not like anyone, other than us, are fishing in the water or invading their territory. I mean, there aren't even any boats on this world, are there?"

"Boats? Of course there are boats, my boy," Michalus answered. "Barges, skiffs and other boats actually do carry a good amount of goods in certain parts of the world. Especially lumber."

"But there are no boats in the ocean, right?" Ethan clarified. He hadn't actually seen any boats at all in this world, on the river or elsewhere. Of course, technically, he'd only seen a small fraction of the world.

"On the ocean?" Michalus looked shocked and glanced behind Ethan to the giant waterspouts. "Are you mad?"

"Probably a bit." Ethan held up his fingers about an

inch apart. "I couldn't imagine how a boat would get through the chaotic waterspouts."

"They can't," Guinevere said. "It's impossible to navigate the spouts. People have tried. Tried and died."

Ethan glanced back at the ocean. "And no one fishes, right? In the ocean, I mean. Right?"

Michalus and Guinevere shook their heads at the same time.

"So then why are they attacking people on land?" Ethan asked. "What are they hoping to gain?"

Everyone was quiet for a long time. Finally, Nia broke the silence.

"Perhaps they are hunting," she offered. "And we are the prey."

Ethan snorted. "A large order of Ethan with a side of Nia please. Oh, and can I get fries with that?"

His friends gave him blank stares and Ethan sighed. "It's a joke from my world. Never mind."

"We don't know that's true," Michalus said. "But regardless of the reason, it does appear that they are active again."

"We sleep in trees?" Par'karr asked, pointing to the forest.

Everyone's heads turned towards the redwoods of Sherwood Forest. There were all sorts of rumors of what befell people who entered the woods. And yet, Ethan and his companions had made it through Sherwood to Camelot - and returned.

Despite making it there and back again, they were all too aware of the creatures lurking in the forest, especially the giant carnivorous Venus fly trap plants. Ethan shuddered at the memory. They would all have died from just one of them who had attacked them, had it not been for the fact that Yuliana had been immune to the creature's hallucinogenic poison.

Then there were the tree lords, the strange sentient, autonomous trees. Now that they were done with their job of keeping Mordred inside Camelot, they could be anywhere in the forest. And without the druid to speak on their behalf, Ethan didn't want to risk encountering them.

"I'm not sure we'd be any safer there." Ethan shook his head. "For now, we'll just have to keep a watchful eye for the fishmen."

Guinevere opened her mouth as if about to say something but then shut it again. She shrugged. "We could set up some sort of fortifications. Perhaps a spiked barricade."

Nia nodded. "Yes, we could cut off some of their avenues of approach."

The blond warrior smiled. "Exactly."

Ethan looked around. "Build it with what?"

They all looked back at the forest. Ethan shook his head. "There is no way we're cutting trees down. Not with those tree lords loose now."

Guinevere growled in frustration. "You have a good point. My father was familiar with the tree lords but neither Arthur nor myself ever spoke to them. I do know they guard their forests jealously."

Ethan looked around the area, noting all the stones in the area. An idea began to form in his mind and he grinned. "Do you know what caltrops are?"

"Cow troops?" Par'karr furrowed his scaly brows.

"Caltrops," Ethan said and looked around at his

companions' faces. It was obvious they hadn't heard of them.

Bending down, Ethan picked up a stone and, channeling a little *Earth* magic, shaped the stone into the shape of a caltrop. At least, he tried to. He was familiar with their general shape from role-playing games but he found that getting the right spacing and angle on the three-sided spike was more difficult than he expected.

The others watched the stone writhing under his mental control until finally he had it good enough that he thought it would work. He stood up and held out his hand.

"It's small," Guinevere said skeptically.

"Yes," Ethan admitted. "But we shape a few dozen of these and spread them on the perimeter of the camp. Anything not wearing boots with tough soles is going to be in for a surprise."

Ethan made a show of throwing it. The caltrops hit the ground, rolled and came up with one of the points sticking straight up. He smiled. "See."

Nia nodded. "We do not call them cow-tropes on my world, but we have things like this. They work well."

Guinevere shrugged. "We can try them. But we shouldn't relax our guard."

"Wouldn't think of it," Ethan said. He bent down and picked up the caltrop and handed it to Michalus. "Think you can make two dozen or so of these before we go back to bed?"

The wizard started to reply but it turned into a yawn. Covering his mouth, he just nodded and bent down to retrieve some rocks.

"Michalus and I will create a few dozen of the caltrops," he told them. He gestured to the bodies and wrinkled his nose. "Can the rest of you drag these bodies down to the beach so our camp doesn't reek of dead fish."

As he bent down and began forming the stones into caltrops, Ethan shook his head. He had hoped this would be an easy journey to find Excalibur. He should have known better. Nothing was ever easy on this world.

2

It continued raining that evening and the entire group was soaked, as was all of their bedding. Ethan tried to dry it with magic, but the effect was temporary. The rain was coming down so quickly, that his bedding was quickly drenched. Between the rain and the double watches, no one slept well that night.

The next morning, it was still raining. The group was tired and soaked to the bone. Despite the downpour, Ethan wandered down to the beach to summon his water elemental so he could do his daily morning fishing ritual.

He was so tired, he nearly forgot the caltrops they'd set out last night until he was about to step on one. Luckily, he caught himself just before he stepped on it. Swerving around the caltrops, Ethan managed to navigate around them.

He strolled down the beach, unsure exactly how they were going to cook the fish he would catch without a fire, but they needed to eat something. Without venturing into the forest, their options were extremely limited. Other than a deer that had wandered out of the forest the first week, they'd been existing only on fish and an occasional edible plant that Guinevere recognized.

It had gotten so bad, that Ethan had seriously considered portaling back to Hawkshead to get some other food. Unfortunately, with the Doemenagg after them, going back to the village only put the entire village in danger.

Ethan cursed. He was tired of fish. They'd eaten almost nothing but fish for weeks and it was definitely getting old. What he wouldn't do for a nice, steaming double cheeseburger... with fries.

Shaking his head to get the image of a cheeseburger off his mind, he summoned his water elemental. As usual, he told it what to do and then sent it on its merry way. The watery creature dived into the water.

A minute or two later, the elemental returned with a dozen fish. It moved in front of Ethan and dropped the flopping fish at his feet. Ethan thanked the elemental and went to dismiss but stopped.

Looking out at the tumultuous ocean, he had an idea. Since he had an elemental that could breathe and move underwater, maybe he could send it to see if there were any Akugyo nearby.

He turned to the elemental. "Go into the water and swim out as far east as you can. Then go as far north and south as you can. Look for any fishmen - uh, things that look like me, only...uh... fishier."

The elemental spun around, went back to the water's edge and then disappeared into the waves. Ethan watched it disappear and then waited for a minute to see if it would immediately resurface.

It didn't, so Ethan bent down and gathered up the fish in the blanket he'd been using for this task since the beginning. It stank of fish and no manner of washing it in the river or the ocean had gotten rid of the smell.

Your lesser elemental (water) has been dismissed.

Ethan's head snapped up as he read the message in his HUD. He looked out at the ocean for any sign of what might have killed his elemental. Had it run into one of the water spouts that constantly formed and dissipated as far as the eyes could see?

He didn't know. Rather than assume, Ethan could find out first hand using his *Clairvoyance* ability. With it, he could see through the eyes of one of his elementals. It was time to do some reconnaissance.

Sitting down cross legged on the beach, Ethan summoned another water elemental. Activating Clairvoyance, his awareness shifted from his own eyes to the eyes of the elemental. It was a strange experience.

Unlike the air elemental, whose vision was crystal clear and almost binocular-like, the water elemental's vision was a bit blurry and constantly wavering. He frowned. It made sense, given that the elemental was made of water. It was just inconvenient.

Shrugging in his own body, Ethan commanded the creature to go into the water. Ethan watched, through its eyes, as it entered the water and then things suddenly changed.

As soon as the elemental was completely submerged, its vision cleared and Ethan saw the underwater world through its enhanced eyes. And it was amazing.

Through the eyes of the elemental, the ocean almost looked as if he were swimming through air. It was as if the water itself was filtered out and fish and other creatures swam through midair. It was so surreal, Ethan blinked several times to make sure what he was actually seeing was real.

There was also much more light than he expected underwater. It was as if the water elemental was either amplifying the light or filtering out the dark. Either way, it allowed Ethan to see much further than he expected. Much further.

It also allowed him to see the brilliant colors of the various coral and shells, as well as the unique colors of the fish and plant life that littered the ocean and ocean floor. The colors were much more vibrant than he knew it should be, so something about the elemental's vision was enhancing everything.

Ethan glanced left, looking down the coast to the south. Then he looked right, up the north shoreline. In both directions, he saw abundant plant life and sea life in vivid color.

Next, Ethan focused his gaze out to the deeper part of the ocean and looked around. It took only a moment for his eyes to focus on something that didn't quite fit in. Then, he froze. Several hundred yards from him were a group of Akugyo who appeared, to the elemental's eyes, to be floating in midair, just above the ocean floor.

Telling the elemental to be very still, Ethan focused on the fishmen. There were fifteen of them in total, but that wasn't all. As Ethan strained his eyes, he caught sight of other shapes behind the Akugyo - large shapes. Shark shapes.

Ethan shuddered as he counted six large sharks. And the sharks weren't just large, they were huge. It was hard to guess their exact length, but he guessed they were at least 25 feet in length, maybe 30.

He was wondering why the shark didn't attack the fishmen until he caught sight of something atop the shark. Straining his eyes, he recognized the figure as one of the fishmen. It was mounted on the shark - like a horse.

His eyes flicked back to the Akugyo as a funnel shape began to form just to the right of them. Ethan knew that had to be the beginnings of a waterspout and the fishmen seemed to know it too. Faster than he would have thought possible, they darted back, closer to the sharks.

Nearby fish realized it too and tried to swim away but the funnel seemed to draw the smaller creatures in. The funnel spun the fish faster and faster until suddenly they shot upward - into the waterspout, he realized.

Consumed with watching the waterspout, Ethan almost missed the funnel appearing to his left. Another waterspout was forming. Cursing, he ordered the elemental to swim right.

Nearly instantaneously, he was suddenly a hundred feet from where he'd just been. He swore. The elemental moved fast. Insanely fast. Turning, he watched the funnel form and then shoot fish up into the sky.

He wanted to look up into the funnel, but there was no way to do that without getting sucked into the waterspout himself. Still, even if his elemental was dismissed, it might be worth it. But that could wait.

Ethan turned his attention back to the fishmen who still floated near the sharks, watching the funnel. The group just looked at each other and towards the shore and Ethan couldn't help but wonder what they were doing.

Could Nia have been right and this was some sort of patrol? Or was there some other reason for them to be there? Maybe humans along the road were prey for them? Or were they food?

Perhaps, like Ethan was hunting fish from the ocean as food, these Akugyo were hunting humanoid land-dwellers for food. Or perhaps it was all sport. He had no way to know and no way to communicate with them.

The fishmen and the sharks suddenly scattered as another whirlwind started to take shape. Their movement brought them closer to Ethan and when they stopped, he saw one of them looked directly at Ethan. He swore.

The Akugyo gestured towards Ethan with its trident and suddenly all of the fishmen looked his way. Even the sharks stopped swimming in circles and turned to face him. He swore again.

Suddenly, as one, the group shot towards Ethan at incredible speed, tridents leading. Panicking, he almost forgot he was in an elemental and started to swim back to the shore. Yet before he even started to move, the lead fishman reached him and buried its trident into his elemental.

Your lesser elemental (water) has been dismissed.

Gasping and reaching down to his chest, Ethan was suddenly back in his own body. He felt his chest to make sure he hadn't actually been stabbed. Once he was sure, he glanced out to the ocean.

It looked like the normal ocean he'd looked at dozens of times. There were waves and waterspouts, with no clue as to what lay just beneath it. Scrambling to his feet, Ethan grabbed the blanket with the fish and hurried back to the group. He had some news to tell them.

3

"More fishmen in ocean?" Par'karr screeched, head swiveling towards the water. His demon rabbits turned as well, lowering their heads and growling. It was still raining and their fur was slick against their bodies, making them look almost comical.

"At least sixteen." Ethan nodded. "But there could have been more riding the other sharks."

"Sharks?" Michalus asked, his brow furrowed.

Ethan was shocked for a moment that the wizard didn't know what sharks were, but then he remembered that there were no boats or ships in the ocean here due to the waterspouts. No swimming either. The people on this world could never have encountered a shark. Lucky them.

"They are like really large fish with rows and rows of teeth," Ethan said. "They are meat eaters and they eat anything."

"And the Akugyo ride these sharks, like we ride horses?" Guinevere asked. Unlike the others, with the exception of Nia, the former queen wasn't alarmed at his story. Her expression remained neutral as he had told the story, and now looked calculating.

He nodded, wiping some rain out of his eyes.

"They must be from a distance then," she said. "You don't ride where you can walk."

She had a point. At least, Ethan thought she did. It was true back on Earth at least. People usually didn't hop in their car to go down to the corner store. He looked from the ocean to Guinevere. "What does that mean?"

"I don't know," she replied, turning her head to scan the beach. "You didn't see any sign of an outpost or fortifications?"

Ethan thought back to his glimpse under the sea. There had been some coral further out but nothing he would classify as a fortification. He shook his head. "I didn't see anything like that. But then again, I have no idea what a fishman fort would look like."

"It may look different from what we might use," Nia said. "But it would still offer some strategic value."

Guinevere nodded, giving the foxgirl an approving nod. "Nia is right. If they are holding this area, then it would offer some sort of protection against enemies."

Ethan scoffed as he remembered the enormous sharks. "That's assuming they have any water-based enemies. As far as we know, they are the apex predators of the ocean."

"That could well be," Michalus added. He looked at Guinevere. "I've never heard of another ocean species attacking us up here on land. Have you?"

The warrior woman shook her head. "No. Not back when Arthur ruled and not since. At least, not up until a few hundred years ago when I was... detained... but Mordred."

He saw the sadness in her eyes when she mentioned Mordred, but there was none when she mentioned Arthur. Ethan guessed that made sense. Arthur had been dead for well over a thousand years, whereas Mordred had died only a few weeks ago.

"So what?" Ethan asked. "Do you think they are some sort of patrol? An advanced scouting party? A war party? Could they be... following us?"

"I don't know," Guinevere replied.

"We should get moving," Nia said. "We can ride until noon. When we stop, Ethan can scout the water and see if they are following us."

The group exchanged glances and Ethan nodded. "That's a good plan."

"Eat first?" Par'karr asked hopefully.

"Yeah buddy," Ethan replied, holding his hands out to gesture at the rain. "I could use some warm food right now."

The group retreated back to the treeline and ducked under the branches of one of the redwoods. Ethan used some *Earth* magic to shape a stone into a flat pan-like shape, then used some *Fire* magic to heat it up until they'd cooked several fish.

He channeled his *Mana* through the Chymera crystal on the trident he'd gotten from the Akugyo wizard. Since he started using it, he felt it was easier to focus his *Mana* through it. He wasn't sure, but it might actually reduce the amount of *Mana* he expended. He still needed to test that part out.

"You're becoming a proper wizard," Michalus commented, gesturing to Ethan's staff.

"It seems easier to channel the Mana through the staff," Ethan replied. "Why is that? Is it because I can see it?"

The wizard chuckled. "Some wizards will tell you that is so, but there has never been any conclusive evidence to support that. In your instance, I would guess it's the size of the crystal."

"So size does matter?" Ethan asked wryly.

Michalus rolled his eyes and Ethan grinned. Apparently the size matters argument had made it to this world too.

Ignoring Ethan, the wizard continued. "When it comes to Chymera crystals, size does make a difference. But also quality. The better quality and the larger the crystal, the easier it is for us to channel our mana."

Ethan thought back to the two large crystals in Arthur's tomb that he'd had to fill in order to open one of the doors. Had he known they could help him channel magic more efficiently, he might have pried them loose and taken them with him.

Looking from the crystal on Michalus's staff to his own, Ethan did notice that his crystal was almost twice the size as the one in Michalus's staff. It also sparkled more, as if it had been cut like a gemstone.

Michalus followed his gaze and nodded. He smirked. "Yes, yours is bigger. Had you not decided to keep the trident, I would have asked to keep it myself."

Ethan grinned. "Had I known larger crystals allowed you to focus mana better, I would have started using it sooner."

"I forget you were never formally trained." The wizard shrugged, then shook his head. "I still find it amazing you learned as much as you did, as quickly as you did."

"Nothing like being thrown into danger, to make you learn quickly," Ethan replied with a grin.

"So I'm learning," the wizard responded. "I've already used some spells I learned centuries ago and never thought I'd need to use."

The fish began to smoke and Ethan swore and quickly flipped them over with his stone spatula. Glancing down at the seared fish, he was happy they didn't look too scorched. He looked up and gave the group an apologetic look. "Sorry."

"It is fine," Nia said, glancing down at the fish. She and Guinevere had been staring out at the ocean, keeping an eye open for any fishmen.

"Par'karr still eat." His kobold friend grinned.

After letting the fish cook for a few minutes on the other side, he felt they were ready and scooped them off onto stone plates Michalus had shaped from rocks and washed with rainwater.

Although he was tired of fish, the steaming meat tasted heavenly and warmed him from the inside. Too soon, his fish fillet was gone and it was time to go. His companions packed their wet gear and ten minutes later, they were back on the muddy trail.

∽

THE GROUP RODE in the rain until what they guessed was noon time. With the clouds obscuring the sky, it was impossible to know for certain but based on his hunger, Ethan guessed it was at least close to noon.

Ethan gave frozen fish to Michalus so the wizard could warm them up, while Ethan started towards the beach to scout out the water again.

As he walked, Nia fell in step with him on his right side and Guinevere fell in step on the left side. Ethan stopped. "What are..."

"We are coming to protect you," Nia interrupted, hands on her scimitars. "If there are fishmen, they may try to attack a lone target."

He opened his mouth to protest but seeing the women's stern expressions, he closed it and nodded. It wasn't an argument worth having and had the places been reversed, he would have done the same. "Sounds good."

Ethan and the women walked to a safe distance before stopping. They all stared out at the ocean and the numerous waterspouts before he sat down cross-legged on the sand. He summoned his water elemental and, after using *Clairvoyance*, moved his awareness into it. Then, he commanded it into the water.

When the elemental entered the water, Ethan was once again treated to the amazing underwater scene through its eyes. Like before, there were fish, plant life and coral littering the ocean floor.

But then movement caught his eye as out several hundred yards, where the ocean dropped off significantly, were shapes floating in the water. He counted the forms before jumping back into his body and dismissing the elemental.

Standing up, he stared out into the ocean. "They're out there."

"Is it the same ones or a different group?" Guinevere asked.

Ethan frowned. "The same group, I think. But a few more."

Nia shared his frown, head swiveling towards the ocean and hands tightening on the hilts of her weapons. "They are following us."

Ethan nodded as he followed her gaze to the ocean of twisting waterspouts. They were being followed. The question was: Why?

4

After a hurried and wet lunch, the group continued along the coastal highway. It rained the entire day again, keeping them all drenched and miserable. Ethan decided he really needed to figure out a way to create an umbrella but wasn't sure how given the technology he had access to.

Near evening, they came to a wide river with a long stone bridge. Ethan called them to a halt as he looked over the bridge. It was wide enough to fit a cart on and over 50 feet long. The bridge looked oddly familiar and brought back bad memories of the Sollasina cthulhu they'd encountered on their way to Camelot.

The Sollasina cthulhu was a squid-like tentacled monster which had attacked from beneath the water as they had crossed the bridge. It had grabbed several of them with its tentacles and upon contact had initiated some sort of mental attack.

Ethan had killed it, but the thing had implanted some

sort of psychic embryo inside Nia which had taken over the foxgirl's will. Had it finished its job, it would have crushed Nia's mind and then transformed her body into a cthulhu.

Luckily, he had used his new *Mental* magic skill to fight it off - if only barely. Yet, the attempt had cost him. He'd burned some of his attribute points to destroy the creature and while the Grail had healed most of the stat damage, he'd permanently lost a point of *Stamina*.

"What is it, Ethan?" Nia yelled over the sound of the rain. She rode up next to him and stopped her horse parallel to his own.

"Remind you of anything?" he asked loudly, nodding towards the bridge.

Nia glanced at the bridge and then a moment later she shuddered. The foxgirl swung her head towards Ethan. "The creature who attacked us."

He didn't know how common the Sollasina cthulhus were, but he didn't feel like taking a chance. Technically, his group, all except Guinevere, had necklaces that would protect them from mental attacks - for a while, at least.

Ethan nodded. "I'm going to scout the water, just to make sure it's safe."

Looking around at the muddy ground, Ethan cursed. He had planned to dismount and sit cross legged, like he usually did when he used *Clairvoyance*. But he couldn't see any place to sit down without getting both soaked and dirty. He cursed again.

"Why are we stopping?" Guinevere asked, riding up next to him.

"I'm going to scout the river," Ethan replied.

The warrior woman stared out at the bridge, sweeping her gaze along the shoreline. "You think the Akugyo will try and ambush?"

Ethan shrugged. "Possibly. Or something else."

"Something else?" the woman asked with a raised brow.

"I'll explain later," he said and then looked between the two women, one on each side.

He held out his reins to Nia. "Can you hold my horse while I summon the water elemental?"

Nia nodded and took the reins, pulling the animal closer to her.

Ethan turned to Guinevere. "Can you make sure I stay in my saddle while I shift my awareness to the elemental."

"Of course," Guinevere answered and put a gauntleted hand on his shoulder.

With his horse and his body steadied, Ethan summoned his water elemental. As soon as it appeared, he willed his conscience into it and commanded it into the river.

The elemental obeyed and quickly made its way to the edge of the river and then dove in. Ethan thought of it as diving, but it was more like "pouring" itself into the river, since his summoned creature really had no solid form.

Once in the river, Ethan was treated to a familiar underwater sight where the elemental's vision seemed to completely remove the water and only show the plant and animal life.

Glancing around the river, Ethan saw nothing out of the ordinary. There were no giant tentacle creatures lurking under the bridge and no Akugyo waiting to ambush them. It looked like an ordinary river bed.

Ethan was about to dismiss his elemental when he saw movement out of the corner of his eye. Turning the elemental's gaze to the east, he saw shapes moving towards him. At almost the same time, he felt someone shaking his body - his actual body. They were trying to get his attention.

With an effort, he released his *Clairvoyance*. His awareness snapped back to his body and he looked around, briefly disoriented. Guinevere was shaking his shoulder. He blinked. "What is it?"

"Look!" Guinevere and Nia both stared wide-eyed down the river while the former queen pointed her other hand down the river, towards the ocean.

He followed the woman's finger and understood their alarm. Sticking up the river, and coming inland from the ocean, were three dorsal large fins. Shark fins.

Ethan cursed. "Those are sharks. And chances are, the Akugyo are with them."

"We should find a more defensible position," Guinevere and Nia said at the same time.

Thinking quickly, Ethan guessed the sharks were about three hundred yards away and closing fast. He looked at the length of the bridge and then back to the sharks. His eyes flicked across the opposite bank and saw that the redwoods ended on this side of the river. On the opposite bank, it was just normal-sized trees.

Did this mean they'd reached the southern edge of Sherwood Forest? Did the dangers of Sherwood end on this side of the forest? Could the tree lords cross the river?

Options and possibilities flashed through Ethan's mind and he quickly made a snap decision.

"Gallop across now!" he yelled. Grabbing his reins from Nia, he spurred his mount into a gallop and turned over his shoulder. "Go! Go! Go!"

The others hesitated only briefly before they spurred their own mounts forward and followed him onto the bridge.

The horses' hooves thundered across the stone bridge, drowning out even the sound of the rain. Ethan looked to the south, eyes fixed on the large dorsal fins as they knifed through the water. It would be close, but they were going to make it.

That was when he felt the tell-tale sensations of magic being used and caught a glimmer of blue from under the water. He swore loudly. The fishmen had a wizard with them this time.

No sooner had he come to that conclusion when a huge watery hand emerged from the water just in front of him. The hand was made completely of river water but was the size of one of their horses. The hand stretched up until it was coming over the bridge, blocking their path. Ethan swore again.

Unsure how to counter a disembodied, watery hand, Ethan did the only thing he could think of on short notice. He yanked his horse's reins and brought the creature to a stop and then created a portal directly in front of them that led to a spot on the opposite shore.

Gritting his teeth as he felt his *Mana* leave him, he channeled his magic through the crystal of the trident and willed the portal open to the size he knew would fit the horses. Just in front of him, a shimmering vertical slit opened and then widened until it would fit a horse and rider.

"Into the portal!" he yelled as loud as he could, hoping his friends heard him. To emphasize his words, he gestured with his arm for them to ride through. "Go! Go!"

Nia had been starting to slow her horse but must have heard him or saw the portal. She nodded as her horse thundered by and went into the portal. As she disappeared through this side of the portal, she instantaneously appeared a hundred yards away.

His eyes told him the trip was instantaneous, but having gone through a portal before, he knew it didn't feel instantaneous to the person going through the portal. It felt longer.

The hand began to move slowly towards them and, at the same time, the sharks were almost to the bridge. Ethan wasn't worried so much about the sharks - not unless he went into the water. He was worried about the Akugyo he knew were riding the sharks.

The hand got closer as Guinevere galloped past him, followed by Par'karr. Ethan realized the hand might reach him before he had the chance to go through and his heart began to pound. If that hand caught him and pulled him into the water, that's where the sharks were. Unbidden, the theme to Jaws began playing in his head.

Michalus came last and the wizard had his staff out, pointing it at the hand. Ethan felt the wizard channeling magic through his own staff and suddenly the watery hand turned to ice and stopped moving only a dozen feet from him.

"Hurry, my boy!" he yelled as he and his horse raced by.

The wizard disappeared into the portal just as Ethan heard a crack in the hand. He cursed and spurred his horse forward through the portal.

As he did, the lead shark leapt out of the water and directly at him. It opened its gaping mouth, revealing rows of razor-sharp teeth.

Ethan screamed just as he entered the portal and the shark's jaws snapped closed on the spot where he had just been. And then he was inside the kaleidoscope-like tunnel that he called the Bifrost.

Colors swirled by as he shot through the tunnel. Like before, he glimpsed stars and possibly even galaxies through the colorful pattern of the tunnel. Faster and faster he raced until suddenly he and his horse were on solid ground with the others, a hundred yards from the portal.

Wheeling his horse around, he just caught sight of the gigantic shark as it sailed over the bridge and crashed into the water on the other side, sending up a spray of water.

Spurring his mount into a gallop, he looked back over his shoulder and yelled to the others. "Let's go! Quickly! I don't want to fight them near the river!"

The rest of his party spurred their own horses and they quickly left the bridge, the sharks and the Akugyo behind them. For now.

5

Ethan and his companions rode for another half hour before stopping. The entire trip, he couldn't stop himself from glancing out at the ocean. He kept expecting to see the dorsal fins of sharks following them. But the rain continued to come down in sheets, and combined with the growing darkness, it was difficult to see. Still, he kept looking and each time he scanned the water, there was no sign of the sharks or the Akugyo.

Once it became too dark to ride, Ethan called the group to a halt. He gestured for them to gather around him. Despite them moving closer, he still had to yell over the rain. "I don't think we can go any further without risking the horses!"

There was a general murmur of agreement among the party members, so he continued. "Michalus, the trees are different here. Is this still Sherwood?"

"No," the wizard shouted back. "Sherwood ended when the large trees did, back at the river!"

Ethan nodded but then realized that with the hood of his cloak up, the others couldn't see the gesture. "Right! I say we camp in the forest tonight, further from the ocean."

Several of the party glanced over to the ocean and there was a general chorus of agreements.

"Do you think we will be safe in the forest?" Michalus asked. "They do seem to be able to traverse dry land."

"Land not dry," Par'karr chimed in, pointing to the puddles that had formed around the road. Of all of them, the kobold seemed the least affected by the rain. His scales seem to provide him some natural resistance to the water soaking into his skin.

Ethan smirked. "True."

"I believe Ethan is right," Guinevere said. "The further we are from the ocean, the more difficult it will be for them. Even though they are able to walk on land, they do not do it well."

"It will also be more difficult for them to sneak up on us and we should have more warning," Nia added.

Everyone agreed so Ethan dismounted and the others followed suit. He summoned some globes of light to light their way. Using the illumination, he led them several hundred yards into the forest before stopping in a small copse of evergreen trees. The overlapping branches of the trees were providing an area that was mostly dry.

Ethan looked around for a better spot but there was nothing within his light's range. At least, nothing his human eyes could see. He turned to Nia. The foxgirl's eyes were like cat's eyes and she saw extremely well in the dark. "See anything better nearby?"

Nia glanced around the area and then shook her head. "This seems like the best spot in this area."

"Let's make camp here!" he yelled to the others and led his horse into the middle of the cluster of trees.

As soon as he did, he noticed the rain dropped off dramatically. The overlapping branches really did reduce the rainfall coming down. Underneath the trees, it was almost a slow drizzle instead of the deluge outside the copse.

"This is nice," Guinevere said as she led her horse inside the protected area. "Though I still wish I had a tent."

"You and me both," Ethan agreed. "Just something to keep the rain off our heads would be nice."

"Ethan do magic?" Par'karr asked hopefully.

Ethan looked around the trees but couldn't think of anything else he could do with his magic to make the area any cozier. His magic only allowed him to manipulate the elements. He could command *Air*, *Water*, *Earth* and *Fire*. He'd also learned to manipulate *Aether* magic, or portal magic, and then *Mental* magic.

Glancing around, he just couldn't see anything he could do. Sure, he could use fire to dry the ground, but it would only be a temporary thing. He could keep it dry for fifteen or twenty minutes by continuously expending *Mana*, but eventually he would run out. Then they'd be wet and he'd be out of *Mana*.

"We can at least dry some wood and build a fire," Michalus suggested. He gestured to the canopy of branches above them. "The majority of the rain is being blocked so we should be able to maintain it."

"Good point," he said. "Everyone spread out and look for firewood. Just keep your eyes open for the fishmen."

The group tied off their horses and quickly searched the area for fallen branches and logs they could use for the fire. In fifteen minutes, they had found enough wood to last through most of the night.

"I will continue to look for wood," Nia said. Ethan started to object but the foxgirl held up her hand. "I can see the best in the dark. I will be fine."

"Just be careful," he told her and gave her a wink.

Nia nodded and then turned and disappeared into the darkness as soon as she was out of the globe of light cast by his light globes and the lightstones.

Turning back to the wood, Ethan and Michalus quickly dried enough to start a fire and within a few minutes, they had a roaring blaze going.

The heat from the campfire felt great after hours of being soaked to the bone. Given the expressions he saw on the faces of his companions, he knew he wasn't alone in his feelings.

Once the initial blaze of the fire died down a bit, Ethan brought out the frozen fish from his portal pouch. As he did so, he realized they only had enough for dinner and then breakfast in the morning. After that, they'd either have to hunt something else or he'd need to go fishing.

Finding a nearby rock, Ethan used *Earth* magic to shape it into a grill. He set the grill over the fire and then put the fish on the grill.

"How are the fishmen following us?" Guinevere asked suddenly.

Ethan blinked. He'd been paying attention to the fish and the former queen's question took him by surprise.

"How are the fishmen following us?" the woman repeated. "Is it by sight? Or are they using some other method?"

"I'm not really sure," Ethan admitted. "I've been wondering that myself but I don't know."

He looked at Michalus. The wizard knew much more about magic - especially magic theory - than Ethan. "Any ideas?"

Michalus rubbed his hands together in front of the fire. He looked into the fire for a long moment before answering. "That's been bothering me, as well. If we are certain that the same group is attacking us, then it's obvious they are following us. Are we certain of that?"

Ethan bit his lip. He'd seen a similar number of them and they'd looked like the others he'd seen but he really didn't know for certain. He shrugged. "I think so, but I'm not sure."

"The group that just attacked us had a wizard," Guinevere stated. "Unless it was one of you who conjured the hand. If they were the same ones who attacked us before, why didn't the wizard attack?"

Ethan and Michalus exchanged looks. She had a good point.

Nia reappeared into the firelight with an armful of wood. "This is all I could find for now."

"That should be plenty." Ethan gave his wife a smile.

Putting her wood with the rest of the firewood, Nia

walked around the fire and sat next to Ethan. Like the others, she rubbed her hands near the fire. "You are talking about the fishmen?"

"Yes," Ethan replied. "We were trying to figure out whether they are following us or whether we are running into different groups."

"I was not able to get the scent of the ones who attacked us today," the foxgirl told them.

"I didn't get a good look at them under the water," Ethan admitted. "But you're right. If this is the same group and there was a wizard with them, why didn't it attack?"

"Ethan kill other fish wizard," Par'karr suggested. "Maybe afraid."

"Maybe," Ethan said and thought back to the bridge. He looked to Michalus. "But the wizard had to be fairly powerful given the size of that water hand it created."

The wizard looked thoughtful and scratched his chin before commenting. "Certainly, they were no novice. But manipulating water isn't as difficult as say, manipulating earth. And I'm sure you noticed most of their magic is water based. The Akugyo may simply have more experience with water magic or some sort of affinity for it."

Ethan sighed. "So we really have no idea whether or not these are the same group or a different group of fishmen."

"We also don't know why they are attacking us," Guinevere stated. "They seem very persistent."

"This may be their territory," Nia told them. "On my world, we defend our territories against any enemy incursions. They may be doing the same."

The group went quiet again and Ethan took that

opportunity to check on the fish. The fillets smelled incredible and he prodded them to make sure they were cooked through. Oh yes, they were done. He quickly gave everyone their fillets and his companions quickly ate the steaming fish on their stone plates.

He moaned as he ate the freshly cooked fish and he wasn't the only one. For several minutes, there was only the sound of moaning and eating from Ethan and his companions.

The hot meat warmed him up from the inside out with every bite. He tried to savor it and make it last, but he was too cold and too hungry. All too quickly it was gone and Ethan wished he had some sort of hot beverage to go with it: a hot coffee, hot chocolate or even tea. He'd take anything right now.

"Is there some magic you have that can mark or track the Akugyo?" Guinevere asked once she had finished her meal.

"I don't think so." Ethan shook his head. He glanced at Michalus. "Do you know of a way?"

Michalus scratched his chin for a full minute before answering. "I seem to recall reading something about a method we might be able to use, but I can't remember the details at the moment."

Ethan sighed. "It looks like that's a no for now."

6

With Michalus unable to recall the exact method to magically track someone, the group began to settle in for the night. Guinevere had the idea to run rope around the trees and hang their waterproof cloaks above them to keep the rain off them.

After a little experimentation, Ethan and the former queen managed to get the cloaks hung at an angle so the little water that did make it through the branch canopy hit the cloaks and was deflected away from them. By the time they had rigged up their makeshift awning, everyone was turning in for the night.

Everyone that was, except Ethan and Par'karr, who had the first watch shift. The two of them huddled by the fire and tried to stay warm and dry as they watched the ocean and surrounding forest for any sign of enemies.

THE NIGHT WAS uneventful and in the morning, Ethan saw that the rain had finally stopped and sunlight was actually breaking through the trees. He was tired, but everyone seemed tired from the constant double watches and damp sleeping conditions.

Unfortunately, it couldn't be helped. Between the Doemenaggs and the Akugyo, it didn't make sense to have only one person on watch. The risk of surprise was just too great. That meant double watches and less sleep for everyone.

He checked his stats in his HUD.

Health: 30
Mana: 103
Stamina: 60

At least Ethan was getting enough sleep to restore all of his stats. That much was good. Still, he certainly wouldn't mind one or two nights' rest in a good inn with an actual bed.

Guinevere seemed to be reading his mind and turned to him as he began packing his bedding. "You can create portals that can move all of us, including the horses, correct?"

Ethan nodded and guessed where this was going.

"Then why are we sleeping out in the rain where we are under constant threat of attack? Why not portal us to your village every night? Or an inn? Or even Camelot?" she asked, hands on hips. She suddenly stopped talking and bit her lip. She gave Ethan an apologetic shrug. "I'm not really complaining. It's not like I haven't slept in the rain before while on a campaign but it seems tactically better to sleep in a defensible position each night and then just portal back in the morning."

The others, even Par'karr, perked up at the woman's words and looked at Ethan. They seemed to share her question. And Ethan admitted, it was a good question.

Once he had realized that he could create a portal large enough for all of them to go through, as well as the horses, he'd considered that very thing. How easy would it be to simply portal back to Hawkshead every night and then pick up their journey where they'd left off.

It would be simple enough. He could create a stone with some unique runes and leave it at the spot where they left off and then portal to it in the morning. It seemed simple and they could all sleep in nice beds each night.

But there was a problem with that idea. At least, he thought there was. It came from his brief contact with the Doemenagg queen, if that had been the alien mind he'd contacted through the assassin insect he'd fought in Camelot.

He couldn't say exactly what it was that made him think it, but he was certain the queen was somehow able to track Ethan and the group through their portal activity. There had been something else too. Something about the portal magic. Something she wanted. He shuddered at the memory of the vast intelligence he'd briefly touched.

If he used portal magic regularly, he had to assume that the Doemenagg would track it either to their location on the road, or to Hawkshead. That meant they could portal into an ambush or they could lead the mantis-like insects back to Hawkshead.

He wasn't about to risk the villagers' lives just so he and his group could be a little more comfortable each night. Especially not with the extra families that had moved in since the kobold attack.

Ethan realized everyone was still looking at him and he cleared his throat. "Ahem. Well, I believe the Doemenagg queen is somehow able to track me through my use of portal magic...."

Michalus's eyebrows shot up. "Like my machine?"

The wizard had built a machine that allowed him to track portal activity and kept it stored in an invisible workshop he had built. He'd shown it to Ethan when they'd first met on their way to Patheos. At the time, he'd thought it more of a novelty but Ethan realized that something like that could be used to track a wizard who frequently used portals.

"Yes," Ethan confirmed. "Like your machine, but I think she does it without any machine."

"Really?" the wizard asked. "That's fascinating..."

"Maybe," Ethan continued. "But when I touched her mind, I got the 'impression' that she was tracking me, each time I opened a portal. And..."

"And what?" Nia asked, eyes narrowed.

"And, I think she wants my knowledge of portals," he admitted. It was a guess, but the sense of hunger he'd gotten from the queen had been powerful and focused. There was something about portals she wanted. She obviously knew the theory of portals and knew what they were, but perhaps she couldn't actually open one herself.

It struck him then that maybe that's what she wanted him for. If he was right and she was sucking knowledge from wizards by eating their brains, then maybe that was the knowledge she wanted from him.

Michalus leaned back and rubbed his chin. "Hmm."

"She cannot have you," Nia growled, her eyes narrowed in anger now.

Guinevere screwed up her face in thought. "So that portal you opened yesterday..."

Ethan sighed. "Yes. The portal I opened yesterday may have told her exactly where we were. But unfortunately, I didn't have any other ideas at the time. That's one of the reasons I wanted to ride as far away as we could get from the portal."

"Portal good," Par'karr said. "It save Par'karr and others from big water hand."

"Par'karr is right. That was quick thinking and you did save us." Guinevere nodded but then the warrior woman gave Ethan a disappointing look that was almost a glare. "Why didn't you tell us this before?"

"Because I'm not 100% sure," Ethan admitted with a small sigh. He'd thought about telling them a few times but he didn't actually have any proof. Just a feeling. "It's a theory. An impression I got from the queen."

"Still," Guinevere said disapprovingly. "You could have shared your theory with us to make us aware."

"Sorry," Ethan apologized. He looked to Nia expecting the same disapproving look and he found it, only it was directed at Guinevere and not Ethan.

"Ethan is the alpha," she told the other woman. "He leads. A leader does not always tell his subordinates everything."

The former queen scoffed. "I am no one's subordinate.

I am here because I feel I can help you recover the sword. And that certainly wasn't how Arthur ran the round table. We were all equal!"

"Ethan is the alpha..." Nia began but Ethan held up a hand.

"Guinevere is right, Nia," he told her. "You all deserve to know what is going on - even if it's just a theory. If for no other reason, any of you might have ideas that I may not think of."

Ethan began pointing at his companions. "Michalus has hundreds of years of experience with magic and knowledge of the land around us. You have battle experience and tactical knowledge - I suspect Guinevere has the same, as well as similar knowledge of the land. Par'karr has a unique perspective from his tribal experience. I don't have any of that."

"You are a powerful wizard," Nia shot back and looked defiantly at the rest of the group, daring them to contradict her. No one did.

"Maybe," Ethan responded. "But so is Michalus."

The elven wizard was powerful and knowledgeable but Ethan knew he preferred the academic study of magic, rather than a more practical hands-on approach. Ethan on the other hand had been forced to learn the hands-on approach just to survive. It always seemed an interesting contrast to Ethan.

Guinevere held her hands up. "I'm not questioning Ethan's skill as a leader or his ability with magic. I would just prefer to have all the facts so I can make up my own mind. After all, I'm over a thousand years old. I may have some insights the rest of you don't."

The former queen had drunk from the Fountain of Youth over a thousand years ago and still looked like a young woman, no more than 23 or 24 years old. It was easy for him to forget that she was actually the oldest one in the group and had lived in this world for a very long time.

"That is a good point," Ethan told her. "Now that you know, do you have any advice?"

"Unfortunately, no," the warrior woman replied with a wry smile. "Your reasoning is sound and I would not put your village in danger just for the sake of a warm bed. And you are right about coming back to an ambush. In the Doemenagg war, we had similar experiences. In fact, now that you mention it, I remember my father expressing a theory like yours. That the bugs could sense our portals."

Ethan nodded. If Merlin had thought the same thing, then that lent credence to his theory. That was both good and bad. It was good to know he might be right but bad if that meant they really were being tracked and he'd revealed their position to the Doemenagg.

"We should eat and then get moving," he told the group. He looked to Par'karr and Nia. "Can the two of you hunt while we prepare the food. I would prefer not to have to go near the water today to fish if I don't have to."

The two of them nodded. Par'karr set off in one direction with his demon rabbits while Nia grabbed her bow and started to head off in another direction. She stopped a few yards away and looked back at him. "Guinevere and Michalus can cook, you can come with me to hunt."

Ethan grinned despite himself. Their "hunting" sessions were an excuse for them to spend a little intimate time together and it had been a long while since they had actually had the opportunity.

Pulling the fish from his portal pouch, he handed them to Michalus with a grin. "They're all yours. I have to go... hunting."

It was clear from the expressions of both Guinevere and Michalus that neither of them thought Ethan was going to be doing any hunting. He grinned and turned to catch up to Nia. Her grin told him hunting wouldn't be all they were doing either.

7

His group set out after eating one of the lizard turkey creatures Nia shot after she and Ethan had their alone time. His companions were so happy to have something other than fish to eat, that no one made any comments about how long they were gone.

Ethan was also glad she had managed to kill something since it meant he didn't have to chance going near the ocean to fish. Despite the lack of any tell-tale signs of the fishmen, he knew they were probably out there somewhere.

The sun stayed with them through their morning ride. He wasn't sure if he actually expected to see signs of the fishmen throughout the morning, but none of them glimpsed the Akugyo or shark fins in the ocean. Ethan didn't know if that was a good thing or a bad thing.

If the fishmen had given up, that was a good thing. If not, that meant they were staying hidden and biding their time. That was a bad thing. It most likely meant an ambush soon and Ethan didn't relish another fight with them. Especially if that involved whatever wizard cast the giant water hand.

When noon came, the group stopped to eat the remainder of their turkey lizard. Once again, Ethan kept a wary eye on the ocean but that wasn't where the attack came from.

He had just taken the first bite of his meat when Par'karr's rabbits all raised their heads at the same time. That's when he noticed the forest to their left was unusually quiet.

Nia sniffed the air and then dropped her food and reached for her scimitars. "Insect men!"

Ethan had grabbed his trident just as four Doemenaggs leaped into their camp, surrounding their party and sending the horses into a panic. The terrified creatures pulled free of the branch they were tied to and ran off back down the trail.

He swore as he saw the horses running but couldn't spare them more than a moment's thought. Ethan had gone over the previous battle in his mind hundreds of times since their last encounter with the critical eye of a MMORPG tactician. He'd analyzed the actions and movements of the creature he had fought and combined with the information he'd gotten from Guinevere, he had come up with a strategy.

"Keep their antennae apart!" he yelled to the others.

One thing he'd noticed in his fight with the previous Doemenagg was that it seemed to need to rub its antennae together to conjure magic. If they could keep them apart, the insect's ability to do magic might be neutralized. The problem was, there were four of them and only two wizards.

Ethan lashed out as quickly as he could with *Air*, pulling the antennae of the two nearest him. The closest Doemenagg hissed and clicked angrily and then came at Ethan with their mantis-like forearms out to impale him.

Nia intercepted one with her scimitars, forcing it back and away from him. The foxgirl danced around the larger creature, meeting its scythe-like arms with the steel of her blades.

The other one barreled towards him with its claw-like appendages aimed at him. Like the previous one he'd encountered, it probably wanted to grab him so it could suck out his brain. No, thank you. Ethan would take a hard pass on that.

Part of his observations from the previous fight was that the creature's exoskeleton seemed nearly impervious to weapons except at the joints. Since he only had a short sword and wasn't particularly good at using it, Ethan had realized he would need something to give him an advantage over the tough chitin of the creature's exoskeleton.

Focusing hard to keep the *Air* between the two creatures' antennas, he summoned the glowing *Manablade* that resembled the laser swords from his favorite sci-fi movie. But unlike the original blade that Michalus had shown him how to create, Ethan created two smaller blades on either end of his trident.

At the same time, he brought up his HUD so he could monitor his *Mana*.

Mana: **89**

He was already down nearly a 10th of his *Mana* and it was dropping quickly. Maintaining the *Air* and then the *Manablade* was taxing on both his *Mana* and his mind. Ethan was already feeling a headache coming on as he struggled to maintain his concentration on what amounted to three spells. Ethan had to push the pain away as the Doemenagg closed with him and he was forced to defend himself.

Charging forward, the mantis creature came in with its forearms out, aimed at Ethan's torso. Ethan brought the trident around in an arc as it closed with him. The Doemenagg brought up its foreclaw to block his strike but didn't understand the nature of the *Manablade*.

You critically strike Queen's Collector for 21 damage.

Like the laser sword from the movies, his white-hot Manablade sliced neatly through the creature's left forearm, severing it completely. The momentum of the blade hadn't been impeded at all from its contact with the first forearm and continued through to slice the tip of the right forearm.

You critically strike Queen's Collector for 13 damage.

The Collector skidded to a halt and brought its foreclaws up to its head level as if unable to process what had just happened. Its large, multifaceted eyes rotated around, staring at its damaged limbs.

Ethan didn't waste any time and followed up his arc with a reverse strike that caught the Doemenagg across the neck, severing it in half.

You   critically   strike   Queen's Collector for 35 damage.
* You gain 50 experience. Experience to next level 11,305.*

Its head and upper neck separated from its body, the mantis creature toppled over and collapsed to the ground.

Mana: 81

Ethan's headache instantly lessened as he no longer needed to hold the creature's antennae apart. He spun towards Nia and the other Collector and saw the foxgirl and the creature going back and forth in a fast paced, intricate dance of blows.

While the foxgirl seemed to be holding her own, Ethan could see that she was breathing hard. The Doemenagg didn't seem to be tiring at all and continued its onslaught.

He was about to intervene when Guinevere suddenly went flying back. Ethan jerked his head over to the other melee to find Michalus and Par'karr squaring off against one of the Collectors while the other one was rubbing its antennae together and pointing them at Guinevere.

Ethan cursed. He realized Michalus hadn't been able to maintain the spell on both of them and one now had command of its magic.

Reaching out with *Air*, Ethan tried to pull the creature's antennae apart but the creature spun towards him and he felt his magic countered. He cursed again and the creature spun back and appeared towards Michalus, rubbing its antennae together.

He had no idea what magic the creature might be conjuring but he knew it couldn't be good. Not knowing what else to do, he pulled back his arm and threw his trident at the creature like a spear.

Instantly, he felt his headache grow ten times worse and watched his *Mana* drop.

Mana: 57

Gritting his teeth as he dropped to his knees, Ethan cursed. Maintaining the Manablade from a distance was straining his concentration to the limits and he squinted his eyes as he forced himself to keep the magic up.

The Collector's eyes rotated towards Ethan and it swiveled its triangular head towards him as it tried to rub its antennae together. He knew the creature would try to deflect it and he pushed himself to counter the creature's spell.

Mana: 42

It hurt, but he managed to stop the Doemenagg from blocking the trident with magic and the weapon hit the creature in its upper body. The Manablade part of the weapon easily penetrated the creature's exoskeleton but then the coral prongs of the weapon slammed into the carapace and bounced off.

You   critically   strike   Queen's Collector for 27 damage.

Unfortunately for the Collector, when the coral bounced off, it did so at an angle, causing the Manablade to nearly sever its upper body in half.

You   critically   strike   Queen's Collector for 31 damage.
     You gain 50 experience. Experience to next level 11,255.

The creature's eyes rotated to look down at its torso, apparently confused at what had just happened. Then, its legs collapsed from underneath it and fell to the ground.

Mana: 31

His *Mana* starting to get dangerously low, Ethan had to let go of the Manablade. The brilliant blue-white blade disappeared from his trident and he felt his headache instantly go down several notches. Instead of an intense, sharp pain, it was barely noticeable.

Guinevere had gotten up and charged in at the creature while Par'karr shot off a double-barrel load of stones from the enchanted shotgun. One of the stones missed but the other one hit the creature with a resounding crack.

Michalus was waving his own Manablade around, keeping the creature away and Ethan could see that the tip of its left forearm was missing.

"Ethan!" Nia cried and he immediately spun towards his wife.

Nia was down on one knee, her scimitars locked with the creature's forearms as the Collector used its larger size to press the foxgirl into the ground.

Knowing he didn't have time for anything elaborate, Ethan grabbed his trident with *Air* and hurled it right at the creature's head.

The Doemenagg's eyes rotated to look at the incoming trident and it tried to duck its head. Unfortunately for it, that moment of distraction was all Nia needed. With a twist of her body, she pushed the creature's arms to the left while side-stepping to the right. Combined with its own motion to duck its head, the Collector was thrown off balance and lurched to the side.

Nia danced to the side, spun around and brought both scimitars around on its neck joint, severing the creature's head from its body, splashing green ichor over her and the ground.

At the same time Ethan saw that Guinevere had flanked the remaining Doemenagg and between her and Michalus, were hacking away at the creature. Fighting off the two larger opponents, it didn't see Par'karr roll underneath it and release both barrels straight up into its head.

The double stone slugs tore through the creature's skull in a spray of green blood. The thing wobbled unsteadily for a moment before collapsing onto the ground in a heap.

Ethan was about to call out congratulations to his little buddy when Nia growled.

"We are surrounded!" she hissed and Ethan looked around for more Doemenagg.

He didn't see any more of the insect men, but a deep guttural voice from the shadows called out. "Well fought... wizards."

8

---

than's head snapped around to where the gravelly voice had come from just in time to see a large, muscular humanoid step out from behind one of the trees. As he did, Ethan caught more movement from around them as eight other man-sized shapes stepped out from behind other trees. Nia had been right. They were surrounded.

The newcomers were about six or seven feet tall and were muscled like human bodybuilders. Their skin varied from a deep olive green to a green-gray skin and all had shaggy mops of black hair, though some were tied in ponytails. But while their bodies might look mostly humanoid, their heads and faces were definitely not human.

They had wide noses and pronounced brow ridges. But the thing that really made them stand out from humans were the two large tusks that protruded from the bottom of their mouths. Combined with their deep set, coal-black eyes, it gave them a dangerous, feral look.

Each of the creatures wore a collection of belts and bandoliers that held weapons of all sorts. The weapons were weapons of killing. These were warriors, not hunters.

They were close enough for Ethan to scan in his HUD and he swept his eyes around them and finally settled on the one who had spoken.

Drorm Thunderflame
  Orc
  Warrior
  Level 8
  Skill increase: Analyze +1%.

"There are more in the trees," Nia whispered to him. As she did, her eyes darted to two spots in the forest. Looking to where the foxgirl glanced, Ethan caught movement in the shadows of the trees. He frowned. How many more were there?

"You are wizards, yes?" Drorm Thunderflame asked in his guttural voice.

Twisting his head back to face the orc, Ethan quickly considered his answer. He knew nothing about orcs, other than what Michalus had told him about orcs taking the city of Avalon. He certainly didn't know what their feelings towards wizards were.

By their proximity and their sudden appearance, Ethan guessed they had witnessed the fight between his group and the Doemenagg. So was there really any point in lying? Probably not and it might start them off on the wrong foot.

"Two of us are," Ethan replied.

Drorm looked from Ethan to Michalus and nodded, then he turned his large head towards Par'karr. "The kobold?"

Par'karr cowed under the orc's gaze and his rabbits gathered in front of him, pointing their horns at the orc and growling.

"He's a summoner," Ethan told the orc.

"Humph," the orc scoffed and then switched his gaze back to Ethan. He scrutinized Ethan for a long moment before speaking. "Why have two wizards, their women and their pet come to our lands?"

"We did not realize these were your lands," Ethan replied. "We are on a... pilgrimage to Avalon."

Drorm snorted and unslung his axe. "Pilgrimage? We are not fools. You are spies!"

"We're not spies!" Ethan protested as he saw the orcs readying weapons. He cursed inwardly. There were too many of them to fight unscathed. If they were going to fight anyway, it wouldn't hurt to tell them the truth. "We're here to find a magical sword called Excalibur!"

The orcs, who had started to advance, stopped and looked at Drorm. The big orc, who obviously seemed to be the leader, stopped as well and arched an eyebrow. "You come for the sword?"

Ethan bit his lip and narrowed his eyes slightly, wondering if he'd just sealed their fate. He nodded to the orc. Then again, the orcs hadn't attacked yet. "Yes."

From the corner of his eye, he saw the other orcs

looking around at each other and heard their low guttural murmuring. Ethan wasn't sure if that was a good thing, or a bad thing.

"Why?" the orc leader asked, staring intently at Ethan.

Briefly wondering whether to lie to the orcs, Ethan quickly decided that, in this case, he may as well tell the truth. "The Doemenagg seemed to return and the sword, Excalibur, was the key to defeating them last time. We think we might need it this time."

There were louder murmurs among the other orcs and even Drorm chuckled. "The sword cannot be drawn. It sleeps until an orc of honor comes to claim it."

Ethan raised an eyebrow. The orc's words were actually fairly accurate. "Who told you that?"

"The shamans have told us this for generations," the orc replied. "Only one who has proven himself can attempt to pull the sword from the stone. You are not orc. You have no claim to the sword."

"But we still wish to see the sword," Ethan protested.

"You are not orc," Drorm replied. "You have no right."

Ethan gritted his teeth in frustration and checked his *Mana*.

Mana: 36

Now that he wasn't using any *Mana*, it was starting to regenerate but he was still far from his maximum. Ethan glanced around at all of the orcs. He could see twelve now but there could be more hidden around them. Even with all of his *Mana*, he wasn't sure they could defeat so many. He cursed silently.

The orc leader looked around at the dead Doemenagg bodies and nodded. "You have fought the Doemenagg and prevailed. It is a difficult thing to survive them. We respect your strength and will allow you to return to your lands. But do not come back."

Ethan knew they needed to find Excalibur and retrieve it if possible. They couldn't give up now. He had to find a way to convince them to let his group see the sword. "We really need to see the sword. Is there a way..."

"No!" Drorm growled sharply. "You are not orc! Now go! We will not extend this offer again."

Ethan struggled to think of something else to say but nothing was coming to mind when he heard Guinevere's voice from behind him.

"We demand the ancient right of parlay," she called out in a loud, commanding voice. It was the voice of a queen, or at least, one who had been queen.

Drorm frowned, making his tusks look even larger, and furrowed his brow. The other orcs murmured to themselves, looking to one another in confusion and then to Drorm. The orc leader continued to frown at Guinevere before finally answering. "Only allies of the orcs may claim the right of parlay. We do not recognize you as an ally."

The former queen stepped forward, head held high. "I am Lady Guinevere, Knight of Camelot, known to some as the Black Knight. Camelot and the orcs swore an alliance to each other in the time of the Doemenagg. I call upon you as a Knight of Camelot to honor our alliance."

There was more muttering this time, louder this time, as the orcs looked from Guinevere to Drorm and then around to each other. Ethan couldn't hear exactly what they were saying or if it were positive or negative.

The orc leader was quiet for a moment, brow furrowed, as he stared at the warrior woman. "Camelot is gone. The knights are gone. The alliance was a long time ago."

"The alliance was permanent," Guinevere countered. "Until the orcs die out or Camelot died out - that included all of the knights. At least one knight still breathes, so the pact remains."

"Impossible!" Drorm scoffed. "Humans do not live that long."

"And yet I live," she replied. "So the alliance is still active and I demand the right of parlay. Or do the orcs forfeit their honor."

All orcs turned to look Drorm, who face flushed dark green. He snarled at Guinevere as his hands tightened on the large axe he held.

If Guinevere was intimidated, she didn't show it. The warrior woman continued to stare at him in challenge.

"Our honor is intact," the leader growled at her, his voice even lower and more gravelly. "But it is not for me to decide whether we still honor the old alliance.

"You and your group will come with us to Gugmirl. The elders will decide whether or not they believe you," he snorted. He grinned wickedly. "If not, you will never leave Gugmirl."

You have received a new quest "Fate of Excalibur - Part I"

You seek the legendary sword,

Excalibur. Drorm has told you the sword can only be seen by those who are orcs or possibly their allies.

Convince the shamans you are allies.

Shaman council convinced (0/1).

Reward: 1000 experience.

Accept quest (yes or no)?

Ethan saw the quest and accepted. Given that he'd received it, he guessed they were on the right track. At least, that's what he hoped it meant.

"Warriors, come!" he yelled out and another ten orcs came out of the trees, bringing their numbers to over twenty.

Ethan whistled quietly. Even at full *Mana*, there was no way they could defeat so many at one time. For now, they were at the orcs' mercy.

Drorm made a few gestures with his hand and the orcs formed up around Ethan and his group. "Put away your weapons. We will go to Gugmirl now. If you try to leave before we get there, you will be killed."

Ethan nodded to his companions and Nia and Guinevere sheathed their swords while Par'karr stowed his magical shotgun away. Michalus kept his staff and Ethan retrieved his trident.

"We had horses but they ran away when the Doemenagg attacked. We need to retrieve them," Ethan said.

The orc leader frowned and then growled deep in his throat, which Ethan guessed was a sign of annoyance. He pointed to two orcs. "Thaggath! Ukzil! Find their animals and then follow us.

"Your animals will be found and brought along," the orc said. "For now, you will come with us. We have many days' journey back to Gugmirl."

Without another word, Drorm gestured to the other orcs and the group began a light jog to the south, forcing Ethan and his companions to start jogging with them or risk being run over.

Nia jogged alongside him, moving close enough so that only he could hear her words. "This is what you wanted?"

Ethan bit his lip and looked at Guinevere's back as the warrior woman ran in front of him. He looked back at his wife. "Let's hope so."

The foxgirl nodded and then glanced down to her scimitars and then her eyes met his. The message was clear. If it came to it, she was ready to fight.

Ethan gave her a small nod. He knew all of his companions would fight, if it came to it. Glancing around at the twenty or so orcs around them, he hoped it wouldn't come to that.

9

His group traveled with the orcs until dusk, when they finally stopped at the edge of a wide river. During the trip, Ethan had taken the time to *Analyze* each of the orcs and had been rewarded by finally getting another level up in the skill. This gave him another point of *Intellect* and further boosted his *Mana*.

He checked out his new maximum *Mana* and his new *Intellect*:

```
Intellect: 42
Mana: 105
```

Ethan grinned at his new totals, then he snickered. If the *Intellect* stat was true intelligence, at this point, he should be on par with Stephen Hawking or Einstein. But he wasn't. In fact, he didn't feel as if he were any smarter than when he arrived. So what was the *Intellect* stat really a measure of?

Taking his mind off his new stats, Ethan glanced around the area near the water. He frowned. Like the site of the last Akugyo attack, this river was wide and had a long, stone bridge as well. He immediately became wary. It seemed like a perfect place for another attack.

Drorm ordered some orcs to set up and build a fire. The orc leader sent others out into the forest to hunt for game. When he was through barking his orders, he came to stand next to Ethan and his group.

"You will eat with us," he told them. He gestured to an area in the middle of the other orcs. "You will camp there."

Ethan and his group exchanged looks, remembering their last crossing of a large river where an Akugyo wizard had created a large watery hand and he had almost become a meal for a shark.

Were the fishmen still following them? Would they attack a group so large? He debated on whether or not to say anything to the orcs but finally decided it was in every-one's best interest if they were aware of the danger.

"Are you worried about attacks from the Akugyo?" Ethan asked the orc leader.

Drorm tilted his head to the side and scoffed. "The fish folk?"

Ethan nodded and gestured to the river and then to the ocean. "That river looks deep and it runs right into the ocean. The fishmen could come right up to the shore here."

The orc leader chuckled. "Ha! The fish folk are

cowards. They do not attack us. We are too strong for them."

Ethan looked around to his companions, who gave him skeptical looks. The fishmen they'd fought hadn't seemed like cowards. Of course, there had always been at least ten of them to his group's five, so maybe they attacked when the odds were in their favor.

"We've been attacked a number of times..." Ethan started but the orc sneered.

"You are not orcs," he sneered. "They do not fear you."

"Last time," Ethan countered. "They had a wizard with them."

That seemed to take Drorm off guard. He stared at Ethan for a long moment before answering. "We have not encountered many fish folk wizards. Are you sure?"

Ethan gestured with his trident. "The first attack had a wizard and I took this from him."

He channeled a little *Mana* so the Chymera crystal glowed a pale blue. "The last attack happened on a bridge similar to this one. The wizard tried to grab some of us with a giant hand of water. At the same time, sharks jumped out of the water and attempted to make a snack out of us."

Drorm's eyes darted to the bridge and the quick-moving water underneath it. He glanced down the length of the river to where it emptied into the ocean. Finally, he looked back to Ethan. "How many attacked you?"

Ethan bit his lip and then shrugged. "I only got a quick glance at them before they attacked. They mostly stayed submerged, I assume so I couldn't target them with spells.

But I'd guess maybe twenty or so Akugyo and a half dozen sharks."

The orc leader frowned. "The sharks cannot come on land, so only the fishmen can attack. We can easily defeat twenty."

"But they also have a wizard," Ethan told him.

"At least one," Michalus corrected, speaking up for the first time. "We know there was at least one wizard, but there could be more than one."

"We have no shamans with us to counter their magic." Drorm's expression darkened. He glanced from Ethan to Michalus. "If they do attack, you will counter their magic."

Ethan resisted the urge to roll his eyes at the big orc. First, Ethan didn't appreciate the orc barking orders at him and his companions. Second, if there was a single wizard, Ethan and Michalus should be able to counter him. If there were two or three, that became a different story.

Still, for the moment, they needed to stay in the orc's good graces. Guinevere had invoked the right of parlay and although Ethan didn't understand what that meant, he guessed antagonizing their "hosts" would be counter-productive to any parlay or negotiations.

He nodded to the big orc. "We will do our best."

"Good." The orc nodded. "Then we are not worried."

He appreciated the orc's bravado, but Ethan wasn't quite as confident. Before the bridge attack, he might have agreed. But the bridge attack had been different. He felt like the fishmen had stepped up their game.

The Akugyo had anticipated where they would go, managed to get there before them and were ready to ambush them when they were most vulnerable - on the bridge. To Ethan, that showed a decent grasp of tactics.

"I can scout the river to see if they are waiting for us," Ethan offered.

Drorm raised a thick eyebrow. "You can look into the water?"

Ethan shook his head. "I can summon an elemental of water, send it into the river and then look through its eyes."

The big orc considered his words for a moment. Drorm stared at the river then out to the ocean before returning his gaze to Ethan. "Do this and report if the fish folk are preparing an attack."

"Sure," Ethan agreed. He quickly summoned his water elemental and the watery creature appeared near him.

Drorm seemed slightly surprised at the appearance of the elemental, as did a few of the orcs around them. Ethan wondered if summoning elementals was not a normal thing for orc wizards. Or perhaps it was just water elementals that were rare. After all, until they started "fishing" in the ocean, he'd never actually summoned a water elemental.

Sitting down cross legged, Ethan used his *Clairvoyance* skill to look through the water elemental's eyes and then commanded it to go to the river. His elemental obeyed his command and slithered over to the river's edge before "pouring" itself into the water.

Ethan blinked his eyes as his vision adjusted to the watery environment. Like his previous underwater viewings through the elemental's eyes, the water itself seemed completely invisible and he saw only the fish, vegetation and other items suspended in midair. He knew everything was actually floating in the water, but the illusion of floating was surreal.

Pushing his fascination to the back of his mind, Ethan scanned the area under the bridge for any signs of the Akugyo but saw nothing. He also happily noted there was no gigantic, tentacled Sollasina cthulhu waiting for them either.

Turning, he looked down the river towards the ocean. Ethan half expected to see a troop of the fishmen and their sharks staring back at him but there was nothing. No sign of any sharks or fishmen as far as he could see.

He ordered the water elemental to go further down the river to get a better look at the area where the river met the ocean. Despite the water elemental's ability to filter out the water, it did seem to have a range limit to where everything disappeared into murky colors.

Ethan moved out towards the center of the river and closer to the ocean when he felt panic from the water elemental. At the same time, he sensed movement from the corner of his eye. He spun the elemental towards the movement and saw a huge gray shape rocketing through the water at him.

He had turned enough to see a large group of the fishmen on the opposite side of the bridge, away from the ocean. Was that a tactical move? Did they realize Ethan and his friends would expect an attack from the ocean side of the river?

As his mind raced with what to do, the gray shape opened its enormous mouth and chomped it down on him.

Your lesser elemental (water) has been dismissed.

"Argh!" Ethan screamed, raising his hands instinctively to protect himself. His heart was racing and he had broken out in a cold sweat at the prospect of being eaten by the shark. He blinked as he realized he was back in his own body. Then, he swore loudly.

Drorm looked down at him in confusion and a bit of amusement. "Is something wrong with him?"

"They're here!" Ethan blurted out. "They're here!"

"The fish folk?" the orc leader asked, searching the river with his eyes.

Ethan shivered, the shark's gigantic, tooth-filled maw still fresh in his memory. He stood up and started to point towards the side of the river further from the ocean. "They're on that side, waiting! And this time, there's at least twenty or thirty of them!"

Drorm's eyes darted from Ethan to the river. He spun towards the other orcs in the camp and made a circle gesture with his arm. "Defensive formation! Prepare for attack!"

Ethan looked to his companions, but they were already readying weapons and looking out at the river.

The fight seemed about to begin.

10

———

The orcs formed up ranks in a surprisingly organized fashion. His initial impression that these were barbaric orcs, similar to what he'd seen in the movies, had been proved wrong. These orcs were obviously organized and disciplined.

Once his orcs had formed ranks, Drorm looked from the river to Ethan. "Why are they not attacking?"

Ethan glanced over to the orc and shrugged. "I have no idea.

"The element of surprise is lost," he said. "If the fish folk would have attacked now, they might have had some small advantage. And yet, they wait."

Looking out at the river, Ethan's gaze wandered to the bridge and he groaned. "They don't need to attack us right now. They can just wait until we cross the bridge and attack when they have more of an advantage."

Drorm frowned. "How does the bridge provide them

an advantage. In a more confined area, any superior number advantage they might have would be negated."

"The sharks," Guinevere said. "They want to use the sharks to even the odds."

"And magic hands!" Par'karr chirped, and then immediately cowered under the orc leader's gaze.

"That would be my guess too." Ethan nodded. "They don't need to attack now. They can just wait until we cross the river and then send the sharks in to take out some of our numbers and, as Par'karr says, pummel us or pull us off with that magical water hand spell."

The orc leader looked at the bridge and his scowl deepened. "How big are the sharks? Perhaps we can fight them off."

Ethan shook his head. "They're huge. It's hard to get a perspective when I see them in the water, but I guess they're at least twenty feet long. But they can jump out of the water and across the bridge. That much weight, moving that quickly..."

"That would make it very difficult to fight them." Drorm scowled. Then his expression turned thoughtful and he scratched his chin. "We might be able to put trees and sharpen both ends to use as a deterrent. If they tried to jump up at us, they would impale themselves."

"Magic hands," Par'karr said. "Magic hands grab trees..."

Once again, the little kobold looked down at his toes when the orc turned to him. Drorm turned to Ethan. "Can you stop the fish wizards?"

Ethan looked to Michalus. The old wizard scratched his own chin as he seemed to consider the idea. Before, he'd frozen the hand, which stopped it briefly. But could they actually counter the spell? And what if there was more than one wizard casting them or one fishman wizard could control multiple hands?

"I'm not completely sure," Michalus responded. "If they use a hand like before, I think we might be able to. But these Akugyo wizards have shown themselves to be very skilled with water magic. They may have other tricks up their sleeves that we cannot counter."

Biting his lip, Ethan knew what he needed to do but he also knew the dangers. He needed to create a portal to the opposite shore and bypass the bridge completely. And yet, if he did, the Doemenagg queen would sense his portal activity and send more of those Collectors.

Ethan glanced around the area, trying to come up with another idea but nothing came to mind. He shook his head and sighed. "I can get us across the bridge safely."

Drorm's head snapped around to look at Ethan. "How?"

"I can create a portal from this side to the opposite bank," Ethan told him and the orc started opening his mouth but Ethan held up a hand. "BUT... doing so will probably reveal our location to the Doemenagg."

The orc leader, who was looking annoyed at Ethan cutting him off, closed his mouth and frowned. "The insects."

Ethan nodded.

"How many will come?" the orc leader asked.

Ethan shrugged. "I have no idea. Last time, we fought four. The time before that, we fought two. If that pattern follows, the next time we might face eight."

"The insects have magic too," Drorm pointed out.

Once again, Ethan nodded.

The big orc brightened. "Can you create a portal back to Gugmirl? There, we have an army. The Doemenagg would stand no chance."

"I can only portal to someplace I've marked, some place I know really well or some place I'm looking at... like the opposite bank," Ethan admitted. He wrinkled his forehead. "What is Gugmirl, anyway?"

Drorm chuckled. "I believe your people called it, Highshire."

Michalus blanched. "Highshire has fallen?"

The orc leader threw his head back and laughed. "Fallen?! Ha! They begged us for our protection. We marched in through open gates."

Ethan cast a glance at Nia and mouthed "truth" to the foxgirl. Unlike the rest of them, she had an unnaturally good sense of smell and could smell a lie.

The foxgirl nodded. What Drorm was saying was true. That begged the question that Guinevere beat him to asking.

"Protection?" the warrior woman asked, her scowl telling the orc she didn't believe him. "Protection from what?"

Drorm smirked at the group's dubious expressions. "From the dragon."

"Dragon?!" Ethan and his companions exclaimed at nearly the same time. He would have thought it comical if he hadn't actually seen a real, gigantic dragon already. Luckily, that one hadn't been interested in them at the time. Now there was another dragon and a city had surrendered to orcs for protection.

As he remembered how enormous the dragon had been, he wondered what sort of protection the orcs could actually provide - if any. The dragon he'd seen was large enough to shrug off any blows these orcs could deliver.

"Yes," Drorm replied to the group with a grim expression. "The dragon, we call it Bal'Furtun, Firestorm."

The name Firestorm gave Ethan a bad feeling in the pit of his stomach. "It can breathe fire?"

The orc leader furrowed his brow. "Breathe fire? No. But it seems to be an adept with fire magic."

"It's a wizard?!" Ethan gasped.

"All dragons have command of magic," Michalus answered before Drorm could open his mouth. "Some have even taught humanoid wizards."

Ethan did a double take. "What?!"

"It is true." The orc nodded. "In the past, it is said that some of our shamans were taught by Bal'Furtun."

"Were?" Nia asked. As she asked, she gave Ethan an almost imperceptible nod, letting him know that the orc spoke the truth.

"The dragon went into a slumber over a hundred years ago," Drorm replied. "When it awoke a few months ago, it began attacking the cities near its lair and refused to speak with us. The shamans do not know why it has suddenly begun to attack orc and human cities."

"And you can fight it off?" Guinevere asked, her expression curious yet doubtful.

Drorm snorted. "We have adapted our weapons of war

to fight the dragon. We shoot arrows the size of orcs up into the sky."

The orc leader's face went grim. "Sometimes it works. Sometimes it does not."

"Do your shamans repel the dragon with magic? Or counter its fire magic?" Michalus asked.

"The shamans stay in Jikhasif, the city you knew as Avalon," he told them. "They rule from there and do not leave."

"Is that where the sword is?" Guinevere asked.

Drorm narrowed his eyes. "The shamans will tell you where the sword is, IF they find you worthy."

A tense silence followed his comment as Guinevere and Drorm had a staring contest. The others looked from the orc leader to the warrior woman to see who would look away first.

Ethan felt the need to diffuse the situation and gestured to the river. "The shamans aren't going to find anyone worthy if we can't cross the river."

Seeming to seize the opportunity to turn away from the unflinching Guinevere, the orc turned on Ethan. "It seems we have two choices. Either fight our way across or use your portal and risk the Doemenagg."

"Pretty much," Ethan agreed. He looked around at his companions. "Unless anyone else has any ideas."

Nia pointed up the river. "Is there another bridge? Perhaps where the water is more shallow?"

Drorm shook his head. "Not that I know of."

Ethan turned back to Drorm. "Then, those seem to be our choices."

"Then let us portal over to the other side and deal with

the insects when, and if, they come," he growled. "At least those, we can fight head on and not have cowards jumping out of the water to snatch us."

Ethan nodded. "Okay, but we need to wait until morning."

"Why?!" the orc leader demanded.

"If we use the portal," he replied, "and it does alert the Doemenagg, we don't want them converging on us anywhere near the river. The last thing we need is a fight on two fronts. We should move on as soon as we portal. Since it's dark..."

"Waiting until morning would give us the light to move on right away," Drorm agreed. "Very well. But we will make preparations, in case the fish folk grow impatient..."

The orc leader might have said more but a commotion arose from the other orcs. Drorm and Ethan's group looked to where the other orcs were pointing and saw a welcome sight.

Coming down the road were the orcs Drorm had sent after their horses. Tied to a rope behind the orcs were their horses. The fading light was just enough for Ethan to count them and confirm that all of the horses had been retrieved.

"They have returned with your animals," the orc leader said.

"And our packs," Ethan smiled.

"Good," Drorm said, gesturing the orcs over to him. "Get your things from the animals and set up your bedrolls in the middle while I set the watches."

The orc leader turned and walked into the middle of

the other orcs and began barking orders. Once he was out of earshot, Ethan turned to the others. "They can set their watches, but we'll set our own. If the fishmen do attack, I want us to be ready."

With a glance at the river and the knowledge of what lay just beneath it, no one in his group argued.

11

Despite their preparations, no attacks came that night. Neither the orcs nor his own companions saw any movement in the river at all. No fishmen had poked their heads up and no shark fins had appeared.

Ethan had sent another water elemental to check up on the Akugyo when it had been his turn on watch and they had still been in roughly the same spot. They'd also sent a shark after his water elemental almost instantly.

No sooner had he stood up from his bedrolls, when Drorm came over him. Like Ethan and his group, the orc leader looked tired and his eyes were bloodshot. His face was turned into a scowl. "Are the fish folk still there?"

"They were last night when I checked," he replied, stifling a yawn. It had been about midnight when he'd checked but Michalus had the last watch. He looked over at the wizard. "Michalus, were they there when you checked?"

The wizard looked at him with bleary eyes and nodded.

"Looks like they've just been waiting all night for us," Ethan told the orc. "Let me see if they're still at it."

Summoning his water elemental, he sent it into the water and managed a quick glimpse at the underwater river before a shark torpedoed into his elemental.

Your lesser elemental (water) has been dismissed.

Ethan shivered at the afterimage of the shark but something else had caught his eye just before his elemental had died. He'd seen several of the Akugyo near the closest support beam for the bridge.

He hadn't gotten a good look at exactly what they were doing, but he had a bad feeling about it. Ethan swore.

"What? They are still there?" Drorm asked.

"Oh, they're still there," Ethan answered, casting a glance at the bridge. "And I think they might be sabotaging the bridge."

"Sabotage? How?" The orc leader frowned as he followed Ethan's gaze to the bridge's first support.

Ethan shrugged. "I only got a glance, but I saw several of the Akugyo around that first support. I'm wondering if they are weakening it so it would collapse as we go across it."

"Then they show a lack of understanding of tactics," the orc scoffed.

"How so?" Michalus asked as he came to stand next to Ethan.

Before the orc could answer, Nia stepped over to them. "You do not sabotage the first support in a bridge. You sabotage one in the middle or towards the opposite side. This way you get more of the enemy."

Drorm gave Nia an approving nod, just as Par'karr and Guinevere joined them. "The foxling is correct. It makes no sense to sabotage the first support. Not only would they get few of us, the others could easily retreat back onto the bank."

Now that it was pointed out to him, Nia's and Drorm's explanation made sense. Sabotaging the first support didn't seem to make sense. They really wouldn't catch many people.

"Unless," Guinevere interjected. "What if the Akugyo are not sabotaging the first support. What if they're sabotaging the first and the last supports. If they can collapse them when we are in the middle..."

She didn't need to finish. They all knew what would happen. If the bridge didn't collapse outright, he and the orcs would be trapped in the middle of the river with no way to get to either shore without going into the river.

"Hmm," the orc growled. "Perhaps they do understand tactics."

"I would not underestimate them," the warrior woman warned. "We did not have many skirmishes with them, but when we did, they showed a surprising grasp of military theory, as well as some unorthodox tactics."

Drorm raised an eyebrow at Guinevere but said nothing. Instead, he turned to Ethan. "But you can create a magic portal to allow us to skip the bridge, yes?"

"I can." Ethan nodded. "But once I create it, everyone

will need to move quickly. It takes a lot of mana to open and then keep open a portal large enough to fit the horses."

"And once on the other side, we must leave the area quickly, yes?" the orc leader asked.

"Yes. If I'm right, the Doemenagg Queen will sense the portal and send her assassin insects to find us," he replied. Ethan bit his lip. What he should have said was, the queen would send her assassins to find HIM.

He remembered back to the brief mental contact he'd had with the queen. Ethan knew the queen wanted him, or rather, his knowledge of portals. Why, he wasn't sure. Unless it was because he'd specialized in Aether magic? Surely there were other wizards who had done so. He blanched. Or were there?

Ethan had unlocked portal magic quite by accident. From his conversations with Michalus, he'd unlocked much earlier than most other wizards. Then, not long afterwards, he'd received the Specialization ability and had to choose which school to specialize in. Had he not accidentally unlocked Aether magic, he would have chosen something else.

He cursed. First, he'd chosen the wizard class, which had automatically made him a target of the brain-sucking Doemenaggs. Then, he specialized in Aether magic and made himself the main course. Ethan shook his head in disgust.

Drorm raised an eyebrow. "Is something... wrong?"

Unsure that he wanted to share the fact that he might be on the top of the Doemenagg queen's hit list, Ethan quickly came up with an excuse. "I... I was just thinking that the reason they may be killing my elementals so quickly might be to prevent us from seeing exactly what they are doing."

"If that is so, then they do have a firmer grasp of tactics that I originally thought." The orc leader nodded. He chuckled and slapped Ethan hard on the back. "Good thing we will be bypassing the bridge altogether."

Forcing a smile, Ethan nodded. The orc was strong and the blow had very nearly knocked the wind out of him.

"I will prepare my troops," Drorm told them. "Where should we assemble?"

Ethan scanned the area before pointing to a spot about a dozen yards from the bank of the river. A partially buried boulder was sticking out from the dirt and, if Ethan stood on it, would allow him to get a better view of the opposite side of the bank. He pointed. "I'll stand there and open the portal next to me."

"Good. I will order them to gather as soon as they have eaten." Drorm grunted and, without another word, he spun on his heel and marched back to his men.

Once he was out of earshot, Nia turned to Ethan with her hands on her hips. "You were not truthful. What are you hiding?"

Ethan kept forgetting the foxgirl could tell when he lied by his scent. He sighed and looked around to make sure none of the orcs were within earshot. Turning back to his companions, he took a deep breath.

"I think the queen is after me specifically," he told his friends.

"Oh?" Michalus asked, raising both eyebrows. "Why is that?"

"I think it's because I specialized in Aether magic," he replied. "During my brief contact with her mind, there was... excitement... about the portal magic."

"An interesting theory," the wizard said as he scratched his chin. "But remember, she came after me first."

Ethan nodded, remembering how the wizard had appeared in Hawkshead, terribly wounded. Michalus had fought one of the Doemenagg and nearly died. It had taken the Grail to bring him back from the brink of death.

"But you must have been attacked near Hawkshead," Ethan countered. "Otherwise, given your wounds, you probably wouldn't have made it to the village."

"That seems like a logical assumption."

"If that's the case, then it's entirely possible that the Doemenagg that attacked you, was actually meant for me."

"Hmm," was all the wizard said, and continued to scratch his chin.

"The Doemenagg came for you?" Nia asked, alarmed.

Ethan gave her an uncertain shrug. "I'm just guessing, but it makes sense. I was in Hawkshead. It must have been on its way and mistook him for me."

The group was quiet for a long moment. It was Guinevere who finally broke the silence. "Do you know why the queen wants your knowledge of portal magic?"

He shrugged. "No idea. All I got from her were impressions. Emotions. No thoughts. I just know she sensed something about the portal magic in me and then got really excited."

"Portal magic would allow her to traverse great distances quickly," Nia said. "It would be a great tactical advantage. No walls could keep her out."

"You think the queen is planning an invasion?" Ethan asked.

Guinevere frowned. "They invaded before. It does make sense. First, eliminate the wizards who were her biggest bane in the first war. Then, learn the secrets of portal magic so that she can send her insects wherever she wants, whenever she wants."

It was a sobering thought. Ethan could be the key for the queen's world domination scheme. Geez. No pressure.

"There is another possibility," Michalus said slowly, drawing out each word as he stroked his chin. The wizard paused, either to collect his thoughts or make sure everyone was listening to him.

Looking around the group, Michalus continued. "It may not be our world she is looking to conquer."

"Yes, but she..." Guinevere started but the wizard shook his head.

"I know the Doemenagg attacked back then," Michalus conceded. "But Ethan has done something I didn't even know was possible. He created a portal from one world to another. It may be THAT knowledge she wants. Not just knowledge of portals. She may not just want one world. If she knew how to portal to other planets, she could jump from world to world."

He saw Guinevere blanch at the thought and Ethan hissed curse. "You really think she could figure out how to do that?"

Michalus shrugged. "It's just a theory. But it does mean

you would be extremely valuable to her. After all, you are the only wizard I've heard of, who created a portal to another planet!"

"No," Ethan contradicted him and the wizard raised an eyebrow. "Whoever created that gate to the other planet did it first. He actually created a portal gateway there!"

The wizard scratched his chin. "You have a fair point. However, that wizard is most likely already dead. You may well be the only living wizard who has done it."

"And it means she won't give up until she gets me." Ethan frowned and shook his head. Great. Just freaking great.

12

"Last call for breakfast!" Drorm yelled, breaking the group out of their conversation.

Ethan looked around at his group and was about to tell them all to gather around when he noticed that Guinevere was still pale. Considering the warrior woman had been alive for over a thousand years and had likely fought countless battles, he thought it out of character.

"Are you alright?" Ethan asked the armored woman.

Guinevere blinked and then nodded. "Yes. I was just... remembering something."

"About the Doemenagg?" he asked, now curious what would make the former queen go white.

"I will... tell you later." She shook her head as if to clear it of bad thoughts. "The orcs are ready and we should not keep them waiting."

The former queen didn't wait for him to reply but

simply turned and headed to the cooking fire, leaving the rest of the group to stare after her.

"I wonder what was that about?" Michalus asked as he stared after Guinevere.

Ethan shrugged. He was curious too, but glancing towards the river, he knew he had other things to worry about at the moment. "Let's get some food before it's all gone and then let's get to the other side of this river."

AN HOUR LATER, both groups had their camps packed away and their gear stowed. Ethan and his group were with Drorm near the boulder he'd pointed out earlier.

"We are ready then?" Drorm asked.

Ethan nodded, but wrinkled his forehead as he saw a group of orcs near the bridge. He tilted his head slightly and frowned. "Those orcs aren't going to try and make it across are they?"

Drorm snorted. "No. But I ordered them to stand near the bridge so it seems like we might be about to go across."

"Good idea," Ethan admitted. He still wasn't sure if the fishmen could see outside of the water, but if they were, the orc leader's deception would have the Akugyo concentrating on the wrong area.

"Do you fear an attack if they realize what we are about to do?" Nia asked.

Hearing Nia's question, Ethan glanced out at the river. He hadn't considered that the Akugyo might actually launch an attack at them on land if they realized what

Ethan was doing. He figured if they were going to attack on land, they would already have done so.

But his wife made a good point. If the Akugyo could see what was going on with them, they might abandon their waiting game and launch an offense on land. Suddenly, being the last person through the portal didn't sound like such a great idea.

The big orc shrugged. "I don't know. But if we can keep them guessing, they will not have time to deploy their troops before we are on the opposite side of the river."

"But you can't know that," Guinevere piped in. "We have no idea how quickly they can redeploy their troops. Ethan has seen them move extraordinarily fast underwater."

"I will stay with Ethan until all the others have gone through the portal," Nia stated in a tone that told him it wasn't up for discussion.

"Par'karr stay too," his kobold companion said, patting his magical shotgun.

"You'll need me if their wizard shows themselves," Michalus told him. "Unless you think you can counter any spells while maintaining the portal..."

Ethan shook his head. Maintaining a large portal took nearly all of his concentration. He doubted he could spare the concentration to even recognize a spell, let alone counter it.

Drorm narrowed his eyes at the group. "You want us to go through the portal, to the other side of the river, while all of you remain? How do I know you won't simply strand us on the far side? If I understand portals, they are one way, yes? We cannot come back through it once on the other side?"

Stopping himself from rolling his eyes, Ethan nodded. "That's correct. They are one way. Once you and your orcs are over there, you can't come back through. That means, if I get attacked while still over here, you can't come back and help. I don't understand. Why do you even care? At least you'll be safe."

The orc leader growled. "She has invoked the right of parlay! I am now honor bound to see her to the shamans! If you leave us now trapped over there, my honor is forfeit!"

Ethan was about to open his mouth to try and talk some sense into the orc but Guinevere stepped in front of Drorm and stared up at him. While he was a good head taller than her, the former queen had a presence that somehow made her seem just as intimidating as the big orc.

"I invoked the right of parlay," she snapped. "I will go first through the portal. Therefore, even if something were to happen and my companions did not make it, your honor would be intact."

The orc leader and the former queen stood locked in a stare for what seemed like minutes before Drorm snorted. "This is acceptable."

Turning from Guinevere, he began yelling orders to the other orcs. Under their leader's direction, they assembled next to the boulder. All except for six orcs, who were hanging out at the entrance to the bridge.

"I guess I'm up," Ethan muttered, looking at the boulder. He glanced at the river before turning to his companions. "Guinevere, can you lead the horses through when you go?"

"Of course," she replied. He could see that something was still bothering her but he knew now wasn't the time to pursue it.

Instead, he turned to his other companions. "I know I can't talk any of you out of staying with me, so thank you. Hopefully, nothing will happen. If it does, our strategy is to get through the portal without fighting if we can. No heroics. We keep the portal open until everyone else is through, then you go, then me last."

Nia bit her lip but gave him a curt nod. He knew she wasn't happy going through before him but there was no choice. As soon as he went through, the portal would collapse. The others nodded or gave him affirmative answers. Ethan hoped things went as smoothly as he had portrayed.

Guinevere reached behind her back and pulled off her shield. She looked at the shield for a moment and then held it out to Nia. "Take this to defend him with."

The foxgirl wrinkled her forehead. "I prefer..."

"I know you prefer your scimitars," Guinevere cut her off and thrust the shield towards her. "But this shield will repel magic. If the Akugyo wizard does appear, you can use it to absorb any magic he throws at you."

Ethan felt his mouth fall open. "You have a magic shield that can't be affected by magic?!"

A slight smile played upon the former queen's mouth. "My father WAS Merlin, the greatest wizard to ever live. You don't think he wouldn't give his only daughter a little advantage, do you?"

Guinevere's smile broadened and she gestured to her armor. "All of my armor repels magic, direct magic, at least. I used to have a magic helmet that also protected me... but I made the mistake of taking it off when I went to try to talk some sense into Mordred. Had I kept it on, he would never have been able to control me."

"Where helmet now?" Par'karr asked, wide-eyed.

"Gone," the warrior woman replied. "Mordred didn't want me to be able to use it to resist him again if he ever lost control, so he had me crush it with a large stone."

Ethan nodded at the woman's words but he was remembering the anti-magic stone in Arthur's tomb. Merlin had made the stone with some sort of enchantment that was far beyond his understanding but somehow made it resist any magic thrown at it. Her armor must work on the same principle.

Nia looked at Ethan, a look of resolve on her face and then took the offered shield. She smiled up at Guinevere. "Thank you."

The former queen winked at her. "Just remember it's just a loan."

"Of course," Nia said and then strapped the shield to her arm.

"Wait a minute," Ethan said as things suddenly stopped making sense. "How have you even been able to go through my portals wearing that armor?! I mean... shouldn't the portal snap closed the moment you touch it with your armor or shield?"

Guinevere shrugged. "I'm not a wizard. I don't pretend to understand how it works. I only know that it does."

"Actually, I think I have a theory that might explain it,"

Michalus said with a raised finger. When everyone looked at him, the wizard cleared his throat and explained. "Ahem, yes, well. You see, the process of opening a portal is an act of magic but the portal itself is not actually magical. That is why she can pass through portals."

"Wait... what?" Ethan asked, confused. How could the portal itself not be magical? He had to focus to keep it open.

"I remember reading a book on how portals are actually opening a doorway into the Bifrost, as you call it, and..." Michalus began to explain but was interrupted by Drorm's shout.

"We are ready!" the orc leader yelled. "Let us spend no more time here. Come!"

Ethan shrugged to his companions and then gave Michalus an apologetic look. "Sorry, Michalus. You can tell us later. All right, people, places!"

Guinevere went to grab the horses, while the rest of them took their positions around the boulder. Ethan climbed to the top of the big rock and looked out across the river to the opposite side.

From his vantage point, Ethan could see a barren area on the far side of the river. Choosing that spot as the target for his portal, he mentally marked the area and turned to look down at Drorm. "Ready?"

"We are ready," the orc leader replied.

Ethan took a deep breath. "Alright. Here goes nothing."

Focusing on a small clearing on the opposite shore, Ethan opened up a portal and felt most of his *Mana* leave him. As it did, a vertical slit appeared in the air at ground level to his right and this opened into an 8-feet-tall by 4-feet-wide portal.

Like the last time, he felt his focus straining to keep the extra-large portal open. He gritted his teeth at the effort. "Go Guinevere!"

His HUD was up and he glanced at his *Mana*.

Mana: 56

The warrior woman wasted no time and walked through the portal with the horses. As she did, Ethan saw her appear on the opposite side of the shore. "She made it! Drorm! Send them through!"

The orc leader barked an order and then went through the portal himself. As soon as he'd disappeared, the other orcs began filing through.

After only half a dozen orcs had made it through, the water of the river began to bubble and Ethan could see shapes in the water. Suddenly, Akugyo launched themselves out of the water and landed on the shore.

Over half of the orcs were through now but the fishmen were running towards them with their awkward gait. Ethan cursed as he realized not everyone would be through the portal before the first wave of Akugyo would reach them.

13

D rorm and the remaining orcs stared at the approaching enemies and snarled. They pulled their weapons out and shifted anxiously. Ethan's companions also readied their own weapons and exchanged worried looks.

Mana: 49

Ethan's *Mana* was draining quickly and it was taking almost all of his focus to keep the portal open. He did spare a glance at the shoreline and saw that there were now at least a dozen fishmen coming towards them, with more leaving the water every minute.

"Keep going!" Ethan yelled. "I can't hold the portal long!"

The orc leader growled as he glanced at the approaching enemies but then barked an order to his remaining orcs. They looked unsure, growling at the approaching Akugyo in challenge. Then Drorm bellowed at his orcs louder and, with a quick look at their leader, the orcs began to once again file through the portal.

Mana: 42

Gritting his teeth against the exertion, Ethan got his friends' attention. "We're going to need to hold them off for a few minutes!"

Immediately, his friends sprang into action. Michalus summoned a large earth elemental that appeared in the shape of a gorilla. At least, that was the closest thing Ethan could think to compare it to - if gorillas had four arms and no head.

The elemental was bipedal but had short, stocky legs and four thick, elongated arms. The thing's torso was thick, with a broad chest that tapered to a slimmer waist. The only thing that was missing was a head.

There was no neck or head of any kind and if the elemental was flesh and blood, Ethan had no idea how the thing would be able to see, speak or eat. But it wasn't flesh and blood. It was a creature from another universe or some other plane of existence.

Michalus gestured at the incoming fishmen and the elemental, despite having no way to seemingly see the gesture or hear any commands, charged off towards the line of Akugyo.

At the same time, Par'karr's rabbits charged off at the approaching fishmen too. As they did, the kobold yanked the trigger of the magical shotgun and a double shot of stones thudded out of the enchanted weapon and hit the closest Akugyo in the chest and stomach.

The fishman staggered as the stone slammed into him. They shattered on contact with the creature's coral armor, but not before the two impacts cracked the Akugyo's breastplate. The thing staggered and one arm reached up to its chest as it tripped over its own webbed feet and went tumbling to the ground.

A few seconds later, Par'karr's demon rabbits reached the downed fishman and, with powerful leaps, impaled the creature's head with their horns.

Mana: 37

The orcs continued to stream through the portal and Ethan thought they might just make it. As if to contradict his optimism, the water near the surface began to bubble as something rose from the depths to the surface.

An enormous shark broke the turbulent surface of the river, its dorsal fin rising a good three or four feet above the water. Atop the creature was a colorfully decorated Akugyo that straddled the shark on some sort of saddle.

While the new fishman's colorful garb set it apart from the others, what grabbed Ethan's attention was the trident it held and the glowing blue crystal embedded in it. A Chymera crystal. This Akugyo was a wizard. Ethan cursed.

Before he'd even finished uttering his curse, another shark rose out of the water next to the first. Like the first shark, this one also had a rider. While not as colorfully decorated as the first, the second shark rider also held a trident with a Chymera crystal. Another wizard. Ethan swore even louder.

"Michalus!" he hissed.

"I see them, my boy!" the wizard yelled. Michalus sent a flaming ball of energy towards the two but the first one gestured with its staff and an arch of water shot from the river and the ball of fire was snuffed out.

"That's not good," Ethan muttered.

The second one gestured and Ethan felt a rendering sensation from the portal, as if someone was trying to rip it away from him. The sudden mental jerking caused him to nearly lose his focus and the portal flickered.

Ethan clamped down on his willpower, forcing the portal to stay active even as he felt something trying to rip it away from him. No, not something, he knew. Someone. The second Akugyo wizard was trying to disrupt the portal before they could get away. And it had almost succeeded!

"The one on the left... it's trying to destabilize... the portal," Ethan said as he struggled to keep his focus and concentration.

Mana: 21

The additional focus and *Mana* it was taking to keep the portal stabilized was quickly draining him. If this kept up, he wouldn't be able to keep the portal going for more than a few more seconds.

Ethan glanced desperately around and saw the last of Drorm's orcs filing through the portal. The orc leader hesitated as he saw the approaching fishmen.

"Go! Now!" Ethan hissed. "Can't... keep... it... going!"

Drorm met his eyes and then nodded, the gesture not just an affirmation but also conveying a respect for him that Ethan hadn't previously seen in the orc's eyes. Turning, the orc leader raced through the portal and disappeared.

The pull on the portal became more intense and it took almost all of his focus to keep it up. He spared a glance at his HUD.

Mana: 13

Looking at his *Mana*, Ethan realized he had only seconds before he would be out of *Mana* and then be forced to use *Overchannel*. Last time he'd used it, he'd permanently lost some of his Stamina. He didn't want to risk losing more stats but he needed to make sure his friends were safe.

The fishmen were only a few yards from them now and there was no way his group could hold off the horde of fishmen. Not with two wizards behind them, supporting them. As it was, Michalus was countering the first wizard but that wouldn't last.

Once Ethan was out of *Mana*, the second wizard could focus on Michalus. When that happened, just like he and the elf had done to the single wizards they'd previously fought, the two Akugyo wizards would overwhelm Michalus - if the fishmen warriors didn't kill them all first.

"Par'karr... Michalus... Go!" he growled. "Nia! You too!"

Michalus and Par'karr glanced up and Nia urged them into the portal. "Do as he says!"

Thankfully, both of them rushed into the portal and disappeared. He knew Nia was beside him, so he didn't look over to her. "Go, Nia!"

Mana: 5

He cursed as he saw his *Mana*. He had two seconds at most before he would need to engage his *Overchannel* and keep the portal up.

As the thought entered his mind, water sprayed up from the river like some sort of strange, reverse rain. Ethan saw the colorful wizard's trident flaring and knew he was working some sort of magic.

"Go, Nia!" he screamed.

The water flew twenty feet into the air and then seemed to turn into crystals that sparkled in the sunlight. No, Ethan realized, not crystals. The wizard had frozen them into ice shards. He cursed as he realized what would come next.

With a gesture of the fishman wizard's trident, the crystals pivoted in midair and shot directly towards Ethan and Nia.

Ethan knew he couldn't counter the spell and keep the portal up at the same time. Now, the tips of the charging fishmen's tridents were only steps away from impaling them.

And why hadn't Nia gone through the portal yet?!

Twisting his head to see where the foxling was, he caught only a blur of motion as something crashed into his back. The sudden jolt of force staggered him and sent him tumbling off the boulder.

As he fell, Ethan could feel his concentration slipping and his *Mana* running out. He tried to activate his *Over-channel* skill but then he was tumbling directly into the portal as it flickered.

"Nia!" he screamed as he realized the portal would wink out behind him and she would be trapped.

And then he was in the Bifrost, spiraling through the kaleidoscope of colors. He felt something shift around him and realized it was Nia's arms around him. Twisting, he saw her grinning face looking up at him. He chuckled as he realized the foxgirl had tackled him through the gate, just in time.

Then he realized this was the first time he'd been through the Bifrost with someone else. Every other time, he'd been alone. Even if he went through a portal a fraction of a second after someone else, he never saw anyone else in the Bifrost.

He was wondering what that might mean when he felt the breath knocked out of him as he crashed into the ground with Nia atop him. A cheer went up from the orcs as they saw them emerge and behind them the portal winked out of existence.

Struggling to raise his head as he gasped for air, Ethan saw the fishmen on the opposite side of the river swarm over the boulder he'd just been on.

The fishmen wizards seem to realize what had happened and turned their shark mounts to face Ethan and the orcs. They made no sounds, but he imagined he could feel their anger from here.

"Can they cast their magic this far?" Drorm asked as he reached down and effortlessly yanked Ethan to his feet.

Abruptly upright, Ethan struggled for a moment to put his feet on the ground before gauging the distance between them and the Akugyo. "I don't think so but let's put some distance between us and them, just to make sure."

Drorm nodded and began barking orders. Guinevere hurried over and handed the party their horses. "Impressive display of magic."

He thanked her and mounted, keeping his eyes on the two fishmen wizards. They hadn't moved, but seemed to stare daggers at Ethan. Ethan wasn't sure why, but he felt like this was personal - like they were looking directly at him.

With a final glance at the Akugyo, he spurred his horse into a gallop and followed after the others.

14

———————

Ethan and his group rode down the road while the orcs ran alongside them. The two groups did this for several miles before Ethan signalled them to a halt. As everyone came to rest, Drorm jogged up to Ethan.

"Why do you stop?" the orc leader asked.

"I thought I would give everyone a breather," Ethan responded, earning a frown from Drorm. Then he gestured out to the ocean. "Plus, I wanted to see if I could spot any sign of them pursuing us in the ocean."

The big orc's head swiveled towards the ocean and he brought his hand up to shield his eyes from the glare. "I do not see any sign of them."

"Me either," Ethan agreed, "but that doesn't mean they are not out there."

He twisted in his saddle to look down at the orc leader. "The other reason I stopped was to ask you whether there are any other large rivers like the one we just crossed before here and Highshire... I mean... Gugmirl."

Drorm scratched his mop of black hair for a moment before shaking his head. "Not that wide. But there are a few smaller rivers we must cross. One about half that size and the other two are much more shallow."

"You think they will ambush us again?" asked Nia, pulling her horse up next to his. She was joined quickly by Guinevere.

"If there was a big enough river, I expect they will," Ethan replied, with a glance down at Drorm. "And they seem to be able to outpace us in the water, probably by riding the sharks."

"The sharks are fast?" Drorm asked, brow furrowed. "But they are so big!"

Ethan nodded. He wasn't sure exactly how fast sharks could swim, but on the week of TV about sharks, they always seemed very fast. Combine that with the fact that Ethan and his group rarely actually galloped the horses and it was no wonder the Akugyo seemed to always be one step ahead of them.

"The river that is half the size of the one we just went over, how far is it and is it deep enough that the Akugyo could hide in it?" Ethan asked.

Drorm shrugged. "I do not know how deep it is. I do not believe I could see the bottom. But it is swift and there are many rocks."

"How do you think they are following us?" Guinevere asked. "Are they tracking us along from the ocean?"

"I don't know," Ethan replied. He scanned the ocean but there were only pteranodons circling the sky around the waterspouts and occasionally diving through them to catch fish. "It's not like they really need to track us, though."

Drorm, Nia and Guinevere gave him quizzical looks.

Ethan smiled. "We've been nothing but predictable. We traveled the same stretch of road, heading south. We haven't deviated from that since we returned to the shore. If they've noticed that, then they only need to get ahead of us and wait."

Drorm considered his answer for a minute before nodding his acceptance. "Then you think they will attack again?"

"It seems that way," Ethan responded and then raised an eyebrow. "Were you attacked on your way north?"

"And why were you coming north?" Guinevere added.

Drorm glared at the former queen for a long moment before narrowing his eyes. "Not that it is any business of yours, but we were patrolling the northern frontier. We had reports of villages burned. We suspected Bal'Furtun, but wanted to be sure."

Ethan exchanged glances with the women. They'd seen the burned villages on their way south and, after encountering the orcs, had assumed they had done it. "Orcs did not burn the villages?"

The big orc wrinkled his face in disgust. "We are not savages. We do not burn villages unless we are at war. And we are not at war."

"Dragon burn villages?" Par'karr piped up from behind Guinevere but then immediately hid behind the warrior woman when Drorm looked his way.

"That was what we were coming to investigate," the orc

leader replied. He gave Ethan and his friends a pointed look. "Before we met you."

Ethan raised an eyebrow. "But you suspect it was the dragon?"

Drorm nodded. "Bal'Furtun has laid waste to many villages around Gugmirl - but no bodies are left. We thought we might find the same."

"Why is the dragon bothering villages at all?" Guinevere asked.

"And why would it take the bodies?" Michalus wondered aloud.

"Maybe eat them," Par'karr offered and then swallowed loudly.

The orc leader shrugged. "We do not know why the dragon awakened after so long or why it went on a rampage."

Ethan was quiet for a moment as he thought of reasons why the dragon could be on the warpath. Unfortunately, he just didn't have enough information to even form a hypothesis.

In the meantime, his main concern was the Akugyo and making sure they were ambushed again. He looked down at Drorm again. "How far is the river you mentioned?"

"A day's travel," he responded. "We should reach it tomorrow afternoon."

"And how far is Gugmirl?" Ethan asked.

"Another two days past the river," Drorm replied.

"Then let's get going," Ethan said. "But I think we should camp in the forest, as far from the ocean as we can."

Casting a quick glance out to the ocean, the big orc nodded. "That seems like a wise precaution. Although they can move on land, their movements are clumsy - like young children."

"If it weren't for their wizards," Guinevere agreed, "they would be no match for your warriors."

"You speak the truth," the orc acknowledged. "We've encountered the fish folk before and they have posed little challenge to us. Occasionally we encounter a group of them with a wizard and then they are worthy enemies."

"How often is that?" Ethan wondered. They'd fought and killed three of the Akugyo wizards, including the one with the first group they'd encountered. Now they'd just encountered two more.

"Very rarely," Drorm replied after a moment. "I have only encountered a single fish folk wizard, though I have heard of other commanders encountering them."

"And just now, we encountered two," Ethan pointed out. "And before we met, we killed three others. That seems odd. They are rare to you and we run into so many recently."

Drorm looked thoughtful. "I agree. It does seem more than a coincidence."

"That's what I was thinking," Ethan retorted.

If fishman wizards really were as uncommon as Drorm would have him believe, then why had they encountered so many of them? Perhaps there were different groups or tribes of fishmen. Perhaps the northern tribe had more wizards and the southern tribe, the one nearest the orcs, had fewer?

"We cannot figure it out here and now," Drorm told him. "We should get moving again."

Ethan nodded and scanned the ocean again. There were still no signs of the Akugyo or their sharks but for all he knew, they were swimming out there, just under the surface. Or, they could be racing along the coast to reach the next river before them and set up another ambush.

"We'll follow your lead," Ethan told the orc commander. Then another thought occurred to him. "Are there any other villages between here and Gugmirl?"

"There are two more, but they are past the larger river." Drorm raised an eyebrow. "Why do you ask?"

"My companions and I have been on the road for months," he told the big orc. "If one of the villages has an inn, I think we'd appreciate a bed for a change."

The orc leader seemed about to object so Ethan sweetened the pot. "I do have some coin and I'd be happy to buy you and your orcs a round or two."

The other orcs, who had been speaking between themselves in hushed tones, suddenly went quiet and looked up at their leader. Drorm glanced back at the eager orcs before facing Ethan with a smirk. "I think my warriors and I would appreciate a good drink. Or two."

A cheer went up from the orcs but a glare from their leader quickly silenced them, though Ethan saw that they still muttered in quiet excitement.

"Great!" Ethan said and saw smiles from his companions. It had been a long time since they'd all slept in beds. Too long. "Let's get going then."

Drorm barked some orders to his troops and half of

them formed up in front of Ethan and his friends while the remaining orcs followed behind them.

Despite being surrounded by orcs again, it felt different. It no longer felt like Ethan and his group were prisoners. He wasn't sure what the new relationship was, but it felt better.

Ethan chuckled as he spurred his horse into a trot. He didn't care if it was facing the Akugyo together or the promise of buying them drinks, he felt much better about things.

He just hoped their new relationship remained, once the group reached Gugmirl.

15

The group reached the river Drorm had spoken about midafternoon the next day. Their previous evening had been uneventful, as had their morning. And despite keeping a close eye on the ocean for any signs of the Akugyo, there were no signs of them in the ocean.

Ethan wished that meant the fishmen had given up on chasing them. Unfortunately, experience had proven that time and time again, the Akugyo seemed to be able to get ahead of them while keeping themselves out of sight.

Thus, when they arrived at the river, Ethan was wary. So was Drorm. The two of them called a halt to the group and had them wait a hundred yards from the river while the two of them went in for a closer look.

The orcs muttered their acknowledgement but Nia immediately objected. "I must go with you!"

"Don't worry," he told her. "I'll be fine."

"Like you were on the boulder?" she retorted with a raised eyebrow.

Drorm chuckled. "I like her. She is feisty. Bring her."

Nia had hopped off her horse before the orc leader had even finished speaking. In a moment, she was next to him, hands on her scimitars.

"You have a fine mate," the big orc said. "If she were an orc, I might challenge you for her."

"You would lose," Nia said quickly, though Ethan did see her try to hide a smile.

Drorm snorted and looked Ethan up and down, his eyes coming to rest on the crystal in the trident. He shrugged. "You are probably right. He is like a shaman. Shamans never lose a challenge unless it is from another shaman."

"Ok, enough of the challenge stuff," Ethan told the two and gestured to the water. "Let's see if our friends planned a surprise for us."

Drorm looked over to the river and frowned. "You could just portal us to the other side now. They could not reach us before we all made it through."

"Possibly," Ethan replied. The three of them continued to walk closer to the river and stopped fifty yards from the river's edge.

Stopping, he turned to the big orc. "But then we'd be marking ourselves again to the Doemenagg. Even if they don't have our exact position, they might just figure out we're traveling along the coast highway and ambush us."

The orc leader was quiet for a long moment. He looked up and down the length of the river. "This one is not nearly as big. It may not be as deep either."

"Possibly," Ethan responded. "But there's only one way to find out."

"How close must you be to summon your elemental?" Nia asked.

"Honestly," he replied. "I'm not sure. It's water, so I'm not sure how far it can actually travel over land."

"Perhaps now is a good time to experiment," she suggested.

Ethan started to reply but a shiver passed over him and the hair on the back of his neck suddenly stood up. At the same time, Nia stood up straighter, eyes going wide and ears twitching left and right.

The orc leader noticed their reactions and furrowed his brow. "Is something wrong?"

He had no idea what this feeling was, but Ethan had a really bad feeling. Nia cocked her head one way, then another before glancing over towards the forest. She stared for a moment, her ears twitching before she spun around, eyes wide. "Dragon!"

Ethan shook his head, convinced he misheard her. "What?"

"Dragon!" she hissed. "It is approaching from the forest."

Drorm's eyes went wide too. "Bal'Furtun! We cannot defeat it!"

Remembering their first encounter with a dragon on the way to Castlehaven, Ethan's eyes darted to the forest. "Quick! We need to get everyone into the forest and hide in the trees!"

The orc leader looked at him like he was mad. "Trees will not protect us!"

"I know," he replied, trying to stay calm. "But we hid from a dragon before. It will work! If it is looking down, the trees will obscure us from its sight!"

Drorm looked skeptical but then he and Ethan both raised their heads as their ears caught the sound of beating wings. Very large beating wings. The orc swore an oath and the three of them rushed back to their companions.

"Bal'Furtun is coming! Into the forest! Hide in the trees now!" the orc leader told his men and gestured for them to go into the forest.

His troops, who now heard the beating wings, rushed to obey his orders. The orcs seemed battle hardened and brave, but it appeared none of them wished to tangle with a dragon. Growling at his troops to be quiet, Drorm rushed in after them.

Ethan didn't blame them for not wanting to tangle with the dragon called Firestorm, or Bal'Furtun to the orcs. If it took siege weapons to ward the thing away from a city, there was nothing these orcs could do.

Guinevere, Michalus and Par'karr didn't waste any time. Once they heard that the dragon was coming, the trio quickly led the horses into the forest. Ethan cast a last glance up at the treetops before grabbing Nia by the hand and leading her into the forest as well.

The two of them huddled near their group, trying to keep the horses calm as the sound of beating wings grew steadily closer. The minutes ticked by and the sound of flapping grew louder until finally the group caught sight of the dragon through the treetops as it flew overhead.

Like the previous dragon they had seen, this one was

enormous. It was hard to say exactly how big the creature was, but it had to be at least 40 or 50 feet long from head to tail. The wingspan of its bat-like wings was at least 75 feet.

Similar to the previous one, this dragon had a large, horned head on a long, thick serpentine neck. The creature had a large muscular body with four powerful limbs that were curled up close to its body as it flew.

The entire body of the creature was covered in slick scales that seemed almost incandescent in the waning sunlight. Unlike the previous dragon they'd seen, which had green scales, the scales of this dragon were a deep red-orange color. Firestorm was both terrifying and majestic at the same time.

Everyone held their breath as the dragon soared overhead. It continued on, apparently oblivious to them and cleared the forest. Firestorm appeared to be heading out towards the ocean but then one of the horses whinnied and the long serpentine neck twisted back to look at the forest.

Ethan cursed under his breath and silently willed the dragon to keep flying to the ocean. It didn't work. Firestorm banked around and began flying back towards the forest.

The orcs tensed and muttered quietly as the dragon approached. Ethan frantically looked around, trying to find better hiding spots. Unfortunately, other than the trees, there was nothing. He cursed again.

Par'karr pushed himself next to Ethan and he could feel the little kobold trembling with fear. "Dragon will see Par'karr."

Ethan wanted to comfort his little friend but he feared the kobold was right. If the dragon landed and looked into the forest, it would see them for sure. The tree canopy provided cover from above. Unfortunately, the tree trunks didn't provide enough cover to protect them from being spotted by someone looking straight on at them.

The dragon was almost to the road and appeared to be dropping altitude to land. He cursed as he realized Firestorm was going to see them.

Then an idea hit him like a slap to the head. Once before, he'd made himself and Nia invisible when they'd encountered creatures in the wastelands that were attracted to movement. It had only been the two of them but Ethan was certain he could do more. But could he do all of them.

"Gather around me!" he hissed as quietly as he could. "Now!"

Drorm threw him a questioning look but Ethan gestured frantically for him to come over. With a glance towards the descending dragon, the orc leader nodded and ordered his men over to where Ethan was.

"I'm going to make us invisible!" he whispered to the group. He made sure not to say "I hope" at the end. "Michalus, if I don't get everyone, you get the rest."

The elven wizard looked like he might object but then the flapping intensified as the dragon came in for a landing. Michalus bobbed his head frantically.

Ethan took a deep breath and prayed it worked. Then, he channeled his *Mana* and spread his invisibility across the group. And amazingly, it worked. Well, mostly. Two of the horses were visible but then winked out as Michalus must have cast his own spell.

"No one move a muscle," he hissed. At the same time, he used his *Mental* magic to send calming thoughts to the horses.

Bringing up his *Mana*, he saw that it had dropped down to nearly half.

Mana: 63

As he watched, another point disappeared. Maintaining the magic was difficult and he wasn't going to be able to do it for long.

The dragon landed near the forest edge with a gust of wind and a thud. The large head glanced one way and then the other, before peering into the forest.

Ethan held his breath as the creature moved its head back and forth as it peered in between the trees. Its serpentine eyes narrowed as it seemed to look right at Ethan. Its head stopped and its gaze lingered on the exact spot where Ethan was. He swore silently and at the same time prayed the dragon couldn't see them.

Just then, a deer broke from cover and darted north through the forest. The dragon's head whipped around faster than Ethan would have thought possible for a creature that size. Then the body followed and the dragon darted away after the deer.

No one moved but they heard the deer make a squealing sound just before there was a meaty crunch and then nothing.

Ethan looked at his stats again.

Mana: 49

The dragon was still out there and Ethan's *Mana* was still dropping. He bit his lip. How long would the dragon take to eat the deer? Could he keep the spell up that long?

After only a minute, the dragon lumbered back into sight, carrying the deer's carcass in its large mouth. It trotted past them and then up the dune and down to the ocean.

As soon as it was out of sight, Ethan dropped the invisibility spell but signaled everyone to stay quiet. For the moment, at least, they were safe.

16

—————

Everyone remained quiet as the minutes ticked by. The dune hid the ocean from their view, blocking any sight of the dragon and what it might be doing near the ocean.

"How long do we wait?" whispered Drorm after several minutes.

Ethan shrugged and motioned Michalus to come over. The elven wizard slipped over and ducked in close. "Michalus, do you know what the dragon might be doing near the ocean?"

Michalus's eyes darted to the dune and then back. "I'm sorry, my boy, I really have no idea. Bathing perhaps?"

He looked to Drorm. "You seem to know about Firestorm. Any idea what it might be doing?"

Drorm wrinkled his forehead. "I know only what all of my people know. Bal'Furtun has not awakened before in my lifetime. I do not know its ways."

Ethan cursed silently. He had no idea what the dragon

might be doing. It could be sunbathing or taking a dip in the ocean for all he knew. Perhaps the dragon drank salt water.

"No one has seen it fly off, right?" he whispered.

Both Michalus and Drorm shook their heads.

"Okay," he replied, careful to keep his voice low. "If it hasn't flown off, then it must be over the dune. The only way for us to know for certain is to go look."

Michalus and Drorm looked at him like he was crazy. He sighed. "Not us. I mean, we send something to look for us. Michalus, I was thinking of an elemental."

"I'm not sure that would be wise," the wizard replied, glancing toward the dune. "Dragons are very knowledge-able about all things magical. If it sees our elemental, it may recognize it as such. If it does, it will know a wizard must be near."

Ethan remembered how quickly the Akugyo had recognized his water elemental and then attacked it. If there was even the remote possibility the dragon might recognize an elemental and then search the area, it wasn't worth it.

"I could sneak over and look," Ethan told them. "Invisibly."

Drorm nodded while Michalus shook his head. "You can't. The invisibility spell is not foolproof. You know what happens when you move."

Ethan did remember. When a person or object covered with an invisibility spell was stationary, it was almost perfectly invisible. The first time he'd encountered it was with Michalus's invisible workshop and none of his group had even suspected they'd passed within feet of the structure.

When the person or object moved, the invisibility wasn't nearly as flawless. It didn't seem to be able to compensate quickly enough to the background. This left tell-tale signs around the subject that reminded him of that alien predator movie in the jungle. Still, what choice did they have?

Drorm looked back into the forest. "Perhaps we can retreat deeper into the forest."

Ethan followed the orc's gaze back in the forest. "That's a lot of feet going through the forest. The noise might attract it. And even if all of us are quiet, the horses are going to make noise."

"What about your mental magic?" Michalus asked. "Can you sense it that way?"

Ethan bit his lip. He'd thought of that several times in the past few minutes. Theoretically, he should be able to reach out and detect the dragon's mind. But he'd dismissed it each time because of the danger. "I could do it, but if the dragon is as powerful and knowledgeable as you say, it might recognize my probe and then..."

"You would give yourself away," Michalus finished.

His two companions were silent for a long time. Finally, Ethan sighed. "I'll go invisibly. If I see or hear the dragon coming, I'll freeze in place and hopefully, it will pass by me."

Michalus seemed like he wanted to voice another objection but instead, he just gave Ethan a resolved nod.

Nia moved in closer and grabbed Ethan's arm. "No. You are not trained to scout as I am. I will go."

He frowned at the foxgirl. While she was right, and infinitely more stealthy than he was, he could literally make himself invisible. "I can make myself invisible."

"Yes," she hissed. "But you are clumsy and noisy."

"You're stealthy, but look." Ethan shook his head and pointed to the dune. "There is no cover for you to hide behind if the dragon comes back."

The foxgirl's eyes darted around the dune and for a second he thought she might have accepted his argument. Then, she faced him and smiled. "Then make me invisible. You did it before."

Ethan opened his mouth to object that he could only make himself invisible, but he had made both Nia and himself invisible in the wastelands. And hadn't he just made the entire group invisible? And yet, he'd simply centered the effect on him and expanded it outward.

He'd never tried doing it on a completely external object. Could he make something invisible at range? He shot Michalus a questioning look.

"Theoretically," the wizard replied with a slight shrug. "It should be possible."

"See." Nia shot him a look of triumph.

He wasn't completely convinced he could make someone else invisible at range, but he knew he had to try or risk an all-out argument with Nia. Bringing up his HUD, Ethan checked his stats.

Mana: 51

Some of his *Mana* had regenerated so he should have

enough to at least attempt it. "Fine. I'll try it. But if it doesn't work, I go. Agreed?"

"Agreed." Nia bit her lip but nodded.

"Okay," he whispered. "Just remember that when you're still, you're completely invisible. When you move, there's a distortion. So if it starts to come near you... freeze."

The foxgirl nodded her understanding.

The chivalrous part of him didn't want to send her into harm's way. Yet, the practical side of him knew she could be much stealthier than he could. He knew it was the right decision. But that didn't mean he had to like it.

Taking a deep breath, Ethan willed Nia invisible. Instantly, he felt *Mana* leave him and the foxgirl disappeared from sight.

"Huh." Michalus raised an eyebrow. "I didn't actually think it would work."

Ethan saw a slight distortion next to his face and felt Nia's warm lips press against his cheek. "I go now."

He saw the tell-tale distortion in the air as the foxgirl moved away from them. She was crouched low and he couldn't hear any foliage crunching beneath her feet.

"Your wife is stealthy, as well as a good warrior," Drorm commented quietly. "You are a lucky man."

"That I am," Ethan agreed, keeping a careful eye on his wife and the other eye on his *Mana*.

Mana: **37**

The initial spell had cost him a good chunk of *Mana*, but

maintaining it wasn't too bad. He guessed he could keep the spell going for at least five minutes. That should be plenty of time for her to look over the dune and then report back.

Nia must have stopped at the edge of the forest because the distortion of the air disappeared and there was no trace of her at all.

Mana: 35

As he watched the area where she had disappeared, he saw the distortion start up again. The distortion broke the cover of the trees and started across the road. It crossed the road and then stopped, briefly disappearing.

Mana: 33

A moment later, it started again, this time starting up the sand dune. The shape of the distortion seemed to indicate she was crawling up the dune on her stomach.

Ethan watched the Nia-shaped distortion slowly climb up the dune and then stop a foot from the top. Once again, she completely disappeared, showing no trace of the foxgirl.

Looking closely, he realized he could track her by the depression in the sand. He hoped it wasn't something the dragon would notice if it came near her.

Mana: 31

After a moment, Nia slowly moved up to the top and appeared to peer over the edge in a slow, fluid motion.

Then she froze and once again became completely invisible.

The seconds ticked by and Ethan didn't see any movement from the foxgirl. He counted thirty seconds and still didn't see any movement. Why wasn't she ducking back down?

Mana: 29

After nearly a minute, he saw Nia's head-shaped distortion raise itself higher and then appear to look up and down the beach. Finally, it ducked back down and began moving back down the dune. In another minute, she was darting across the road and into the trees.

As she entered the forest, Ethan dropped the invisibility and the Nia-shaped distortion dissolved away into the real Nia. He let out a breath he hadn't known he'd been holding and flashed her a grin.

"What's it doing?" he asked quietly.

"Nothing," she replied. "It is not on the beach. The dragon is gone."

17

"It's not there?" Ethan repeated, casting a glance from Drorm to Michalus.

"I think we would have heard it fly away," Michalus agreed.

"Did it wander down the beach?" the orc leader asked.

"No." Nia shook her head. "I saw its tracks. It went INTO the ocean."

Ethan blinked. "Into the ocean?"

He looked at Drorm, who seemed to know more about Firestorm than any of them. "Does it... swim?"

Drorm opened his mouth and then closed it. He made a face and then shrugged. "I have not heard of Bal'Furtun swimming before."

Ethan turned to Michalus. "Do dragons swim?"

Michalus scratched his chin for a moment. "I can't say that I recall reading anything about them swimming."

"Perhaps we should continue south while the beast is swimming," Drorm suggested.

"Maybe," Ethan replied, staring out towards the dune and the waterspouts beyond it. Ethan didn't like losing track of a fifty-foot dragon. And why had it gone into the ocean. Food? Or maybe it had a lair there.

"Do you know where the dragon's home is? Is it in the ocean?" Ethan asked Drorm.

The big orc shook his head. "No. Bal'Furtun does not live in the water. It lives in the mountains to the south. At least, that is where the shamans traveled in the past to meet it."

Ethan cursed. "So why is it..."

He instantly went quiet as a huge spray of water erupted from the other side of the dune. Over the top of the dune, Ethan saw the tips of crimson wings moving up and down. He motioned everyone behind them and went to reactivate his invisibility spell. Then he saw his *Mana* level and cringed.

Mana: 27

Ethan cursed silently. He hadn't had enough time for his *Mana* to regenerate after making Nia invisible.

"I don't have enough time to regenerate mana!" he hissed.

There were mutters of fear from the orcs but Drorm silenced them with a look. Everyone fell into silence as more water sprayed into the air from the opposite side of the dune and then with a roar, the dragon launched itself into the air.

The giant, bat-like wings flapped, spraying sand all around the area as the serpentine body rose steadily into the air. As the dragon continued to rise, it seemed to scan the forest with its large reptilian eyes.

Ethan held his breath as the creature's gaze went past the place where they hid. Luckily, the dragon glanced over them and looked further north and then turned its gaze south. Wings pumping up and down, it continued to gain altitude until it was sixty or seventy feet above them. Then, with a twist of its body and a push of its wings, it darted forward and headed east over the forest.

Everyone stayed quiet as they listened to the sound of the dragon's wings fading off into the distance. Ethan waited until he no longer heard the wings before he turned his head and gave Nia and Michalus a questioning look. He knew their hearing was better than his.

"It's moving away," Michalus said and Nia nodded.

Ethan and the others let out a sigh of relief. That had been close. Too close. Ethan had no idea how to fight a dragon, let alone a wizard-dragon. If it was truly thousands of years old and taught magic to the orcs, he had no illusions that his feeble magic could challenge it.

"We should go now," Drorm insisted, "before Bal'-Furtun returns."

"Give me a few minutes to recharge my mana," Ethan told the orc. When Drorm looked impatient, he explained. "I will send up an air elemental so we can see where the dragon went and make sure it's not headed back."

"I still have mana," Michalus told him. "I'll scout."

Ethan nodded, feeling foolish for not thinking to ask the elven wizard. "Good idea! Just go above the treetops. The last thing we want to do is attract its attention."

"A sensible precaution," Michalus agreed and sat

down. The elf closed his eyes and a moment later, a distortion in the air appeared, in the shape of a bird. Drorm and the other orcs gasped when it appeared so close to them, hands going for weapons, before they realized it was friendly.

"It's just the elemental," Ethan assured them. "It's under his control."

The elemental hovered for a moment, looking at the wizard and then launched itself skyward. Ethan lost track of the air elemental as it circled the trees. He finally gave up and looked down at Michalus. All he could do was wait for the wizard's report.

Only a minute later, Michalus opened his eyes and stood up. He pointed to the east. "The dragon is flying east, over the forest. It is many miles away and does not appear to be coming back."

Ethan frowned and furrowed his brow. "What was it doing in the ocean? Taking a bath?"

"Ethan!" came Nia's voice from behind him. "I know what it was doing in the water."

Spinning, he saw the foxgirl standing on the top of the dune, looking at the other side. Ethan hadn't even realized his wife had left. He shook his head and then left the cover of the trees to see what she was looking at.

Once they saw Nia and then watched Ethan leave the safety of the forest, the rest of his group and the orcs left as well. Drorm shouted some orders to his orcs and then joined Ethan and his companions on the dune. Ethan whistled as he saw what Nia had meant.

"Apparently," Ethan told them. "The dragon likes seafood."

Scattered around the beach were pieces of Akugyo. Small pieces. Had Ethan not been familiar with them, he might have thought the pieces were parts of large fish but he knew better. One of the arms still had a coral buckler attached to it.

"It appears the dragon did us a favor," Guinevere said in an emotionless voice.

"Indeed," Drorm agreed with a grunt.

Ethan bit his lip. "But why?"

"Why what?" Drorm asked.

"Why did it attack them? And how did it know they were there?" Ethan wondered aloud.

"Does it really matter?" Guinevere asked with a shrug. "It may have just saved us a fight."

Nodding, Ethan stared out into the ocean. A million questions were buzzing through his mind. "Yes, why were the Akugyo there? Were they the same group that followed us? If so, how did they find us? And why did the dragon attack them? How did it know they were even there?"

"Perhaps the fish-folk and Bal'Furtun are enemies," Nia suggested.

"Maybe," Ethan said, but he didn't think that was it. The dragon had stopped on land, grabbed the deer and THEN headed into the water. "But why was the dragon roaming so far from its lair?"

Drorm grunted. "Bal'Furtun has been roaming up and down the coast since it awoke. It attacks towns and burns villages - even parts of fields and forests. No one knows why. None of the shamans remember this happening before."

Ethan tried to make sense of it in his mind. "So, the dragon was flying out here, looking for a village to burn and then what... saw the fishmen from the air and decided to drop down for a snack?"

His companions exchanged looks but no one answered him for a long moment.

"Maybe," Par'karr said with a shrug.

"It doesn't matter now," Guinevere snorted. "We are alive and the dragon may have scared the Akugyo away."

Michalus put a hand on Ethan's shoulder. "I agree, there are many questions. But I don't think we will find the answers here."

Ethan frowned and nodded. He did have many questions. That's all he seemed to have lately. More questions. Why did the Akugyo seem to be following them? Why did they seem so intent on killing him and his group? Why had the dragon come this way? How had it known about the Akugyo and why had it attacked them?

But Michalus was right. Standing here on the beach wasn't likely to give him any answers. Maybe the shamans would know more about the dragon and its relationship to the Akugyo. And that was all the more reason to continue their journey.

"You're right," he said finally. "Let's get moving and see how far we get before dark."

"What if dragon come back at night?" Par'karr squeaked. "Campfire bright in dark."

Ethan looked around at the rest of his companions. "Par'karr has a point. I suggest we sleep in the forest without a fire."

Drorm nodded. "This seems like a wise suggestion.

The kobold is right. A campfire would give away our location for miles."

"Good thinking, Par'karr," he told the kobold and Par'karr beamed.

"We're wasting light," Ethan said. "Let's get this show on the road."

"Show?" Drorm frowned and the others looked equally confused.

Ethan sighed. "Let's move out."

The rest of the group agreed and, in a few minutes, they were back on the road, headed to Highshire.

18

———

The next day, the group passed several farms before they reached the first intact village they'd seen since Sherwood. Drorm told him its name was Riverford and it was situated next to one of the two rivers they had passed since the dragon.

Riverford was a human village about twice the size of Hawkshead. There were at least two dozen homes and businesses, including an inn. Luckily, the inn had vacancies but only four rooms - not nearly enough for Ethan's group and the orcs.

"Did you stay at the inn when you came through last time?" Ethan asked the orc leader.

Drorm frowned and shook his head. "There is not enough room for all of us and we are not given coin for lodging."

"I can pay for a room for some of you and a few of your orcs," Ethan offered. "If you don't mind sharing a room or two."

The big orc shook his head. "If there is not room enough for all of us, then we will sleep on the outskirts of town."

"Are you sure?" Ethan asked.

Drorm nodded and let a smile play on his lips. "But if your offer to buy us drinks was genuine..."

Ethan grinned. "Absolutely. Let me talk to the innkeeper and see what he's got."

The innkeeper was a portly, middle-aged woman named Maeve who watched the group warily from the door of her inn as they discussed the accommodations.

Walking over to Maeve, Ethan gave the woman his best grin. "Do you have ale?"

"Yes, inside." The rotund woman narrowed her eyes and then glanced around at the large group. "Ain't room enough for everyone."

Glancing back at Drorm's orcs, Ethan scratched his head. The innkeeper had a point. The orcs would never fit in the small common room in the inn. He chuckled to himself as an idea came to him. If you couldn't bring the orcs to the ale, bring the ale to the orcs. He turned back to the innkeeper. "How much for a keg?"

After negotiating the price for the two kegs the innkeeper had, Drorm had four of his men carry the kegs to their camp on the south side of town. Ethan thought that it would be enough ale for the orcs to have at least two drinks each.

Once Maeve had seen Ethan's money, her attitude had changed significantly. His group had rented three of the four rooms. Ethan and Nia shared one, Michalus and Par'karr shared another and Guinevere got the third room.

Once they dumped their gear and left their horses in the small stable behind the inn, the group gathered in the common room and ate a meal of bread and venison stew. The stew was simple enough. In addition to the chunks of meat, it also had potatoes, carrots and onions. Despite its simplicity, after eating weeks of nothing but grilled meat, Ethan thought it tasted amazing.

As they were finishing up, Maeve walked over and sat down near them. "You like the stew?"

"So good," Ethan said as he scraped the bottom of his bowl with the last crust of bread. The bread too was wonderful. None of them had eaten bread since leaving Hawkshead and he realized how much he missed it.

"Stew good!" Par'karr agreed.

"It's my mum's recipe." Maeve beamed. The innkeeper's expression turned serious. "Any news from the north or news about the dragon? We haven't had any merchants travel through here in months. Just the orcs."

Ethan saw the twist of the woman's lips as she mentioned orcs. He glanced around the common room to make sure none of Drorm's crew had entered when he wasn't looking. "Are the orcs treating you poorly?"

"Did they really surrender Highshire to the orcs?" Guinevere asked.

Maeve sighed and slumped down in her chair. "The

orcs treat us fine for the most part. Though they do tend to take some livestock as they go through - on their patrols. The villagers don't take kindly to that, but they ain't about to say anything."

"So they haven't hurt anyone here in the village?" Ethan followed up.

"No," she replied with a small shrug. "Can't say anyone's been hurt. They're just a bit... scary, you know."

Par'karr nodded vigorously. "Par'karr scared of them."

"What of the dragon, Firestorm?" Maeve asked.

"We ran into it yesterday," Ethan told her.

The innkeeper's eyes went wide. "You ran into the dragon... and survived?!"

Ethan gave her a sheepish grin. "We actually hid from it."

"You were lucky then!" the innkeeper told them. "Firestorm destroyed two villages further north, Woodpine and Crestville. Nothing left of them from what I hear. Though..."

He raised an eyebrow. "Though what?"

Maeve bit her lip. "Last we heard, Woodpine was almost abandoned. People kept disappearing."

"Disappearing?" Guinevere asked. "Taken by the dragon?"

The innkeeper shrugged. "No one knows. We've had a few people disappear here as well. But it's been a hard year. They could have just gone down to Highshire."

Guinevere leaned towards Maeve. "What about Highshire? Did they really surrender themselves to the orcs?"

"From the little bit of news we got, they did." Maeve nodded. She seemed happy to stop talking about the disappearance. "The dragon burned part of the city and killed the prince. After that, the steward negotiated an alliance with the orcs down in Avalon."

"An alliance?" Michalus raised an eyebrow.

"It doesn't sound like an alliance," Guinevere snorted. "It sounds like they took the city over."

Maeve shrugged. "That's what it seems like."

"And everyone was okay with that?" Ethan asked.

"I don't think most people are okay with it," the innkeeper replied. "But it's keeping the people of High-shire alive. At least, that's what I hear."

"Drorm, the orc leader, said the orcs brought in siege weapons to repel the dragon. Is that true?" Ethan asked. He was starting to like Drorm, but he wasn't sure if the orc told him the truth. Or maybe, not all the truth.

"I heard the orcs brought some sort of weapons with them," she replied. "I hear they sent the dragon running a couple of times. I also heard it's come back and burned more of the city too."

"Perhaps the weapons are not as effective as the orcs make them out to be," Guinevere offered and Ethan couldn't help but agree.

"They may not be effective at all," Michalus suggested and everyone turned to him.

Ethan furrowed his brow. "What do you mean?"

The wizard cleared his throat. "The dragon is a wizard. An extremely powerful wizard. Just like you and I can grab things with air magic, I would be surprised if the dragon couldn't grab or stop the missiles their weapons are throwing at it."

"So you two are wizards," the innkeeper said with a raised eyebrow. "I heard you all got killed or something."

Ethan and Michalus looked at the innkeeper curiously but she rolled her eyes. "I'm an innkeeper. It used to be that people actually stopped here, including wizards. I know you folk carry those staffs. Although, I have to admit I never seen one like yours."

"Mine's a bit different." Ethan replied, glancing at his trident. "Is us being here a problem?"

Ethan knew how people didn't even like to be around wizards, for fear of becoming collateral damage from whatever was killing them. Of course, now Ethan knew what was trying to kill him - the Doemenagg. They wanted to kill him and suck his brain out to feed to their queen.

Maeve shrugged. "Don't make no difference to me. I never had any problems with a wizard."

"Glad to hear it," Ethan told her. "We won't be any trouble."

The innkeeper smiled and then changed the subject. "What about news from the north? Has the dragon attacked Castlehaven?"

"Not as of a couple of months ago," Ethan answered. He looked to Michalus. "Right?"

Michalus shrugged. "I skirted Castlehaven when I came south. I also stayed away from the villages too because of... obvious reasons."

Ethan knew the "obvious reasons" Michalus spoke of was the fact that Castlehaven had instituted slavery of elves and foxlings. Had the wizard actually gone into the city, someone might have tried taking him as a slave. Not that they would have been able to. The wizard was formidable and had hundreds of years of experience to draw on.

Maeve nodded sadly. "So it's just us down south."

"As far as we know, the dragon is just down here," Ethan told her. "I mean, we didn't hear anything about Firestorm until we ran into the orcs."

"I was hoping you might know why the dragon decided to start burning villages down," Maeve sighed. "And if you knew whether it was coming for us."

"I'm afraid not, my dear," Michalus replied. "We're as much in the dark as you are."

The innkeeper wrapped her arms around herself. "Most of the people in this village go to sleep, not knowing if we're going to wake up. We're afraid the dragon will burn down the village while we sleep."

Ethan wanted to say something reassuring but the words didn't come to him. He'd seen the dragon close-up. If he lived in one of the villages, he would probably leave rather than put up with the constant threat of a possible dragon attack.

Then again, he had magic. While Ethan could make it out on the road, he doubted most villagers could. Especially not ones with families.

"Well," the innkeeper said, getting to her feet. "I have cleaning up to do and dishes to wash. You all have a good night."

As the innkeeper retreated into the kitchen, everyone looked around at each other. It was clear they all had the same idea. Like the villagers, all of them would wonder if they would wake up tomorrow or if the dragon might come in the dead of night and burn down the village.

It was not a comforting thought.

19

O nce Nia was done with him, Ethan slept fitfully that night, plagued with dreams of dragons and insects. In his dreams, both the dragon and the Doemenagg pursued him. He ran and ran but couldn't lose them. He'd slip and fall and each time he did so, they'd get a little closer. Luckily, right when they caught him, he'd wake up.

Despite his dreams, the dragon did not appear and the village wasn't burned to the ground. Ethan awoke tired, but he did awake. He couldn't imagine how the villagers lived with the continual threat of a dragon attack.

Nia insisted on a little alone time in the morning and Ethan wasn't about to say no, even if he was tired. They were the last ones to come down for breakfast, but he didn't care. It was worth it. Plus, without Ainslee there to eat all the food, he guessed there would still be some left for them.

After a breakfast of eggs and smoked meat, Ethan and

his group rejoined Drorm and the orcs. Drorm stopped giving orders to his men when they approached. Walking over to meet them, the orc leader pointed south.

"We are about a day from Gugmirl," Drorm told them. The orc looked up into the sky. "Provided Bal'Furtun does not appear."

"How often does the dragon fly around the coast?" Ethan asked.

Drorm shrugged. "The dragon flies where it wishes, when it wishes. Then it returns to the mountain."

"Its lair?" Ethan with a raised eyebrow. Images of a dragon's lair, filled with gold and treasure suddenly popped into his mind.

Once again, Drorm shrugged. "I do not know for certain. But it is the mountain where the shamans would meet with Bal'Furtun to be taught magic."

"Fascinating," Michalus said. "Is it where the dragon slumbered?"

Drorm turned to the wizard. "Perhaps. None of us dare enter the mountain itself. The shamans who wish to learn present themselves at the base of the mountain. If the dragon finds them worthy, it flies from the mountain and speaks to tell them to come up the mountain."

"But you did say it slumbered, right?" Ethan asked. He was certain the orc had said the dragon had slept for a hundred years or so. "If no one enters the mountain, how do you know?"

The orc leader grunted. "That is what the shamans tell us. If the dragon does not appear for some time, it is sleeping."

Ethan and Michalus exchanged looks. Michalus asked

the question Ethan was thinking before he could get it out. "But no one has actually seen the dragon sleeping?"

Drorm shook his head. "No. No one enters the mountain."

"Why not enter mountain?" Par'karr asked, eyes wide at all the talk of the dragon.

The orc leader looked down at the kobold, who instantly withered under Drorm's gaze. "It is forbidden by the shamans."

"Why is it forbidden?" Ethan asked.

Drorm let out an exasperated breath. "You ask many questions!"

"Sorry," Ethan apologized. "The curse of being a wizard."

Michalus nodded and they both looked at the orc expectantly, waiting for an answer.

The big orc rolled his eyes. "I do not know why it is forbidden. I only know that it is. If you wish to know the answer, you will have to ask one of the shamans."

Ethan pushed down his frustration and looked around at the orcs. They were packed and ready to leave. Some of the orcs looked a little bleary eyed and he couldn't help but notice that the two kegs were completely empty. He smiled. "Let's get going then."

"Yes," Drorm agreed, obviously glad to be done with the conversation. "We have many miles to cover today."

THERE WAS no sign of either the Akugyo or the dragon throughout the day. Despite not seeing them, the group was still tense. Everyone scanned the sky and the ocean regularly, half expecting to see the dragon flying towards them or the fishmen emerging from the water. Yet, no attack came.

Then, just after lunch, the wind picked up, blowing hard from the east. Ethan spotted dark storm clouds in the east, moving quickly their way. These didn't appear to be normal clouds either, but reminded him of the storm they'd weathered on the way to the library in Patheos.

Pointing to the clouds, Ethan called out to Drorm and his companions. "Is that what I think it is?"

Michalus followed his finger and his eyes went wide. "Mana storm!"

"Mana storm?" Ethan repeated. Then he remembered how the storm seemed to recharge his *Mana* - while simultaneously trying to kill him.

"No one really knows why they form," Michalus said. "But they happen when too much Mana accumulates in the sky. It comes down like lightning into the earth! Very dangerous!"

"Very dangerous!" Par'karr bobbed his head.

"I agree with the kobold," Guinevere said, looking towards the rolling clouds. "These magical storms are extremely dangerous. We do not want to be caught without shelter."

Ethan cursed. "Then we need to find shelter!"

He remembered finding some loggers after the first storm. They had been stuck out in the open and almost all of them had been killed by direct lightning strikes. He doubted his group would fare any better.

"There is no shelter!" Drorm growled. "The trees will

provide no protection!"

Remembering the lightning that had struck a nearby tree repeatedly during the first storm, Ethan agreed. "How long until it's on us?"

Drorm looked at the approaching clouds. "An hour, maybe less."

Guinevere. "Probably less."

Ethan looked up and down the road. Drorm was right. Other than the trees, there was no cover. To their right was the ocean and to the left was forest. They were completely exposed.

"Any rivers with stone bridges around?" Ethan asked.

Drorm wrinkled his forehead. "Rivers? You do not hide from a storm in the river!"

Resisting the urge to roll his eyes, Ethan took a deep breath. "No, not the river. But if there's a stone bridge, Michalus and I could shape it into a shelter."

The orc leader scratched his head but then shook it. "No, not within an hour's ride."

Ethan cursed again, desperately looking for any sort of rock formation or something they could shape into a shelter. He spun in his saddle to face Michalus. "Any ideas?"

The wizard had been staring at the approaching clouds. When he heard Ethan's voice, he turned towards him. He slowly shook his head. "None. There is nothing around here that will protect us."

Cursing, Ethan scanned the area one more time. He thought back to their earlier ride but he couldn't remember passing any large rocks or boulders they could shape into any sort of protection.

He was about to order them to move out, in the hope

that they would find something in the next hour when Par'karr suddenly spoke up. "Rabbits!"

Hearing the word "rabbits" from the little kobold at such a stressful time made Ethan chuckle involuntarily. He turned to his friend. "What?"

"Rabbits!" Par'karr repeated. "We be like rabbits!"

Ethan blinked at the kobold, unsure what Par'karr was trying to say. Be like rabbits? Was that some sort of Zen thing? Or did he mean they needed to move as swift as rabbits?

Par'karr growled softly in frustration, scratching his scaly head. After only a moment, he brightened. "Rabbits go inside burrows. We be like rabbits."

Burrows? Rabbits? For a second, Ethan didn't understand but then it hit him. Tunnels! Par'karr was telling him they should make some tunnels in the earth. "You mean, we should tunnel into the earth, right? Make a burrow, like a rabbit."

The little kobold bobbed his head up and down enthusiastically. "Yes! Be like rabbits!"

Spinning back to Michalus, Ethan raised an eyebrow at the wizard. "Do you think we can do that? Use earth magic to form a tunnel?"

The mage scratched his chin and frowned. "This area is very flat. If we dug tunnels..."

"They would flood," Ethan finished, understanding exactly what the wizard was getting at. And he was right. He remembered how much water there had been in the first mana storm. "We need an area that is raised, then we can dig into it and it will be above the waterline."

"There was such a place!" Nia exclaimed. "A half hour

ago, we passed an area where the forest was raised six or seven feet from the road."

Ethan's head swiveled to his wife. "Are you sure?"

She nodded. "I was watching it closely as I thought it would be a good place for an ambush."

"A half hour back?" Drorm growled. "We will be cutting it close."

"I don't think we have a choice!" Ethan told the group. He pointed to the clouds. "Those clouds will be here soon. Burrowing a tunnel seems the best way for us to hide from the storm. We need to at least try."

Drorm looked skeptical but finally nodded. He looked at Nia. "I hope you are right."

"I am," Nia told him. "I remember it very clearly."

"Alright," Ethan told them. "We're wasting time. I say we go for it. At this point, unless someone has a better idea, it's the best chance we have."

There were muttered agreements among the group and Ethan spun his horse around the way they had come. He looked down at Drorm. "I suggest you see how long your orcs can double time it. The quicker we get there, the more time Michalus and I have to actually dig the tunnels."

Drorm flashed him a sly smile. "Two kegs of ale says we can keep it up the entire way."

Ethan returned the grin. "You're on!

"Come on, you orcs! You wanna live forever?!" Ethan yelled and spurred his horse down the road. They were in a race against time and failure meant being caught out in the open when the storm hit. And there was a good chance that meant death.

20

His group rode for fifteen minutes before reaching the area Nia had described. The wind had picked up speed and the dark clouds that they had thought might take an hour to reach them had caught up to them.

But they were still on the periphery of the storm. It was impossible to tell exactly how far away the main part of the storm was from the group. Even now, they heard the crack of lightning and the boom of thunder from the east. And it was getting closer by the minute.

Glancing from the storm above to the embankment, he thought this might be the area Nia had in mind. Or at least, the beginning of the area. Seeing it again, Ethan remembered passing it. At the time, he had noticed this part of the road had been washed away or hidden under sand.

Now, as Ethan looked closer, he realized the truth. The treeline at this location was much closer to the ocean.

Because of the proximity to the water, it appeared that the tide had come in and washed away the road and the soil around the trees. The same erosion had left a ten-foot-tall embankment consisting of the gnarled roots of the trees above.

Ethan squinted as he reined in his horse in front of the embankment. The wind was picking up the sand and swirling it around. Ethan had to shield his eyes with his hand to stop from being blinded. He turned to Nia. The wind swirling around them was so loud, he had to yell. "Is this the place you were talking about?"

"Yes," she called back, her voice barely audible over the howling of the wind. Like him, she was squinting and shielding her eyes with her hand. She gestured to the rooty embankment. "Is this enough space to make tunnels?"

Spinning to his opposite side, Ethan looked at Michalus and gestured to the area Nia had indicated. "What do you think?"

Michalus furrowed his brow and looked up at the dark clouds swirling above and then down at the embankment. He said something but Ethan couldn't make out what it was. He held his free hand to his ear. "What?!"

"I said," Michalus shouted, "I don't think we have much choice! But I think we will run into problems with the roots! "

Ethan had thought the same thing but he was already thinking of a plan. He and Michalus could start forming the tunnel while the orcs could cut the roots enough to allow them to get into the tunnels.

Turning to Drorm, he raised his voice again. "Michalus

and I will form the tunnel! You and your orcs need to chop the roots so we can get through them."

Rather than try to shout over the storm, the orc leader just nodded. He turned to the other orcs and began shouting orders. Ethan saw the orcs bring out their weapons but then looked up and down the embankment in confusion.

Realizing they were waiting for him to start making the tunnels, Ethan slipped off his horse and handed the reins to Par'karr. Michalus did the same and came to stand next to him. The wizard leaned in close. "How do you want to do this?!"

"I will shape the earth into a tunnel!" Ethan shouted and then immediately spit out some sand that had blown into his mouth. The wind was getting worse and the sand was now coming at him from all directions. He swore. "You harden the dirt so it doesn't collapse!"

Michalus nodded rather than reply. The wizard's eyes were slits and his hand was trying to cover both his mouth and his eyes at the same time.

Squinting at the embankment, Ethan focused his *Mana* through the trident's Chymera stone and began to will the earth into the shape he needed. Slowly, it began to bend to his magic and a round hole began to form.

He stopped after only a few seconds. Ethan cursed and looked back at the horses. He had started making it large enough for his group and the orcs but realized it would be too small to accommodate their horses. It would need to be taller and either wider or longer - or both.

Ethan cursed again as he realized it was going to take longer to form it both taller and wider. Shaking his head, he began again. This time he formed a hole seven feet wide and seven feet tall.

As the earth slowly moved to accommodate his will, Ethan could feel Michalus's magic. Fighting the Akugyo wizard's and countering their magic had made him more sensitive to the different types of magic. Not only could he feel the wizard's magic, he could easily tell that it was *Earth* magic, as well.

Once again, he'd been forced to learn on the fly. Learn or die. Trial by fire wasn't his preferred method of learning, especially when the stakes were so high. And yet, as Michalus had pointed out, Ethan had progressed much more quickly than other wizards. But Ethan couldn't linger over his preferred learning method at the moment. There was a task that needed to be done or people were going to die.

Bringing his focus back to the task at hand, he blinked sand out of his eyes and looked at the hole he was creating. Ethan realized it was starting to go more and more slowly because he was having to move the dirt out of the hole. The further he went back, the further the dirt had to travel to get out of the hole.

He stopped and Michalus looked over at him. "Why are you stopping?!"

The crack of lightning split the dark sky only a few miles from them, causing everyone to flinch. Ethan bit his lip as he looked at the hole he'd formed. It was only about six feet deep. To make it deep enough to hold everyone, he'd have to go back twenty or more feet.

"This isn't going to work!" he shouted to Michalus and the wizard looked shaken.

"What do you mean?! It's working!" the wizard yelled back.

"It's taking too long to move the earth from the back of the hole to the front of the hole," he told Michalus, as loud as he could.

The wizard looked from Ethan to the hole and then back. "We don't have a choice! Maybe we should both dig out the tunnel!"

Ethan shook his head. He had thought of that but he knew the tunnel would collapse if the walls, and especially the ceiling, were not hardened. He looked up and down the embankment before making a snap decision.

"We make multiple holes!" Ethan yelled. "This one needs to be bigger for the horses but the other ones can be smaller so they won't take as long!"

Michalus started to answer but coughed as sand must have gotten into his mouth. Instead, he nodded and gestured for Ethan to start again.

Now that he had a new plan, Ethan quickly dug the first hole slightly deeper to accommodate the horses and then hurried over to Drorm and Guinevere. The two had been watching the hole form and jumped as he put a hand on each of their shoulders.

"Why do you stop?!" Drorm yelled.

"It will take too long if we make it go deeper!" he shouted back. "We're going to make more holes. Have your men start chopping the roots on this one. By the time they're done, hopefully we'll have the next hole dug!"

The orc leader grunted and Guinevere nodded. The two of them went over and began directing the other orcs.

Bringing up his HUD, Ethan checked his *Mana* level after the first hole.

Mana: 73

Ethan felt a squeeze on his arm and looked over to see Nia. She squinted up at him, a piece of cloth like a bandana tied over her mouth. From the look of it, she had cut it from one of her blankets. She reached up and tied one around his head, covering his mouth.

He grinned down at her before realizing his mouth wasn't visible. Instead he yelled, "Good idea! Thank you!"

His wife held up other pieces of cloth and gestured to the others. He realized she had made enough for their entire group. "Yes! Give them to our group, then show Drorm. They can make their own if they want!"

Nia hurried off and then Ethan began forming the next hole. Rain began to pour down around them and he realized they were running out of time.

As if to prove him right, a large bolt of lightning split the sky less than a mile to the east, followed by a huge boom of thunder that seemed to shake the very air around them. He swore and stared at the hole he was digging. They needed to move faster.

Yelling to Michalus, he and the wizard began going as fast as they could. Ethan dropped the hole size to around four feet, knowing the orcs would have to crouch down but also knowing they probably wouldn't survive long in the open.

Working with the wizard, they formed three more holes before the lightning got so close, then Nia began dragging him into the hole with the horses. He started to object but then a bolt of lightning slammed into the beach less than a hundred yards away.

Eyes stinging and half blind from the afterimage of the lightning, Ethan allowed himself to be dragged into the large hole with the horses. As he passed Drorm, he shouted. "We're out of time! Get as many as you can into the holes!"

Drorm nodded and barked some orders before he and several of his orcs joined Ethan, his group and the horses in the large hole. They were squeezed in like sardines, and the stench of horses, sweat, and fear permeated the hole. Yet, despite the discomfort, it was better than being in the open.

Trying to keep the horses calm, the group stared out of the hole as the storm raged around them, thunder shook the earth and lightning lit up the sky.

21

The storm lasted for several hours by Ethan's estimation. Without a watch, it was impossible to say exactly how long. With the clouds obscuring the suns, they simply weren't able to see the sky and guess the time. Even when the darkest of the clouds had passed them by, it was still overcast. Ethan heard his stomach rumble. Judging by how hungry he was feeling, he guessed it was dinner time.

Once it had passed them, the storm continued over the ocean and they watched the play of the lightning on the water until it was out on the horizon. Looking at it from such a distance, Ethan thought the play of the lightning on the water was beautiful. Beautiful but deadly.

The rain was the last to move on and although it might have been safe to leave their shelters once the lightning passed, everyone stayed inside until there wasn't even a drizzle.

"Storm over?" Par'karr asked from the back of the tunnel.

"I think so," Ethan replied. It had been at least ten minutes since they'd heard lightning and even then, it had come from the ocean.

He saw that everyone was looking at him expectantly. Ethan sighed and stuck his head out of the shelter and glanced around. When he didn't feel any drops of rain and no lightning struck him, he stepped out into the open.

Ethan took a deep breath. The air was thick with humidity but it was a welcome relief from the confines of the hole. Several hours of sweaty orcs, humans, a foxling, an elf and a kobold - not to mention the horses - didn't exactly make for a pleasant odor.

The others began to emerge from the holes as well. Drorm came to stand next to him as Ethan stared out at the disappearing storm. "Had we been caught in the open, not all of us would have survived. We owe you a debt of honor."

Turning to the orc leader, he shrugged. "I'm sure you would have done the same."

"No," Drorm grunted. "We had no way of creating shelter. Neither I nor my orcs could have saved you."

Ethan frowned. "What do you do if a storm comes up on you like that? That has to have happened before."

"It happens from time to time," the big orc replied. "If we are in the city, we seek shelter. The lightning does not penetrate houses. If we are in the open, we do our best to seek shelter. If no shelter is available, we dig holes."

"Dig holes?" Ethan repeated, his brow furrowed. "And that protects you?"

Drorm shrugged. "Sometimes it does. Sometimes it doesn't."

Nia came to stand on Ethan's other side, opposite Drorm. The foxgirl looked out into the churning ocean and the waterspouts that littered it. "We should move from this place."

"Oh?" Ethan asked.

"It is too close to the ocean. We would not have much time to react if the Akugyo attack," she explained, gesturing along the shore.

"Good point," he told her. He turned to Drorm. "You good with moving back down the road before we set up camp?"

"Yes," the orc leader replied, giving Nia an appraising look. "Your wife makes a good point. This area is not very defensible."

Turning from them, Drorm began barking orders to his orcs, getting them ready for a march. Ethan talked to his companions and explained that they were heading south. Then the group mounted their horses and waited for the orcs to join them. He didn't know how far they would get before it became too dark to see, but he would feel better being further away from the narrow strip of beach.

THE GROUP TRAVELED for an hour before finding a suitable campsite. Once they had, Drorm sent two of his orcs to hunt. Ethan turned to the orc.

"You want Michalus and I to cook the meat with magic

or are you planning a fire?" he asked the big orc. They had been careful about a fire since their encounter with the dragon. Was he planning to risk it now?

"We will build a fire," Drorm told him. "The dragon will not have ventured out during the storm. We should be safe tonight."

Ethan didn't like the sound of "should be safe." He shot a questioning look at Michalus but the wizard just shrugged.

"Do not worry," Drorm told him, obviously picking up on his discomfort. "We will put the fire out once we are done cooking. In the meantime, I suggest drying your blankets and anything else you have that is wet."

"That sounds good," Ethan replied. He still wasn't sure about the wisdom of having the fire, but he did have to admit that it would feel good to warm himself.

"It appears that we may need your help," the big orc said sheepishly and pointed to the pile of wet wood that his orcs were assembling.

Ethan knew what Drorm wanted him to do. Because of the storm, all of the wood was wet. He and Michalus had done the same thing before when there was no dry wood. The two of them immediately set to drying the soaked wood with a bit of *Fire* magic. Once enough of the wood was dry, the orcs had started a bonfire and waited for the hunters to return.

Whether due to the storm or something else, the orcs came back with only a few of the lizard turkey creatures. It wasn't much for the orcs and Ethan's group but the orcs shared what they had. No one went to bed that night with a full belly, but at least everyone had some food.

THE NEXT DAY the group set off south again. They'd lost time backtracking because of the storm but shortly after lunch, they crested a large hill. As the group reached the top, they looked down on a city the size of Castlehaven that stretched out before them.

Like Castlehaven, and Camelot for that matter, the city was ringed by a tall, stone wall. He couldn't be certain from this distance, but it looked to be a similar height to Castlehaven's walls. Given its size, it had to be Highshire.

"We have reached Gugmirl," Drorm said from beside him. "Here you will speak to the shamans and they will hear your case."

Ethan bit his lip for a moment, unsure whether he should ask the question in his mind. Drorm seemed like an honorable man... or orc, as the case may be. He didn't doubt the orc leader's words, but he wondered how the shamans would receive them and if they would be so accepting.

He debated asking the question for a full minute before finally deciding to risk insulting the orcs. Ethan looked down at Drorm and held the orc's gaze. "Will my friends be safe in Gugmirl?"

Drorm frowned for a moment and Ethan saw several emotions play across his face before he relaxed and nodded. "You will be safe, especially if this one can prove her claim."

The big orc indicated Guinevere and the warrior woman spun towards him. "Oh, I can prove it."

"Then the shamans will have to recognize the right to parlay," Drorm said.

There was something about the orc's tone that seemed to indicate he was either hiding something or holding something back. He had a guess as to what it was, based on what Drorm hadn't said to them.

"Parlay?" Ethan repeated. "So, they will let us state our case. But that doesn't mean they will let us see the sword, does it?"

Drorm looked down and shook his head. "It does not. I told you before, only the worthy may attempt to draw the sword."

"How do we prove our worth?" Nia asked.

"Through great deeds," the orc leader replied, "in combat or in service to the orc nation."

Guinevere nodded. "Trial by combat?"

Drorm nodded. "That is one way."

"What are the others?" Michalus asked.

The orc leader shrugged, looking back to the city. "That is for the shamans to decide. But know that their word is law and their decisions are final."

"So"—Ethan frowned—"we have to impress them and get their permission or this whole trip was for nothing."

"I am sure they will hear your request," Drorm told him confidently. "I will put in a good word for you."

"They will hear our request?" Guinevere asked with a raised eyebrow. "You seem very certain you can persuade them. Why is that?"

Drorm snorted and looked at the warrior woman. "I am certain because one of the shamans is my mother."

22

From the hill, it took an hour for them to reach the gates of the city. Then another half hour to reach the keep inside the city. As they walked through the city, Ethan caught sight of a mix of races. The civilians seemed mostly human, with a bit of elves, halflings, foxlings and dwarfs.

There were also a lot of orcs, and every orc he saw was armed. The orcs moved in groups of five or six and seemed to be patrolling the streets. Ethan watched them as they moved along but the citizens of the city paid them no mind.

Ethan also managed to catch glimpses of the wall and the enormous crossbow mounted on some sort of base. It reminded him of the Greek ballista or scorpion weapons from Earth history but it was bigger.

"Are those the weapons you use against the dragon?" Ethan asked Drorm, pointing to the gigantic crossbows.

The orc leader grunted. "Yes."

Drorm's tone and short answer seemed unlike the big orc and Ethan raised an eyebrow. "Is something wrong?"

Twisting his head around, Drorm growled. "Nothing."

Then the big orc rolled his eyes and sighed. "We do not speak of our weapons or give our secrets to outsiders. To do so is forbidden."

He raised his hands in a gesture of peace. "I wasn't trying to pry, I was just curious."

"I do not remember the orcs being so secretive," Guinevere commented. Her tone was neutral, but the disappointment on her face was unmistakable. "The orcs I knew were great warriors, proud and fierce. They paraded their strength before others. They didn't hide it."

Drorm growled but said nothing. He kept walking, leading the group through the throngs of people, towards the main keep.

When they reached the keep, Drorm called a halt about ten feet from the entrance. Ethan looked up and took in the twenty-foot-tall stone walls that enclosed the inner keep of the city. He could just make out the forms of orcs walking patrol on the parapets above.

Moving his gaze down, he saw that the large, thick wooden doors that led into the keep were open. They were also guarded. Ethan counted eleven heavily armed orcs to either side of the door.

From the right side of the door, a larger orc stepped forward and raised his hand in the air with a fist. "You return, Drorm."

He was close enough that Ethan could bring him up in his HUD.

Captain Melturl Battlearm
  Orc
  Warrior
  Level 7

"You bring prisoners?" the captain asked, glancing at Ethan and his party.

"Guests, captain," Drorm replied. He gestured to Guinevere. "This one has invoked the ancient rite of parlay."

"Parlay?" The orc captain frowned. "She is not orc. We have no allies at the moment."

"She claims the ancient alliance," Drorm said with a glance at the woman. "The alliance with Camelot."

"Camelot!" the captain barked a laugh. The orcs around the gates to the keep also chuckled but continued to watch Ethan's group warily. "Camelot is gone - if it existed at all. There are no knights left."

"There is one," Guinevere snapped.

Melturl glared at her and snickered. "She is mad."

"She claims she can prove it," Drorm added.

"How?" the orc captain scoffed.

"I will prove myself to the shamans," Guinevere said, returning the captain's glare.

"The shamans?" Melturl smirked. "She is mad. If she cannot prove her claim, she will be stripped naked and paraded through the city as penance. And that's if the shamans are feeling generous today."

Ethan saw a little color in Guinevere's cheeks but wasn't sure if it was anger or embarrassment. Knowing what he did of the warrior woman, he guessed it was anger.

"Take me to the shamans and I will prove myself," the former queen growled.

"Her head may be mad, but she has heart." The captain snorted. Melturl turned to Drorm. "Are you sure you wish to disturb the shamans with this foolishness?"

Drorm nodded. "Her companions are wizards. If nothing else, the shamans will want to question them."

Melturl shifted his gaze from Guinevere to Michalus and then darted to the wizard's staff. Then the orc captain glanced at Ethan and he raised his eyebrows as he saw Ethan's trident. "That is from one of the fishfolk."

"It is," Ethan replied.

"They are rare," the captain told him. "You are fortunate to take such a trophy."

"Not so rare, it would seem," Drorm broke in. "That is another reason I must see the shamans. We were attacked by fishfolk. They set traps for us and lay in ambush."

"Fishfolk?" the captain's eyebrows shot up again.

"Yes," Drorm nodded gravely. "And they brought great beasts called shacks!"

"Sharks," Ethan corrected and both Drorm and Melturl glared at him.

"Sharks," Drorm growled.

"It sounds like you have much to report," the captain said. "You should go before it gets late."

The captain stepped out of the way and gestured for the orcs at the gate to let them through.

Drorm pointed to six of his men. "You, come with us. The rest of you, return to the barracks."

"Come." The big orc gestured to them and started into

the keep. Ethan glanced at his companions, shrugged and then followed the big orc through the large doorway.

As they followed Drorm through the keep, Ethan couldn't help but notice that he only saw orcs inside the keep. And all of the orcs appeared to be soldiers.

Ethan felt a poke in the side and turned to his wife. Nia pointed to the furthest part of the inner keep on the right. Following her finger, he immediately saw what she was pointing out.

The entire right corner of the inner keep was blackened. The walls appeared to have been scorched by fire. He also saw the silhouettes of bodies that had been burned or melted into the walls like leftover shadows.

"The dragon," Drorm said, noting where he was looking. "That time, our weapons did not drive it away."

"Dragon come back?" Par'karr asked quietly.

"The dragon has attacked the city over a dozen times," the orc leader told them. "I do not doubt it will attack again."

Par'karr swallowed and closed his mouth.

Drorm led the group through the courtyard. They passed more orc soldiers who were engaged in various activities. Some were unpacking carts, others were packing things into crates while yet others were engaging in some sort of training exercises. The orcs gave them curious looks but no one challenged them.

The orc leader stopped in front of a large stone building. It had three stories that he could see and two towers on either side. The towers were only ten or twelve feet taller than the main building and just fifteen feet wide.

Even from down below, Ethan caught a glimpse of part of a ballista jutting over the edge of the towers.

Drorm turned around, face grim. "You must wait out here. I will go in and address the shamans and ask for an audience."

Nia glanced around at the thirty or more orcs in the courtyard, eyes narrowed. "And what if they do not grant us an audience."

"Then I will escort you back," Drorm said firmly.

"No parading naked?" Guinevere asked with a smirk.

"Not if they do not grant the audience," the big orc replied, face still grim. "But if they do grant the audience and you cannot prove you are who you say you are..."

There was a momentary silence before Par'karr piped up. "Par'karr not mind parading naked. Par'karr never in parade before."

Ethan bit his lip to stop from chuckling. He looked down at the little kobold and smiled. "Let's hope it doesn't come to that."

Par'karr shrugged but Ethan thought he detected a bit of disappointment.

"The kobold is not far from the truth," Drorm said. "If they do not accept her proof, you will all be held guilty and be punished."

The big orc looked from Ethan to Guinevere. "Are you sure you wish to make this claim before the shamans?"

"I do," Guinevere said and then smiled and winked at Ethan. "And don't worry, I can prove it."

"I hope you are right," Drorm sighed. "Because if not, you will all be punished. If that is the case, I cannot help you."

Drorm gave Ethan one last questioning look. The message was clear: Are you sure you want to do this?

Ethan glanced over at Guinevere. The woman hadn't lied to them that he knew of. And if she had, Nia would have smelled it. He didn't really want to be paraded around the city naked or undergo some other equally humiliating punishment.

Unfortunately, he didn't have a choice if they wanted to try to get a chance to see Excalibur. They needed to talk with the shamans and they needed to somehow prove their worthiness to be able to see the sword.

"We will try to see the shamans," he told Drorm.

The big orc nodded. "Wait here. I will return with word of their decision."

With that, the orc barked a command to the orcs at the thick wooden door and they pulled it open and let Drorm pass through. Once he was inside, the orcs pulled it closed, the sound echoing around the courtyard.

Ethan swallowed. There was no turning back now.

23

The group waited outside for nearly an hour before Drorm returned through the thick wooden door. The orc didn't leave the doorway but instead motioned for them to come forward. When he spoke, his voice sounded tired. "The shamans have agreed to hear your request for parlay."

Everyone started forward but Drorm held up his hand. "Only Ethan and Guinevere. The rest of you must remain until the shamans have decided."

Ethan narrowed his eyes. "Decide what?"

"They have agreed to hear her claim to be a member of the old alliance," the orc leader said, gesturing to Guinevere. "Then they will render a judgement whether it is valid and then they will decide whether to honor the parlay."

"I will go with you!" Nia hissed, her eyes darting around the courtyard. "My place is at your side!"

Drorm shook his head. "They will only allow Ethan and Guinevere. I am sorry."

Ethan stared at Drorm for a long moment. The orc looked unhappy and apologetic, but also resolute. The orc shifted uncomfortably at his gaze, eyes dropping to the floor. "I am sorry. I argued that you should all come before them but they do not know you."

Turning to his wife, Ethan lowered his voice. "Is he lying?"

Nia gave him a little pout, which made her look absolutely adorable, but shook her head. "He is not."

Keeping his voice low, he moved his head closer to her. "Stay here. Stay on guard and be ready to go if I appear."

The foxgirl looked up at him, forehead wrinkled. "Appear?"

"If anything goes wrong," he told her quietly, "I'll portal here and then get us all out of here."

As he spoke, Ethan channeled a little *Fire* magic through the hidden Chymera stones in his pocket. He was so used to using the stone in the trident he almost forgot he still had other Chymera stones. But in this case, he didn't want to alarm the orcs. He didn't want anyone to know what he was doing.

With a thin line of fire, Ethan burned three runes into his wife's leather backpack. They were small, but in this case, size didn't matter. Only the unique runes and their sequence mattered. With them, he could portal back to her in an instant.

His wife wrinkled her nose. "You are burning something?"

"Just making sure I can get back to you." He smiled and then kissed her.

Turning, Ethan stepped towards Drorm and Guinevere came up next to him. Not knowing what else to say, he grinned. "Take me to your leader."

Drorm turned without comment and led them into a large hallway. Two more guards were inside the doors, one on each side. The hallway itself was nearly ten feet wide and at least thirty feet long. There were doors every ten feet and an orc guard stood to either side of each door.

Ethan flinched when he heard the door slam behind him but resisted the urge to turn around. Instead, he focused on the hallway and the orcs that lined it, standing at attention. He wondered what was behind the doors that they needed to be guarded.

The hallway ended in a set of double doors, guarded by a pair of burly orcs as large as Drorm. The two eyed Ethan and the others for a moment before opening the doors and allowing them to enter.

Straining his eyes, Ethan could see that the room ahead was large and dark, lit by only a few candles. From where he stood, he could see that there were six candles, arranged in a semi-circle in the dark room. Looking closely, Ethan could see orcs illuminated by the candles. Judging from the candles' height and the little bit he could see, he guessed the orcs must be sitting at tables or desks.

The orc to the right of the door spoke in a hoarse voice. "The shamans will see you."

Drorm continued to the doorway and then stopped. He turned to Ethan and Guinevere and sighed. "I am not permitted to be with you while you make your plea. I have vouched for you and your deeds but I hope - for all of your sakes - that you can prove your claim."

Ethan's eyes shot to Guinevere but the woman only smirked. "Oh, I can."

He admired the woman's confidence but wished she would have told him exactly how she was going to prove herself. As it was, he might be putting his life in her hands. Possibly the life of his friends too.

"Good luck," Drorm said and thrust out his hand.

"Thanks." Ethan clasped the orc's large hand and pumped it several times. "And thanks for vouching for us."

The orc shrugged. "Had it not been for you, many of my men would have died in the storm. I owe you much."

Not sure what to say, Ethan just smiled. "I'm sure you would have done the same."

The big orc released his hand. "Perhaps."

"The shamans do not like to be kept waiting," the orc to the left of the door growled. "Enter. Now."

Drorm stepped back from the door and gestured for them to enter. Ethan took a deep breath and stepped forward into the darkened room. As soon as they had cleared the doorway, the door closed behind them with an audible thud.

Ethan stopped and looked around at the candle-lit room. He couldn't see much of it, but he did see candles on the walls. Based on where the wall candles were located, he estimated the room was forty feet wide by sixty feet long.

In the center of the room were seven tables, or perhaps they were simply desks, it was hard to tell in the dim illumination. Behind each of the tables sat an orc. All of the tables, that is, except for the center table. That table was empty.

Among scattered papers and other objects, each table held a single, wide candle. The candle on each table was lit. All except for the center table. The candle on that table was not lit. Was another shaman supposed to join them?

He scanned the darkness again, wondering if there were guards hidden in the darkness. Given the poor visibility, there could be a dozen orcs hidden in the shadows and he would have no clue. Then again, these were six shamans - wizards by all accounts. Did they really need guards? Anything that could take on six wizards probably wouldn't be stopped by a dozen warriors.

"You may approach," one of the orcs said. The voice was guttural, like the other orcs, but also sounded old and female.

Guinevere started forward again and Ethan took a few steps to catch up with her. She stopped ten paces from them and stood there, hands at her sides. To him, she looked almost relaxed. Then again, she was over a thousand years old and a veteran of wars and countless skirmishes. She'd probably faced worse. Ethan wished he shared her confidence.

The orcs were close enough for Ethan to Analyze them so he pulled up his HUD.

Unandum Thunderflame
>   **Orc**
>   **Wizard**
>   **Level 8**
>   **Shohma Blackaxe**

```
Orc
Wizard
Level 7
Ranezim Nosecleaver
Orc
Wizard
Level 7
Doklar Starkbrass
Orc
Wizard
Level 6
Senamm Stonelash
Orc
Wizard
Level 7
Suk Wolfsorrow
Orc
Wizard
Level 6
```

The same female voice spoke again but this time Ethan identified the speaker as Unandum Thunderflame, the orc just to the left of the center of the semi-circle. And given her last name, he guessed this was Drorm's mother. "You claim the ancient alliance with Camelot but this cannot be. Prove your claim or be judged!"

Guinevere took another step forward, head held high and eyes defiant. "I do claim the ancient alliance. I am Lady Guinevere, Knight of Camelot, known then as the Black Knight. My husband was Arthur Pendragon, King of Camelot. My father was the wizard Merlin."

"Liar!"

"Deceiver!"

"The old alliance is gone!"

"She tries to trick us!"

The orcs erupted into sounds of disbelief and some of outrage. It might have gone on longer, but Unandum picked up a large metal ball next to her hand and slammed it down the table three times. The voices died down and then went silent.

Drorm's mother glared around at the other orcs before turning her eyes on Guinevere. "Your claim is impossible. The Queen of Camelot was human. She would have died a millennium ago. What proof can you offer us to back up your words?"

Guinevere smirked, her expression one of triumph. "I have the brand."

Ethan had no idea what she meant, but once again the orcs erupted into shouts and cries of disbelief. The shamans yelled and argued with each other more than yelling at Guinevere. Once again, Unandum slammed her metal ball down on the table three times and the orcs went silent.

Unandum stared at Guinevere with narrowed eyes. "Show us the brand."

Guinevere nodded and turned to Ethan. "Help me with my armor."

Ethan moved closer and followed her instructions to help her remove her pauldrons, vambraces and finally her chestplate. Under the armor, she had a padded tunic which she shrugged out of, revealing nothing more than a thin, and quite sweaty garment that clung to her rather large chest.

He did his best not to stare at her breasts through the nearly see-through fabric but he was only human. Unfortunately, she caught him looking and raised an eyebrow. "What would Nia think?"

Feeling his face grow hot, Ethan forced himself to look away but then he caught sight of a black mark on her otherwise-flawless skin. At first, he thought it was a tattoo. But looking closer in the dim light, he realized what he was looking at - a brand.

A sword, crossed with an axe in a large fist had been burned into her rear, left shoulder. When she saw him looking at it, she gave him a crooked smile. "Do you have any idea how difficult that is to hide in a gown?"

Then she turned around and let the orcs see the brand. There were gasps from the orcs and once again the shamans erupted into arguments.

"Liar!"

"Fake!"

"It's not real!"

Unandum called the shamans to order again with her steel ball but some of the orcs continued to speak.

"She cannot prove that is real."

"It is a fake."

"Silence!" the female shaman growled and the others went silent. Unandum stared at the brand for a full minute and then glanced around at the other shamans. "That was the mark of the old alliance but it could be easily duplicated."

Guinevere rolled her eyes. "Do you remember what

made the mark? And how the shamans of old made sure it couldn't be duplicated?"

There was a low murmur among the orcs and they looked around at each other before turning to Unandum. The female shaman nodded. "Come forward."

Guinevere did so and then bent down near Drorm's mother. The female shaman held out her hand for a moment and then snatched it away, eyes wide. "She speaks the truth. It is the ancient brand."

The other shamans stood up from their seats and moved to Guinevere, holding their own hands over the brand for a few seconds each. The warrior woman just stood there, facing Ethan and smiling triumphantly.

Ethan, for his part, kept his eyes locked on her face. He occasionally moved his gaze to one of the orcs, or anything else except her chest. He mostly succeeded.

"You may step back while we discuss this," Unandum announced, gesturing for the former queen to return to Ethan's side.

Guinevere did and seemed to move her torso deliberately so that her breasts bounced, causing Ethan to flush an even deeper crimson and deliberately look into the darkness.

He heard her chuckle as she reached him and then bent down, grabbing her padded tunic.

Ethan's curiosity beat out his embarrassment and he turned around to face her, careful to keep his eyes on her face. "What were they feeling on the brand?"

Guinevere nodded. "The high shaman who gave this to Arthur and the rest of us knights, used some sort of small crystals in the brand."

"Chymera crystals?!" Ethan asked, wide-eyed.

"Yes," she replied. "The same crystals you use to channel your magic."

"May I?" he asked, holding out his hand.

"Sure," she replied and turned her back to him so he could move his hand over the brand.

Ethan did so and opened his awareness to any crystals or magic the same way he did when filling a crystal or channeling his *Mana*. It was faint, but he definitely detected the crystals. But not only were there weak crystals, he could actually sense the pattern of crystals that exactly matched the brand. "Woah!"

"Yeah, hurt like the devil when they did it," Guinevere said and slid her padded tunic back over her torso. Ethan was both relieved, and a bit disappointed, to see her back in her tunic. She chuckled at him. "I rarely get out of my armor anymore, but it's nice to see I can still turn a man's head. Now help me get the rest of my armor back on. I feel naked without it."

The two of them worked quickly to replace her armor. As they got the last strap buckled, Unandum cleared her throat.

"Ahem. We accept that you are one of the knights of Camelot," the orc said. "And we grant you the right of parlay."

Quest Complete.
Fate of Excalibur - Part I
Shaman council convinced (1/1).
Reward: 1000 experience
You gain 1000 experience.

24

Ethan and Guinevere both swiveled their heads to the female shaman. Guinevere inclined her head politely and smiled. "Thank you, esteemed shamans. I come before you to ask to examine the sword Excalibur, which we understand you are in possession of."

Once more, the shamans erupted into pandemonium and Ethan had to physically prevent himself from rubbing his forehead.

"The sword is not yours!"

"You plan to steal the sword!"

"You are not orc!"

The shouts went on for several minutes, some directed at Ethan and Guinevere while others were directed at each other. It would've been almost comical if he didn't really want to examine Excalibur.

Finally, Unandum banged her metal ball on the table for silence and, after another minute of the shamans slowly quieting, Drorm's mother glared at the other shamans before turning the glare on Ethan and Guinevere. "The sword belongs to the orc nation now. You have no claim over it."

Guinevere ground her teeth for a second, her face flushing, but then she released a breath and smiled. "The sword was created by my father, for my husband. It should have gone to my son..."

"Your son, the demon?" snorted Doklar, as he twisted his lips in disgust. He was a sourly-looking orc with long, braided hair and many battle scars on his face and hands. Ethan wondered if he'd been a warrior at some point before becoming a shaman.

The former queen's face flushed again but she quickly got control. "You know of my son?"

"We know many things," Shohma snapped. The female shaman was thin for an orc, with a shaved head and several tattoos on her neck, head and face. Her nose was pierced and she wore a nose ring that seemed a bit too thick to be comfortable.

"Then you know my son is dead," Guinevere said flatly.

The orcs looked surprised at her revelation and began speaking to each other in hushed tones. After a couple of minutes, they quieted and looked back at the warrior woman.

The orc on the far right spoke to them for the first time. Ethan's HUD had identified him as Suk Wolfsorrow. He was a burly orc who looked more like a warrior or bodybuilder than a shaman. Yet, despite his impressive physique, his eyes glittered with intelligence. His voice was deep and commanding. "You killed your son?"

Pain flashed across Guinevere's face for an instant but

was gone as quickly as it appeared. She kept her face neutral. "I did not. This man, Ethan, did."

All eyes turned to Ethan and, feeling a bit self conscious, he smiled nervously. The shamans said nothing but eyed him up and down, taking time to pause on the head of the trident where the large Chymera stone was embedded.

"A human wizard," one of the shamans snorted. Ethan's HUD identified the speaker as Ranezim Nose-cleaver, the smallest orc present. She was petite and actually attractive, for an orc, but the look of disgust on her face ruined the effect.

"My son tells me you are a powerful wizard," Unandum said. "Is that true?"

Ethan considered the question. He had no idea how much these orc wizards knew and he had no basis to compare himself, other than Michalus. He shrugged. "I'm not bad. I'm still learning."

There was some snickering from the orcs but Unandum gestured and the snickering died out. She stared at Ethan for a moment, locking her eyes on Ethan.

Skill increase: Mental Magic +1%.

He saw the message in his HUD at the same moment he felt a probing at his mind. Without really thinking about it, he snapped his mental firewall into place, slapping the mental probe away.

Unandum flinched. Her eyes opened wide, mouth falling open. The other orcs noticed and their heads turned to her.

"What is it?"

"What happened?"

The female orc snapped her mouth shut and then narrowed her eyes at Ethan. "He knows the magic of the mind. He cast me out... forcefully."

The orcs' heads swiveled back to Ethan. Unsure whether he had just offended, insulted or assaulted the shaman, he squirmed in place. He shrugged apologetically. "Sorry. I've had some... bad experiences... with mind magic recently."

"Perhaps I should have made you aware of my attempt first. So few are familiar with the magic of the mind." Unandum stared at him for a moment before shifting her eyes. "My son says you opened a portal large enough for a horse...."

"Ridiculous!"

"Your son was mistaken!"

"No one opens portals that large!"

Ethan took a calming breath, starting to get seriously annoyed with these shamans. He knew it was a waste of *Mana*, but rather than argue with them, he created a portal right in front of the assembled orcs. He made it six feet tall and four feet wide, large enough to easily fit a horse through.

The orcs looked alarmed, probably sensing his magic. Before they could do anything, the portal fully formed, filling the room with shimmering light from the Bifrost. The orcs froze and there was a moment of stunned silence as all of the orcs stared at the portal, then there was a collective gasp. Then, pandemonium once more broke out.

"That's impossible!"

"How?!"

"Thor's hammer!"

Gritting his teeth against the strain of keeping the portal up and against the throng of orc voices, Ethan checked his *Mana.*

Mana: 53

He smiled to himself as he saw he still had half his *Mana* left. He remembered a time, not so long ago, that opening a portal this large would have drained him dry. Now, he still had *Mana* to spare.

Dismissing the portal with a small effort of will, Ethan watched it collapse quickly and then disappear. The light from the portal gone, he blinked against the sudden darkness.

The orcs continued to argue and debate the portal, the size of the portal and one even argued that the portal had been an illusion.

"Geez," Ethan said under his breath.

"They cannot believe it's real. No one creates portals that large." Guinevere turned to him and lowered her voice. A shadow of sorrow passed over her face. "Not since my father."

Ethan blinked. "What?"

"Portals that large are impossible for most wizards to create," she said. "My father was the only other wizard I've ever seen create one so large."

He didn't know how to respond to her statement. Being compared to Merlin was mind boggling. It was also, he had to admit, very cool. But he knew the only reason he was better at portal, or Aether magic, was because he'd chosen it as his specialization. His other magic, while decent, wasn't nearly as impressive.

Three loud thumps against the table by Unandum and the room dissolved back into silence. All of the orcs were staring at Ethan but it was Drorm's mother who spoke. "Your demonstration was... impressive. And you killed the demon, Mordred?"

"I did," Ethan replied, remembering the fight in the ruins of Camelot. "He was trying to kill me and my friends. I had no choice."

The orc shaman shrugged. "The demon is dead. That is all that matters."

From the corner of his eye, Ethan saw Guinevere flinch but the former queen said nothing. She just stared straight ahead.

There was a moment of awkward silence and then Unandum continued. "The sword is ours now. You are not orc. You are not worthy to see the sword or try to pull it from the stone."

Ethan suppressed a sigh of disappointment. He had been ready for this answer, but it was still disappointing. His mind raced as he tried to think of something else he could say.

"We have fulfilled the obligation of parlay," Drorm's mother said. "This meeting is..."

"Wait," Ethan said quickly. "I wish to prove myself worthy. You said I am not worthy. Drorm said I can prove my worth through challenge or by service to the orcs. Who do I need to challenge?"

Unandum stopped talking, mouth still open and stared at him. She closed her mouth and turned to the others, who looked equally taken back - if not outright disgusted. The female shaman shook her head. "Those are ways that orcs can prove themselves worthy. You are not orc, you cannot..."

An orc his HUD identified as Senamm Stonelash spoke up. He was a slim orc with finer features and a long, braided beard. He spoke to Unandum but his narrowed eyes never left Ethan. His tone reminded Ethan of a slimy used-car salesman. "There is a task he could do to prove his worth. Even if he is not orc."

The shamans erupted into arguments again, yelling and gesturing but Senamm didn't flinch. His narrowed eyes continued to bore into Ethan. It actually made him feel uneasy.

Unandum rapped her steel ball on the table for silence and then turned to Senamm. "You know the laws..."

"I do," the slender orc interrupted, finally turning his gaze away from Ethan. "A normal task would not suffice. As a non-orc, he must perform a truly great service."

"No such task..." the female orc began to say but then her eyes went wide for only a second before narrowing at her eyes at Senamm. "That is suicide."

Ethan raised an eyebrow. What type of task could they be talking about?

"It would be a task that, if done, would make him worthy to try the sword," Senamm said, his face breaking into a predatory grin.

There were muttered agreements and several of the

other orcs were sizing him up now. Ethan didn't like to feel like a piece of meat in the butcher's window and he was starting to worry about exactly what they would want him to do. He cleared his throat and looked from Senamm to Unandum. "What is this task?"

Drorm's mother stole a last glance at Senamm, who continued to smile like a snake. She sighed in resolution and then turned back to Ethan. "There is a task that you could do that would prove your worth, orc or not."

The shaman paused and Ethan waited for her to continue.

"The dragon, Bal'Furtun," she started and Ethan felt his heart sink and his stomach do a flip flop, "has been attacking our cities since he awakened."

"You want me to kill the dragon?!" Ethan sputtered, his eyes wide. He wanted to add "Are you freaking insane?" but stopped just short of saying it.

The orcs all looked aghast. "Kill Bal'Furtun?! Are you mad? Of course not."

Ethan opened his mouth to ask what the heck they wanted him to do but then shut it when the orc shaman continued.

"Your task would be to go to the dragon's lair and find out from him why he is attacking us," Unandum continued. "So that we may remedy whatever wrong we committed against him."

You have received a new quest "Fate of Excalibur - Part II"

You seek the legendary sword, Excalibur. After convincing the shaman council you were allies, they have given you the task of speaking with the dragon, Bal'Furtun, to prove your worth to see Excalibur.

Speak to the Dragon (0/1).

Reward: 2000 experience, +1000 reputation with Shamans of Tal'Rae, +1000 reputation with Orcs of Tal'Rae.

Accept quest (yes or no)?

After a moment of shock, Ethan's brain kicked in and he remembered Drorm saying that the dragon had taught the shamans magic. That meant the dragon had talked to others before. Maybe it would talk to him.

"We have spoken," Unandum said, banging her metal ball on the table. "You will find out from the dragon why he is attacking us and we will allow you to see the sword. Return when you have completed the task. Or do not return at all."

"Wait!" Ethan said, causing the orcs to look at him in annoyance. "Has anyone else tried talking to the dragon? What did it say?"

The orcs exchanged glances and then looked to Unandum. "We have sent others."

Ethan waited for her to continue and when she didn't, he gestured for her to go on. "And?"

Drorm's mother looked him in the eye and held his gaze for a long moment. "And none have returned."

25

Ethan and Guinevere met Drorm just outside the shamans' room. The big orc stopped fidgeting with his weapon belt when he saw them and raised both eyebrows. "What did they say?"

"They'll let us see the sword." Ethan grimaced, casting a glance at Guinevere. "All we have to do is talk to the dragon."

"What?!" Drorm growled, brows furrowed. "But..."

"But no one has returned from trying to speak with the dragon," Ethan deadpanned. "Yeah. So we heard."

"Then you must give up on the sword," Drorm said grimly.

Ethan bit his lip and cast another look with Guinevere. The warrior woman's face was expressionless, her eyes straight ahead. He guessed she was waiting until they were out of the keep before she would tell him her real thoughts.

"I told them we'd do it," Ethan confessed.

"What?!" the orc leader bellowed, earning harsh looks from the guards at the door. Drorm shook his head. "No sword is worth your life."

"That's what I told him," Guinevere said through clenched teeth. The former queen didn't bother looking at Ethan, but continued to stare ahead.

Ethan nodded meaningfully at the orcs near the door. "Let's discuss this when we get back to the others."

Without waiting for anyone to reply, Ethan walked past Drorm and began retracing his steps to the entrance-way. After a moment, he heard the hard leather boots of Guinevere and the softer, padded footsteps of Drorm fall into step behind him.

As he walked, he brought up his HUD and read the quest again as he slowly shook his head.

You have received a new quest "Fate of Excalibur - Part II"

You seek the legendary sword, Excalibur. After convincing the shaman council you were allies, they have given you the task of speaking with the dragon, Bal'Furtun, to prove your worth to see Excalibur.

Speak to the Dragon (0/1).

Reward: 2000 experience, +1000 reputation with Shamans of Tal'Rae, +1000 reputation with orcs of Tal'Rae.

Guinevere was right, of course, and Ethan knew it.

Excalibur wasn't worth losing his life over. And yet, he felt the sword was important if they were going to fight the Doemenagg. And considering the insect assassins had come for them twice, he knew a fight was inevitable.

It was inevitable for Ethan. The Queen, whose mind he'd briefly touched, knew him now. Just as he'd touched her mind, she had touched his too. Somehow, she'd seen the memory of him using a portal to another world. And that's what she wanted.

Ethan wasn't sure how he knew the Doemenagg queen wanted that ability. It was a feeling more than a memory of anything he'd learned from her. And even though it was just a feeling, he knew it was true.

He sighed as he reached the double doors that led out. The two orcs at the doors stepped inward and grabbed the large, metal rings that acted as door handles. With a grunt, the two orcs tugged on the ring and the doors swung inward.

Looking out the doors, Ethan could see the suns had set and the moons had yet to rise. Only the ringed gas giant marred the dark, starry sky. He also noticed that his companions were no longer waiting for them.

Drorm shouldered past him and then paused, turning to face Ethan. "Curfew has started. Your companions were escorted to lodging for the evening. I will take you to them."

The big orc spun and began to walk swiftly towards the main gates of the inner keep. Ethan hurried to keep up with the orc, with Guinevere next to him. Neither of them said a word until they were through the gates.

Once through the thick double doors of the inner

keep, they were back in the main part of the city. Drorm continued to walk swiftly. He led them several blocks and then turned left onto a wide street.

The entire time, Ethan noticed that the streets were empty except for the orc patrols they passed. The patrols glared at them but once they spotted Drorm, they continued on their route with a second glance.

Drorm walked halfway down the street and then stopped in front of a painted door to a large, three-story building. Above the door was a rusted copper sign in the shape of a tusk with a chunk missing. Beneath the symbol were the words "The Cracked Tusk Inn" in painted white letters.

The copper sign wasn't tarnished and, in Ethan's untrained eye, looked new. Given the name, he wondered if the tavern had been renamed since the orcs took over.

"Your companions are inside," the orc leader told them. "I must get back to the barracks, but I will stop by tomorrow morning."

Without waiting for a reply or a thank you, Drorm spun on his heel and strode back the way they had come.

Ethan shook his head in frustration. Now, he had Guinevere and Drorm upset with him and he was about to go in and explain to the others what he had agreed to do. It was not going to be a good night. Pushing open the door to the Cracked Tusk, Ethan stepped into the inn.

The door opened to a large common room with a half dozen long tables that reminded Ethan of picnic tables back on Earth. There were no tablecloths and the wood of the table was stained by ale and food. They looked much older than the copper sign outside.

The smell of stale hops and the aroma of cooking food filled the room. Ethan couldn't quite place the food by its smell, but his growling stomach reminded him it was long past their normal dinner time.

Glancing around, he noticed the walls of the common room were decorated with weapons of all sorts. There were a pair of swords, a halberd, a section with daggers and then several axes. Ethan noticed discolored wall areas where something else had clearly hung on the wall before the weapons. It seemed to reinforce his earlier theory that this inn had been converted to cater to orcs.

The tables were arranged in two semi-circular rows around the large fireplace at the far end of the room. There was currently a fire in the fireplace and it cast flickering light around the room. There was an open doorway to the left side and a narrow staircase leading up to the right side.

Looking around, Ethan didn't see any orcs at the tables. In fact, the inn was completely empty other than a foxling, a kobold and an elf sitting in the leftmost table closest to the fire. Their faces were silhouetted by the fire behind them, but he knew exactly who they were: their friends, of course.

Nia stood up and beckoned them over. "Come. Sit. We have food coming!"

Guinevere strode past him, towards their friends and he hurried after her. The warrior woman stopped several feet from the group and gestured to Ethan. "Someone talk some sense into this idiot."

Par'karr perked up and Nia cocked her head. Michalus

massaged his temple with his hand. "Why? What has he done now?"

"He..." she started but Ethan took a step closer to his friends.

"They will let us see the sword if we do them a favor," he interrupted, earning a glare from Guinevere.

Nia and Michalus narrowed eyes and Par'karr furrowed his brows. The foxgirl shook her head. "What favor?"

"They -" he started but it was Guinevere's turn to interrupt.

"They want us to go and talk to the dragon!" the warrior woman snapped, glaring at Ethan. "And he said yes."

No one in the group said anything for several seconds. Instead, they just stared at Ethan, mouths open until he began to feel uneasy.

"They know you are a fool," Guinevere hissed.

Nia's mouth closed and it looked like she might say something but she looked down and shook her head.

"My boy," Michalus said finally. "Why would you agree to that? You saw the dragon. We have no hope to defeat it if it doesn't wish to talk."

"Did I forget to mention," Guinevere growled, "that they've sent others to talk to the dragon but none have returned."

Par'karr leaned back against the wall. "Par'karr need drink."

Ethan frowned. It seemed like this time, everyone was against it. "I think we can succeed."

He did actually believe they could succeed. Ethan had

come up with a plan the moment they mentioned it. Unfortunately, he hadn't had a chance to actually tell anyone about it yet.

"How?!" Guinevere demanded. "How are we going to get the dragon to talk to us if it won't talk to the orcs?"

Forcing a smile, Ethan looked from Guinevere to his friends. "I think we can succeed because we don't actually have to get near the dragon."

Everyone looked at Ethan, confusion written on their features. Nia cocked her head. "How can we talk to it without getting near it?"

"We shout!" Par'karr offered with a toothy grin.

"From someplace far away," Michalus groaned.

"No," Ethan replied and tapped his finger to the side of his head. "I can use mental magic to talk to it telepathically."

26

There was silence for a moment and then Guinevere opened her mouth to speak. Before she could get a word out, an orc appeared from the open doorway. The orc was over six feet tall, with long dreadlocks pulled back and tied together. He might have been a soldier or guardsman at one time, but now it looked like any muscle he had once, had long since turned into fat. The newcomer was dressed in plain pants and shirt, over which he wore a dirty apron.

"I'm Rodor, the innkeeper," the orc said, wiping his hands on his apron. "This is all of you then?"

The orc was close enough that Ethan could scan him in his HUD.

Rodor Deeprunner
   Orc
   Warrior
   Level 3

Ethan nodded. "Yes, this is all of us."

"Good, dinner's almost ready," Rodor replied, then licked his lips. "Drorm said you have money to pay."

It wasn't really a question and Ethan sighed. "How much for dinner and rooms for the night?"

"Dinner will be a silver each," he replied. He gestured to the mugs in front of Ethan's companions. "Ale is another silver each. How many rooms do you need?"

"Par'karr and I can share," Michalus suggested.

"Par'karr no trouble." The kobold grinned. "Par'karr sleep on floor."

"Three rooms," Ethan told Rodor.

"Four silver a night," the orc replied quickly. Ethan could see Rodor's fingers twitching as his mouth moved silently and guessed the orc was counting up how much silver he was about to get. "2 gold, 2 silver. Any more ale will be more."

Rodor held out his right hand expectantly and Ethan fished through his coin purse and brought out 3 gold. Walking over to the orc, he dropped the coins into Rodor's outstretched hand.

The orc retracted his hand and, one by one, held the coins up to the light with his left hand, looking at each one. When he was done looking at them, he bit down on them. After nodding at each one, he made the coins disappear into a pouch on his belt. "Thank you. I will finish the meal and bring it shortly."

As soon as the orc disappeared through the doorway, Ethan heard Guinevere's voice from behind him. "I still don't like it."

Ethan took a deep breath and turned around. "I don't

like it either. Even if I can communicate with the dragon, it doesn't mean it won't fry us or eat us..."

"See!" Guinevere interrupted. "You are making my case."

"But," Ethan continued, "Excalibur was on the carvings in Arthur's tomb and it's also mentioned in the journal. Plus..."

He trailed off, remembering the feelings he'd gotten from the Doemenagg queen. It was just a feeling. Back when he'd been in touch with the queen's mind, he'd seen an image. Just for a moment, he'd gotten an image of Excalibur - or what he thought was Excalibur - from the queen, along with a feeling of fear, maybe even terror.

"Plus what?" Nia asked.

"Plus, I think the Doemenagg queen is afraid of the sword," he replied. "And if that's the case, I want to get it."

"You don't even know you can draw the sword," Guinevere countered. "I couldn't."

Ethan bit his lip. The truth was, he was hoping he could draw the sword. Excalibur was a legend back on Earth, a fairy tale. What child who heard the story didn't dream of pulling the sword from the stone and becoming king - or queen. And yet, he knew it was hubris to believe he could do it.

But even if he couldn't draw the sword from the stone, he could at least study it. Maybe he could learn something about the enchantment. Perhaps he could figure out why the queen seemed terrified of the sword.

"Even if I can't draw the sword," Ethan explained, "I still want to study it."

Michalus perked up with the mention of studying the sword. "Oh, I agree. Imagine what we could learn from it."

Guinevere rolled her eyes and let out an exasperated breath. "Wizards!"

"Will what you learn from the sword be worth the danger?" Nia asked, locking eyes with Ethan. It was clear to him that she didn't think so.

"It might be," he told her, though he really didn't know the answer. He hoped it was true. "The queen really is afraid of the sword. If I can learn why, even if I can't take the sword, I might be able to replicate whatever it is about the sword that scares her."

"You believe the Doemenagg will keep coming for you?" Nia asked.

"Yes."

Nia's face became hard. "Then we must have every advantage."

"Yes," Guinevere growled, "but facing a dragon is much more dangerous than facing a Doemenagg!"

"For now," Nia countered. "But more and more Doemenagg will come. Next time, there may be 8, 10 or a dozen. They want Ethan, but they cannot have him!"

"It would be safer if you just left, headed in some random direction and just kept going!" Guinevere said. "It's better than trying to face the Doemenagg queen! Or a dragon!"

"I thought you came along to help us," Ethan said.

"I did!" the former queen shouted. Guinevere must have realized how loud she was because she looked slightly embarrassed and stood up straighter. She took a deep breath and let it out. "I am trying to help you. I'm trying to help you not end up like my husband."

"But..." Ethan started but Guinevere didn't let him speak.

"You're good with magic," she continued. "But Arthur was the best of us. He was a brilliant tactician and an amazing fighter. He had Excalibur! And still, the queen killed him!"

The warrior woman deflated a bit, pulled out a chair and slumped down in it. She looked up at Nia. "You don't want to know what that feels like. To have that pain... for eternity."

Guinevere looked down at the table and fell silent. No one else spoke for several minutes and then Rodor returned with several plates. He stopped, possibly sensing the tension in the room. The rotund orc looked from person to person before making a sour face. "Bad time?"

"Par'karr hungry!" his kobold friend said, leaning forward in his chair. "Good time for dinner!"

Rodor took another look at Ethan and his companions, shrugged and walked over to the table. He set the three plates he was carrying on the table, then spun and started back towards the doorway but Guinevere's arm snaked out and caught his wrist.

"What's the strongest stuff you've got?" she demanded.

"Dwarven spirits, from the north." The orc grinned. "It's a gold a glass."

"Bring me two," she said and, fishing in the pouch at her belt, produced two gold coins.

When Rodor had disappeared through the doorway,

Nia spoke up. "I will be with him. If he dies, I will die fighting by his side."

Guinevere flashed her a bittersweet smile. "Then at least you will be spared a long lifetime of pain."

Ethan blew out a breath. "Hey! It's not a foregone conclusion that I'm going to die. I'm pretty good with magic, in case you haven't noticed."

The former queen snorted. "My father was with my husband and, no offense, but you are nowhere near the level of my father. Not even close."

He grimaced at the barb but Ethan knew she was right. He'd barely scratched the surface with magic. Merlin was quite literally a legendary wizard, probably the most powerful wizard who ever lived.

"You should forget the dragon, forget the sword, forget the queen and just pack up and get as far away as you can," Guinevere told him. "Go somewhere where no one can find you and the two of you can live a long, happy life... together."

Rodor picked that moment to return. He dropped off two more plates and a small tray with a glass bottle and a pewter cup. He looked down at Guinevere and smiled. "Looks like you could use the bottle. The rest of the bottle's on me. "

The orc looked slightly embarrassed and cleared his throat. "I'll be in the kitchen. If you need something else, just holler."

Once he was gone, Ethan looked at Guinevere. "I don't think I can walk away from this. Those Doemenagg found me...well... Michalus in Hawkshead, they found us in Camelot and then they found us on the road. I don't know if there's any place that would be safe. The queen seems to be able to figure out where we are."

"Scrying," Michalus said.

"What?" Ethan asked, turning to the wizard.

"The queen may have learned scrying and could be using that to find you," he said, rubbing his chin. "It could be how she found the other wizards too."

Ethan remembered Michalus mentioning scrying before but had never bothered to get an in-depth explanation of it. That may have been a mistake. "So she can find us anywhere?"

"Scrying allows you to see the subject and their surroundings," Michalus replied, "but not the exact location. For instance, if she were scrying us now, she would see us here... in an inn, but unless she recognized the inn, she would only know what she could see of the inn and a general direction."

"But all she would need to do would be to keep scrying us until she recognizes something and then send her minions after us."

"Or," Michalus said, holding up a finger, "if you use a portal. If you're right and she has some ability like my machine, then she will have a direction and an approximate distance."

"I'm not going to live my life, hunted like a dog. I don't want to be looking over my shoulder all of the time." Ethan shook his head. "I'm going to go and see if I can talk to the dragon, find out why it's attacking and then go examine the sword. I'm going to kill this insect queen and be done with it!

"Just like before," he continued. "No one has to come

with me. We have enough money that you can stay here in the inn until I return."

"Par'karr come along to talk to dragon," the little kobold said.

"Where you go," Nia snapped, "I go."

Ethan flashed them both a smile and then turned to Michalus. "You don't want to miss a chance to talk to a dragon do you? Who knows what lost lore they might be able to share."

"Indeed," the wizard replied. "The thought had occurred to me since we learned that the dragon used to teach the shamans. Very well, I will come."

He smiled at the elf and looked to Guinevere. She had poured herself a cup of the dwarven spirits and looked down at the cup intently. Bringing it to her lips, she downed the contents in one swallow and didn't flinch.

"Fine, I'll go," she said, reaching for the bottle. Guinevere poured herself another cup of the dwarven spirits. She lowered her voice as she took the now-full cup and brought it to her lips. "What the hell do I have to live for anyway."

27

After they finished eating, they all retired to their rooms. It had been a long day and everyone was tired. Well, almost everyone. Nia seemed to be full of energy. The foxgirl insisted on recharging his *Mana* several times, despite the fact that it was completely full. But Ethan didn't mind. Not one bit.

When they were finished, it was Nia who fell asleep first and Ethan who couldn't sleep. His mind was on Excalibur. Despite his earlier words to the group, he began to wonder if the sword really was as important as he thought.

He even pulled out Merlin's journal and re-read the passages about the death of the Doemenagg queen. Unfortunately, it didn't mention much of the sword at all. It only mentioned that Arthur had killed the queen with the sword, but had been mortally wounded in the process.

Closing the book, Ethan tossed the book into his backpack next to the bed. With a thought, he extinguished the dim light he'd been using to read. The room went dark. He lay back and stared into the darkness.

Was the sword worth the risk to himself and his friends? Physically, the dragon was the largest, most powerful creature he'd encountered on this world. More than that, it was a powerful wizard as well. If it came to a fight, Ethan knew he had no chance.

He was betting everything on his ability to communicate with it telepathically from a distance. To talk to it first and somehow convince the dragon he was a friend - or at least friendly. Ethan felt confident that he could. He just didn't know how yet.

Closing his eyes, Ethan listened to the sounds of Nia's breathing and thought about the dragon until sleep finally overcame him. Then he dreamed of dragons for the remainder of the night. In one dream, he was running from a dragon. In the next, he was riding a dragon through the air.

After that, he had a long dream of being the dragon and soaring through the night sky towards snow-capped mountains. It was an oddly realistic dream that felt almost as if he were really there.

He flew over forests, following a giant river that led all the way to enormous, snow-covered mountains. He circled the largest of the mountains for several minutes before gliding down and into a cave opening large enough for his entire wingspan.

And then he woke up.

"Ethan!" Nia said loudly, shaking him. "Wake up!"

Groaning, Ethan opened his eyes. He felt like he'd barely slept. He yawned. "I'm up! I'm up! What is it?"

Nia frowned and pointed to the window where the sun shone in. "You have been asleep for a long time. I was worried."

He blinked and yawned again. "What do you mean? What time is it?"

"It is nearly noon!" she replied, looking him up and down. She sniffed him. "You do not smell ill. Are you well?"

Ethan blinked again and shook his head to clear it. "Wait? What?"

"It is almost noon!" she repeated, her face now worried. "I could not wake you earlier. You made sounds but would not awake."

Frowning, Ethan furrowed his brows. How could he have slept until noon? He never did that. At least, he couldn't remember doing it since he arrived on this world. He looked at the window and could tell from the angle of the sun that Nia was right. It was nearly noon.

"Are you sure you are well?" Nia asked. She sniffed him again. "You do not smell sick but you still look tired."

"I still feel tired." He nodded, bringing his fist to his mouth to stifle a yawn. "I can't believe I slept that long and still feel tired."

A thought occurred to him and he brought up his HUD to look at his stats. That's when he saw the new messages.

You have gained: Scrying magic.
　Skill increase: Scrying magic +1%.
　Skill increase: Scrying magic +1%.
　Skill increase: Scrying magic +1%.
　Skill increase: Scrying magic +1%.
　Skill increase: Scrying magic +1%.
　Skill increase: Scrying magic +1%.
　Skill increase: Scrying magic +1%.
　Skill increase: Scrying magic +1%.

Ethan swore, eyes going wide as he read the messages. He twisted his head towards Nia. "Go get Michalus! Quick!"

"What?! What is it?" Nia demanded, her face a mask of concern.

"It's not bad," he reassured her. He glanced at his HUD again to make sure he had just read what he thought he had. "I'm not sure how... but I think I just gained a new magical skill."

Nia cocked her head. "You learned... in your sleep?"

He gave the foxgirl a crooked smile. "I have no idea either. That's why I want to talk to Michalus."

Smirking, Nia's eye darted up and down his body. "Do you wish to get dressed first?"

Ethan blinked and then looked down at himself. He smiled sheepishly as he realized she was right. He was still naked from last night. "Fine. You go get him while I put some pants on."

"You are sure you are well?" she asked again with a glint in her eye.

He narrowed his eyes. Ethan didn't need to use his *Mental* magic to know what she was thinking. "Yes, why?"

Roaming her eyes up and down his body again, she grinned playfully. "Are you sure you do not want to recharge your mana first?"

He realized then that Nia was only covered by a blanket she was holding around her. She let it drop and suddenly he realized telling Michalus could wait. He returned her smile. "You know, I can tell him later."

Without another word, Nia pounced on him.

A half hour later, both of them were dressed walking down the steps to the common room. Just like the previous night, the room was deserted except for his friends - and Drorm. They all had mugs in front of them and were talking as they came into view.

The big orc looked up at the pair as they got halfway down the stairs. He sneered. "You spend half the day frolicking while there are things to be done?"

"We weren't... frolicking," he replied and then stopped between steps and shrugged. "Well, not all the time. Something else happened."

Drorm snorted and gave a knowing smile. "I'm sure."

"No," Ethan replied. Reaching the common room, he walked over and took a place at the table. He turned to Michalus, who was sipping a mug. "I woke up late this morning because I gained the scrying magic skill last night... while I slept."

Michalus had been bringing the mug to his lips but suddenly stopped and stared at Ethan. "You did what?"

"I fell asleep thinking about the dragon," he related.

"Then I had a couple of dreams about the dragon, normal dreams I mean. Then, I had this dream that I was the dragon and I was flying. I followed this really big river to some snowy mountains and then went inside a cave. When I woke up, I had gained the scrying skill."

Ethan had almost said HUD but had stopped himself at the last minute. He didn't want to explain a heads-up display to Drorm.

"How extraordinary. In your sleep, you say? I've never heard of someone learning a magical skill like that," Michalus marveled.

Guinevere bit her bottom lip and then spoke. "I did. My father. He learned magic so easily."

"Really?" Michalus asked, turning to the former queen. "While he slept?"

"Maybe," she said, wrinkling her forehead. "It was a long time ago. Magic came very easy to him."

"It is not known by many." said Drorm. He stared intently at Ethan. "But Bal'Furtun's lair is in the Akyl'Ovop mountains. The Salg'Medh river runs from those mountains, west to the ocean. It is one of the largest rivers in the west."

Ethan cocked his head. "Wait. Are you saying what I saw with the dragon was real? That I was scrying on Bal'Furtun?"

"Unless you are deceiving me somehow," the orc leader replied. "I do not see any other explanation."

"So you actually used scrying without even knowing you were doing it?" Michalus asked, shaking his head.

Ethan shrugged. "I guess so. But I don't know how."

"That is truly remarkable," the wizard told him. "You really are some sort of magical savant."

Drorm snorted. "I came to tell you that I will accompany you to the dragon since I know the way but now it appears that you do not need my help."

"Why would you do that?" Guinevere asked. "Did the shamans put you up to it?"

"The shamans did not put me up to it," growled Drorm. "In fact, my mother argued against it. She would have ordered me to stay here but knew I would just disobey and get myself in trouble. That would make her look bad."

"Why do you want to come with us?" Nia asked.

"I owe you," Drorm said. "You saved my men during the storm. Possibly from a fishfolk attack, as well. An orc always pays his debts."

The big orc looked back at Ethan. "But now it appears you do not need my help."

Ethan shook his head. "No, we could still use your help. I just saw from a bird's-eye view - okay, a dragon's view. The landscape was tiny from the dragon's perspective. I don't think I could find it again from just an aerial view."

Guinevere turned to Ethan. "How do we know the orcs haven't ordered him to come along to keep an eye on us? Spy on us?"

The orc leader growled and Ethan looked at Drorm. "We're doing this for them. Does it really matter if they have someone watching us?"

"Fine. Bring him." The former queen crossed her arms over her chest. "I'll keep an eye on him."

"Fine," Drorm hissed.

Just then, Rodor came out of the doorway with his hands full with plates of steaming food. The innkeeper stopped, possibly sensing the tension in the room. After a moment he grinned. "Lunch time?"

28

"I must go make preparations," Drorm told the group. "I will return tomorrow morning."

The big orc turned to Ethan. "If you want to make haste, I suggest you buy supplies before we leave."

Not waiting for Ethan to answer, Drorm spun and walked out the door, slamming it behind him.

Ethan let out an exasperated breath. "Why did you have to antagonize him? He hasn't done anything to us? If anything, he helped us get here."

Guinevere twisted her head around to glare at Ethan, but then her eyes darted to Rodor. The innkeeper laid the plates of food on the table, looking uncomfortable at the previous tension. He cleared his throat. "I'll just... ah... go get the rest of the food."

The warrior woman frowned the entire time she watched Rodor retreat back into the kitchen. Once he was out of sight, Guinevere snapped her attention back to Ethan. She leaned forward and spoke in a low tone, just above a whisper. "I wasn't going to tell you until we got out of the city."

Guinevere stopped and glanced around the room, seemingly to make sure no one else could hear. Then she turned back to Ethan. "The orcs guard their relationship with Bal'Furtun very jealously."

Nia furrowed her brow. "What do you mean? Jealous of what?"

"The dragon has taught their shamans for centuries," she started to reply and then stopped. Guinevere gave him a mirthless smile. "Actually, I guess it would be millennia by now. The shamans had been learning from the dragon for centuries when we first allied with them."

"Really?" Michalus gasped, eyebrows raised. "Exactly how old is that dragon? I've read a little on dragons but research is hard to come by."

Guinevere snorted. "You want to know why?"

"I assume it is because they are rare and dangerous to observe." Michalus shrugged.

"You're partially right," she snickered. "Like I said, the orcs are jealous over their relationship with the dragon. Any non-shaman heading to or from the dragon is killed."

"Killed?" gulped Par'karr. "Why killed?"

"The shamans don't want the magic they are taught to get out to others," she replied. "Only one person I know of has talked to the dragons and lived."

Ethan sighed, guessing the answer. "Merlin."

"My father," she confirmed. She glanced back to the doorway as Rodor emerged from the kitchen with more food. She remained quiet as he dropped off the additional plates and then looked around. "I'll be back with some ale for you."

Once the innkeeper had disappeared, Guinevere leaned in. "My father knew the orcs would try and ambush him and he simply opened a gateway and returned to Camelot. It was one of the contentious issues when we approached them about the alliance. But by that time, they didn't really have a choice."

"The orcs kill anyone who visits the dragons?" Nia asked with a frown. "And you believe they will kill us?"

Guinevere nodded. "I was going to wait until we left the city and then suggest we gate back to Camelot or back to your village."

Ethan rubbed his temples. "Why would they send us to talk to the dragon if they were just going to kill us? That makes no sense. Or do they think the dragon will get rid of us?"

"I don't know for certain," the former queen replied with a snicker. "My guess is, they're hoping the dragon kills us. And if we actually succeed, they'll kill us afterwards."

"Either way, they plan to kill us," Nia growled. "They have no honor."

Rodor came out with a pitcher of ale in one hand and two pewter mugs in the other hand. He set them in front of Ethan and Nia, placing the pitcher in the middle of the table. The orc looked at Ethan expectantly.

Michalus shrugged sheepishly. "You have the money, my boy."

"Oh! Right!" Ethan smiled. "How much, Rodor?"

"1 gold," he replied, wiping his hands on his apron.

Ethan fished out two gold and handed it to the orc. "Bring out another pitcher of ale in a little while."

Rodor nodded and returned to the kitchen.

Thinking about Michalus's statement, Ethan reached into the coin purse and pulled out a fistful of coins. He quickly divided them into equal stacks, as best he could. Then, he set a stack of coins in front of each person. "Sorry, guys. We've been together the entire time and haven't really needed money so I just kept it with me. Take this and let me know when you need more."

Guinevere shook her head and pushed the stack of coins back to Ethan. "Thanks, but I don't need it."

"You need some money!" Ethan insisted.

Guinevere gave him a sly smile and patted one of the pouches on her belt. "You don't think you two are the only ones with magic pouches, do you? My father WAS Merlin."

Ethan chuckled. "Why didn't you say something?"

"A girl's got to have secrets," Guinevere replied with a wink.

Nia started to push hers towards Ethan. "I will be with you. I do not need coins."

"Take them," he told her and then smiled. "Please. In case we're separated, like last night. This way you have money too."

The foxgirl stared down at the coins for a moment but finally reached out, took them and stashed them in one of her pouches. Ethan glanced around at the others, but Par'karr and Michalus had already made their coins disappear.

"You're wrong by the way," Guinevere told Nia. "They do have honor. It's just not the same as yours, or mine."

"What honor do they have if they agree to let Ethan see the sword in exchange for talking to their dragon, but then plan to kill us?" Nia demanded.

Guinevere shrugged. "They do normally stick to the letter of their agreements, as we learned with the alliance - usually slanted in their favor."

"Are you saying they will let us see the sword?" Ethan asked. He was confused. First, the former queen said the orcs would kill them, now she was saying they would keep their word.

"I have no idea how they'll interpret it," she told him. "I still say they don't think we will come back, so then they won't have to do anything."

"But if we do come back?" Nia asked.

"They may take you to the sword and kill you there," Guinevere said. "That would be strictly within their agreement."

"Or," Michalus said, rubbing his chin. "They could allow you to try and pull the sword from the stone. If you don't pull it from the stone, they kill you. If you do pull it from the stone..."

"They kill him anyway," Nia growled.

Guinevere nodded. "They have fulfilled their bargain and either way, they keep the sword."

Ethan bit his lip. "Are you sure? I feel like Drorm has been straight with us this whole time."

"He was in there for an hour," Guinevere sneered, "talking to Mommy. And then she happens to send us to the dragon? Do you think it is a coincidence?"

"You think it was Drorm's idea?" Ethan gasped. He hadn't gotten that vibe from the big orc at all. If anything, he had begun to think of Drorm as a friend. Would he really have sent them on a quest that could mean certain death? Was he part of the orcs that would try to kill them?

He swore. If that was true, he'd really misjudged the orc. But how would they know if it were true? Maybe Drorm's mother had done it despite her son?

"I've dealt with orcs in the past," Guinevere replied. "They're true to their word, but how they interpret their word is not always how we would interpret it. That's one of the reasons I was angry at you last night. You agreed before I had a chance to explain it."

"Why did you not say something before?" Nia demanded. "Before we reached the city?"

"When?" Guinevere snapped back. "The orcs showed up out of nowhere and were with us until we reached the city. Exactly when was I supposed to have that conversation? In front of the orcs?"

Nia snarled, glaring at the former queen and hands dropping to her weapons. Guinevere returned her stare and didn't back down.

"Ladies," Michalus intervened. "It doesn't really matter now, does it? We are in a pickle and we need to figure a way out."

"Pickle?" Par'karr cocked his head.

"We're in a jam," Ethan explained.

"Jam?" Par'karr perked up, looking around the table. "Par'karr like jam!"

Ethan sighed. "I mean, we are in trouble."

Looking disappointed, Par'karr bobbed his head up and down. "Big trouble!"

"The question is," Ethan asked, "is how do we get out of this situation alive?"

"And what is Drorm's purpose in coming? Wouldn't they just wait until we got back and kill us, if what you said is true - that they stick to the letter of their bargain?" Michalus added.

"If I had to guess, I'd say he's there to make sure we don't talk to the dragon and then leave." Guinevere shrugged. She looked from Ethan to Michalus. "And probably to see if the dragon teaches either of you any magic."

Ethan threw his hands up. "Why are they so afraid of anyone learning magic from the dragon? I haven't seen them do anything extraordinary. I mean, look how impressed they were by my portal - and I learned that on my own."

"Actually, my boy," Michalus told him. "You are a bit of an anomaly. Most of us wizards don't learn as quickly as you do. It takes years of research and experimentation to learn a new type of magic."

"So why can I learn it so fast?" Ethan asked the wizard. "What's so special about me?"

Michalus gave him a little shrug. "I don't know. But my prevailing theory is that it has something to do with you being an outworlder and your... what did you call it... HUD?"

Frowning, Ethan sat back in his chair. He'd figured that most wizards were like him and could learn new magic easily. Michalus was extremely knowledgeable about magic, but Ethan kept forgetting the elf was hundreds of years old. He'd had centuries to study magic and even then, he couldn't do *Scrying* or *Mental* magic.

His thoughts went back to the dreams, visions or memories - whatever they were - of the aliens and the room. Obviously, the aliens had done something to him. The quests and the HUD was proof of that. Had they modified him in other ways? Had they altered him to more easily learn magic?

It was a scary concept. He still felt like himself. Yet, the aliens that had brought him here had made changes to him - possibly at the genetic level. But why? Why alter him at all? Why the HUD and the quests and everything?

"Ethan?" Nia asked, looking concerned. "Are you well?"

"I'm fine," he replied and pulled his thoughts back to the matter at hand. "I was just thinking."

"About a plan to get us out of this mess, I hope," Guinevere said.

"I don't have a plan yet," Ethan told the group. "I'll think about it and see if I can come up with something on the way. Everyone else do the same and let me know if you think of anything."

"And how are we supposed to do that with Drorm around?" Guinevere asked with an arched eyebrow.

Ethan grinned and tapped the side of his head with his finger. "Don't you remember? I can read minds."

Guinevere rolled her eyes. "You're as annoying as my father sometimes."

29

———

True to his word, Drorm met them at the inn the next morning with their horses at first light. Ethan hadn't had any *Scrying* episodes the previous night and had gotten a good night's sleep.

"You have clothing for the mountains. And a tent. That is good. But you did not get supplies?" the orc said in disbelief as he looked at the party.

He understood the orc's confusion. His group held bundles of clothing and poles for a tent they had purchased. What they didn't have were any bags of food.

Ethan smiled and nodded. "We did. They're in our... wizard pouches."

Drorm had been right the day before. If they didn't have to hunt every morning and every evening, they could get several more hours of traveling in each day. That would speed up their journey.

There hadn't been a time limit on the quest itself. Yet, time was of the essence. The longer it took them to find the dragon and ask it why it was on the rampage, the more villagers and townspeople would suffer.

He thought back to the burned-out villages they'd passed. How many villagers had died or been displaced? Ethan had no way of knowing, but now that he had a chance to help, he certainly didn't want more people dying because he was too slow.

Of course, there was no guarantee that they would even find the dragon at its lair. Despite having scrying magic and having the dream of the dragon, Ethan had no idea if what he had seen was real. It had seemed real. But for all he knew, it had just been a dream.

The fact that he'd picked up the *Scrying* skill at the same time did make him believe it had been real. Otherwise, it was too much of a coincidence.

After lunch the previous day, the group had wandered the city and picked up as much dried fruit and jerky as they could find. They'd also bought hardtack. The tack looked like a cross between a flat biscuit and a cracker but the vendor told them it would last for weeks.

They'd bought some waterproof bags as well to store it in at the suggestion of one of the vendors. According to him, it would preserve it longer by not letting humidity get to it. Now, two weeks' worth of food was safely stored inside their portal pouches.

Having seen the dragon flying in his scrying dream, Ethan also knew the area they were headed was in the mountains - snow-covered mountains. It was going to be cold up there, so he told everyone to buy the warmest clothes they could find. He just hoped they hadn't forgotten anything.

Drorm grunted and held out the reins to their horses. The big orc had his own horse this time, a large black horse of some breed Ethan didn't know. He looked around the area before facing Ethan. "Come. Let's begin our journey. It is a long way to Bal'Furtun's lair."

Ethan and his companions loaded their supplies and they divided the pieces of the tent between them so they didn't overburden any one horse. When they were done, they mounted up and followed Drorm through the city to the eastern exit from the city. As they rode through the gate, the group could see miles of lush, hilly farmland stretched out in front of them.

More striking was the huge river that snaked through the farmland, splitting the land in two. Ethan had seen wide rivers before on Earth, but this rivaled any river he'd seen before. He couldn't be sure, but he guessed the river had to be five miles wide.

He whistled. "Wow. That's a big river."

"That is Mag'Nokk, the great river," Drorm told them. "We will follow it to the dragon's lair. It is an easy journey from here. The orcs used to travel months from the south to get to Bal'Furtun. Now it is a straightforward journey. It is easy until we reach the mountains."

"Easy... but no one who has tried visiting the dragon lately has returned, right?" Guinevere smirked.

Drorm frowned. "That is true. None of the shamans who have gone have returned."

"Wait," Ethan said, turned in his saddle to face the orc. "Only shamans have gone to talk to the dragon?"

"Of course," Drorm replied. "Only shamans may speak to the dragon."

"How many shamans have gone?" Ethan demanded. He suddenly had a bad feeling about this.

The orc flushed and he scowled. "That is not your concern..."

"And you believe the dragon killed them?" Ethan interrupted. He knew he might be making the big orc mad, but his bad feeling was getting worse. "Just tell me."

Drorm snarled. "Yes, the dragon found them unworthy and killed them."

"How many shamans have gone? And how many at one time?" Ethan asked.

"Why does that matter..." the orc started to ask but Ethan held up a hand.

The big orc narrowed his eyes. "They went in groups of three. It is always in groups of three. But the dragon found them unworthy and slew them."

"But no one knows for certain, right?" Ethan prompted. "What I heard you say was: the shamans go to talk to the dragon but none return. Everyone is just assuming they made it to the dragon and that the dragon was upset and ate them, right?"

Ethan saw the muscles of the orc's jaw clenching and unclenching and his knuckles were white on the reins of the horse. "Yes. The journey there is straightforward. There is no doubt they made it to the dragon. But they were deemed unworthy."

"Or," Ethan said, and then paused for dramatic effect. "They never made it, which means no one has actually made it to the dragon."

Drorm furrowed his brow and opened his mouth to speak, but Ethan continued.

"The Doemenagg are hunting wizards. Shamans are wizards," he told the orc. "And you have been sending a small number out into the wild since this happened."

The big orc rocked back in his saddle as if struck. He opened his mouth and then closed it, a mixture of emotions playing over his face. Finally he spoke. "We have had killings among the shamans for the past two years, as have the other lands. The shamans now sleep in a heavily guarded area, warded by magic, so there have not been any slayings in months."

Drorm paused and looked back at the city and then to the east, where their destination lay. "But you are right. It is custom that the trio of shamans approach the dragon. They have not even been getting an escort."

"You really think it is the Doemenagg who have been killing them?" Michalus asked, scratching his chin. "I mean, it does make sense."

Guinevere chuckled mirthlessly. "They don't even have to work for it. They probably just lie in wait and kill them as they come."

"That means, they will be waiting for us," Nia pointed out.

Ethan nodded. "If I'm right, somewhere along the road to the mountains is probably a Doemenagg ambush - just waiting for the next group of shamans."

"To suck their brains," Par'karr added helpfully and made a sucking sound.

Drorm scowled at the kobold and Par'karr cowered on his horse. The big orc turned to Ethan. "You really believe this is possible?"

"I think it's more than possible," Ethan replied. He

remembered the sense of hunger he'd gotten from the queen. Not hunger for food, but hunger for more magical knowledge. And she was intelligent.

If she had consumed an orc brain before, she might have absorbed knowledge of the dragon and of the orcs' tradition of sending the shamans to the dragon. At that point, she just needed to have some of her minions stationed at some point to intercept any shamans.

Ethan swore and looked east. "I think that at some point, we will run into a Doemenagg ambush."

"How many?" Drorm asked. His face was no longer angry, but was resolved and calculating. "Can we defeat them? Perhaps I should bring my orcs with us."

Guinevere shot Ethan a warning glance and flashed him a tiny shake of her head. He understood what she meant. With more orcs around, they might decide to get rid of Ethan and his friends after they talked to the dragon - assuming they were successful.

If it were just Drorm, chances are they would at least get back to the city. With an entire troop of orcs, they may just decide to kill Ethan's group right after the quest was done - honor or no honor.

"I think we can handle them," Ethan told him. "After all, when you first met us, we took on quite a few of them and survived."

Drorm nodded slowly but cast a glance at the city, brows furrowed. He looked through the gate for a long moment before finally nodding again. "Fine. It will go faster if there are fewer of us. If you are sure you can handle them..."

"I'm not sure of anything," Ethan admitted and then

seeing a glare from Guinevere, he gave the orc a grin. "But I believe we can handle a small number of them."

"And if it is not a small number of them?" Drorm asked flatly.

"I'm not sure if all Doemenagg can use magic," Ethan replied. "But the ones that go after wizards can use magic. If ten or twelve Doemenagg ambush us, I don't think your orcs would be much help. It would be like 30 of your orcs going up against 10 shamans."

"That would not be a good fight," Drorm admitted. He let out a long breath. "Fine. Let us go as we are then."

"And keep a watchful eye out," Nia said.

Ethan nodded. "Absolutely. We need to have as much warning as possible."

"Good," Drorm said and turned his horse back around to face east. "Then let us go and be on guard."

Kicking his heels into his mount's side, the big orc's horse started east.

"Drorm is right. Stay on your guard," Ethan said and then nudged his own horse forward and listened to the sounds of his companions' mounts as they fell in line behind him.

30

———————

The road quickly cut sharply to the south and then ran parallel to the river. The group followed the road east through miles of fields. Despite previously living in a rural farm area on Earth, Ethan only recognized wheat. He had no idea what the other crops were.

All of the fields looked to be in good shape and Ethan guessed it was from the nearby river. He didn't know much about farming, but he knew that water played an important part of growing. As he thought about it, that was probably the reason there were farms along the river near Hawkshead. The river provided the moisture for the crops.

When he tried to ask Drorm about the farms or crops, the orc shrugged. "I am a warrior. I know nothing about the farms or the farmers of the lands around this city."

Drorm seemed different, almost agitated. Ethan almost asked if something was wrong, but dropped back in line, instead. He had a feeling that even if there was something wrong with the big orc, he wouldn't share.

Ethan shivered suddenly as the hairs on the back of his neck stood up and a feeling of icy cold went up and down his spine.

Skill increase: Scrying magic +1%.

An unmistakable feeling of being watched came over him and he brought up his HUD to read the message that flashed across it. He frowned as he read the message. Why had he just received an increase in his _Scrying_ skill?

He suddenly had a bad feeling. Ethan wondered if the _Scrying_ skill increased the same way that the _Mental_ magic skill did. With _Mental_ magic, he'd gotten skill increases not only when he used the skill himself, but also when the skill was used against him.

Ethan certainly wasn't scrying on anyone. The only other explanation he could think of was that someone was _Scrying_ on him. But who?

His first thought was the dragon. After all, he'd seen the dragon in his dreams and he had guessed that he had been _Scrying_ at that time without even knowing it. Was it possible the dragon had become aware of him _Scrying_ and was now _Scrying_ back at him?

If that were true, then the dragon might know they were coming. Was that a good thing or a bad thing? What would it do if it did know? As he thought about the dragon, another possibility occurred to him. The orc shamans.

The shamans had already demonstrated _Mental_

magic. According to Michalus, that was a rare magical skill among wizards. The wizard had also said that *Scrying* was equally rare. And yet, shamans were trained by a dragon who appeared to be some sort of master of magic. Could they have learned *Scrying* as well?

Another shiver passed over him and another message flashed across his HUD.

Skill increase: Scrying magic +1%.

Someone or something was definitely *Scrying* on him. Ethan wasn't sure what else it could be. The problem was, he didn't know who it was or why they were doing it.

Ethan wondered if there was some way to block the *Scrying*, like he'd done with the *Mental* attacks. He'd created a *Mental* wall around his mind to combat the Cthulhu and Mordred's attacks. Was there a way to do that with *Scrying*?

Unlike with *Mental* magic, Ethan couldn't figure out how to put up any sort of wall with *Scrying*. When he'd put the wall up against the Cthulhu, he could feel it going up - almost see it. When he thought about a wall against *Scrying*, nothing happened. He sensed nothing and the hairs on the back of his neck still stood up.

He glanced over his shoulder at Michalus, riding between Par'karr and Guinevere. He might know if it were possible to block *Scrying*. He was over eight hundred years old and had studied magic his entire life. If anyone would know, it would be him.

Although he was tempted to ride back and talk to Michalus, Ethan continued riding. He could sense that someone was *Scrying* on him. If they weren't aware that he knew they were doing so, maybe he could use that to his advantage somehow.

Ethan knew very little about *Scrying* itself. Could it be used to eavesdrop on conversations? If he went back to talk with Michalus and they could hear him, he'd give himself away. They would know he could sense them. Any advantage would be lost.

Luckily, he had a way to communicate with people without talking: *Mental* magic! He doubted anyone could pick up on any telepathic communications through *Scrying*. At least, he hoped they couldn't.

Reaching out to Michalus's mind, he initiated a link and heard an exclamation from the wizard behind him.

It's okay, Michalus, he sent to the wizard. *It's me, Ethan.*

"Michalus okay?" Par'karr called back to the wizard.

Don't let on that we're communicating. We need to keep it a secret, Ethan told Michalus.

"Um... I... ah... a fly just flew in my mouth," the wizard replied.

"Flies tasty!" Par'karr said and then turned around to face ahead with his mouth open.

A fly? That's what you thought of? Ethan asked the wizard.

Well, my boy, you have someone screaming in your head with no warning and see if you can think of an excuse quickly, the wizard snapped back. There was a pause. *Not that this isn't fascinating, but why are we communicating like this?*

Someone is scrying on us, he replied. *I can sense it, plus I've gotten some skill-ups.*

Do you know who? the wizard asked.

No idea.

And you're sure someone is scrying on us?

Yes. I mean, I'm pretty sure. Ethan couldn't explain exactly why, but he was certain what he was feeling was someone *Scrying* on them.

Interesting, Michalus replied. *Do you think it is the shamans?*

It could be. Drorm's mother had mental magic. It's possible the dragon taught them scrying too.

Hmm. That seems plausible. But why would they scry on us only an hour from the city?

Ethan resisted the urge to shrug. *I don't know. It could also be the dragon.*

The dragon?!

Well, I did scry on it in my dreams or whatever that was. If the dragon could sense me scrying on it, it might be returning the favor.

If that is true, then it may know we are coming.

Yes, he replied to the wizard. *But we don't know if it's the dragon. It's entirely possible it is the shamans.*

There was a moment of silence from Michalus, so Ethan pressed on. *Can wizards hear sounds through scrying?*

From everything I have read, no, they cannot.

That was good news and Ethan started to relax. Then he heard Michalus add, *However... I have read many instances where the wizard learned to read lips or had someone who read lips. This was especially true with wizards who worked for the princes.*

Ethan cursed silently. *Then whoever is watching us could figure out what we're saying.*

Theoretically, Michalus replied. *I do know that there*

were issues with the method. Something about the angle of the viewing.

That makes sense. When I was seeing the dragon, I was only seeing from a single angle. I wasn't able to see anything behind the dragon.

A very skilled scryer can change the angle of his viewing, but not quick enough to see both sides of a conversation if two people are facing each other.

That made sense to Ethan. It was like on TV, where the camera angle kept switching between two people who were having a conversation. If the camera only ever stayed on one person, you'd only see that one side of the conversation.

Ethan remembered his second question. *Is there a way to block scrying? Like how I blocked the mental attacks?*

Hmm, the wizard replied. *There might be, if the scrying is centered on you. I remember reading an excellent treatise on the subject a couple hundred years ago. The wizard - I forget his name now - definitely said it was possible.*

Centered on me? Ethan asked. *If I can sense it, doesn't that mean it's centered on me?*

Now necessarily. You can center scrying on anything or anyone that you know well. A favorite tactic about four hundred years ago was to send the person some sort of gift and then center the scrying on the gift.

Like a magical trojan horse, huh?

A what horse?

Nevermind, Ethan sighed. *You're saying the scrying could be centered on one of us or on some item we're carrying?*

Yes.

Ethan cursed. *And since I tried to disrupt it already and failed, that means it probably isn't centered on me.*

That seems a fair assumption, the wizard replied. *Although you are still very new at scrying. Perhaps you are not yet strong enough or skilled enough to block it.*

And if it's not centered on me, then there's no way for me to block it at all.

That is what the treatise said and I do remember reading the same thing in several books, the wizard told him.

But at least we know someone is watching us. And knowing is half the battle, right?

Is it? Michalus asked. *I hadn't read that before. What is the other half?*

Ethan sighed. *Nevermind. Maybe me knowing gives us some advantage. Perhaps we can exploit that somehow.*

Perhaps, my boy. I can't think of how to use that to our advantage at the moment, but perhaps something will occur to you or I later.

In the meantime, I will contact everyone mentally and let them know we are being watched.

Drorm?

Ethan hesitated. Part of him trusted the orc, but something had been different since they'd reached the city. He wasn't sure what it was or why the orc was acting differently, but if it were the shamans watching them, could he really be trusted?

I think it's best if we don't say anything to him, at least, not at the moment, Ethan told the wizard.

That does seem like the prudent choice at the moment, Michalus sent back.

Ethan cut the mental link. He took a deep breath and

let it out. The hairs on the back of his neck were still up and checking his HUD, he saw that he had two more messages.

Skill increase: Scrying magic +1%.
Skill increase: Scrying magic +1%.

As he was looking at the messages, a shiver went through him again. This time, the hairs on the back of his neck seemed to relax and he no longer sensed anyone watching them.

He hoped that meant no one was scrying on them any longer, but who knew when they would resume. Ethan needed to warn the others before the scrying happened again. He looked at his *Mana*.

Mana: 87

Checking his messages, he saw that his *Mental* magic skill had improved from using it with Michalus. He noticed it was also taking less *Mana* to use. That was good. Taking another deep breath, he began mentally reaching out to his other companions.

31

———

Fom all of the mental communication with his group, Ethan received a skill level increase in *Mental* magic. The increase came with a boost to *Intellect*. That meant more *Mana*. Bringing up his HUD, he checked out his new maximums:

```
Strength: 12
   Agility: 17
   Hardiness: 15
   Intellect: 43
   Intuition: 15
   Charisma: 12
   Health: 30
   Mana: 107
   Stamina: 60
```

Ethan appreciated the new *Mana*, though once again

he noted that the increase in his *Intellect* didn't seem to translate feeling any smarter.

He also received several more *Scrying* skill ups as someone or something *Scried* them two more times. Each time, he tried blocking the *Scrying* but it was like grasping smoke. It appeared that Michalus was correct. There was no way to block it. At least, not for now.

The group continued east along the river and passed dozens of farms and two small villages. There had actually been three villages, but the third one had been completely burned down. The work of the dragon, no doubt.

Unlike other villages he'd seen, these two villages that remained had large round structures that Ethan guessed were some sort of grain silos. Living in the country back on Earth had gotten him used to seeing silos, though he thought he remembered one of his neighbors telling him that their silos were mostly for corn feed and not grain.

These silos were very similar, though smaller than the ones on Earth. Plus, instead of being built from aluminum or steel, these silos were crafted from stone and mortar. In fact, the silos seemed to be the most well-constructed buildings in the villages.

Ethan briefly thought of asking Drorm about it but remembered the orc's earlier comment. Chances are, he knew nothing about them. And even if he did, the big orc had been sullen the entire trip.

Given the orc's behavior, Ethan was starting to believe that maybe Guinevere was right. Maybe Drorm knew the shamans would kill them. Maybe he was even part of it.

That irritated Ethan. No, that wasn't true. It pissed him off. He had thought that the big orc was, if not a friend, at least becoming friendly. But, he had been wrong about people before. He rolled his eyes as he thought of a few of his girlfriends. Oh yes, he'd been wrong about people before.

When the twin suns sank down under the horizon and the elongated shadows turned to darkness, they finally stopped. Since there was no need to hunt, they immediately found wood for a fire, broke out their rations and ate around the campfire.

The group was silent, most of them lost in their own thoughts or staring into the flames of the campfire. Ethan noticed that Guinevere kept her eyes on Drorm but the orc stared wordlessly into the fire.

Ethan thought he saw emotions playing across the big orc's face but it could have just been the flickering light from the flames. He quickly finished up his salted meat and turned to his bedroll.

"Wait," growled Drorm and Ethan stopped and turned to face the orc.

This time he did see emotions flickering across the orc's face before they settled on a look of resolution. The big orc growled. "There is something you must know."

The orc stopped and Ethan cocked his head, waiting for the orc to finish. Drorm took a deep breath and opened his mouth to continue.

Before Drorm could speak, Ethan shivered. The hairs on the back of his neck stood up and he had that all too familiar sensation of being watched. Someone was *Scrying* on them.

As if to prove his point, his HUD flashed with a new message.

Skill increase: Scrying magic +1%.

Holding up his hand, Ethan shook his head. "Someone is watching us."

Everyone froze and looked around, hands going for weapons. Ethan shook his head. "They're scrying on us."

Just in case there was someone who could read lips, Ethan moved his mouth like he was saying things, feeling a bit like he was in one of those foreign martial arts films with translations that didn't match what they were saying.

Drorm went pale and his head snapped from side to side as if he could see where the scrying was coming from. "You... you are sure?"

Ethan nodded and reached out to Drorm with his mind. *I'm sure. They've been watching us all day.*

The big orc started, eyes going wide and his head snapping to Ethan. His mouth opened to say something but Ethan shook his head and then pointed to his temple. *Think it. They may be reading our lips.*

You can hear me? Drorm asked.

Well, I can hear what you're thinking, if that's what you mean, Ethan replied.

This is not natural, the big orc muttered in his head.

Ethan gave the orc a skeptical look. *You've never had someone communicate with mental magic?*

No, Drorm replied and then cocked his head. *No one except my mother.*

And can they scry too? Ethan asked the orc, raising an accusatory eyebrow at Drorm.

The orc narrowed his eyes at Ethan. *The shamans?*

Ethan snorted. Was Drorm still playing a game with them or did he really not know? And how would he not know? Scrying would give the orcs a huge advantage. He looked at the orc. *I don't know. My mother cannot but I do not know what the abilities of the others are.*

Drorm looked down at the base of the fire for a long moment before looking up. *You know the shamans' plan?*

Locking gazes with the orc, Ethan nodded. *If we find the dragon and talk to it, they are going to kill us to preserve the secret of its lair so no one else can learn from the dragon.*

The big orc was quiet and then nodded. *I was about to tell you.*

Ethan cocked an eyebrow. The orc had been ready to tell him something before Ethan had sensed the scrying. But had he really been about to tell them the shamans intended to kill them?

Momentarily shifting his mental focus to Nia, he established a link with her. *Has Drorm lied at all since he stopped speaking? Can you tell if he's telling a lie mentally?*

Nia started and then frowned at him, brow furrowed. *I have not smelled a lie on him but I do not know if it works if he merely thinks a lie.*

Keep your nose open and raise your left hand if you smell him lie, he told his wife. He had an idea but wasn't sure if it would work. But at the moment, with someone watching, it was the best he could come up with.

The foxgirl nodded and Ethan turned his attention back to Drorm. *Okay, I'm going to ask you a question mentally, but I want you to answer aloud. Don't worry, anyone scrying will have no idea what's going on.*

Fine, ask, the big orc told him.

Were you about to tell me that the shamans were going to kill us if we succeeded?

Drorm locked eyes with him. "Yes."

Ethan glanced over to Nia. The foxgirl shook her head.

After flashing his wife a smile, Ethan turned back to Drorm. *I assume you didn't say anything earlier because others were watching.*

"Yes," the big orc said aloud.

I argued on your behalf, Drorm said mentally. *I pointed out that you saved me and my orcs from the storm. I also pointed out that Guinevere is part of the old Alliance. I was... unsuccessful.*

So they decided to kill us all once we complete the quest? Even though Guinevere had told them this before, hearing confirmation just made him angry all over again.

"Yes," the orc said aloud and hung his head in shame. "They have forsaken our honor."

Ethan glanced at Nia again and his wife shook her head again. He felt himself grinding his teeth together and forced himself to stop.

That is why I came with you, the big orc said. *To warn you. If you succeed and we survive, you must not go back.*

Ethan swore aloud. He didn't care if someone read his lips - let them. After a moment, he calmed down a bit. He looked back at Drorm. *When were they going to kill us?*

I'm not certain, but I believe after they take you to see the sword. The shamans will keep their word.

How do they plan to kill us?

I don't know.

No ideas at all?

Drorm shook his head. *This has not happened in my lifetime.*

Ethan swore to himself. He would get so close and then have to fight for his life. And even if he won, he'd probably have an entire orc army after him. Unless he portaled away. But if he fled, he wouldn't get a chance to try and pull Excalibur from the stone, or at the very least, study the sword.

He swore again and then felt a shiver as the hairs on his neck returned to normal. He made a face. "Whoever was scrying on us has stopped."

"You're sure?" Drorm asked.

"Yeah," Ethan replied. As sure as he could be.

"I take it you were using your mind magic on Drorm during that bout of silence?" Guinevere asked with her hand on her sword. "What did you find out?"

"He tried to convince the shamans to let us live but they still plan to kill us," he replied. "Just like you said."

Everyone tensed up but Ethan continued. "He was actually about to warn us, right before the scrying started."

"That's an odd coincidence," Michalus noted.

"You're sure?" Guinevere asked with narrowed eyes.

Ethan winked at Nia, who gave him a sly smile. "As sure as I can be."

"So then we should leave these honorless dung heaps to the dragon and head back north," Guinevere scowled.

Drorm's face flushed and he cracked his knuckles but then sighed. "Please do not go. If you truly think you can speak with the dragon, please find out what we have done to anger it."

"You expect us to risk..." Guinevere started but Ethan turned a hard glance on her.

"Is that really what a knight of the round table would do?" he asked.

Now it was Guinevere's turn to flush and she snapped her mouth shut. Her face became an expressionless mask. "The round table is broken."

"Not as long as you are alive," Ethan shot back.

Guinevere said nothing but turned her eyes back to the fire.

He waited for a few seconds to see if she would say anything else and then faced Drorm. "Why shouldn't we leave?"

"You saw what happened to the villages and the city," Drorm replied. "This will continue and get worse unless we find out what we did and make amends. No one else has returned to tell us what we did to anger Bal'Furtun. Please. You must help if you can."

Ethan heard the sincerity in the orc's voice and he knew that Drorm was right. If he just abandoned them to their fate, he would be haunted by guilt.

"Fine. We'll see if I really can talk with the dragon mentally. If so, we'll see if he tells you what's going on," Ethan said. "And afterwards, we'll figure out a way for us to get the sword and NOT be killed."

32

Ethan thought he'd sleep a bit more soundly that night. After all, he'd been right about Drorm and he felt good that the big orc hadn't betrayed them. On the other hand, they'd gotten confirmation that the orcs did intend to betray them.

The next morning, he was tired. He also had several messages waiting for him in his HUD.

> ***Skill increase: Scrying magic +1%.***
> ***Skill increase: Scrying magic +1%.***
> ***Skill increase: Scrying magic +1%.***
> ***Skill increase: Scrying magic +1%.***

There were at least two dozen messages, all the same. Someone had been *Scrying* on them during the night. Given the number of messages, they'd either done it for a long time or had looked in on them several times while they slept.

Ethan frowned and turned to Drorm. He paused and felt for the signs of *Scrying*. There were none of the telltale signs that someone was watching. For the moment, it seemed they were alone.

"Someone was scrying us last night," he told Drorm, but said it loud enough that the entire group could hear.

Everyone stopped what they were doing and turned to Ethan. Nia glanced around and sniffed the air. "You are sure? Could they be near?"

"I have no idea." Ethan shrugged. He twisted his head to look at Michalus. "Is there a way to tell how far away they are? Whoever is scrying us, I mean."

The elven wizard scratched his chin. "I don't remember reading anything about distance."

"That stinks," Ethan said. "It would be nice to know how far they were, maybe even what direction they were."

Michalus was still scratching his chin. "While I don't remember anyone mentioning that they could tell distance or direction, your question did jog a memory. I think I remember a rather interesting passage about the dangers of scrying on another wizard."

Ethan perked up, as did the others. "Oh?"

"It was a long time ago." The wizard bit his lip, brow furrowed. "I'm afraid my memory isn't what it used to be."

"Try," Ethan encouraged him. "If there is some way to prevent scrying or block it, that would be super helpful."

"No." Michalus shook his head. "It's not blocking it."

Rubbing his temples with his fingers, the wizard closed his eyes in concentration. "It was talking about the dangers of scrying a wizard... and... ah yes! There was something about the wizard scrying back."

"Scrying back?" Ethan repeated.

"What does that mean?" Drorm asked.

Guinevere nodded. "That sounds familiar. I think my father said something about that once."

"Do you know how he did it?" Ethan asked the former queen.

"He never really discussed magic with me." She shook her head and frowned. Then, she sighed. "Or maybe I should say, I never really cared for it, so he stopped talking to me about it."

"So neither of you know how I might be able to scry back?" he asked, head swiveling from Guinevere to Michalus.

Both of them shook their heads and Ethan cursed.

"You possess the scrying, yes?" Nia asked.

"Yes," Ethan asked, turning to his wife.

"Have you used this ability?" she continued.

He shook his head. "Not yet. Honestly, I'm not even sure how. So far, all I've been able to do is detect when they're scrying."

"To understand how to counter different weapon styles," the foxgirl told him. "I learned the styles first so that I understood their strengths and weaknesses. Once I understood the new style, I was able to better counter it. Perhaps the same would work with this scrying."

Ethan smiled at his wife. "That actually makes a lot of sense."

She grinned back at him.

He scratched his head. "Though, I'm not quite sure how to start scrying."

Both Guinevere and Michalus shrugged. The wizard

gave him an apologetic look. "As I said before, there wasn't much writing on actually using scrying. The wizards who knew the skill were secretive with it. What I've read has been mostly theory."

"Ethan good with magic," Par'karr said with a toothy grin. "Ethan figure out."

Smiling despite himself, Ethan looked down at his little friend. "I hope you're right."

"We should get moving," Drorm said, looking up at the suns. "We still have several days to Bal'Furtun's lair."

Ethan agreed and the group packed up their belongings, ate a breakfast of dried rations and then set off on the horses.

As they started east along the river road, Ethan let his horse fall back alongside Michalus. The wizard arched an eyebrow as Ethan moved parallel to him.

"Any ideas on how I can scry?" he asked the wizard. "Nia's right. I need to practice scrying so I understand it more. I know you said you didn't know how it worked, but is there anything you read that can help me?"

Michalus looked thoughtful for a long moment before answering. "The only thing that the accounts are consistent on is that the wizard who is scrying must focus on a specific object or person and they have to know that person or object very well."

"But if it's the shamans scrying, they don't know any of us..." Ethan began to say and then trailed off, looking at Drorm at the head of the procession. "Drorm."

The elf nodded. "That would be my thought."

Ethan cursed quietly and glanced back up at the orc. "Not much we can do about that then."

"Not at the present," Michalus agreed, then he cocked his head. "Although, it may not even be Drorm they are scrying, but something he carries."

"Something he's carrying?" Ethan frowned. "You mentioned that before. Scrying can be centered on an object?"

Michalus nodded. "That was the most common way of scrying in the past. Create a small item that is very familiar to the wizard. Have that item secreted on someone's person or even left some place important, then the wizard can scry for the object, rather than a specific person."

"Like a bug," Ethan noted.

"A bug?" The wizard furrowed his brow at Ethan and cocked his head.

"On my world," Ethan explained, "there are small devices that spies or sometimes law enforcement plant on people. Some allow the person to be tracked and others can actually allow them to listen in on the person's conversations."

"And this is magic?" Michalus asked.

"No, it's technology," Ethan replied with a smile.

"Fascinating," said the wizard. "You will need to tell me more about how these 'bugs' work."

"Later," Ethan promised. "Right now, any idea how to initiate the scrying?"

"I only know they mention focusing on the object or person," he replied. "Other than that, I'm afraid not."

"Okay, thanks," Ethan said and then gave the horse a tap with his heels to move up alongside his wife.

He pulled his horse next to Nia. "I want to try and

practice scrying as we ride but I'm not sure what to expect. Can you take the reins and lead my horse?"

"Of course." She smiled. Then, her face became serious. "Be careful."

"You know me." He gave her a lopsided grin.

She rolled her eyes. "Why do you think I told you to be careful."

He chuckled and handed her the reins. The foxgirl wrapped them around her hand and then nodded.

"And...uh..." Ethan gave her a sheepish look. "Try to make sure I don't fall off my horse."

Nia nodded. "I will make sure you do not fall."

Ethan flashed her another smile and then leaned back in his saddle. It was time for him to try *Scrying*.

He didn't know nearly as much as Michalus about magic, but he guessed that *Scrying* had to be similar to both *Clairvoyance* and *Aether* magic.

When he opened a portal, he had to be very familiar with the area. In fact, Michalus had taught him the trick of creating unique runes to mark a spot where he wished to teleport. It ensured that he opened a portal to the correct place instead of someplace that just looked like the place he was thinking of.

If that was the same for *Scrying*, then he needed an object or person he was very familiar with. Ethan briefly thought about it before deciding on the runes in Arthur's tomb. They were unique and he knew them well. They should make the perfect target. Now the hard part.

Not knowing exactly what he needed to do, Ethan shut his eyes and focused on the runes he knew were in Arthur's tomb. He focused intently, just as he did when he opened a portal. He knew magic worked on the will of the wizard, so he willed himself to see the runes.

Skill increase: Scrying magic +1%.

Ethan saw the message on his HUD and got excited but he saw nothing. His eyes were still shut and all he saw was blackness.

For a moment, he thought maybe the chamber itself was dark, but then he remembered the shaft above the sarcophagus that they'd used to escape. Since it was day, light from the shaft would be illuminating the tomb. That meant it hadn't worked.

He cursed. He had hoped it would be easy but apparently, it wasn't as simple as he thought. So much for being a magical savant. And yet, he had gotten an increase in the *Scrying* skill. He must be doing something right.

Ethan blinked his eyes open, took a deep breath and began trying different variations of concentration. It would only be a matter of time until he figured it out. He hoped.

33

———

The group stopped for the evening at a campsite near the river. Unfortunately, neither the crackling of the fire nor the calming sounds of the river helped Ethan relax.

He had been working on his *Scrying* skill all day with no success. While he had actually gotten a skill increase in *Scrying*, along with the accompanying *Intellect* increase, he hadn't actually been able to *Scry* anything.

Ethan was about to say something to Michalus when the familiar shiver and the feeling of being watched came over him as the hairs on the back of his neck stood up. He sighed. This was the fourth - or was it fifth - time today someone was *Scrying* on them.

After the second attempt, late in the morning, Ethan had created a signal to let the others know they were being watched. He cleared his throat and then rubbed at his right eye. The others glanced at him, giving him small nods of confirmation.

The *Scrying* went on for a few minutes and then ended. Ethan growled. "Why are they looking in on us so often? They know we can't make it there so quickly."

Drorm shrugged. "I do not know. Perhaps they are making sure you do not just kill me and flee."

Guinevere snorted and Drorm looked at her. "What?"

"I have to admit," the woman said with a smirk. "The thought did cross my mind at first."

The big orc scowled. "You would dishonor yourself while under parlay?"

The former queen chuckled. "Parlay is over. I knew what the shamans had in mind. They tried to do the same thing to my father over a thousand years ago."

Drorm frowned. He sat back and went silent.

"Do you have any idea why they are keeping such a close eye on us?" Michalus asked the orc leader. "I admit, it doesn't really make sense to me."

"No," the orc replied, scratching his head. "They seem to check in on us several times a day."

"Maybe shamans make sure we not get lost," Par'karr offered.

Drorm shook his head. "They know I am familiar with the path. I have guided some of the newer shamans to the mountain to speak to the dragon."

"They let you go to the mountain?" Michalus asked. "I thought someone said it was for shamans only."

"Not all the way to the mountain," the orc admitted. "There is a small village at the base of the mountain called Rag'Orr. We would stop there for the night and then the shamans would leave first thing in the morning to finish the trip up the mountain. It usually took a full day for them to go up the mountain and then return."

Ethan raised an eyebrow. "That doesn't seem like much time for the dragon to train them."

Drorm nodded. "This was before the dragon awoke. The shamans would go up to the stone door. If it opened, it meant Bal'Furtun would see them. If not, then they returned."

"Interesting," Michalus commented. "How long do they train if the dragon did see them?"

The orc shrugged. "I have no idea. It has not happened in my lifetime. Sometimes, they never return. It is the risk of becoming a shaman."

"Could the shamans have someone following us?" Nia asked, looking at Drorm. "Ready to ambush us after we speak to the dragon."

Drorm flushed and scowled but then he sighed and hung his head. "Two days ago, I would have said no. Now... I do not know. The shamans must protect their secrets, but what they have planned is not honorable."

Ethan shook his head. "I don't get it. The shamans know I can create a portal large enough for us to escape. Even if they have a small army, we can just portal out."

"Unless they planned to have you disabled or killed before they attacked," Guinevere said, looking at Drorm.

"That would be a good strategy," Nia snarled, turning to the orc. "Remove the means of escape before attacking."

"You kill Ethan?" Par'karr asked, his scaly face hurt.

Drorm growled, looking between the two women and then down at the kobold. "I would not do that, even if I was ordered! I owe Ethan my life! I honor my debts!"

Ethan looked to Nia with a raised eyebrow and gave her a questioning look.

Nia relaxed and gave Ethan a small nod. Guinevere saw and scowled.

"I believe you," Ethan told the orc. "I believe you are an honorable orc. But my friends are, shall we say, overprotective."

"Then can we dispense with the accusations?" Drorm scowled, glancing between Nia and Guinevere.

Ethan turned to the two women. "I think we've established that Drorm is honorable. I think that's enough accusations."

"Drorm not kill Ethan?" Par'karr asked, obviously still confused.

"No, Par'karr," Ethan assured his friend. "Drorm is not going to kill me."

Par'karr grinned. "Good. Par'karr like Drorm."

Drorm looked down at the kobold and gave him a smile.

Nia nodded. "I agree."

Ethan looked to Guinevere, who was still silent.

"Fine!" the warrior woman snapped. "He's honorable. But that doesn't change the fact that the shamans are watching us several times a day. They could still be planning an ambush."

"Are we sure it is the shamans who are scrying us?" Michalus said. The elf had been quiet during their conversation, staring into the fire.

"Who else would it be?" Guinevere asked. "Drorm already admitted they plan to kill us."

"Very true," the wizard conceded, "but it occurred to me that they really have no need to spy on us."

"Oh?" The warrior woman cocked her head.

"We went to them with the request to see Excalibur," Michalus explained. "They have no reason to believe we won't come back. They also have no reason to suspect that we know they plan to kill us. Why bother spying on us then?"

Everyone was quiet for several minutes.

Finally, Drorm broke the silence. "What are you suggesting? That someone other than the shamans are watching us?"

"It stands to reason that if the shamans have no reason to scry us, they would not waste the time or resources," Michalus replied. "If that is true, then it is logical to assume that someone else is scrying us."

"Someone or something," Ethan breathed, remembering his dream about the dragon.

"The dragon?" Michalus guessed.

"I first got the scrying skill that night I dreamed about the dragon," he explained. "I'm pretty sure most of it was dreaming, but that last part might have actually been me subconsciously scrying. If that's true, then it's possible the dragon scried me back."

Par'karr swallowed and looked around. "Dragon is watching us?"

Ethan shrugged. "If it's not the shamans, it could be the dragon."

"But that's not the only possibility," Michalus said.

Furrowing his brows, Ethan looked at the wizard. "If not the dragon, who else could it be?"

"The Doemenagg queen," Michalus replied flatly.

Ethan felt a shiver run down his spine and this time it wasn't from scrying. He hadn't even thought of the queen but if she had absorbed magical abilities from wizards she'd killed, she could definitely know how to scry.

"Do you think that is how the Doemenagg continued to find us?" Nia asked.

"It would make sense," Guinevere said. "From what you've said and what I've seen, they do seem to have an uncanny ability to find us."

"But why wasn't I sensing her scrying before?!" Ethan growled, angry with himself that he hadn't thought of that earlier.

"Because you didn't have the skill," Michalus reminded him. "You only received the skill in the city. Before that, you would have been as blind to the scrying as I am."

"Are you saying a wizard can't detect scrying unless he knows how to scry?" Ethan asked.

Michalus shrugged. "I'm afraid I don't know. And I don't think there are any wizards alive in the west who do."

Ethan swore. "If the queen has been scrying us, then she may know where we're at and where we're going..."

"And if she already has some of her assassins waiting for the next group of shamans to head up the mountain..." Guinevere filled in.

"We could be walking into a trap," Drorm finished.

Feeling a sense of dread, Ethan looked around at the others. "If the queen can communicate with them over long distances, the assassins could be on their way here now."

Par'karr's hand inched towards the magical shotgun. "They come here?"

"We have no way of knowing," Guinevere said, then looked between Ethan and Michalus. "Unless one of you two know how to track them."

The two wizards shook their heads.

"Wait," Ethan said as a thought occurred to him. He turned to Michalus. "Didn't you say that you could only scry an object or person you knew well."

"Yes, that is what my research indicated," the wizard replied. A moment later, the wizard looked up, eyes wide. "If that's the case, then how is she scrying on you?"

Ethan smiled and nodded. "I just thought of that too. There's no way she would know me well enough to scry on me."

"How would the dragon know you to scry on you?" Nia asked.

He opened his mouth to answer but then closed it when he realized he had no answer to that. Ethan frowned and looked around at the group. "If what Michalus is saying about scrying is true, then technically, neither the Doemenagg queen nor the dragon should be able to scry on us."

"If what he read is true," Guinevere pointed out. She turned to Michalus. "Are you certain it's true?"

Michalus scratched his chin and then shrugged. "I don't have the ability to scry. I only know what I've read and it is possible that the accounts I read are not accurate."

Ethan slumped and let out a frustrated breath. "Then we really have no idea whether it's possible and that means, we have no idea if it could be the shamans, the dragon or the Doemenagg queen."

"Or it may be more than one of them," Nia added. "Never assume only one enemy is plotting against you."

The group stared around the fire at each other, and then looked around the area. They all seemed to come up with the same idea at the same time.

Drorm was the first to actually speak what they were all thinking. "If one or more enemies are watching and probably hunting us, we should post double watches. Just to be safe."

No one disagreed.

34

———

No one slept well that night, knowing something or someone was hunting them. Ethan hadn't even practiced *Scrying* during his watch with Drorm. Instead, both of them had stayed as alert as possible.

He did receive several more skill-ups from *Scrying* that evening and then again in the morning before they left. Ethan nearly cringed every time it happened now.

He imagined the Doemenagg queen *Scrying* him and then directing her assassins to him and his friends. Each time the Doemenagg had found them, there had been more of them. How many would the queen send the next time?

It only took one to slip through and kill him or one of his friends. They needed to be careful. They needed to be alert. And he needed to figure out how to *Scry* back on whoever was watching them!

Once again, they ate their dried rations and then

started east along the road. Ethan rode alongside Nia again so he could practice *Scrying*. He hoped he'd have better luck today.

THE GROUP CONTINUED to follow the river road all day. They passed a few more farms but they had begun to thin out as the terrain became more hilly. The road became rougher, even as it narrowed.

Unable to concentrate as his horse navigated the less-traveled trails, Ethan resumed his position behind Drorm as the afternoon wore on.

As the group rounded a particularly steep hill, Drorm brought his horse to a stop and pointed eastward. Ethan pulled his own horse to a halt and followed the orc's finger to a mountain range far in the distance.

The mountains were tall and jagged, their tops covered in snow. They reminded Ethan of the Rocky Mountains back on Earth. At least, they reminded him of photographs of the Rocky Mountains. He hadn't actually seen them in person.

As the others gathered around, Drorm pointed to the largest mountain in the range which towered over the others. "Bal'Furtun's lair. We will reach the base in two days. From what my mother told me, it will be another day to reach Bal'Furtun's lair."

"You've never been there yourself?" Guinevere asked.

"No," the orc replied with an annoyed look. "As I said before, only shamans may go up to the dragon's lair."

The former queen rolled her eyes.

Drorm ignored her and gestured around the wild hills and forest that stretched out before them as if blocking their approach to the dragon. "It will get rougher from this point. Other than trappers, humans do not go into the Great Forest."

Guinevere snorted. "With good reason."

"Oh?" Ethan frowned. "What reason?"

Guinevere looked at Drorm with a raised eyebrow. "Do you want to tell him or should I?"

Drorm grunted. "She is right. The Great Forest is home to many creatures... including giants and trolls."

"Trolls?" Par'karr squeaked. "Par'karr hate trolls."

Ethan remembered when they'd been attacked by trolls on their way to find the library of Daemonium. They had been a tough challenge for his party. Much like their RPG namesakes, the trolls of this world regenerated any wounds very quickly.

"Yes," Michalus agreed. "I do remember reading a tome or two on the Great Forest. Trolls in the forest and giants as you get closer to the mountains."

The wizard suddenly looked pale as he stopped talking and looked out into the forest that loomed in front of them.

"What is it?" Ethan asked him.

"I remember reading about other things too," he murmured, eyes on the forest.

Nia cocked her head. "Something more powerful than a giant or a troll?"

Ethan saw Guinevere and Drorm exchange glances but he couldn't quite read their expressions. Did they know something or were they just as confused as he was.

He gestured for the wizard to continue. "What else is in the forest, Michalus?"

The wizard looked at Ethan and blinked. "I'm sorry, what did you ask?"

"What... else... is... in... the... forest," Ethan asked again, emphasizing each word.

"Fae," Guinevere replied before the wizard could reply.

Drorm nodded soberly.

"Fae? Like fairies?" Ethan asked.

"Ooh," Par'karr said wide-eyed. "Par'karr want to see fairies!"

"No, you don't," Guinevere snapped. "No one wants to run into these fairies."

Nia's ears twitched. "What are fairies?"

"Mischievous creatures who wield strange magical powers," Drorm responded. "But they are usually rare to encounter."

Ethan frowned. "Mischievous how? Will they attack us?"

"Not exactly," Guinevere said. "They steal things."

"What things they steal?" Par'karr asked, looking down at his rabbits protectively.

"Magic," Michalus answered grimly. "They steal magic."

Cocking his head, Ethan furrowed his brows. "What do you mean? They'll steal our enchanted items?"

"No, my boy," the wizard said, keeping his eyes on the forest. "They steal magic from wizards."

Ethan frowned deeply. "Steal magic? You mean mana?"

"Yes," Michalus replied. "They can suck the magic right out of a wizard, enchanted items too."

"Wait?! What?" Ethan shook his head. "Are you saying they can steal the enchantment from an item? Any item?"

The wizard nodded gravely. "Any item."

Ethan's first thought was his portal pouch. Currently, all of their food was divided between his and Michalus's portal pouches. If something happened to either or both pouches, they would lose access to all of their food.

Then there was the portal pouch to the Grail. If that pouch lost its enchantment, they'd have no access to the Grail. Without it, they had no healing. This was sounding worse and worse.

"What happens when they suck the magic out of an item?" he asked.

"They suck the magic from the Chymera stones themselves, leaving them completely empty," Michalus replied. "And destroying the item in the process. Though, you could technically re-enchant the items since the crystals would be empty."

"Great! Ethan growled. "So we have to make it through a forest with magic-sucking fairies?!"

"Did you not say that the orc shamans go there regularly?" Nia asked. "Can we not follow their path? If they travel this path often, it should be safe. Is that not so?"

The big orc shook his head. "We only took the city recently and only one group of shamans have used this path. Before that, the shamans would come from the south, skirting around much of the forest."

Ethan furrowed his brow and looked at the river to his right. Even though it had narrowed, it was still at least a mile in width. Ethan could trace its route through the hills to where it disappeared into the forest. "How do your people cross the river?"

"There is an ancient bridge a day and a half ride from here," Drorm replied. "The shamans and their escorts have used the bridge for generations to reach the dragon. It was a perilous journey through the Great Forest as you can imagine. If they encountered fairies, the shamans would lose all of their power. This is why they needed escorts."

"So, basically what you're saying," Ethan reiterated. He hoped he was wrong but unfortunately, he didn't think he was. "Fairies can suck out my mana and destroy all of our magic items. Is that what I'm hearing?"

Drorm, Guinevere and Michalus nodded at the same time.

"And there's no way to prevent them from doing it?" he asked. "Can we kill them?"

Guinevere chuckled. "You can't kill a fairy. They are beings of pure magic."

"There are fairies until we reach the mountain?" Nia asked.

"No," Drorm replied with a shake of his head. "At least, we have never encountered them east of the bridge."

"I do not like this," Nia told Ethan. "We must travel for a day and a half without the magic of you or Michalus?"

"What else can we do?" Ethan shrugged. "There's no other way around, right, Drorm?"

The big orc shook his head. "I know of no other way around."

Guinevere frowned too. "I told you I'd come with you and I'll keep my word, but I don't like it."

Ethan looked out over the forest again. What had once seemed like a thing of beauty, now became a thing of dread.

Unfortunately, Ethan had no choice. Not if he wanted to see Excalibur. He swore. He needed to get to the dragon and try to speak with it. He couldn't let fairies stand in his way. But, he also didn't want to speak for the others.

He let out a heavy breath. "I need to go on, but the rest of you don't. You can wait here."

"Where you go," Nia said immediately, "I go."

Drorm shrugged. "I have nothing to fear from fairies."

Michalus bit his lip and looked down at his belt. Ethan knew he was thinking of his own portal pouch.

"Par'karr go," the kobold said but then pulled out the magical shotgun Ethan had created. "Par'karr leave shotgun. Fairies not eat."

Ethan smiled. "That's an idea, Par'karr. We could leave our magic items here and then come back for them."

"Just leave them here?" Michalus asked.

Looking around, Ethan pointed to a boulder. "We can store them in that boulder. I can shape it to be hollow, we can put our items in it and when we come back, I can take them out."

Everyone looked at the boulder. Guinevere sighed. "If I go into a place with fairies, I need to leave my sword, shield and armor here."

"I thought your armor repelled magic," Ethan said, confused.

"It does," she replied. "But it's still magic. The fairies will strip it of all of the enchantments my father placed on them."

"Then we're all going?" he asked and, one by one, they nodded.

Ethan was glad everyone was coming but he knew they would be at a severe disadvantage if they ran into any fairies and had no magic at all. He nodded, maybe more to himself than anyone else. "Okay, let's hide our items and see how far we can make it."

35

Ethan used *Earth* magic to shape a stone boulder so that it was hollow inside. The extra mass he used to make the boulder larger. This meant the hollow area would hopefully be large enough to accommodate all of their items.

"We can store everything in here," Ethan told them. "But I suggest we camp here for the night and set off first thing in the morning. That way, we only have to spend one night in the forest."

Almost as one, the group nodded.

"Good." Ethan grinned and looked out to the river. "Since we have extra time today, I'm going to get us some fresh fish."

There was a general murmur of approval from the group. Ethan guessed that, like him, they were sick of dehydrated food.

"I will go look for any edible berries or plants," Guinevere said.

"Take Drorm with you," Ethan told her. "And keep your eyes open."

The warrior woman started to object but then nodded. "Right, people watching us. Possibly Doemenaggs."

Ethan nodded and Drorm walked over and stood near the former queen. After a moment, they disappeared into the forest.

"If you're going after fish," Michalus said with a smile, "you'll need a fire. Par'karr and I can gather some wood."

"Come on, Par'karr," Michalus called to the kobold, who quickly scrambled over the wizard.

"Par'karr help!" The little kobold grinned up at Michalus.

"I think that will be good." The wizard smiled down at the kobold and then looked up at Ethan and winked. "It might take us some time to find enough wood. At least twenty or thirty minutes."

Ethan furrowed his brow for a second before understanding the wizard's not so subtle hint. He grinned from ear to ear. "That would be great!"

The wizard smiled and nodded knowingly before turning and hurrying off to the forest.

Ethan smiled at Nia. "They're going to be gone for twenty or thirty minutes..."

"Yes." She nodded, glancing after the two figures. "That is what he said."

He rolled his eyes. "So we'll be ALONE for twenty or thirty minutes."

"Yes...oh...OH!" She smiled as she realized what he was saying. She grabbed a blanket from her saddle, hurried over to him and grabbed his hand. "Come! We must make the most of this time!"

The two of them did make the most of the time and then quickly dressed. Ethan sent his water elemental into the water to get some fish and had over a dozen by the time the Drorm and Guinevere came back empty handed.

"I hope you had some luck," Guinevere growled in frustration. "We found nothing."

"Nothing edible," Drorm said sourly.

Ethan frowned. "Is that normal?"

Guinevere shrugged. "It could be for this area. Drorm?"

"I have only been this way once," the orc admitted. "I really could not say."

Par'karr and Michalus returned with the wood and soon they were feasting on grilled trout. After several days of nothing but dried food, the trout was heavenly. Soon afterwards, Ethan and Drorm took first watch and the others turned in early.

THE NEXT MORNING, Ethan used his water elemental to gather some more fish and grill them out. After they were done with breakfast, the group was ready to leave. But before they could, they had a task to perform. They had to hide all of their magical items.

Ethan began to take much of the food from the portal pouches and pack it on the horses. They hadn't brought any extra saddle bags so they couldn't fit it all. But they should have enough.

After that, he put most of his own magic items in the portal pouch. Next he retrieved the items he'd created for the others, like the shotgun and the stone crowns that protected against mental attacks. He added the heater and the lightstones as well.

Ethan looked at his trident and the large Chymera crystal embedded in it. He also remembered the other Chymera stone in another pouch. He turned to Michalus. "What about my trident and your staff?"

"They should be fine," the wizard replied. He gestured to the crystal on his own staff. "We only channel mana into the stone. The stone does not have any enchantment or mana of its own."

"That makes sense," Ethan admitted. He'd been thinking along the same lines, but he noticed the wizard's expression. "Do you hear a but?"

Michalus shrugged. "I'm not sure if I want to take a chance."

"Oh?" Ethan arched an eyebrow.

"The crystal in this staff is finely cut," the wizard explained. "If the fairies were to somehow ruin it, I don't think I could easily find another one."

"Cut?" Ethan asked. "That makes a difference?"

"Yes." Michalus nodded and pointed from his medium-sized crystal to the larger crystal in Ethan's trident. "Well-cut crystals channel mana better. Less mana is lost as you channel your mana through it."

"That's news to me!" Ethan said, looking up at the crystal in the trident. He'd thought he'd imagined how much easier it was to channel *Mana* but it seemed like he hadn't.

"I keep forgetting that you've had no formal training," Michalus told him. "Otherwise I would have mentioned it. The crystal you have in that trident is one of the largest, most well-cut crystals I've ever seen."

"Really?! You're kidding. A crystal in this fishman trident is really one of the biggest and best Chymera crystals you've seen? Seems... odd," Ethan asked.

Michalus nodded. "It is. It must have killed a human wizard and taken it from him."

"Huh." Ethan looked back up at the crystal in the trident. "Knowing that, I would be upset if anything were to happen to it."

"I don't think it's worth the chance," the wizard agreed.

Ethan sighed, shoulders slumping. "Fine. It'll go in with the rest."

He took his spare crystal from his pocket and put it and the trident in the boulder. After him, Michalus followed suit.

Looking at Drorm, Ethan gestured to the hollow boulder. "Do you have anything that needs to go in here?"

The orc shook his head. "I have nothing magical."

"I guess it's your turn, Guinevere," he told the warrior woman and then stepped away from the boulder to give her room. "There should be room for all of your gear."

Nodding, the former queen walked over and, giving her armor one last look, pushed the pieces of armor into the boulder. Then she slid her shield atop the armor. Finally, she took her sword belt, stared down at the sword and then gingerly placed it inside the hollow. "I feel naked. And wet."

Ethan looked the queen up and down. She was wearing a pair of cotton trousers and the padded gambeson that looked worn from years of use. Both were soaked with sweat from being under her armor.

"I can dry that off for you," Ethan offered, gesturing to her soaked clothing.

"That would be great." The former queen smiled.

Ethan grinned sheepishly. "You'll have to take it off first."

Both Guinevere and Nia looked at him with raised eyebrows.

Realizing what he had said, Ethan felt his face grow warm. He waved his hands back and forth across his body. "No... no... I mean... uh... if I, you know, dry it with you... uh... in it... that might create... um... steam... which might... you know... burn you."

Ethan gestured towards the trees. "You know... you can ... uh... go behind a tree... and... take it off. "

Nia cocked her head and then shrugged. She grabbed a blanket from her horse. "Come, I will help you."

Guinevere gave Ethan a smirk before turning and following Nia over to a large tree. Ethan watched her go before realizing what he was doing and then spun to face the boulder. He looked around at the other men and pointed at the boulder. "I'll just seal this up now."

He started to will the magic when he realized his crystals were all inside the boulder. He shook his head and then reached in and took out his spare crystal. "I won't be able to seal this up all the way without a crystal. I'll use this one and then hide it."

Focusing his *Mana*, Ethan started to seal up the boulder but immediately noticed how much more difficult it was and how much more *Mana* he used. Michalus was right. The bigger the crystal and the more well cut, the easier it was to focus *Mana* through it.

A few minutes later, Nia appeared from behind the trees and held up Guinevere's clothes. She smirked at Ethan. "You can dry these now."

Ethan nodded and, using his crystal, he used a bit of *Fire* and *Water* magic to remove the moisture from the warrior woman's clothes. "Done."

Giving the clothes a pat down, Nia nodded and then returned them to Guinevere behind the tree. After a few more minutes, the two women returned to view.

"Thank you," the former queen told him. "This is much better. Without my sword, I'll need another weapon."

Ethan walked over to his horse and retrieved the two shortswords Nia had given him when she began using the scimitars. He handed them to Guinevere. "You can have these. I'm sure you'll put them to better use than I will."

"Not quite what I'm used to," the warrior woman said as she took them from him, "but I'll make them work."

He looked down at the crystal in his hand. It was the same crystal Ethan had taken from the kobold witchdoctor's wand during the attack on Hawkshead. He knew he should hide it, but if he did so, he would not be able to tap into his *Mana*. Like Guinevere without her sword and armor, he'd feel naked.

Ethan made up his mind. He would keep the crystal with him. If the fairies ruined it, so be it. He'd still have the trident back here when he returned. He slipped the crystal into his pouch.

"Let's get everything packed and get out of here," Ethan announced.

There was a murmur of agreement and within a few minutes, they were heading into the Great Forest.

36

Although the forest had looked close, it still took them several hours to reach the outskirts. When they did, Ethan called the group to a halt.

"We're at a disadvantage right now," Ethan told the group. "Our magic will be limited and Guinevere is without her armor and weapons. Let's do our best to avoid any confrontations if we can."

When no one said anything to the contrary, Ethan turned to his wife. "Nia, you take the lead and keep your nose open for anything. The more forewarning we have, the better chance we have of avoiding it."

Nia nodded but then looked around. "We will be noisy with the horses."

Ethan nodded. "True, but without them, we'll spend more time in the forest."

"This is true," she replied and then moved her horse in front of Drorm.

"Anyone else have any ideas on getting through this area?" he asked. He'd asked the previous evening too and hadn't gotten any answers but there was no harm in asking again.

"Stay to the trail," Drorm said. "It runs along the river and will take us to the bridge. From there, the path is more traveled."

Ethan nodded. "You heard him, Nia. Stick to the path. Lead us in."

Nia spurred her horse forward and everyone followed suit. The column of riders slowly entered the forest and Ethan couldn't help but feel a sense of foreboding. Memories of their encounters in Sherwood Forest were fresh in his mind. Back then, he'd at least had his magic. If they met up with fairies, he may not have any *Mana*.

There was always the option of using *Stamina*. However, since losing a point of *Hardiness* saving Nia from the Cthulhu, Ethan had been loath to use it. He didn't need to lose any more stat points.

Once inside the forest, Ethan noticed how much different it was from Sherwood. The trees here were normal trees, not the giant redwoods they had encountered previously. In fact, the forest looked so normal, it could be from Earth.

But they weren't on Earth. Despite the forest looking normal, he knew from the others that it was the home to trolls, giants and fairies - possibly Doemenagg or other creatures too. They had to keep on their guard.

Thinking about keeping on guard, he realized something he hadn't given any thought to yet today. So far, there had been a complete lack of any *Scrying*. It was midmorning already and normally by this time, they'd have been *scried* at least once. Yet, he'd felt nothing so far. It was odd. And perhaps a bit disconcerting.

The Scryer had been consistently looking in on them and now suddenly, it had stopped. He frowned as he tried to guess the reason. One reason that came to mind was that the scryer already knew where they were.

Ethan glanced around nervously. If it were the Doemenagg queen, did that mean she already had her minions in place to ambush them? Perhaps she knew where they were going and had placed them in the best spot for an attack.

"Hey guys," Ethan called out. "Keep an extra eye out."

"Do you sense something?" Nia asked, turning to look back at him.

"I haven't sensed anyone scrying us yet today," he explained. "It worries me."

"No scrying good!" Par'karr called from behind him. "Scrying bad."

"Yeah, I guess," Ethan replied. "But they've been scrying us several times a day since we left the city. Why stop now?"

"You think they know where we are?" Michalus asked. "So they don't need to scry us any longer?"

"Hey Drorm, you said there was only one trail to the dragon's lair from here, right?" he asked the orc.

Drorm didn't bother swiveling in his saddle. "Yes. This is the only trail that I know of. It will intersect the path our shamans take at the bridge."

"Then if we are on the trail," Nia noted, "they will know where we are going."

"That was my thought," Ethan confirmed.

The foxgirl called the party to a halt. "Then we may be walking into an ambush."

Ethan nodded. "That was also my thought."

"We don't know for certain it is the Doemenagg," Guinevere pointed out.

"This is true," Drorm agreed. "If it is the shamans, then perhaps now that they see we are on the trail, they no longer have a need to watch us."

The companions exchanged glances, then everyone turned to Ethan. Once again, they all seemed to defer to him. He shrugged. "We don't know who it is, so let's just stay on our guard and look for any ambushes. Perhaps we can turn the tables."

Ethan looked up into the trees. He remembered the Doemenagg attack in the ruins of Camelot. The creatures had jumped down from the walls, so they could either leap very high or they could climb very well. "Keep an eye up in the trees too. If it is the Doemenagg, they could try hiding and dropping down on us."

At his words, everyone glanced up into the branches of the trees, looking for any danger. When there was none, Nia nudged her horse into motion again and the procession continued.

THE GROUP CONTINUED for two more hours and stopped at what Ethan guessed was noon. Or at least, noonish. The forest canopy made it difficult to see the twin suns, but occasionally there was a large enough gap that he could see.

So far, there hadn't been any sign of either monsters or an ambush. He felt himself and the others starting to relax a bit but then tried to force himself to pay close attention to the surroundings.

The group let the horses drink from the river, while they filled up their waterskins. Then, as the horses nibbled on grass, Ethan and his friends ate their dried rations.

Ethan had just finished eating his jerky when movement caught his eye out in the forest. At first, he thought it was the play of sunlight coming through an opening in the tree canopy. Then it moved in an odd pattern that couldn't be the work of sunlight.

"I think the fairies have found us," Guinevere said, pointing out at a different spot.

Turning his head, Ethan saw a globe of light move through the forest. As he watched, he saw a second, then a third move from tree to tree. He watched for another minute and he was able to count dozens of the small globes of light moving around the forest, gradually getting closer.

"Other than stealing our mana," Ethan whispered, "can they harm us in any other way?"

Drorm nodded. "Yes. The ones our shamans have reported have shot lightning, created rain and even made orcs disappear who attacked them. We must not attack them or attempt to prevent them from getting what they want. If we do, it may provoke them."

Ethan watched the glowing lights get closer. He hated

to sound like a baby, but he wanted to prepare himself. "Does it hurt?"

The orc chuckled. "No. None of the shamans reported that it was painful. Just wet."

"Wet?" Ethan asked, furrowing his brow.

Guinevere rolled her eyes. "They kiss the mana out of you."

Ethan blinked. "Kiss?"

"Yes." The orc nodded. "The shamans did say the fairies put their lips on someone with mana and draw it out."

He wasn't sure how he felt about little kissing fairies, but it was better than giant mosquito fairies. Wet little kisses he could handle.

The fairies came closer and closer until they reached their makeshift circle. The little globes of light, flitted around the horses then moved to Ethan and his companions. There seemed to be about a dozen of them, though it was hard to keep track of them due to their erratic movements.

Briefly buzzing around his companions, the fairies quickly settled on Ethan, Michalus and Par'karr. Five of them landed on him, while another five landed on the wizard. The remaining two landed on Par'karr.

He wondered briefly why they were drawn to the kobold, but then Ethan realized his friend must use *Mana* to summon his demon rabbits. If that were the case, he probably had more than the others, though not nearly as much as Ethan and Michalus.

Squinting at the little balls of light, Ethan managed to catch a glimpse of tiny little humanoids that seemed composed completely of light. They were actually kind of cute - in a *Mana*-eating sort of way. And then they began to kiss him.

```
You lose 1 point of Mana.
  You lose 1 point of Mana.
  You lose 1 point of Mana.
  You lose 1 point of Mana.
  You lose 1 point of Mana.
```

He shivered as they kissed him and drained some of his *Mana*. It definitely didn't hurt. If anything, it sort of tickled.

"Oh my," Michalus muttered as his fairies began kissing him too.

"Fairies tickle," Par'karr giggled.

```
You lose 1 point of Mana.
  You lose 1 point of Mana.
  You lose 1 point of Mana.
  You lose 1 point of Mana.
  You lose 1 point of Mana.
```

"How much mana will they take?" Ethan asked.

"I do not know," Drorm replied, watching the fairies on him.

"They'll drain you dry," Guinevere said.

```
You lose 1 point of Mana.
  You lose 1 point of Mana.
  You lose 1 point of Mana.
```

You lose 1 point of Mana.
You lose 1 point of Mana.

The fairies continued to kiss him and drain away his *Mana* at a surprisingly fast rate and he couldn't help but believe the warrior woman. As quickly as they were draining him, he'd be empty in two or three minutes.

"And you are sure we cannot attack them?" Nia hissed, her ears back and her hands on her scimitars.

"You could kill a few," Guinevere said with a shake of her head. "But more would come and they would not be happy."

"And they can really harm us?" the foxgirl asked skeptically.

You lose 1 point of Mana.
You lose 1 point of Mana.
You lose 1 point of Mana.
You lose 1 point of Mana.
You lose 1 point of Mana.

"Yes." Drorm nodded. "They can definitely hurt us."

Ethan motioned Nia to stand down. "We knew this would happen. Let's just let them have the mana and then be on our way."

Nia made a face but moved her hands away from her weapons. Ethan nodded to her and then sat back and waited for the fairies to be done.

37

———

The fairies didn't take long. Within a few minutes, Ethan, Michalus and Par'karr were completely drained of *Mana*.

Ethan had kept his HUD up as the fairies drained his *Mana*. He had been concerned that the fairies might suck his *Mana* into the negative but the little creatures stopped as soon as he hit zero. When the fairies were finished, they flew off to a distance of about twenty feet and then flitted around in intricate patterns.

"You guys okay?" Ethan asked Michalus and Par'karr.

"Par'karr okay." The kobold frowned and looked around at where his rabbits had been. Par'karr hung his head. "But rabbits gone."

The demon bunnies had disappeared shortly before the fairies had flown off the kobold. Ethan suspected that his friend needed some *Mana* to maintain the summons. Once his *Mana* had dropped below a certain level, the rabbits had been banished.

"If they let our mana levels regenerate," Ethan offered, "you may be able to summon them again."

Par'karr looked up at Ethan and nodded listlessly.

"They are finished?" Nia asked, keeping a wary eye on the fairies. "You are completely out of mana?"

"For the moment." Ethan nodded. "I wonder how much they'll let us regenerate before they come in for seconds... and thirds... and fourths..."

As Ethan watched a point of *Mana* regenerate, his question was answered. One of the fairies darted in and kissed him on the cheek. Immediately, the *Mana* disappeared from his HUD. A few seconds afterwards, two more flew in and kissed Michalus and Par'karr.

He frowned. "I guess we know the answer to that."

"It appears they will be keeping us drained as long as we are in their territory," Michalus said. The wizard shrugged. "Not that it matters to me, since I left my staff in the boulder."

Ethan raised an eyebrow. "Good point. I didn't see any of them going for the pouch with my Chymera crystal."

"Perhaps they aren't interested in it after all," Michalus conceded. He frowned then. "Which means I could have brought mine with me."

"It's only been a few minutes," Ethan noted. "Let's give it a bit more time before we draw any final conclusions."

"It looks like the fairies don't harm you. That's good," Guinevere said, breaking her silence. The warrior woman had been tense the entire time the fairies flitted around them. Like Nia, her hands had been on the hilts of her weapons.

The only one who hadn't been nervous was Drorm.

The big orc leaned back against a tree, arms folded across his chest as he had watched the fairies move in. He'd just watched with an unconcerned, almost bored, expression.

"I take it, this is what you were expecting?" Ethan asked the big orc.

Drorm shrugged indifferently. He looked around at the glowing fairies as they danced through the air around them. "When I came with the shamans last time, the fairies did not harm them. I thought it may be the same for you, but I did not know for certain. I did know there was nothing we could do to stop them if they wanted to harm you."

Guinevere scowled. "You don't know that for certain."

"My people have come through the southern part of the Great Forest for hundreds of years," he replied. "For a long time, it was considered a test to reach the dragon. Before the Doemenagg began attacking the shamans, they used to make the journey alone. If they could not make it to the dragon without their magic, then they were deemed unworthy."

"No magic against trolls and giants?" Guinevere asked, forehead wrinkled. "If they weren't warriors, it sounds more like suicide."

Drorm snorted. "Maybe for human wizards, not for orc shamans. Shamans are trained to be warriors from childhood, like all orcs."

"I've fought giants," Guinevere growled. "They are nearly impossible to take down, certainly not with three to one odds. You need more like twenty to one."

"And yet, very few shamans failed," the orc snickered.

"Perhaps orcs are just naturally superior to humans in battle."

Guinevere rolled her eyes, turned and mounted her horse. "Come on. We're wasting daylight."

The others mounted and, with Nia once again in the lead, they set off down the trail again. The fairies followed them, keeping their distance until one of them regenerated a point of *Mana*. Then, like before, they'd swoop in, drain the *Mana* with a kiss and dart away.

As they darted in and out, Ethan remembered something. He turned around in his saddle to face Michalus and raised his voice. "Even non-wizards and summoners have Mana. I know, because I've siphoned some from Nia. Why aren't they going after them?"

Michalus, who appeared to have been deep in thought, started and then looked up at Ethan. "I'm sorry, what was that, my boy?"

"Even non-wizards have mana," Ethan repeated. "Why aren't the fairies going after them?"

The elf blinked and then looked around at Drorm, Guinevere and Nia. "You know, I have no idea. Even though they do not use their mana, you are correct, they still have mana. It would make sense that it would drain them too."

"I do not have mana," Drorm said. "I am not a shaman."

"Everyone has mana," Ethan replied. "Not everyone uses it."

The big orc furrowed his brow, but said nothing.

"It is true," Nia told him. "I allowed Ethan to use my mana before."

"What good is it if we cannot use it?" Drorm scoffed. "It's like not having it."

"Except wizards with the siphon ability can pull it from a willing person," Ethan countered. "And do more. Don't shamans do the same to power enchantments?"

Drorm shrugged. "If they do, I have never heard of it."

"Probably part of the orc culture," Guinevere quipped. "Orcs rarely admit they can't do anything themselves. Asking for someone to share mana would be showing weakness. Isn't that right."

The big orc turned around and faced forward and did not reply.

"That's a yes," Guinevere said with a wink to Ethan.

"I believe we are straying from the topic at hand," Michalus said. "We still do not know why the fairies are not feeding off the others."

"No warriors who have accompanied the shamans have reported being bothered by them," Drorm said without turning around. "If you are right and we all have mana, the fairies do not want ours."

"I guess it doesn't matter," Ethan said. "But if we need mana in a pinch, maybe we can use it to our advantage."

"Perhaps," Michalus said, rubbing his chin.

The group faded into silence then and there was nothing but the clip-clop of horses, the sound of the river and buzzing of fairies.

For their part, the fairies followed them, always staying twenty feet away and then darting in every time Ethan or one of the others regenerated *Mana*. After a while, Ethan closed down his HUD and just ignored the fairies.

As he focused on where they were going, Ethan did notice that the terrain was getting rougher and more hilly. He also caught glimpses of the ice-covered mountains occasionally through the tree canopy. They were getting steadily closer.

Nia held up a fist and pulled her horse to a halt. The others did the same and watched in silence as the foxgirl sniffed the air. She moved her head around as she sniffed and then began to dismount.

"What is it?" Ethan said softly.

The foxgirl whipped her head towards Ethan and put her finger over her lips. The message was loud and clear. Shut up.

Closing his mouth, he and the others watched the foxgirl look around the ground and then sniff the air. Then, she dropped to all fours and sniffed the ground.

Ethan began to feel uneasy and noticed the others were equally tense. Drorm had pulled his axe from its holder on his back and now held it across his lap.

If the fairies noticed anything wrong, they gave no indication. While Nia moved around the ground, they darted in to steal some *Mana* from Ethan, Par'karr and Michalus.

Ethan's *Mana* was at zero. Unless he wanted to channel *Stamina* to work his magic, there wasn't much he could do. He didn't want to use his *Stamina*, especially after permanently losing a point of *Hardiness*. But if it came to a choice between dying and possibly losing some stats, he'd take the stat loss. He just hoped it didn't come to that.

Finally, Nia stood up. She peered into the forest to

their left for a long moment. She sniffed again and then turned to face them. Her face was grim and Ethan got a bad feeling.

"What is it?" he whispered.

Nia glanced over her shoulder and then back at Ethan. When she spoke, her voice was low. "Trolls."

38

"Trolls?!" Par'karr gulped behind him.

"Are you sure?" Drorm asked, his grip on his axe unconsciously tightening. The orc looked around the area, trying to spot the danger.

"I am sure," the foxgirl said. "There are at least a dozen of them."

"A dozen!" Ethan exclaimed and, realizing how loud he'd been, immediately lowered his voice as everyone glared at him. "Sorry. A dozen?!"

Nia nodded. "The trail is faded but there are a dozen different scents."

Ethan glanced from Drorm to Guinevere. They were both natives to this world and from their comments, they had faced down trolls before. "Can we take a dozen trolls?"

Drorm's expression darkened. "No. Not without magic. Wounds from our weapons will heal quickly without a killing blow or fire."

Nodding, Ethan turned around to look at Guinevere. The warrior woman was looking around the area, her face impassive. After a moment, she locked eyes with Ethan. "Unless we find defensible ground or the two of you can summon some fire, Drorm is right. We cannot defeat so many."

Ethan cursed. Then a thought occurred to him and he pivoted his head back to his wife. "Which way are they?"

Nia's face looked even grimmer. She swept her hand to the side of the trail. "They came from that direction. You can see the broken foliage here and here."

The foxgirl pointed to some bushes next to the trail but they looked like any other bushes he'd seen. He nodded anyway. "Which way did they go?"

"They ran across the trail and over to the river," she continued.

"Probably to drink," Drorm noted.

She nodded. "When they were done drinking, they came back to the trail."

"Where did they go then?" Ethan asked, the sinking feeling in his stomach getting worse.

His wife bit her lip and waited a moment before answering. "They turned here and went down the trail. They are ahead of us."

Ethan cursed again. "Ahead of us?!"

"Yes," she replied. "Two or three hours ahead of us."

"We could run into them anytime," Michalus noted. "They could even turn around and come back this way."

"Do you get the sense that this trail is used by them often?" Guinevere asked.

Nia shrugged. "It has rained here within the last few days. If there were any signs before this, they are gone now."

"What are you thinking?" Ethan asked the warrior woman.

"Look at the trail," Guinevere said, pointing to the trail in front and behind them. "I've been wondering who made this trail. Drorm, you said your people just started using it, right?"

"Yes," he replied. "Since we took the city."

"I doubt the humans of those villages we passed are brave enough to venture this far into the forest," the woman explained.

"You think these are... troll trails?" Drorm asked, his brow furrowed.

"Something travels this trail regularly or it would have grown over," she said.

Ethan frowned. "If that's the case, then why did it take Nia so long to smell trolls?"

Guinevere shrugged. "Nia said it rained here a few days ago. I'm sure they don't just run back and forth on the trail. We just happened to reach an area they just used."

"So there could be even more of them behind, in front or on the side of us," Ethan said, rubbing his temples.

Nia nodded. "I did not smell them until now, but if Guinevere is correct, they could be anywhere."

"Anywhere?" Par'karr squeaked. A fairy darted down and kissed the little kobold on the top of his scaly head before retreating back to its original position.

Ethan felt the kiss of one of the fairies on his ear before the glowing creature flitted away and resumed its position with the other fairies. He thought it was strange that the creatures didn't all swarm him, competing for the *Mana*. It almost seemed they were taking turns. Did that mean they were intelligent? Did they have some sort of hierarchical system that determined who went next?

Of course, once they resumed their positions in the group, Ethan immediately lost track of them as they bobbed and weaved in their intricate little flying dance. For all he knew, it was the same one coming down each time.

Shaking his head, he snapped his attention back to the situation at hand. He looked at Drorm. "Are there any other trails or any way to cross the river before that bridge you told us about?"

"Not that I remember." Drorm shook his head. "Though I have only been this way once."

"I'm open to ideas." Ethan let out a breath. "Other than walking into a tribe of trolls."

"Go back?" Par'karr asked hopefully.

Ethan understood his friend's fear. At the moment, the little kobold was at as severe a disadvantage as he and Michalus. Without the magical shotgun he'd given the kobold and without his demon rabbits, Par'karr would stand no chance against even one troll.

"Even if that were an option," Ethan told his friend, "we could run into another group on our way back."

Par'karr deflated, his scaly face showing his obvious fear.

"As you say," Drorm told him, "we risk running into them either way. I say we continue ahead and hope they stay in front of us."

"You realize that we have only encountered a single group," Guinevere pointed out. "We could easily become flanked if another group picks up our scent."

Ethan cursed again. He hadn't thought of that.

Nia shook her head. "I doubt there will be another group until we move further."

Guinevere raised an eyebrow. "How can you be sure?"

"The ones we encountered before were very primitive. They are most likely territorial creatures," the foxgirl said. "I do not think one group will enter another group's territory."

"But you don't know for sure," Guinevere observed. "Do you?"

Nia stared defiantly at the former queen. "I do not know for certain. But I believe it is true."

"Even if we don't encounter a second group," Ethan said, trying to break the tension between the two women. "We still have a group of a dozen trolls ahead of us."

Guinevere let out an exasperated breath. "If we want to stay on the trail, we either turn around and head back or we go forward. We can also go off the trail, which I don't think is a good idea."

Ethan nodded but before he could comment, the former queen continued.

"If we go ahead, we either press forward and hope we don't run into them, or we look for some sort of defensible position where we can either hold them off or defeat them," she finished. She smirked. "Unless one of you has a better idea."

No one spoke up with a better idea and after a moment Ethan realized everyone was looking at him to make a decision. He cursed silently. Having everyone defer to him was fun, most of the time. When it came to decisions that might get them all killed, it wasn't fun at all. It was nerve wracking. If he made the wrong decision, they might all die. He shook his head. No pressure.

Unfortunately, there were risks with any option he chose. If they turned around and went back, they could be attacked by some other group on the way back. Plus, going back would also mean that he would not talk to the dragon and would never get to see Excalibur.

Ethan only saw one real option, keep going. With any luck, Nia was right and there was only one troll group in this area and they would keep going east and stay ahead of Ethan and his companions.

He nodded to himself. If it came to a fight, he'd use whatever *Stamina* he had to burn down as many trolls as possible. Hopefully, it would be enough to sway the odds in their favor. Hopefully.

"Let's continue on," he told the group. "But let's be careful. Nia, stay in front and keep your nose alert for any trolls. Hopefully, you can smell them before they become aware of us. The rest of you, stay alert. Keep your eyes open for defensive spots. If we have advance warning, we can turn around and backtrack to a defensive spot by staying ahead of them with the horses."

The group muttered their agreement and Nia

remounted her horse. Nia spurred her horse forward, followed by Drorm.

Just before Ethan got his own horse moving forward, he heard Guinevere's voice. "I hope you know what you're doing."

"Me, too," Ethan said softly. "Me too."

39

Nia led them east along the trail. They went cautiously, with the foxgirl frequently stopping them and sniffing the air. Occasionally, she'd dismount and look at the ground at tracks, before remounting and resuming their journey.

The entire time, Ethan and the others tensely watched the forest around them. While they trusted Nia's nose, a second set of eyes never hurt. Plus, they were all looking for any defensible areas.

The suns were starting to dip and soon it would be dark. Ethan didn't enjoy the prospect of camping out in the open with a band of trolls wandering the forest. Magic or not, if a dozen trolls attacked with the element of surprise, he wasn't sure they'd make it.

Ethan bit his lip. Not for the first time, he wondered if he should just call it a day and go back to Hawkshead. Was seeing Excalibur really worth all of this trouble? It certainly wasn't worth one of his friends dying over.

Had he known about the giants and trolls, and the fairies, he would probably have told the shamans what they could do with their quest. Now, he was kicking himself for getting them all into a situation that could result in them being the main course on the troll all-you-can-eat buffet.

Since he'd gotten to this world and discovered how to use magic, he'd felt powerful. Maybe even invincible. He'd killed powerful creatures with nothing more than magic and his will. He was like some superhero from the movies or comics. But this wasn't a movie and he wasn't some hero with unbreakable plot armor.

Without his magic, he was next to useless on this world. He'd practiced with Nia to learn the basics of the short sword and actually knew enough that he wouldn't impale himself in a fight. But he'd given the short swords to Guinevere, so he didn't even have those. Instead, he had two daggers.

He hadn't practiced any knife fighting techniques and even if he had, they wouldn't do any good against trolls. They would heal any simple wounds from a dagger in seconds.

Another fairy flicked in and kissed away his *Mana* and he had to fight the urge to bat it away. He had barely noticed them for the last couple of hours but his recent train of thinking made him wish there was some way to make them go away. But there was no way he knew of.

For the first time since he'd realized he had magic on this world, Ethan felt truly powerless. And he hated that feeling. Despised it. It reminded him too much of his life on Earth. A life he realized he thought he had left behind.

Bereft of his magic, he was just an ordinary guy, just like he was on Earth. Only now, the stakes were much more dire than worrying about making sure all his bills were paid or that he had enough money to go out to the bar and try to pick up a girl. This was literally life and death.

Ethan was pulled away from his thoughts by a roaring sound that he recognized. He turned from the forest to the river side of the trail and looked ahead. Sure enough, it was exactly what he thought. A waterfall.

Given the river's width was still nearly a mile wide, it was a very large waterfall. It reminded him of Niagara Falls back on Earth. At least, it reminded him of pictures of Niagara Falls, since he'd never actually seen them in person.

Nia had obviously seen the same thing and called them to a halt. "I have never seen a waterfall so large."

"It's huge. It reminds me of one back on Earth." Ethan nodded.

"My people call it the Mor'Cha'Thargar or, the Dragon's Teeth Falls," Drorm said, gesturing to the waterfall. "You cannot see it from here because of the mist, but at the bottom of the falls, there are tall jagged rocks that look like giant teeth."

"So no going over in a barrel then?" Ethan grinned.

Everyone turned to stare at him open-mouthed.

Par'karr looked at him. "Ethan go over waterfalls in barrel?!"

"And you survive that experience?" Michalus gasped.

Given the seriousness of the expressions on his companions' faces, Ethan had to stop himself from laughing. Instead, he forced himself to keep his expression neutral. "Uh... no. Back on my world, some people have tried but I don't think too many of them survive."

"Why do they do it?" Guinevere demanded. "They must know it is suicide."

Ethan opened his mouth and then closed it, unsure what to say. From what he read, quite a few people who went over the falls were actually committing suicide. He tried to think of the ones who had other motivations. "I think it's mostly for fame."

Drorm frowned. "Why would stupidity bring them fame?"

Unable to help himself, Ethan burst out laughing. Given the completely idiotic things people did on social media and video streaming services, just for a moment of internet fame, he had asked himself that same question so many times. "You know, Drorm, I really don't know."

His companions shook their heads and then glanced back at the magnificent waterfall. Ethan traced the path they were on with his eyes and saw that it got much more steep as it wound its way along the side of the falls.

He pointed at the base of the waterfall and then at the zig-zagging trail. "Do you think there's a defensible spot either at the base of this waterfall? Or maybe up there at the top?"

All eyes turned to follow his finger. Michalus scratched his chin, while Nia cocked her head one way and then the other.

"That might be possible," Guinevere said after a moment's pause. "The top would give us a vantage point to look down and see anyone coming from the west."

"But if we were forced to retreat," Drorm pointed out, "we would be at the disadvantage. The horses will need to be walked up those trails. We could never outrun the trolls if we had to walk them back down."

"We will have the same issue if we camp at the bottom. We will be alerted if anything comes down the trail from the east," Nia said. "But if they come from the west, we have no avenue of escape. We will be caught on the trail up."

Ethan frowned and looked up and down the trail alongside the waterfall. "What about halfway up?"

The group gave him questioning looks.

"If we're halfway up, we would have plenty of advance warning, right?" he asked rhetorically. He already knew Nia would either smell, see or hear them approaching. "And the trail looks narrow there. The trolls would need to come at us single file - two at a time at the most."

Michalus scratched his chin some more. "There is a certain logic to that idea."

"Unless we're attacked from both sides at the same time," Guinevere offered. "Then we're boxed in."

"How would they get around us to flank us?" Ethan asked.

Guinevere shrugged. "A rival tribe, who knows. The bottom line is, we'll be cutting off our avenues of escape."

"Do we really believe we could outrun the trolls?" Drorm asked. "Even on horses, we will need to stop sometime. Trolls can march for days."

"It's hard to make plans from this distance," Guinevere cut in. "Let's continue on and see what things look like when we get closer."

"Fine." Drorm snorted. He shrugged and turned around.

Guinevere rolled her eyes at the orc's back and Nia shook her head before rotating in her saddle and moving their group forward.

IT TOOK another hour to reach the bottom of the falls and by then, the shadows were starting to get longer. He knew they'd need to find someplace to camp soon since only Nia could see in the dark and without torches or magic, they had no way to make light.

From where they were on the trail, the mist from the waterfall quickly soaked through their clothes, leaving them all cold and wet.

Par'karr shivered, wrapping his arms around his chest. "Water cold."

"It comes from the thawing snow on the mountains." Drorm nodded. "It is very cold and can rob you of feeling if you are in it too long."

Drorm wasn't lying. Ethan was freezing. He had to fight to keep his teeth from chattering. "Oh yeah... it's cold alright. I don't see how we can camp down here. We'll freeze."

"Ethan!" Nia exclaimed and Ethan spun towards his wife and drew his dagger in a fluid motion. Yet he saw no threat.

"What is it?" he asked, looking around.

The foxgirl cocked her head and pointed behind him.

"The fairies! They are not swooping in on you, Par'karr and Michalus."

Ethan blinked and let his dagger fall to his side. He turned and looked at the fairies, who had gathered about fifty feet away and were bobbing and weaving in their intricate flying dance. Though, as he watched them, he got the impression that their dance had become... irritated.

He pulled up his HUD so he could check his stats.

Mana: 5

"You're right!" he said with a grin. "I've regenerated 5 mana."

Looking up at the fairies, he waited for several minutes to see if any would dart in to steal his *Mana* away. None came.

"That's strange," he said.

"Perhaps not," Michalus interjected. "Some insects cannot fly in the rain. The water weighs down their bodies too much. I never had the chance to show you, but I do keep a few hives of honey bees not too far from my cabin. I use the honey to treat the jerky I make, amongst other things."

Ethan looked around at the mist caused by the water-fall and grinned more broadly. "You're saying they can't come any closer because of the mist?"

"I believe that's as plausible an explanation as any," Michalus said with a shrug. "I'm not familiar with fairy anatomy, so it's just a theory."

"Or there is something around here they're afraid of," Guinevere suggested.

That was a sobering thought. Ethan spun back to Nia. "Do you smell anything?"

Nia sniffed the air for several moments and then sneezed. She scratched her nose and then shook her head. "I cannot smell anything, but this mist has erased any scents that were here. I cannot smell anything."

Ethan checked his *Mana* again.

Mana: 7

He was continuing to regenerate magic. Unfortunately, the moment they left the mist, the fairies would likely be on them in an instant and drain them dry. Still, it did give Ethan a few ideas.

"I say we camp somewhere around here," he told them.

"Camp here?" Drorm frowned. He gestured around at the mist, which was visibly in the air. "In this?!"

"Hear me out," he said, holding up his palms in a placating gesture. "If Michalus and I have our magic back, we shape one of the rocks into a shelter - maybe two shelters. I think I can cause the rocks to heat up and provide us heat throughout the night."

"There are no real avenues of escape here, except back the way we came," Guinevere pointed out.

Ethan smiled. "If Michalus and I have our magic back, we may not need to escape. If we have stone shelters and magic, we can fight them off."

Drorm and Guinevere looked skeptical. Nia just

nodded and glanced over the waterfall, examining what she could see of the shoreline.

"You forget," Michalus said, holding up his empty hands. "I don't have my staff with me."

"We can take turns with my spare crystal," Ethan said, fishing it out of his pouch. He gave the wizard a sheepish look. "It does mean the two of us will have to take double watch shifts."

"I can live with that," Michalus agreed.

"Let's hope we all live with this crazy idea." Guinevere frowned as she dismounted. "Because if it doesn't work, we're sitting ducks."

40

———

As Ethan waited for his *Mana* to regenerate, he suggested that they move closer to the waterfall. "The further we are from the trail, the less likely we are to be seen - or smelled - by any passing predators, including the trolls."

The group agreed. Michalus and Par'karr stayed with the horses, while Ethan, Drorm, Guinevere and Nia followed the shoreline towards the waterfall to look for better camping spots.

The mist made it difficult to see and also made the rocks slippery. As they got closer to the waterfall itself, the path became rockier, but also much more slick with water. More than once, one of them nearly slipped off the rocks they climbed over. Luckily, one of the other group members was always there to catch them before they slipped into the water.

"There's no point in looking further," Guinevere finally said, after she nearly slipped into the water a second time.

"Even if we find some great place for you to make a shelter, we'd never get the horses back here without one of
them breaking a leg or going into the river."

Ethan frowned and looked down at the wet boulders.
She was right. The horses would never make it this far
back. At least, not the way it was now. He checked his
Mana.

Mana: 21

Taking out his Chymera crystal, he channeled *Earth*
magic causing the boulders in front of them to merge
together into a flat surface. It took less than a minute and
only used a quarter of his *Mana*, but once it was finished,
a 4-foot-wide by 8-foot-long section of the boulders was
now a stone road.

He grinned. "How about that?"

Guinevere and Drorm exchanged looks and then carefully stepped out onto the flat stone section. Guinevere
moved back and forth a few times before nodding. "This
should do. But do you want to waste your mana on a stone
road?"

"Even if I use up all of my mana," Ethan replied,
"Michalus can take over and we can go back and forth
until the job's done."

"This seems like much work for a single night," Drorm
pointed out.

"Maybe," Ethan agreed. "But at least we'd be safe."

"As long as the trolls do not find us here," the orc
retorted. "If they do, we have no escape."

Ethan grinned. "But here, Michalus and I can use

magic. Not only that, but they would not be able to approach us, except on stone - which for us, would be a weapon."

"Like the werewolves," Nia commented.

Remembering back to their encounter with the pack of female-only werewolves, Ethan nodded. Werewolves had been chasing them and they'd made a stand on a stone bridge. He'd been able to shape the stone to form both spikes and bars and effectively stop the werewolves from getting to them.

They'd have a similar situation here. With all the stone around, Ethan could easily impale a dozen trolls. He grinned. If they attacked while the group was this close to rock, it wouldn't even be a contest.

"Werewolves?" Drorm asked with a raised eyebrow, looking around the faces of the other companions. Guinevere furrowed her brow and shrugged.

Realizing neither of the two had been with them when they'd encountered the werewolves, Ethan gave them a quick summary of their encounter and how he'd used the bridge's stone to effectively cut off their pursuit.

"And you can do that here?" the orc asked.

"Are you kidding?" Ethan chuckled. "With this much stone around, they wouldn't stand a chance."

Guinevere nodded. "My father did similar things. If you're sure you can defend this area, then it seems the further we go back, the safer we will be."

Drorm snorted. "And the wetter."

Ethan shrugged. "I don't know what I can do about that."

"Can we make a fire? Would that not keep us dry?" Nia

asked.

"I guess we could," Ethan replied with a shrug. "I could make a hole in the top of the shelter for the smoke to go out. But we'll need to collect firewood."

"There is plenty of wood around," Guinevere pointed out. "We are in a forest, after all. You'll have to use magic to dry it."

"I can do that," Ethan said and then gestured towards the waterfall. "Let's see how far this goes back and if there's actually room to make a large enough shelter back there. We can worry about the firewood later."

The group agreed and continued on. Ethan used magic to flatten more boulders into what was effectively becoming a stone road.

After about a hundred feet, the path they were following started curving inward towards the waterfall even as the cliff loomed up on the left side.

"This is about as far as we can go!" Drorm yelled over the roar of the water. The waterfall had gotten progressively louder and now required yelling to be heard.

"It's too narrow here to make a shelter!" Guinevere bellowed.

Ethan pointed at the cliff wall. "What if we carve the shelter out of the cliff?!"

"Can you do that without bringing the cliff down on us?" Guinevere yelled back.

"Only one way to find out!" Ethan replied. He wished Ainslee was here. The dwarf would no doubt be able to tell him whether it was safe, or at least point out any weak spots or structure flaws in the cliff face.

"Move back!" he yelled to the others. "And be ready to

run!"

The others exchanged looks and then quickly retreated back down Ethan's stone path. For his part, Ethan backed up as far as he could and still cast his magic.

"Here goes nothing," he said under his breath, knowing no one could hear him over the cascading waters.

Then, using his Earth magic, he began to carve out a hole in the side of the cliff. It was slow work because he had to move stone from where it was to the outside instead of just forming it into a shape.

He used the excess stone to actually create a small hollow tower next to the cave he was creating, complete with a stone ladder. He grinned as he did it. Not only was he creating a cave, he was creating a guard tower too. One that would give them an unobstructed view of the stone road that led to the cave.

Ethan frowned then and stopped as he looked around at the mist. While the watchtower was a good idea, the mist simply made it impractical since it obscured visibility beyond five or six feet. He sighed. What was that they said about the best-laid plans of mice and men... and wizards.

Finally, he was forced to stop with the cave only half formed. He looked at the others. "Out of mana. Let's head back and I'll bring Michalus back here so he can continue!"

Guinevere nodded and then pointed to herself and Drorm. "Drorm and I will go collect some wood if Nia wants to watch the horses with Par'karr."

The four of them began making their way back to the others when a small shape moved in the mist. The group quickly came to a stop, hands reaching for weapons. After only a moment, the shape of a small kobold materialized through the mist.

Par'karr looked startled at their sudden appearance but then Ethan realized his friend wasn't just startled. He was afraid.

Wide-eyed, the little kobold pointed down the path. "Trolls is coming!"

Ethan cursed. It was too early! They weren't ready! He cursed again. "How long?"

Par'karr just stared wide-eyed at him. Ethan raised his voice over the sound of the falls. "How long, Par'karr?!"

"Trolls is coming down cliff," Par'karr croaked. "Not take trolls long!"

Cursing again, Ethan turned back to the others. "Come on! We need to get the horses down this trail and out of the open!"

Moving past Par'karr, Ethan gestured for everyone to follow him as they quickly made their way back to the spot where they had left Michalus and the horses. When they appeared out of the mist, he could see the look of relief on the wizard's face.

"The trolls are coming down the path from the top of the falls," he said and Ethan realized he could hear hooting, growls and snarls coming from up the path. The path was shadowed now with the sinking suns and he couldn't see any signs of trolls - just hear them.

Ethan cursed again and thrust out his hand with the Chymera crystal. "Take it! We need to smooth out the stone and get the horses back where I've started carving out a cave!"

Michalus nodded and took the crystal from Ethan. He cast a look up the cliff face to where the sounds were coming from.

"We have fifteen minutes before they are down," Nia said. The foxgirl was staring up at the path and Ethan remembered she had excellent night vision.

"You're sure?!" he asked.

Nia shrugged. "I am guessing based on how quickly they are moving. They are making noise, but I do not think they are aware of us yet."

"What makes you think that?" Guinevere asked.

"If they knew we were down here," she replied, eyes still on the paths above, "they would move faster."

"Let's go with that!" Ethan told the others, getting their attention. "Drorm! Guinevere! See if you can get any wood nearby! Don't wander! Get whatever you can and get back here!"

The two of them nodded and moved off. Ethan turned to Par'karr and Nia. "You two stay here with the horses. Nia, keep your eyes on them. If they start to move faster, yell for Drorm and Guinevere to get their butts back and then start walking the horses down the path!"

Ethan turned to Michalus and gestured towards the waterfall. "We need to shape as much stone as possible before they get here! Come on!"

Not waiting for the wizard's reply, Ethan turned and hurried back down to the water's edge. They had fifteen minutes to create some sort of defensible fortification before the trolls reached them. If they couldn't, it might be a really short fight.

41

Michalus's *Mana* had recovered to a point where he was able to easily flatten the remaining boulders. The wizard created a four-foot-wide path that led from the edge of the river, all the way back to where Ethan had started to shape the rock. The result was a flat, stone path that led to the shallow cave Ethan had begun to carve out.

"I'm afraid I don't have much mana left, my boy," Michalus said, holding out the Chymera crystal.

Nodding, Ethan took the Chymera crystal from the wizard. "That's perfect! We now have a path that we can lead the horses back on."

"And perhaps lead the trolls back here as well," Michalus retorted with a meaningful look.

Ethan opened his mouth to speak but before he could, Guinevere materialized through the mist with an armful of wood. Her expression was grim and Ethan guessed what she was about to say before she even said it.

"They're almost down," the warrior woman said as Drorm materialized behind her. Like Ethan and Michalus, they were forced to yell, just to be heard over the crashing water.

"I hope you had time to make some defenses," the orc added, stopping just short of running into Guinevere.

Shaking his head, Ethan glanced back at the shallow cave and cursed. "We just finished the path."

Drorm and Guinevere both muttered their own curses and hurried past Ethan with the wood. The two of them dropped it unceremoniously just inside the cave entrance and then turned towards him.

Guinevere looked up and down the area. "At least we have a choke point."

"We may still not be able to hold them." The big orc nodded in agreement but his face was still grim. He looked at Ethan. "How much can you two help with magic?"

An embarrassed expression crossed Michalus's face and he glanced at Ethan before looking back at them. "It will take me a bit to regain enough mana to be helpful."

Drorm growled and looked at Ethan. "Tell me you have mana."

Ethan brought up his HUD.

Mana: 19

Grimacing Ethan gave the big orc a sheepish look. "Not much. Depending on how long it takes them to get here, I may have more."

Guinevere blew out a breath. "So what you're saying is: you may or may not be any help."

Before Ethan could answer, Nia emerged from the mist, leading the horses. She looked right at Ethan as soon as she saw him. "They will be here in minutes."

"Take the horses to the cave," Ethan told her. "There should be just enough room for them."

It was true. The shallow cave would have just enough room for the horses, but no room for them unless he used some of his *Mana* to make it bigger. But if he did that, then he would have no magic to help with the defense.

Ethan took a deep breath. If it came to it, he'd use his *Stamina* to power his magic - even if that meant he might take permanent stat damage. After all, as he'd concluded earlier, living with stat damage was better than dying without stat damage.

Pressing himself against the cliff wall, Ethan let Nia lead the horses past him. She no sooner went past than three rabbits bounded down the trail. Demon rabbits. That meant Par'karr had regained enough *Mana* to re-summon them. That was something at least.

A few seconds later, the kobold appeared leading the remaining horses. Par'karr's eyes were wide and he gestured behind himself. "Trolls down! Trolls see Par'karr and horses! Trolls coming!"

Cursing, Ethan gestured back towards the cave. "Get the horses in with the others."

Ethan checked his HUD again.

Mana: 21

Seeing his *Mana*, he cursed again. He barely had any and he doubted it would be enough to defeat a dozen trolls.

"Get behind us!" Guinevere yelled as Par'karr hurried past them. "Drorm and I will try to hold them back!"

Turning, he saw the warrior woman and the big orc with their weapons out, their expressions serious.

"Can we hold them?" he asked them.

Drorm and Guinevere exchanged looks but it was the warrior woman who replied. "Maybe. This is a narrow choke point, so their numbers advantage is minimized. At most, only two can attack at a time. But with their regenerative ability... I don't know."

The big orc nodded. "If we inflict enough damage, maybe they will retreat."

Grunts and howls sounded from somewhere in the mist and Ethan realized the trolls had found where they had gone. Given their feral nature, he guessed they had probably smelled them.

Ethan cursed and turned to retreat behind Drorm and Guinevere when he suddenly paused and spun back around. A plan formulated in his head as he looked down the path.

"Ethan!" Drorm yelled. "Get behind us!"

"Hold on," Ethan said with a grin. "I have an idea."

Channeling Earth magic, Ethan sloped the outer half of the stone road down at a steep angle, making it impossible to traverse. With the slick mist coating it, if the trolls even tried, they'd slip into the water and be carried away by the current.

Mana: 14

Next, Ethan slanted the nearest ten-foot section of the road completely, making it effectively impassable. This meant, if the trolls wanted to reach them, they'd need to leap the five feet separating them. Hopefully, it would make them easy targets for the fighters.

Mana: 9

Gesturing Drorm and Guinevere to back up, Ethan backpedaled and then formed the road in front of him into a wall of spikes. He grinned. They could try to jump across, but they'd end up impaling themselves on spikes. That would make them very easy targets. Even he could handle an impaled troll. Maybe.

Mana: 3

Looking at his *Mana*, he nodded. It was the best he could do for now. He just hoped it would help.

As he pivoted to retreat behind Drorm and Guinevere, the first of the trolls appeared out of the mist. It resembled the trolls he'd fought before, on the way to the library of Daemonium, though he thought their fur might be darker.

The creature came bounding out of the mist on all fours, like a gorilla. As it reached the section Ethan had slanted down, it lost its footing and went sliding into the water with a howl. The one following it was moving too fast to stop and suffered the same fate. Both trolls were swept away by the current and disappeared into the mist.

Ethan checked his HUD but there were no damage messages or kill messages. He frowned. He hadn't killed them - hadn't even hurt them - but they were out of the fight for the moment.

A large hand gripped Ethan's shoulder and he jumped until he realized it was Drorm. The orc nodded in approval. "That was good thinking but you should get behind us now before they figure out a way around."

As if to emphasize his point, two more trolls materialized out of the mist but these did not fall into the water. Instead, they bellowed at Ethan and his friends and beat on their chests.

Slowly backpedaling, Ethan watched as the two trolls stopped posturing and began to look at the slanted area, the gap and then the spiked wall on the opposite side.

Ethan frowned as he could almost see the gears turning in the trolls' heads. They were trying to figure out a way to get across. He cursed. Apparently, they weren't as stupid as he thought.

Even as he thought it, the troll closest to the cliff wall looked up and down the wall. It then tried to use its massive claws to climb the wall but hundreds or even thousands of years of rushing water had created a very smooth cliff face and the creature found no purchase.

Above the sound of the roaring water, Ethan could hear the creatures growling to each other and watched their eyes move from their side of the path to his side. He nodded. They were contemplating jumping across. At least, that's what he guessed they were doing.

Drorm pulled him back and this time Ethan let him. As he went past Guinevere, the woman gave him a nod of approval. "Not bad. We might actually have a chance."

Ethan returned her nod and hoped she was right. Once behind the pair of warriors, Ethan spotted Michalus and handed him the crystal. "It's all yours. Do what you can if one of them makes it across."

Michalus frowned, looking around. "I don't know how effective fire will be in this mist."

"Maybe," Ethan said, biting his lip. "But I wonder if they can regenerate if they're dead."

The wizard furrowed his brow. "What do you mean? You need fire to kill them."

"Maybe," Ethan said, thinking of basic anatomy. "What can they regenerate from a brain wound? If you kill the brain, will the body still regenerate?"

Michalus looked thoughtful. "An interesting hypothesis."

"Only one way to find out," he replied. He pointed to the base of his skull. "Try to hit them here with a stone spike. If I remember my anatomy lessons right, that's the brainstem and the part that controls autonomic functions like breathing, your heartbeat... and maybe regeneration."

"Fascinating," Michalus said. "You'll have to tell me about the brainstem later."

Ethan was about to say "sure" when a howl sounded and one of the trolls leaped across the ten-foot distance, only to impale itself on Ethan's spiked wall.

"Quick!" Ethan said, gesturing at Michalus. "Create a spike and send it into the brainstem! Uh... base of the skull."

Michalus hesitated for a moment and then, held out the hand with the crystal. The Chymera crystal glowed blue and then a spike erupted from the wall and into the struggling troll's mouth and then out the back of its skull.

The creature twitched for a moment before its limbs went limp and dropped to its sides. The only thing holding up the troll was the spike through its head.

Drorm and Guinevere both turned to stare at the wizard. Guinevere whistled, just barely audible over the sound of the waterfall. "Nicely done."

"We may have just proved your hypothesis," Michalus said, flashing Ethan a smile. With a gesture, the spike retracted and the troll's body fell into the water and was swept away by the current.

Ethan nodded but then frowned as another troll took its place on the opposite side. The fight was far from over.

42

The battle with the trolls, if it could truly be called that, didn't last long. Two other trolls tried leaping across, meeting a similar fate as the first. The only difference was, their heads were lopped off by Drorm or Nia. It seemed that removing their heads also stopped the regeneration process.

After three of their number had been killed and two others had been carried away, the trolls stopped trying to jump across. There was a lot of hooting and howling, lasting almost a half hour before the trolls just suddenly vanished back the way they had come. One moment, they were beating their chests and howling, the next moment, they were gone.

By that point, both Ethan and Michalus had recovered a fair bit of *Mana* while the trolls had been posturing. They both stood ready to use their magic up until the point where the creatures disappeared.

For several minutes, no one said anything. Everyone

just stared at the opposite side of the path, waited and listened. But once the minutes continued to tick by and there was no more sign of the trolls, Par'karr spoke up.

"Trolls gone?" the kobold said. The kobold was back with the horses, speaking soothing words to them and scratching their heads.

Ethan looked from the path, back to Par'karr. "I'm not sure."

"Trolls do not give up easily," Drorm said and Guinevere nodded her agreement. "They can be relentless hunters - IF you manage to escape."

"You think they're coming back?" Ethan asked.

Guinevere shrugged. "No idea. They might wait us out. Sit out there and assume that at some point we'll come back out."

Ethan shivered, realizing he was soaked to the bone. Looking around, he could see that they all were. The mist from the freezing mountain water was nearly as cold as the water itself. They needed a fire or they would all probably get some sort of hypothermia.

"Keep an eye out to see if they come back," he told the two warriors. "I'm going to go back and make the cave larger and see if I can get a fire going."

Drorm and Guinevere nodded and turned around to continue to watch the gap. Ethan retrieved the crystal from Michalus and then retreated back to the cave.

There, he regenerated *Mana* to further hollow out the cave. He ended up making it twice the size, giving them enough room for the horses and all of their bedrolls - not to mention a fire.

He managed to taper the ceiling and then form a

hollow chimney of sorts that led back outside. Ethan wasn't an engineer, but he hoped it would prevent the smoke from filling the makeshift cave.

With barely any *Mana* to spare, he finished up the final touch by enclosing the cave so that only a man-sized door allowed entrance. He hoped this would keep most of the mist out and keep the heat in. Or so he hoped.

His own magic depleted, he turned the Chymera crystal over to Michalus and let him dry the wood and then start the fire. The wizard did so and within a half an hour, most of them were huddled around the fire, drying off and eating their evening meal.

They set triple watches that night. Drorm, Ethan and Nia and then Guinevere, Michalus and Par'karr. Each group took turns watching the path while the other group slept. They all knew it was going to be a long night.

THE NEXT MORNING, everyone was exhausted. The only good thing was that the trolls hadn't appeared at all. Unsure if the trolls were simply waiting for them back on the shoreline, Ethan summoned his air elemental and had it scout around.

Ethan just managed to see that the shoreline was clear of trolls when he saw the glowing forms of the fairies. It was easy to see them because they all swarmed towards the air elemental and moments later, his connection with the creature was severed.

Frowning, Ethan stood up. "I think they drained whatever mana was keeping the elemental together."

Michalus scratched his chin. "I should have realized that would happen. After all, the mana forms and maintains your bond with the elemental..."

Before the wizard could go on with a lengthier explanation, Ethan added the rest of the news. "But it looks like the trolls are gone."

"You're sure?" Guinevere asked.

Ethan shrugged. "I didn't get a really good look around before the elemental was uh... eaten, but the area where we entered the path seemed clear."

The group exchanged looks. None of them seemed particularly convinced.

"I will scout it out," Nia said, stepping forward. Ethan opened his mouth to object but snapped it closed as she glared at him definitely. "The rest of you are like cubs in a briar bush. I will sneak in and out without being heard or seen. Also, I will smell them if they are nearby."

The rest of the group looked around at each other. If anyone took any offense at being called "cubs," no one showed it. Additionally, his wife had a good point. She had a much better sense of smell than any of the other members of the group.

"Fine!" Ethan said. "But be careful!"

"I am always careful." The foxgirl nodded. Then, looking at the broken path, she gestured. "Can you fix the path until I am back."

"Oh, right," Ethan said and, with an effort of will and some *Earth* magic, he restored the path. Without another word, the foxgirl drew her scimitars and hurried down the stone path and disappeared into the mist.

The group waited nervously for ten minutes before

Nia re-emerged from the mist. He noticed her weapons were sheathed and took that as a good sign.

Nia stopped just in front of them and shrugged. "They are gone. I cannot tell which way they went, but they are gone."

"What do you mean you can't tell which way they went?" Drorm asked, eyes narrowed.

"They tore up the clearing last night," the foxgirl explained. "And there are fresh tracks going both back up and going west. I cannot say which is the freshest since the mist still obscures much of the scent."

"Guinevere, Drorm, Nia and I will go have a look," Ethan told them. "Michalus, you and Par'karr stay here with the horses."

Michalus and Par'karr both nodded and Ethan gestured to the others to go back down the trail.

Following the stone path back to the shoreline, Ethan immediately found himself swarmed by fairies the moment he stepped out of the mist. He growled as he saw his *Mana* level plummeting and in only a few minutes, his *Mana* was gone.

He cursed as the fairies darted away. "No more mana."

"We figured." Drorm chuckled.

"Ravenous little things," Guinevere observed.

"We weren't attacked," Ethan pointed out. Had they been, he would have been no help since the fairies completely obscured his sight while they were feeding off him.

Drorm and Guinevere had searched around while he was being fairy food. They both shrugged.

"Nia's right," Drorm said. "There are tracks all around this area but I cannot tell where they went."

"Same here," Guinevere confirmed. She looked thoughtful for a moment. "I do find it interesting that they took the time to stomp around. It's almost as if they were purposefully trying to obscure their trail."

"Why would they do that?" Ethan asked.

"Good question," the warrior woman said.

"They do not want us to know where they went," Nia stated. "My people do this. Create many sets of tracks to obscure our true destination."

"Great! Just great!" Ethan murmured. He looked west and then up the hill. "So we don't know if they're in front of us or in back of us."

The three others all shook their heads.

Ethan cursed. "We can't just stay here. I say we move on and hope they went west. We'll have to stay alert for an ambush."

"You really think the trolls are capable of setting an ambush?" Drorm asked incredulously. "How would they even know which way we were going?"

"Maybe they're not as dumb as we think they are," Ethan offered. It was a sobering thought and he hoped he was wrong.

"We should get going then," Nia said. "We are wasting light."

Ethan and the others agreed and after retrieving Par'karr, Michalus and the horses, they started up the steep zig-zag trail that would take them up the top of the waterfall.

The climb was tough, but the path was wide enough

to easily accommodate both riders and their horses. But after thirty minutes, they made it to the top of the waterfall. After that, the trail leveled out and continued to parallel the river.

The fairies were still following them, swooping in every minute or so to kiss away and *Mana* they regenerated.

"We are only a half day away from the bridge," Drorm told them all. "We will be out of this area by nightfall."

"And in giant country," Guinevere muttered under her breath. "That's like out of the pan and into the fire."

Despite knowing what was ahead, Ethan would be glad to be away from the fairies. He was anxious to have his *Mana* back and once again be useful. Nodding to Nia, he gave the signal to get them moving.

The group hadn't gone far - maybe only twenty minutes - when Nia suddenly called everyone to a stop just as they entered a small clearing. She seemed about to say something when forms burst from the foliage on all sides of them.

Ethan swore! Trolls! They'd walked right into the ambush and now they were completely surrounded by hooting, snarling trolls.

"Form up!" Guinevere yelled, trying to steady her horse and draw her weapon. "Before they can attack! Form up a defensive circle!"

He wasn't sure if the trolls understood her or if they just chose that particular moment to attack. As one, the creatures lumbered forward, murder in their eyes.

The trolls were almost on top of them when suddenly

fairies swooped down to surround his group, forming a protective circle.

The trolls, who had been charging forward, skidded to a halt. The trolls didn't look afraid, merely confused - possibly even curious - at the glowing little forms that flew intricate patterns between the trolls and his party.

"What are they doing?" Guinevere asked.

Ethan shrugged. "No idea."

Hungry, bored or both, one of the trolls reached out to grab the fairy in front of it. Ethan started to cry out a warning to the little creature when suddenly the world became white.

A bright flash blinded Ethan and then he heard a deafening clap of thunder. As he blinked away the after-image of a lightning bolt that had come from the fairy, he saw it had burned a gaping hole in the chest of the troll who had just reached for it.

The troll had enough life left to look down at its ruined chest before collapsing backwards. Around them, other lightning bolts erupted from fairies, killing or maiming trolls until, within only a few seconds, the remaining trolls turned tail and fled into the forest.

The fairies maintained their positions for a minute longer before darting over to Ethan, Michalus and Par'karr to kiss away the *Mana* they'd regenerated. Then, they resumed their normal positions in the air, as if nothing had occurred.

Drorm's mouth was open as he looked from troll corpse to troll corpse and then up to the fairies. "What just happened?!"

"I think they just protected us," Guinevere said with awe. "But why?"

Ethan was still in shock for a moment, the afterimages of the lightning bolts still burned into his retinas. He looked up at the fairies, then down at the trolls. A thought occurred to them and he chuckled. Everyone's head turned to him.

"What is funny?" Guinevere demanded. "Do you know why they saved us?"

Still chuckling, Ethan nodded. "I think so."

"And?!" Drorm growled when Ethan didn't immediately continue.

Ethan grinned. "And, I think they were protecting their food."

Drorm furrowed his brow. "Their food?"

Michalus scratched his chin. "You're saying we're their food?"

"Or rather, we produce their food - mana," Ethan said. "And I think they must know that if we're dead, they won't eat."

They all looked up at the fairies with new respect, and possibly a bit of fear.

"I'm willing to accept that," Guinevere said. "But let's get out of here, just in case."

No one disagreed. Keeping a wary eye on the fairies, the group spurred their mounts forward down the trail and away from the still-smoking troll bodies.

43

―――――

No other trolls bothered them the rest of the morning, though the fairies continued to follow them. The glowing creatures acted the same way the group had become accustomed to. The fairies gave no indication at all that earlier that day, they'd killed several trolls with lightning bolts.

Ethan, on the other hand, couldn't get it out of his mind. Judging by the furtive glances from the rest of his companions, they couldn't forget either. They may be small, but they packed quite a magical punch.

The group rode in silence until just after noon. At that point, the hilly terrain suddenly flattened out into a long, rocky plain with no trees. In fact, there was no vegetation at all, just a barren plain that reminded him of the desolate plain they'd crossed to get to the library of Daemonium.

As the group exited the cover of the trees, Ethan

noticed that the fairies did not follow them. He stopped his horse and turned around in his saddle.

He could just make out the glowing forms of the creatures a few feet inside the treeline. The fairies hovered and flitted around but did move past the last tree.

"The fairies aren't following," Ethan said loudly, getting everyone's attention. The others stopped as well and turned to see what he was talking about.

"I wonder why they don't follow us." Michalus surveyed the area. "Not that I'm complaining, mind you."

"Does it really matter?" Guinevere asked. "At least you'll have your mana back."

"Guinevere is right," Nia agreed. "Now you will have your mana back if we need to face any foes."

Ethan nodded and brought up his HUD as he continued to watch the darting forms of the fairies.

Mana: 1

He frowned. His *Mana* was not regenerating. He watched his HUD for several minutes, growing more and more confused, the longer he watched. His *Mana* was definitely NOT regenerating, despite there being no fairies to keep him drained.

"Uh," he said, after watching the score for several minutes. "My mana isn't regenerating. Par'karr, Michalus... do you feel your mana regenerating?"

Par'karr shrugged and then he scrunched up his face. He shook his head. "Par'karr not able to summon rabbit."

Michalus cocked his head one way and then the other

before shaking it. "I think you're right, my boy. I don't feel my mana returning."

"Any idea why our mana might not be regenerating?" Ethan asked aloud. He doubted anyone knew the answer, but it couldn't help to ask.

As expected, no one offered any suggestions.

"On the opposite side of the river, there is a similar section of desolation that stretches for over a hundred miles." The big orc gestured around to the barren area around them. "We do not know why, but the fairies will not cross it. Neither will the trolls. I have not heard the shamans complain about their mana not regenerating, but they may not share that with us."

"That's weird," Ethan said.

Drorm shrugged.

"Let's get going then," Ethan said. "I'll keep an eye on my mana. Par'karr, Michalus, you guys do the same."

The two of them made affirmative noises. Ethan gave the signal for Nia to continue along and the foxgirl urged her mount into motion.

Nia led them across the barren earth, keeping a sharp eye out and occasionally sniffing the area.

Ethan also kept a wary eye out but saw nothing. Literally nothing. There were no woodland creatures scurrying around. No plants swaying in the wind. Nothing. It was like everything in the area was... dead.

Worse, it had been nearly fifteen minutes without a single point of *Mana* regenerating. Something was wrong. He wondered briefly if the fairies had done something to him - permanently.

Looking around the desolate area around him, he

wondered if perhaps it was something about the environment that prevented his *Mana* regeneration. Either prospect was disturbing.

"Do you know what caused this desolation?" he called out to Drorm.

"No one does," Drorm answered without turning around, "but it has been here as long as my people have been coming to the dragon. Thousands of years."

"And it's been this desolate this entire time?" Ethan asked. He found that extremely strange. He knew areas on Earth that had been wiped out by forest fires or volcanoes that had eventually grown back in a few hundred years. Why hadn't this area?

"Yes," the orc replied.

"My father knew about this area," Guinevere called out from behind him. "He asked the same questions you're asking. If I remember correctly, he said something about a corrupted lay line or something like that."

"A ley line?" Michalus spoke up. "Are you sure?"

Ethan frowned. He had no idea what a ley line was, though the name did vaguely sound familiar. "What's a ley line?"

"They are invisible lines of mana that criss-cross the planet," the wizard explained. Then, seeing Ethan's look of confusion, Michalus continued. "They are like magical blood vessels in the planet. Instead of blood, they pump mana."

"Are they like longitude and latitude?" Ethan asked, unsure if the concept of longitude and latitude even existed on this world.

"Yes." Michalus nodded. "You could think of them like

that. But, even though they are invisible, they can be felt by some and measured with the proper equipment."

"Hmm," Ethan mumbled as he looked around. "So could a corrupt ley line be causing us issues regenerating mana?"

Michalus looked thoughtful and then shrugged. "I've never read anything like that, but it's certainly possible."

"If that's the case, then when we get away from this area, we might start regenerating mana," he said, half question and half statement.

"Possibly," the wizard responded noncommittally.

"Then let's get through this as soon as possible," Ethan said and signalled to Nia. "Let's get to the other side of this area as soon as possible."

Nodding, the foxgirl spurred them forward and picked up the pace, urging the horses into a trot. Ethan spurred his own horse forward, wanting to get out of this strange area.

After another fifteen minutes, they finally approached the line of trees on the far side. Not only did he see the treeline, he also spotted a large stone bridge that spanned the river. Oddly, it was almost perfectly parallel to the treeline.

"This is the bridge you spoke about?" Ethan asked as they stopped just shy of the treeline.

"Yes," Drorm confirmed. "My people used this bridge for thousands of years to make the journey to the dragon."

Nodding, Ethan checked his HUD.

Mana: 3

"Yes!" Ethan exclaimed, doing a little happy dance in his saddle.

"Ethan okay?" Par'karr asked, his scaly brows furrowed as he watched Ethan's strange movements.

"My mana's regenerating!" he grinned. "Given enough time, I'll be back to full capacity."

An idea occurred to him and he turned to the others with excitement. "Hey! If the fairies aren't a problem anymore, once my mana regens, I can portal back to the other side of the forest and get our stuff."

Drorm grunted and shook his head. "I wouldn't do that just yet."

"Oh?" Ethan asked with a raised eyebrow.

"There may be fairies on this side too," the orc explained.

"Are you serious?!" Ethan groaned. Ethan heard Par'karr and Michalus do the same.

"Yes," the orc confirmed. "They are not as common, but I would not risk it. Not until we reach the base of the mountain. There are no fairies on the mountain."

"At least there's that," Ethan said sourly. He looked at the mountains, looming much closer now. "You said we should be at the village at the bottom of the mountain by nightfall?"

Drorm nodded.

He was still tempted to portal back and grab his trident and Michalus's staff but decided against it. Just because the fairies they encountered so far didn't affect his Chymera crystal, didn't mean the next batch they encountered wouldn't do anything. Ethan just didn't feel it was worth the risk.

Ethan looked into the forest that loomed ahead. He saw no sign of fairies, but he hadn't seen the other fairies until they were further into the forest. He threw his hands up.

"Fine," he said. "Let's just get there and then I can portal back."

Nia got them moving again and it was only as Ethan crossed into the forest that he realized he didn't remember being scried the entire previous day, at least, not since they had entered the forest. He also hadn't felt anyone scry him today.

Was his lack of feeling the scrying due to being so low on *Mana*? Or was there some other reason?

He hadn't enjoyed it when he knew someone was spying on them. Now, Ethan was worried that they weren't spying on them. It was a strange situation but the way it suddenly stopped worried him.

They still had no idea who had been scrying them the entire time but he couldn't help but feel a sense of dread, the closer they got to the mountain. He cursed silently. He hoped he was wrong, but Ethan just felt like something was about to happen. Something bad.

44

Ethan's premonition proved to be true only an hour later as the horses suddenly became skittish at the same time Nia called the group to a halt.

"The horses have gotten wind of it too," Drorm growled, struggling to keep his own horse under control.

Trying to calm his mount as it whinnied nervously beneath him, Ethan looked ahead to his wife. "What is it?"

"There is a strong scent in the air," the foxgirl hissed, glancing around nervously and sniffing the air. "I have not smelled it before."

The entire party scanned the forest and the river bank around them, also struggling to control their horses.

"Trolls?!" Par'karr asked.

Drorm shook his head. "There are no trolls on this side of the desolated area. It will be a giant."

"Giants?!" the kobold squeaked. Ethan wasn't sure, but he thought Par'karr's scales actually seemed to pale.

Ethan cursed, redoubling his efforts to see through the trees. They'd faced ogres before and they were ten or twelve feet tall. How large would giants be?

Behind him, he heard Guinevere cursing too. "And I don't have my armor or sword!"

"How big are giants?" Ethan demanded, looking from Drorm to Guinevere.

Drorm opened his mouth to answer but at that moment, Ethan felt a tremor in the earth. Having watched all of the Jurassic dinosaur movies, he recognized it as an impact tremor. That meant, either a Tyrannosaurus Rex was coming, or - more likely - a giant the size of a T-Rex.

The same moment he felt the impact tremor, the horses went crazy. They reared back, tossing Ethan to the ground. Hitting his head on the ground hard enough to see stars, he barely had the presence of mind to roll to the side as Michalus's horse's hooves came down on top of him.

Pain exploded in Ethan's head as he rolled to the side. The horse's hooves came down an inch from his head and he was forced to roll up into a fetal position as the horse thundered over top of him.

Squinting through slitted eyes, Ethan saw that the rest of the party had been thrown from their horses. All of them, that is, except Par'karr. His horse was racing away with the little kobold still in his saddle, desperately trying to stop the horse.

Perhaps learning his lesson from the Cthulhu fight, where he had gotten carried away, Par'karr jumped from the saddle. The agile little kobold hit the ground and rolled in what appeared to Ethan to be a decent somersault.

Ethan pushed himself up, staggering a bit as his balance seemed off. At the same time, he felt another impact tremor. The vibration was followed by a loud, deep sound.

"Ohhhhhh," the thunderous voice groaned as a crack resonated through the forest. Ethan had seen enough monster movies to know exactly what that sound was - a tree being split or knocked over.

He cursed as he glanced from side to side, trying to find the source of the voice. Sharp jolts of pain exploded in his skull as he turned his head and he wondered if he had a concussion.

Everyone had their weapons drawn at this point, backing into a circle as each person continued to look for what Ethan imagined could only be a giant.

"Uhhhhhh," the deep voice intoned again and another tree cracked, then another. As a group, they turned to Ethan's right, away from the river as their eyes caught the movement of a tree being pushed down.

Ethan struggled to look through his slitted eyelids. He didn't dare open them further, lest the pain threaten to overwhelm him. Even through his narrowed vision, he caught a huge shape moving through the trees.

It was hard to make out the details, but as he watched, a tree directly in front of the shape toppled over with a crack. Ethan scrambled to pull his Chymera crystal from his pouch so he'd be ready to do whatever he needed.

"It is... gigantic!" Nia hissed.

"That's what she said," Ethan muttered under his

breath with a chuckle. He instantly regretted it as the motion made his head pound.

"What?" asked Nia, turning toward him. She noticed the look of pain on his face and her face became concerned. "Are you unwell?"

"I hit my head when I fell," he replied, wincing as the act of even talking caused him pain. He cursed, then cursed again when his first curse caused him even more pain.

"Are you okay to cast?" Michalus asked from beside him.

Ethan flinched as he twisted his head to look at the elven wizard. His first reaction was to say yes. Then he forced himself to be more practical, even with his pain-fogged brain.

Currently, he was staring through slitted eyes and the slightest movement of his head caused him sharp pain. In addition, his brain felt sluggish, as if he were recovering from a hangover. As much as he hated to admit it, Michalus was in much better shape to cast than he was.

With a sigh of regret that sent sparks of pain through the front of his head, he held out the Chymera stone. "You'd better take this."

Michalus gave Ethan a sympathetic look before nodding and taking the crystal from his outstretched hand.

Two more cracks split the air as trees toppled, causing Ethan to jerk his head in that direction. He gritted his teeth against the pain that shot through him and tried to make out the shape now that it was more revealed.

While there were still a few scattered trees between

them and the giant, it was evident that the giant was humanoid. Ethan was able to make out thick, tree-trunk-size legs that disappeared under some sort of furry leggings. The fur leggings, which came down just below the giant's knees, were rough-looking and appeared to be made of different-color animal hides.

The ground trembled again as one of the huge legs lifted and then came down with a boom, pushing over another of the trees in front of it. The tree crashed to the ground with another bone-rattling thud, revealing more of the giant. Looking up, Ethan could now make out the torso of the giant through the few remaining trees between them.

Ethan cursed. The creature had to be a good twenty feet tall, perhaps more. Its chest was the size of a small house and its long, heavy arms were themselves the size of tree trunks. But even the creature's size couldn't detract from the most bizarre characteristic of the giant. It had two heads.

While Ethan had played games with multi-headed creatures - and even multi-headed giants - the reality of seeing was much different. He had to blink his eyes several times, just to make sure he wasn't seeing double. Sadly, he wasn't.

"The giants have two heads?!" Nia gasped as she caught sight of the creature's torso.

Drorm flickered a glance at the foxgirl. "Of course. How many heads do giants have where you are from?"

"None!" Nia shot back. She looked up at the giant. "There are no giants on my world."

"Lucky you," Guinevere snickered.

Whether their movement or their talking attracted the giant's attention, both heads pivoted their way. The giant's eyes focused on Ethan's group and then, slowly, both mouths split into broken grins.

"Foooooooooddddd," it bellowed with both heads, the sound coming through in a strange version of stereo.

Grimacing with the pain of speaking, Ethan growled to Drorm and Guinevere. "How do you fight these things?"

Drorm chuckled. "With enough orcs, we can sometimes take them down. Or several shamans working together can take them down."

"Mostly," Guinevere said, looking up at the giant. "We usually just ran, or rather rode away."

Ethan turned to her. "Are you serious?"

The warrior woman shrugged. "They are slow and stupid. There was really no point in killing them unless they stumbled into civilization. When that happened, we'd lead them back into the forest before losing them with horses."

"But we don't have horses," Ethan stated, feeling like Captain Obvious. "Can we outrun it on foot?"

"No," she replied. "Now that it has our scent, it will keep tracking us. If we could get far enough away, it would forget about us, but that won't happen without horses."

The creature finally took another stride forward and Ethan could see that a single step for the creature was nearly ten feet. He realized she was right. His group wouldn't outrun the giant on foot. With the horses gone, they had only one choice now. They would have to fight.

45

___

"Any strategies?" Ethan asked, flinching as pain blossomed in his head with every word. He felt like he was getting worse, instead of better.

He swore, realizing he would be healed already if he still had access to the Grail. Instead, the portal pouch that he'd enchanted to link to the goblet's resting place was still back inside the boulder.

"Fooooddddd!" bellowed the giant again, though Ethan thought it might be the other head who spoke this time.

"When they come out of the forest," Drorm growled, "we try to set up our siege weapons. Several of them can take one down."

Rolling his eyes, Ethan turned to the orc. "Siege weapons? Are you serious?"

Drorm shrugged. "You asked me how we dealt with them."

"Is that the only way?" Ethan asked, once again cringing at the pain that shot through his head.

"If there were shamans nearby, they would work together to kill them or drive them back with fire," the orc retorted.

"Can you try throwing some fireballs at the thing's head...er... heads," Ethan asked Michalus, "and maybe we can scare it off?"

"Of course," Michalus replied.

Without further comment, the wizard raised his hand holding the Chymera crystal and sent a large flaming ball at the giant's right head. The flaming ball streaked towards the creature, hitting it in the cheek and then exploded into a larger ball of fire.

The right head flinched and the right hand came up to rub its blackened cheek. At the same time, the left head looked from the right head down to Michalus. The left reddened in anger.

"Baaaddddd!" the left head snarled.

The giant lurched forward with a massive step, bringing it much closer to Ethan's group. Everyone took an involuntary step backwards.

The wizard cleared his throat nervously. "That was... uh... surprisingly less effective than I had hoped."

"The shamans bombard both heads with fire, spreading out so it cannot focus on only one!" the big orc yelled.

"In other words"—Ethan grimaced—"Michalus just painted a target on himself."

"What?!" the wizard exclaimed, going wide-eyed as he looked at the giant.

"It's not that intelligent!" Guinevere snapped. "It only knows that something hurt it and that something came from this direction. It doesn't understand things like magic or wizards."

"It will come for all of us," Nia said, "because we are all prey to it."

"Yes," Guinevere said with a shrug.

"Make giant go in water!" Par'karr squeaked. "Kobolds do this sometimes with big enemies! They get stuck in mud."

"What do you mean?" Ethan asked, regretting speaking the moment the words were out of his mouth.

The giant took another thunderous step forward, now only fifty feet away. They took another step backwards.

"Kobolds trick big enemies into mud," the little kobold explained, pointing at the nearby river. "Big enemies sink in mud. Then kobolds throw spears until dead."

Ethan frowned at the simple strategy and looked around at the others. They all had skeptical looks on their faces. Par'karr saw their expressions and his shoulders slumped. His hands dropped down to his large demon rabbits that were right against his legs.

Since they hadn't encountered any fairies yet on this side of the desolation, the little kobold had been able to re-summon his rabbits. Now the three creatures rubbed against him, staring up at the approaching giant.

"Actually," Guinevere said with a glance back at the river. "That's not a bad idea."

Par'karr perked up. "It not?!"

"They aren't very intelligent," the warrior woman continued, her eyes on the giant. "If we can somehow get it in the water and it sinks into the muddy bottom, we might be able to put enough distance between us before it works its way out."

"How do we do that?" demanded Drorm.

Grimacing at the pain in his head, Ethan gritted his teeth. He pointed to a nearby log. "We grab the log, drag it to the water, hang on and swim out as far as we can. If we're all in one place, it will make a more tempting target for it."

Another huge step and the giant was only twenty-five feet away. Both angry heads glared down at the group.

They were out of time and they all knew it. Drorm swore and rushed over to the fallen log. He looked at Guinevere. "Help me!"

The two of them grabbed the log and they all ran to the river. When they reached the edge of the water, Drorm and Guinevere tossed the log in, and they all jumped into the water.

The water was ice cold and the sudden cold, combined with the pain in his head, nearly made Ethan lose consciousness. He felt a hand grab him and haul him further up on the log.

He looked over to see Nia looking at him with a concerned look. Teeth chattering, she spoke to him. "You must stay awake!"

Nodding, Ethan draped his upper body across the log as the others began to frantically kick with their legs to put some distance between themselves and the shore.

Unfortunately, they hadn't counted on the current being so strong and they began to drift west with the river.

Ethan groaned. "Try to kick at an angle... so we don't get... carried down."

"The river is too strong!" Drorm yelled back. "The water is moving too swiftly!"

"Fooooodddd!" two heads bellowed in stereo as the giant reached the river.

Trying to think, Ethan thought about what Drorm had said. Water. The water is moving too swiftly, the orc had said. Water. Yes, that was it! His water elemental! It was an ability and he didn't even need the Chymera crystal to activate it!

With a thought, which ended up being more painful than he anticipated, Ethan summoned a water elemental. He looked at the watery dolphin which had appeared next to him. He pointed to the opposite side of the river. "Get us away from the giant."

The dolphin hesitated for only a moment, seeming to look from Ethan to the giant and then to the opposite shore. It submerged and the next thing he knew, the log lurched away from the giant.

"Elemental," Ethan hissed to Michalus through his gritted teeth.

"Ah... excellent thought," the wizard said and summoned his own elemental. "Push us to the opposite bank."

Michalus's elemental disappeared under the water and the log suddenly picked up speed. They were quickly moving out of the giant's arm reach, towards the opposite shore.

The giant watched the log moving away and howled in frustration. "Foooooddd!"

"We should just go to the opposite side of the river," Guinevere said. "I doubt the giant will come all the way across."

"What about the horses?" Nia asked. "Without them, we will spend more time in the forest."

The giant showed no sign of coming into the river, instead standing on the shore, looking out at them. It didn't appear their plan to lure it into the water was working.

"It doesn't appear to be cooperating with our plan, anyhow," Drorm pointed out. "It's just standing there."

"Maybe giant afraid of water," Par'karr ventured.

Ethan chuckled, instantly regretting it as fresh pain assaulted his head. He wasn't sure why he found the idea funny, but he did.

A grunt sounded behind them and Ethan turned just in time to see a huge tree flying towards them, apparently thrown by the giant.

"Incoming!" he yelled, nearly passing out with the sudden pain. He felt his grip slipping on the log and then was suddenly drenched as the tree impacted the water about twenty feet in front of them, causing a huge splash.

Coughing water out of his lungs, he looked back to see the giant was already hefting another log in its left hand. As he watched, the giant cocked its left arm and sent the impromptu missile soaring towards them.

The group was hit by another tremendous splash as the other tree splashed into the water fifteen feet to their left.

"It's throwing trees at us!" Guinevere spat.

"And it's getting closer!" Drorm observed.

"Kick faster!" Par'karr squealed.

"The giant is going for more trees!" Nia yelled.

Ethan was quiet. An idea came to him. Something he'd done before - sort of. He turned to Nia. "Help me get to the other side of the log."

The foxgirl furrowed her brows. "Why?"

"Please, just do it," he told her.

She paused for a moment later and then nodded. Taking hold of him, she held onto him as he went under the log and then re-emerged on the opposite side, now facing the giant.

Looking back, Ethan saw the giant lumber back into view carrying two more trees, or rather, portions of trees.

"Give me the crystal," he grimaced, looking at Michalus.

The wizard flashed him a concerned look. "I don't think..."

"Trust me," he told his friend. "I don't think you can do this."

"Do what?" Michalus asked.

The giant was hefting the tree in his right hand, preparing to throw it.

"Quickly!" Ethan insisted, thrusting his hand at the wizard. "No time!"

The giant cocked its arm and launched the tree into the air just as Michalus handed Ethan the Chymera crystal.

Ignoring the pain in his head, Ethan forced himself to focus and opened a portal just in front of the tree as it came hurtling directly at them.

He felt *Mana* leave him and watched as the tree disappeared as it sailed into the portal's entrance.

There was a groan from the giant as both heads looked down at the tree protruding from its chest, neither head seeming able to comprehend what had just happened.

Ethan smiled. He'd created a portal just in front of the tree that led directly to the giant's back. Like the time he'd used a similar trick with a fishman mage, the giant had essentially just killed itself.

```
You critically strike Mountain Giant
419 for damage.
   Mountain Giant dies.
   You     gain     150     experience.
Experience to next level 10,105.
```

The giant fell face first into the river, its body half on land and half in the water.

Feeling darkness closing around him, Ethan slipped the crystal back into Michalus's hand as everyone started to congratulate him. "I think... I'm going to..."

And then Ethan was slipping away into darkness: a cold, wet darkness that welcomed him down... down... down...

46

Ethan blinked his eyes open. The act of doing so allowed light to enter his eyes, burrow into his brain, causing him to flinch. Shutting his eyes quickly, he groaned. Pain. Pain meant he was alive but the piercing pain in his head almost made him wish he wasn't.

"He's awake," Nia said from above him and he realized the back of his head was lying on something. Moving his head very slowly, he realized it felt like a lap. Yes, his head was on a familiar lap, Nia's lap.

"Can you open your eyes?" another voice said from his left. It sounded like Michalus.

He groaned again but didn't open his eyes. "I can but it hurts. Probably a concussion."

"I don't have the runes to the tomb memorized," Michalus's voice said. "You will have to create a portal to the tomb so that we can get the grail."

Ethan nodded but immediately stopped as the smallest motion caused pain to explode in his head.

"Keep him awake," Guinevere's voice said. "Don't let him fall asleep again."

"Ethan!" Nia said again. "Open your eyes."

With maximum effort, Ethan opened his eyes to slits, barely able to see anything but knowing that if he opened them any more, the pain would return.

His wife's big eyes were staring down at him. "Can you create a portal to the healing cup?"

"Crystal," Ethan groaned, at least having the presence of mind to remember he should use his *Mana* and not his *Stamina.*

"Here you go, my boy," Michalus said and Ethan felt a hard object placed in his opened hand and then his fingers were closed over it.

He started to nod again but stopped himself just in time. Instead, he tried to recall the runes in the tomb. It was hard. His mind was foggy and it was hard to think.

Finally, the images came to him and he tried to fix them in his mind. It was difficult, because his addled mind kept losing focus. He cursed and concentrated on the runes.

After several attempts to keep the images in focus, he felt his mind lock onto them and then he willed a portal to open but something didn't quite feel right. Instead of a portal opening up to Arthur's tomb, he felt his stomach lurch and everything around him dissolved.

The next thing he could see was the prismatic colors of the rainbow bridge, the Bifrost. He cursed as he realized he'd somehow entered the Bifrost on his own instead of opening a portal.

"Ethan!" came Nia's voice from above him.

Opening his eyes more, Ethan realized Nia was with him! Without intending to, he'd brought both of them into the Bifrost. He tried to smile up at her. "The things... I have to do... to get you alone."

He saw her smile down at him and then suddenly they were in a dimly lit chamber, with a shaft of sunlight streaming down from the ceiling. The light illuminated a familiar tomb. King Arthur's tomb. And atop the tomb, was the object Ethan needed most right now - the Holy Grail.

"I got us here," he muttered weakly, eyes fluttering. He felt weak and drained suddenly and all he wanted to do was go back to sleep.

"Do not close your eyes!" Nia hissed, gently moving his head off her leg.

Right. Don't close his eyes. Sleeping with a concussion was bad. Ethan felt his head laid against a cold stone floor. He saw movement through his slitted eyes and after a moment, felt cold metal pressed against his mouth.

"Drink, Ethan!" Nia urged him. "You must drink!"

Ethan opened his lips and felt cool liquid poured into his mouth until he started to cough. The first cough caused him excruciating pain, but then he felt warm all over and the pain melted away. At the same time, his mind cleared and he was suddenly able to think clearly again.

He smiled up at Nia and then pushed himself into a sitting position. He moved his neck around, testing how his head reacted. There was no pain. He smiled at Nia. "Thanks! I needed that!"

Letting the goblet fall to the ground, Nia rushed to embrace him. The foxgirl squeezed him tight and planted kisses on his neck. "I was very worried. Guinevere said you had a bad head injury, that you had to be healed soon. I was worried we were too late."

Hugging his wife back, he stroked her hair. "It's okay. I'm fine."

Nia continued to hug him but Ethan's mind was on something else. His wife felt him tense beneath her and stopped kissing his neck. She pushed herself away and looked at him with a concerned look.

"What is it?" she asked.

Ethan cursed and brought his fingers to his forehead, slowly massaging it.

"Your head is still hurting?" the foxgirl asked, concern evident in her voice and on her face.

He let out a breath as he continued to massage his forehead with his fingers. "I screwed up."

The foxgirl furrowed her brow. "What do you mean?"

"Instead of opening a portal to the Grail," he explained, "I somehow brought us here. It's like the first time I discovered portal magic. I literally just... teleported from one spot to another."

Nia cocked her head, confusion etched into her features. "Why is this bad? You needed the cup. We have gotten you the cup and you are better. This is good."

Sighing, Ethan bit his lip. "If I had just opened a portal, someone could have reached through and grabbed the Grail and used it on me. Then I could have opened a portal back here and we could have returned it."

"But we can return it," she said with a slight wince. "The noise it makes is starting to hurt my ears, so I will do it now."

Before he could say anything else or stop his wife, she reached over and snatched up the Grail. Bounding to her feet, she hurried over to the tomb and gingerly replaced the Holy Grail atop the tomb.

Spinning around to face him, she gave him a grin. "See, it is replaced!"

He nodded and stood up, giving her a halfhearted smile.

She furrowed her brow. "Something is still wrong?"

"Nia," he told her, gesturing around the chamber. "Instead of opening a portal to this place, I brought the two of us here. I keyed in on the runes I placed on the tomb the first time we were here and used that to come here."

The foxgirl was clearly not understanding his point. He didn't blame her. She wasn't a wizard and, despite being one himself, he didn't fully understand the whole teleportation/portal thing. He tried to make it crystal clear to her.

"Since I was out of it, I didn't make any runes before I left," he told her. "That means I have no anchor point to portal back to."

Realization dawned on the foxgirl's pretty face. Her eyes widened and her mouth opened into an "O" shape. "We cannot get back to the others?"

Ethan nodded. "I don't have anything to portal to."

"Nothing?!" Nia asked. "Can you not portal to the clearing we were in?"

"It has to be very specific," Ethan explained. "Something unique. If not, we could end up in a similar-looking place - who knows where..."

"You do not remember anything unique?" she asked, shoulders slumped.

Ethan bit his lip as he thought back. "I might be able to get us back to the bridge. It was fairly unique and I think I still have a decent memory of it."

"That is still far from our companions," she pointed out.

"I know." He shrugged. "If I had been more alert, maybe I would have been able to memorize the surroundings - or create some runes to portal back to. Unfortunately, there was nothing unique enough that stood out in my..."

Ethan stopped mid-sentence. He'd been wracking his brain to think of anything that was unique about the area they had been in - some small detail he'd noticed. He hadn't thought of anything until he remembered the battle.

He flashed Nia a grin.

She raised an eyebrow. "You have thought of something?"

"I have." He grinned even wider. He had thought of something he could use as an anchor point. Something he remembered that was unique enough that he could focus on and open a portal to.

"What is it?" she asked, curiosity getting the best of her.

"How many places on this planet do you think have a freaking huge giant with a tree hanging out of its chest?" He grinned.

"You can open a portal to the giant?"

"I think I can," he answered and held out his hand. In his mind's eye, he conjured an image of the giant in his mind's eye. Then, he pictured it with the tree trunk stuck through its chest. Locking the image in his mind, he willed the portal open.

A door-sized opening appeared in the air in front of him. Through the portal, he spotted the giant he'd killed lying face down in the water.

"I did it!" Ethan exclaimed with a huge grin. "There's the giant!"

His wife turned his head, causing him to lose focus on the portal. With a hiss, the portal shrank quickly and then disappeared.

Ethan looked down at the foxgirl with a questioning look. "I had the portal open. Why did you..."

He caught the mischievous look in his wife's eye and realized what she had in mind. He smiled down at her. It had been a while since they'd had some alone time. "Good point. They can wait a bit longer. And it would be nice to get out of these wet clothes..."

47

———

After a little alone time, Ethan opened a portal back to the fallen giant and the two of them stepped through. Remembering how he'd brought her through the Bifrost with him, Ethan decided to do a little experiment. He held her hand as he stepped through.

Ethan blinked as he entered the portal. Once more he found himself in the swirling rainbow tunnel. He could still feel Nia's hand in his and looking back, he saw her just behind him.

Before he could say anything, they were stepping onto the uneven shore near the river, right next to the dead giant.

"You did it," the foxgirl said with a smile. "We are back."

"Yeah," Ethan agreed, looking around. He didn't see any signs of their companions. "But where is everyone?"

"I do not know," Nia replied.

Ethan cupped his hands to his mouth to call out to

their friends, but his wife's slim hand pulled them down. Brow wrinkling, he looked down at her.

"Do not call out," she told him. The foxgirl glanced over at the dead giant nearby. "If there are other giants, we do not wish to alert them."

His wife began sniffing the air, turning her head one way and then another.

"Do you smell more giants?" he asked warily. Ethan had gotten lucky with the last giant. Had it not thrown the trees, he doubted they could have killed it. He certainly couldn't count on using the same trick twice.

After a few minutes of walking around the beach and sniffing the air, Nia returned to him. "I do not smell any other giants, but the wind has shifted. It blows west now. It may be us who are downwind now."

"What about the others?" Ethan asked. "Do you smell them?"

"Not them," she said. "But I smell smoke. Someone has made a fire not far from here."

Ethan looked around and sniffed the air. Now that she mentioned it, he was able to discern the smell of burning wood.

He'd used magic to dry their clothes after their love-making but knew the others would have had no such ability. Since he still had the only Chymera crystal, Michalus couldn't have been able to dry their clothes. They would have had to resort to the old-fashioned way. At least, he hoped it was them and not some giant roasting his friends over an open flame.

"Let's go find them," he told her.

The two of them quickly found them only a few dozen

yards up the embankment, inside a small copse of trees. They huddled around a small fire, naked, except for their short clothes.

Drorm turned his head at their approach. "They return."

"Ethan alive!" yelled Par'karr, jumping to his feet. Almost immediately, the others shushed him.

"No yelling," hissed Guinevere. "There could be more giants around."

Looking chagrined, Par'karr nevertheless raised a hand and waved enthusiastically at Ethan and Nia. When he spoke again, his voice was much lower. "Par'karr glad Ethan back."

That was when Ethan noticed that Guinevere, Drorm and Michalus all had demon rabbits on their laps. He raised an eyebrow and pointed at the rabbits. "What's with the rabbits?"

"They're keeping us from freezing after that lovely little swim in the ice-cold river," Guinevere growled.

"Rabbit warm!" the kobold said with a big grin.

Drorm looked Ethan and Nia up and down. "You are dry. Did you use magic to dry yourselves?"

Ethan nodded.

"How about you use some of that on our clothes," Guinevere said.

"Yes, my boy," Michalus said. "That would certainly help with this chill."

Realizing how cold and miserable his friends were, Ethan quickly obliged and used a combination of *Fire* and *Water* magic to dry the clothes. As soon as he did, Guinevere grabbed her clothes and began putting them on.

Ethan didn't realize he was staring at the warrior woman's fit body until he heard his wife make a sound next to him.

Expecting to be chastised by Nia, he found her shaking her head at him. "You males are all the same."

Then the foxgirl looked at the former queen with an appraising eye, cocking her head one way and then the other. "But she is acceptable as a second wife. She is a good warrior."

Ethan blushed at her words. Then he saw Guinevere giving them both a hard stare and he felt his face grow even hotter when he realized the warrior woman had heard his wife's comment.

Clearing his throat, trying to ignore the heat in his face, he looked down at his wife. "Maybe we should go look for the horses while they get warm."

It took them until nightfall before they found all the horses. Ethan and Nia had found the first one, Drorm's horse, and returned to the others. Then they had split up and went after the other horses until, one by one they'd found them.

Now, it was dark and they were all tired from their encounter with the giant and running after the horses. With the horses returned, along with their food and supplies, the group decided to camp for the evening.

The copse where they'd used to build their fire worked as a campsite too, providing some cover against giants - they hoped. They kept the fire going all night and Ethan insisted they set double watches. Luckily, no other giants disturbed them.

The next morning, the group immediately resumed their trek towards the mountain. Only two hours into their journey, Ethan noticed that the ground had steadily been getting steeper. Not only that, but it was getting colder. Much colder.

Because of the trees, Ethan hadn't been able to see exactly where they were in relation to the mountain. When the trees finally broke, he realized they had reached the foot of the mountain. He called the group to a stop.

Ethan looked up at the snowcapped peaks towering high above them. He whistled. "That's a big mountain."

"We go up mountain?" Par'karr asked dubiously. "Snow on mountain!"

"Almost to the top," Drorm told them. Shielding his eyes with his hand, the big orc looked lower on the mountain and then grunted. He pointed to a cluster of tiny buildings at least ten miles away, higher up the mountain. "The village. We can rest there and then start up the mountain tomorrow."

"You're sure we'll be welcome there?" Guinevere asked. "Even though we are not shamans?"

"You are on a mission from the shamans. They will let you pass." Drorm shrugged.

"How will they know we are on a mission?" Michalus asked, intrigued. "Have the shamans sent some sort of magical message?"

Snorting, Drorm patted his saddlebag. "No, I have the orders here."

"Good thing we didn't lose the horses," Guinevere said softly, rolling her eyes.

"Yes," Drorm agreed. "Good thing."

"Are the villagers that vicious?" Ethan asked.

"They are not villagers," the orc replied. "They are all soldiers. And yes, they are vicious. It is their job to prevent the dragon from being bothered by outsiders."

"Good thing you have orders then," Guinevere said, her voice dripping with sarcasm. "Do they say to kill us after we talk to the dragon?"

"I do not know. They are sealed." Drorm scowled at the warrior woman. After a moment, he sighed. "But that is a possibility."

"Great," Ethan said, rolling his eyes. "So you're going to hand them the orders that tell them to kill us."

Drorm shrugged. "They will wait for you in the village but you can portal away. There will be no reason to return to the village."

"Let's hope you're right," Ethan said. He turned around and looked back the way they'd come. He looked over the forest and the large river that cut through it. "Any more fairies?"

"No," Drorm told them. "They do not leave the forest."

"Good," Ethan replied. "Let's get to the village and then we can portal back to the boulder and get our stuff."

"About time," Guinevere said. "I feel naked without my armor."

The warrior woman's words brought back the memory of her in nothing but her short clothes and Ethan suddenly found everyone looking at him. He blushed. "What?"

"I asked," Drorm repeated, "shall we continue on?"

Ethan cleared his throat and nodded. He purposefully didn't look at Guinevere. "Yes. The sooner we get there, the better."

"There will be accommodations there, correct?" Michalus asked. "Surely, we are not expected to camp out."

Drorm chuckled. "Yes. There are extra cabins for the visiting shamans. They will let us use them."

"Thank the gods," Michalus responded with a smile.

"I wouldn't say no to an actual bed," Guinevere admitted.

"Come," Drorm said, moving his horse to the front of the pack. He looked up at the twin suns. "If we hurry, we may get there just in time for dinner."

48

As Drorm predicted, the group arrived in Rag'Orr as the suns were getting low on the horizon. The trees having thinned out, the soldiers of the village had a clear view of them as Ethan's group approached.

They'd had to stop and put on their warmer gear as they continued to climb in altitude and given their bundled appearance, Ethan guessed the soldiers at the village might not realize they weren't orcs until they got closer.

When they finally did draw near, a group of twenty, well-armed orcs met them several hundred yards from the village. A grizzled-looking female orc, with a scar across the left side of her face, stepped out and raised a hand. The orc's hair was a salt and pepper mix, but braided and spilled out of her hooded parka-looking jacket.

All of the orcs were dressed in warm-looking furs, but Ethan noticed all carried long spears in addition to swords or axes hanging on weapon belts girded around their cold-weather apparel. They appeared ready for a fight.

The lead orc and the others were just out of Ethan's range to identify them in his HUD, so he had no idea what level they were.

"Who are you and why have you come?" the woman barked.

"Hail, Brodtha. I am Drorm Thunderflame," Drorm answered. "The shamans have sent me on a mission."

The female orc, who Drorm had identified as Brodtha, stared hard at Drorm before finally nodding. Her frown didn't fade. "You, I know.

"I do not know the others." Brodtha then looked over Ethan's companions, her face unreadable. Her voice became hard. "They aren't orcs and they are not shamans. Why have you brought them?"

Not answering her, Drorm reached into his saddlebag. Ethan saw the orcs tense but the female orc, most likely their commander, held her hand up and the other orcs relaxed slightly.

Acting as if he hadn't noticed, Drorm withdrew a scroll case and held it out. "Orders."

Brodtha stared at the offered scroll case for a moment before walking forward and taking it from Drorm. She returned to stand in front of her orcs before opening it and pulling out a scroll. She read through it quickly, looking up at Drorm and the others several times. Finally, she rolled the scroll back up, slid it back into the scroll tube and then stashed it away inside her own jacket.

The female orc looked up, gaze roaming across them.

Her face remained as stony as before. "You are to speak to the dragon. This is unheard of."

"You saw the seal," Drorm retorted.

"I saw the seal," Brodtha responded, still eyeing the group. "You know what the orders say."

Drorm nodded. "I was told what the orders are."

"By Mommy, no doubt," the female orc sneered. Some of the orcs behind her snickered, causing Drorm's face to go red and his hand to drop down to his axe.

The female looked at Drorm with amusement before snorting. "Still more balls than brains."

"Shall I return to the shamans," Drorm hissed through clenched teeth, "and tell them you have abandoned your duty and forsaken your honor then?"

This time it was Brodtha's face which turned red, though her hands never reached down to the weapons at her hips. She snorted. "I will follow orders. We'll see if you follow them too, when the time comes."

Without another word, the grizzled female orc spun and stalked back to the village. As she passed her orcs, she shouted "fall in" and the others orcs spun in place and then marched after her.

"Warm reception," Guinevere said, her voice dripping with sarcasm.

"Not the most inviting welcome I have ever received," Michalus agreed.

"Do we go into the village now?" Ethan asked, not quite certain what had just happened. He wasn't sure what he'd expected, but that hadn't been it.

Drorm watched the other orcs retreat back to the

village and then turned in his saddle. "Brodtha's a hard one but she will follow her orders."

Guinevere lowered her voice. "And do those orders involve killing us?"

The orc's face flushed with anger for a moment but then he hung his head and nodded. "Most likely. They will help us until you return from the mountain. Either on the way back or once we reach the village, they will carry out their orders."

"They kill Par'karr?" the kobold squeaked. "Par'karr nice!"

"Once you finish talking to the dragon," Drorm said, looking around the area to make sure no other orcs were in earshot, "you can open a portal and escape. I can come back empty handed and let them know you escaped with magic."

"Which allows you to save face," Guinevere sneered.

"You may go back to your human cities or your human village," Drorm retorted. "This is my home. I must live here once you have gone."

"That's fine," Ethan said in what he hoped was a soothing voice. "We knew this was coming."

"And you're helping them, why?" Guinevere demanded, rehashing her old argument.

"If there's any way I can communicate with the dragon and find out why it's attacking villages and cities," Ethan responded. "Then I have to do it. Hopefully, that means we'll still get to see Excalibur. Even if it doesn't, you know as well as I do, it's the right thing to do."

"Even if the orcs will betray us?" Nia questioned.

Ethan nodded, looking at his wife. "There are other

people being affected by the dragon. People who have nothing to do with the orcs. If I turn around and leave now, without knowing if I could somehow have helped to bring an end to the dragon's rampage, any future deaths would be on me."

Nia ground her teeth but nodded curtly. "You are alpha. It is your decision."

Par'karr shivered in his saddle. "We go to cabins now? Par'karr cold."

Drorm nodded. "It looks like they won't be helping us. But they won't hinder us either."

"So no hot meal?" Michalus asked.

"I wouldn't count on it," Drorm answered with a look towards the village.

"Then we will cook our own," Nia said, slipping off her horse and throwing her reins to Ethan. She pulled her bow and quiver from her horse and started into the woods without a glance back.

Guinevere snorted, watching the foxgirl disappear into the trees to the side of the wide trail. She turned to Ethan. "I know that look. I gave it to Arthur many times. Someone's in trouble tonight."

Ethan watched his wife disappear into the trees and nodded absently. He remembered her earlier expression and realized the warrior woman was probably right. Later, he and Nia would have a "conversation."

"Let us see what cabins are available," Drorm said, bringing Ethan's thoughts back to the issue at hand.

Not waiting for an answer, Drorm spurred his horse forward into the village and Ethan and the others fell in behind him.

As they entered the village proper, Drorm stopped at guards who stood watching the trail. "One of our number went hunting. Send her to our cabins when she returns."

"Yes, sir," the orcs responded. They were close enough that Ethan could examine them in his HUD.

Gach Clanedge
   Orc
   Warrior
   Level 6
   Bavtuld Nosebrass
   Orc
   Warrior
   Level 6

Skill increase: Analyzed +1%.

"Which cabins are available?" Drorm asked them.

Gach turned and pointed to three cabins on the far side of the village. "Sir, those three are reserved for visitors. Wood for a fire is stacked on the side."

"Thank you, soldier," Drorm replied and spurred his horse onward. The soldiers didn't watch him go, but instead stared at each of his companions as they passed by.

The group stopped in front of the three cabins. Drorm dismounted and motioned the others to do the same. "The cabins sleep four. Normally, the shamans take one and their escorts take the other two."

The big orc pointed to the one furthest to their right. "Ethan, you and Nia take that one. Michalus, Par'karr and

I will take the next one and Guinevere, you can have the final cabin."

Guinevere rolled her eyes. "I'm a knight. I've slept in tents and camps with men before. There's no reason for three of you to crowd one cabin, while I get one to myself."

Drorm opened his mouth to say something but Guinevere continued but the warrior woman motioned to Par'karr. "Come on, Par'karr, you and the rabbits can stay with me."

"Okay." Par'karr grinned and hurried over to Guinevere with his rabbits hopping after him. "Rabbits cold though. Need fire."

"Of course," Guinevere said as she tied off their horses. With the horses secure, she pushed the door to the cabin open, letting him inside.

Ethan, Drorm and Michalus watched the door close and then looked around at each other as they tied off their own horses.

"Well then, Drorm," Michalus said cheerfully. "It looks like you and I will be roommates. Ethan, would you mind if I use the crystal to light the fire, first?"

He handed the wizard his crystal and then watched Michalus and Drorm disappear into their cabin. That left Ethan by himself out in the cold.

Sighing, he pulled his pack and Nia's pack from their horses and then let himself inside the cabin. He wasn't sure why Guinevere had insisted on having a cabin-mate or why she'd chosen Par'karr. Then again, in a village full of soldiers, most of which had probably not seen a female - other than their commander - for some time, perhaps it was best to have a roommate after all.

He went about making a fire, after getting his Chymera crystal back from Michalus and once the fire was roaring in the fireplace, sat on the bed. He waited with growing dread for Nia to return so they could have a "talk." A talk he knew he probably wasn't going to enjoy.

49

———

An hour later, Nia burst into the cabin and slapped a large piece of meat on the small table near the door, startling Ethan as he warmed his hands near the fireplace. He'd used the time she was gone to haul in wood from the pile outside and build a nice fire. He looked at the scowl on her face. Apparently, the nice, warm fire wasn't going to be enough to dissuade her from having a conversation with him.

"You are risking your life for those who would betray you!" the foxgirl said without preamble. She tossed her bow and her quiver onto the floor and then stood there facing him with her hands on her hips.

Ethan motioned her to lower her voice. He spoke in what he hoped was a quiet, soothing voice. "Shh! We don't know who is listening."

Nia fumed at him, gritting her teeth, before speaking again, this time more softly. "Why are you risking your life - and ours - for those who will betray us?"

Sighing, Ethan stood up from the fire and faced his wife. He'd explained this all before but he realized he mustn't have done a good job.

"It's not just the orcs who are affected by the dragon," he answered. "It's everyone in the region."

"And so you would do the bidding of honorless curs who intend to betray us?" the foxgirl demanded.

Ethan tilted his head, unused to the venom in his wife's voice. It felt like there was something more than just her worry for his safety going on. He took a deep breath. "Nia, is there something else going on?"

"Other than watching my mate, my alpha, walking into a trap?" Nia retorted.

"Yes, but we know it's a trap," Ethan replied with a smile. "So it's not really a trap."

"It is still a trap!" his wife growled. "These orcs plan to kill you... kill all of us."

"No," he responded. "THEY think it's a trap. We can bypass this entire village with a portal."

"Yet you are bargaining with those without honor!" she retorted.

Once more, his wife had mentioned honor. Was that what this argument was about? If so, how come she hadn't brought it up before when they'd first learned of it. Ethan needed to know if that was the root of her anger.

"Is that what this is all about? Honor?" he asked.

"Of course it is!" Nia growled.

"Why didn't you say something before? Back when Guinevere first said something? Or when Drorm admitted it?" he asked.

Nia gritted her teeth. "Because I was being Tal'Cha! I

was supporting you in front of the others! You have not changed your mind, so now I am being Tal'Cha and giving you counsel!"

Giving counsel? Was that what she called this? And it sounded like she had disagreed the entire time but was staying silent because she was being a good wife. Ethan resisted the urge to shake his head in frustration.

Ethan tried to think of the best way to diffuse the situation. Luckily, from being a computer tech, he'd dealt with plenty of irate customers. It was time to put some of that experience into practice.

First, thank the customer for their "valuable" feedback, so they feel that their opinion is important. While he'd often just played lip-service to the customer's feedback, he was genuinely glad that Nia was giving him her opinion. And he was certainly glad she had supported him at the time.

"Nia," he said in the best soothing voice he could muster. "I appreciate you supporting me when we first found out about the orcs' plans. It means a lot to me that you supported me in front of the others."

He saw the foxgirl's stance relax slightly, though it was evident she was still upset. Ethan moved on to step two. Repeat their concern back to them, to make sure you understood it.

"It sounds like you are upset because I am continuing to deal with the orcs and that they appear to have no honor, is that correct?" he asked.

"Yes," Nia answered curtly. "You should have no dealings with those without honor."

Ethan nodded. The easy part was over. Now he had to

find common ground and come to an understanding with her. Given the level of anger she had about the orcs, he wasn't sure what that would be.

He certainly didn't want to give up on the chance to examine Excalibur. Although at this point, he didn't really believe that was going to be a possibility. If the orcs truly were planning to kill them after they spoke to the dragon, then they certainly weren't about to reveal the location of Excalibur to him.

Suppressing a bit of his own anger, he forced himself to deal with the issue at hand. "You are right."

"Of course I am right!" she retorted.

"Despite making an agreement with us," he continued, trying not to let himself grow angry, "it appears they plan on reneging on the deal, not showing us Excalibur and then kill us after we've completed the mission. Or showing us Excalibur and then killing us."

"Exactly!' Nia spat. "They are without honor. You should allow the dragon to continue rampaging the area!"

"But then innocent people will get hurt too," he protested. "Remember the villages?"

He saw a flicker of doubt pass over her features but then it disappeared. "If they do not wish to suffer the orcs' fate, they should move on. When the drought is in the land you have made home, you do not stay and starve. You move to a new area. They can do so too."

"It's not that easy for a lot of these people," Ethan told her. "You've seen them. They aren't warriors. Just like the farmers in Hawkshead, they'd never make a journey through the wilds. Especially not with children. Just look at all the attacks we fought off."

"They should train themselves so they can defend themselves and their families," she countered.

"Maybe." Ethan shrugged. He wondered what Nia would have thought of him and his life back on Earth. He certainly hadn't been capable of defending himself.

Thinking back to when he first arrived, he realized he'd barely been able to defend himself then. It had taken him some time before he'd learned how to really use his magic. What had she thought of him then?

Pushing the thoughts to the back of his mind, Ethan forced himself to focus on the matter at hand.

"Nia, I'm not going to try and talk to the dragon because of Excalibur," he explained to his wife. "I can't just leave those people to their fate..."

"Even if the orcs did something to the dragon?" Nia asked. "Perhaps the dragon is angry because they broke their word to it."

Ethan opened his mouth to respond but then closed it. He hadn't really considered that possibility. The way the shamans had talked, they were completely in the dark as to why the dragon started attacking villages and cities. What if they were lying? Or what if they were responsible somehow, by breaking some promise to the dragon?

"I hadn't thought about that," he admitted.

"What if you go to the dragon and it attacks you - attacks all of us," the foxgirl said in an exasperated tone, her voice breaking. "I cannot defend you against a dragon."

He cocked his head. Was that what this was really about? Was she angry because she couldn't defend him against the dragon? Was this all about his safety?

"Nia," he told her. "I don't expect you to defend me against a dragon!"

"I am Tal'Cha! It is my duty to protect my alpha!" Nia responded.

"Nia, it's a dragon... no one could defend me against it," Ethan told her. "But it's something I have to at least try."

"Even if it means your death?" Nia asked, an almost-pleading tone to her voice.

Ethan didn't really feel like he was the overly heroic type, but he couldn't just stand by and do nothing. He certainly didn't want to die, but he hadn't really considered that it would come to that.

After all, he could open portals and even teleport away. Plus, he had his *Mental* magic. He didn't even need to get close to the dragon. If anyone had a chance to try and talk with the dragon and live to tell the tale, it was him.

"Nia," he started. "I don't plan on any of us fighting the dragon. I'm going to try to get close enough to use my telepathy on it. If it even starts to get near me, I'm going to portal away."

"Us," Nia growled.

"What?"

"Us," Nia repeated, her voice hard. "I am coming with you."

He was about to argue with her, but realized it would be pointless. He also realized that if the roles were reversed, he wouldn't let her go without him.

"Us," he agreed with a nod. He raised an eyebrow. "Does this mean you are okay with me talking to the dragon?"

"Of course not! But you are stubborn as any other alpha." Nia rolled her eyes at him but then her face softened. "You must promise me that if the dragon comes after you, you will use your magic to go far away."

"Nia..." he started but she held up a hand.

"Promise me," she repeated.

Ethan nodded. It was an easy promise to make since that had been his intention all along. "I promise."

"Then it is settled," Nia said with a nod. She gestured at the meat she had brought. "Then we should cook this and eat."

"Sounds good," Ethan agreed with a smile. "How about you cook the food, while I portal back to the boulder and get our stuff."

Nia raised an eyebrow at him.

"We're away from the fairies," he explained. "And regardless of what happens, I don't plan to trek back through those woods. No point in not having all of our gear with us."

"That is a good idea," Nia said, grabbing the meat and pulling out her knife.

Smiling, Ethan took the Chymera crystal from his pouch and focused on the runes he'd carved in the boulder. He fixed them in his mind and then willed the portal to open. Nothing happened.

Actually, that wasn't true. He felt the *Mana* trying to obey his will but then, instead of focusing on the point where the portal would open, it seemed to dissipate before it could actually create the portal.

Brow furrowed, Ethan tried again. Once again, he felt the *Mana* moving to open the portal and this just... disappeared as it tried to open it. He quickly tried a third time, with the same results.

Skill increase: Scrying magic +1%.

Without warning, the sense of being watched suddenly blossomed in Ethan's mind. It had been days since he had felt it and the sudden feeling took him by surprise. Unconsciously, he looked around the small cabin and then swore.

There was something different this time. The feeling felt much stronger than the previous times. Not only was it stronger, it seemed more directed at him. He wasn't sure why he felt that way. It was as if this time, whoever was scrying was looking at him directly. He swore again.

"What is wrong?!" Nia asked, looking around the small cabin for any hints of danger.

Ethan looked at his wife, feeling a sinking feeling in the pit of his stomach. "I can't form a portal and someone is watching us again... or should I say, watching me."

50

_____

Nia's hands instantly went to her weapons as she too scanned the cabin. "Is it the orcs?"

"No idea." Ethan shrugged. He once again tried to focus his own scrying skill around the area in an attempt to see if he could get any hint at who was scrying them. Michalus had said it was possible, but so far his efforts had been a bust.

Just as he was thinking that, his eye caught something shining in the corner of the room. He squinted at it, wondering if it was the reflection of the light on something metallic. It wasn't. The shining spot almost seemed to be radiating its own light.

"Nia," Ethan said in a whisper. Michalus had told him that scrying couldn't pick up sound, but he wasn't taking any chances.

The foxgirl looked over at Ethan and he nudged his head to the corner where the point of light was. He kept his voice low. "Don't be too obvious, but look in that corner and tell me if you see anything."

Nia didn't move her head, but her eyes glanced up at the corner he had indicated. She moved her eyes back to him. "I see nothing. Do you see something?"

"You don't see a point of light up there?" Ethan whispered.

His wife shook her head slightly. "There is no light in the corner."

"I see something. It might be the scrying point," Ethan whispered, still feeling the strong sense of being watched. As he focused, he realized the feeling seemed to be emanating from the point. If that were the case, could he look through it and see who it was who was scrying?

Taking a deep breath, he willed himself to look through it. At first, nothing happened. Then, it was as if he was being sucked towards the point of light.

Beginning to panic, Ethan was about to draw back when suddenly he was looking at some place else. He was in a large cavern, with light streaming in from areas he couldn't see. But that wasn't the thing that caught his attention.

Staring back at him was a large reptilian face of a dragon. Ethan tried to backpedal, but he wasn't physically there - just his consciousness. He began to will himself back to his body but a booming voice cut through his mind as the dragon cocked its head at him.

Ethan noticed that the creature's scales were a deep red-orange color, the same as the dragon from the beach. The same as Bal'Furtun - Firestorm. He felt his body swallow nervously and he silently cursed.

A human, the voice thundered, causing Ethan to mentally wince. *How interesting and unexpected.*

```
Quest Complete.
  Fate of Excalibur - Part II
  Speak to the Dragon (1/1).
  Reward:  2000  experience,  +1000
reputation  with  Shamans  of  Tal'Rae,
+1000  reputation  with  orcs  of
Tal'Rae.
  You gain 2000 experience.
  You  gain  +1000  reputation  with
Shamans of Tal'Rae.
  You  gain  +1000  reputation  with
orcs of Tal'Rae.
```

He quickly debated on whether to sever the connection or try to respond. With the dragon's huge head filling up his vision, Ethan really just wanted to just leave. Despite knowing the dragon wasn't really there, it was nerve-racking being so close to something that could probably swallow him whole.

On the other hand, it would be extremely rude to just leave. The dragon might get offended at that. And the last thing he needed was an offended dragon. He swore silently, knowing what he needed to do.

Using the head of the dragon as a point of reference, Ethan pushed out with his own thoughts using his *Mental* magic. *Uh... hello.*

The dragon squinted at him, or perhaps at the scrying

point. Ethan had no way to know since this was all new to him. *It speaks. Also unexpected.*

You were expecting someone else? Ethan asked.

Truly, I did not know what to expect, the dragon responded. *No one has tried to portal on our mountain for over a thousand years. I thought perhaps one of the orcs had finally learned a new trick.*

Before Ethan could respond, the dragon narrowed its eyes. It seemed to be looking right at him, making him feel like squirming in place. *Who are you? And why are you portaling on our mountain?*

The dragon's words thundered in his mind, causing him to mentally shudder. Despite this, he did notice that the dragon had used the word "our" twice now, and not "my" when referring to the mountain. Did that mean there were other dragons there? If so, that was an unexpected twist.

Feeling the dragon waiting for his answer and loath to make the creature angry, Ethan replied. *My name is Ethan. I'm a wizard. The orcs asked me to find out why you are attacking the villages and cities.*

The dragon's head snarled and Ethan guessed he had said something wrong. He cursed inwardly, trying to figure out what he had said that might have set the dragon off.

The orcs sent you?! the dragon thundered in his mind. *Why do they not come themselves?*

They did. They sent some shamans. They just figured you... uh... killed them. Ethan replied. He had meant to say "eaten them" but figured he shouldn't.

The dragon snorted. *Is that what they told you? No orcs*

have been to our cave - not that I would have allowed them, the dragon retorted.

Ethan felt his brow furrowing. The shamans had definitely told him they'd sent shamans. Not only that, but Drorm had personally escorted a group here. Was one of them lying? Both of them?

He shook his head, or thought he did, since he couldn't see his body. Nia could smell lies. She would have known if Drorm had lied. And if Drorm was telling the truth, then either the shamans never made it to the dragon's cave, or the dragon was lying.

If the dragon was telling the truth, Ethan had a pretty good guess what had happened to the shamans - Doemenaggs. The creatures might have found the shamans and eaten their brains. Just great.

Firestorm was looking at him expectantly and he realized the dragon was waiting for Ethan to speak. Clearing his throat and belatedly realizing it wouldn't translate through the mental link, he quickly said the first thing that came to his head.

Why are you attacking the area? he asked and then immediately regretted his bluntness.

Anger filled the dragon's eyes and a reptilian scowl marred its head. It was quiet for a long moment before finally answering. *That is not something I will discuss with you like this. If you wish to know, then we will speak face to face.*

Ethan swallowed again. He'd been planning on speaking to the dragon from afar using his *Mental* magic - and so he had. Getting up close and personal with a dragon hadn't been on his to-do list.

Yet, now that the dragon had set the terms, he guessed it was either go in person or call off the whole thing. Given the dragon's anger over his question, Ethan wasn't sure that a face to face meeting would be in his best interest.

Well, little human? the dragon spoke, annoyance creeping into the booming voice.

I...uh... have some friends, he told the dragon.

No! the dragon blasted into his head. *Only you! You and I will speak alone.*

My wife... Ethan started and then trailed off. He had meant to say "My wife will never let me go alone" but realized that might be giving away too much information. Unfortunately, the cat was out of the bag now.

Your mate is with you? the dragon asked, moving its head closer to Ethan. Once again, he wanted to backpedal but there was no place for his consciousness to go unless he wanted to sever the connection.

The foxling? She is your mate? the dragon asked.

Ethan cursed as he realized that the dragon would be able to see everyone in the cabin through its scrying. He cursed again as he tried to decide whether to lie or be honest. In the end, he decided on honesty. After all, if Nia could smell the truth, perhaps the dragon could too.

Yes, Ethan said finally.

The dragon backed up slightly, tilting its head to the side. Then it looked to a different part of the room that Ethan couldn't see, before turning its attention back on Ethan. When it spoke, Ethan thought he detected a hint of sadness in the dragon's voice. *Bring your mate. Mates should not be separated. But only the two of you may come. Come now and I will await you.*

Remembering it was dark out - and cold - Ethan grimaced. While Nia might be able to navigate in the dark, he certainly couldn't. Climbing up a mountain in the dark was a good way to get yourself killed.

He sighed. *Can we wait until the morning to visit you? It's dark and...*

The dragon rolled its eyes and made a sound that might be a chuckle. *It has been a long time. I forget how frail humans are. Very well. You and your mate will visit me tomorrow.*

Ethan nodded, not sure if the dragon would see the gesture through the scrying. *Uh... we will leave first thing in the morning.*

Make sure that you do, the dragon responded, looking directly at Ethan. *I don't want to come looking for you.*

You have received a new quest "Fate of Excalibur - Part III"

You seek the legendary sword, Excalibur. You have spoken to the dragon and must now meet the dragon in its lair to discover why it is attacking the orcs and surrounding countryside.

Discover why the dragon is attacking (0/1).

Reward: 3000 experience.

Accept quest (yes or no)?

With that, the connection was suddenly gone and

Ethan found his consciousness back in his body, inside the cabin. A worried-looking Nia was shaking him.

"Ethan! Ethan!" she repeated. "Are you okay?"

Blinking, Ethan focused on his wife. "I'm fine."

He brought up his HUD.

Mana: 17

His conversation with the dragon and possibly the scrying itself had taken a huge toll on his *Mana*. A bit longer and he might have run into problems.

"What happened?" the foxgirl demanded. "Why did you not respond?"

"I just had a little chat with the dragon. And it invited us up to meet it," Ethan replied numbly, still coming to grips with what had just happened. He just hoped they wouldn't be the main course.

51

"Ethan and Nia not go alone." Par'karr was the first to speak up after Ethan had gathered everyone in their cabin and related his conversation with the dragon.

"I don't think we have a choice," Ethan said, giving his little buddy a smile. "The dragon seemed quite adamant about it just being the two of us. If more of us show up, it might be... uh... upset."

"And eat the rest of us," Guinevere pointed out.

"I find it absolutely fascinating that you were able to converse with the dragon while it Scried you," Michalus said, rubbing his chin. "I mean, I had read that such things were possible, but there are so few wizards..."

"Focus, Michalus," Guinevere interrupted him. "Dragon. Ethan and Nia. Going alone."

Michalus blinked and then gave the group a sheepish look. "Sorry, of course, I am concerned. But I believe Ethan is correct. If the dragon said only the two of them, I think it would be foolish to show up at a dragon's home uninvited."

"On that we agree," Drorm said, looking around the room. "Bal'Furtun has not been in the most forgiving mood lately."

The group went quiet, thinking about the recent attacks and how much destruction the dragon could wrought when provoked.

"And it said nothing else as to why it has been attacking us?" Drorm said after a minute.

Ethan shook his head. "Nothing. It purposefully didn't say anything. When I brought it up, that's when it insisted on a face-to-face meeting."

"I find it interesting that it allowed you to bring Nia," Guinevere said.

"How so?" Michalus asked before Ethan could ask the question.

"Why her?" the warrior woman asked, looking at Nia. "Why allow anyone other than you to come? What was that business about mates being separated?"

He bit his lip for a second before voicing his suspicions. "I'm not sure if the dragon is alone."

Drorm's head snapped to look at Ethan. "What do you mean?"

"Just that," Ethan replied. "The dragon called it 'our' mountain several times. I don't think it's alone."

"Another dragon?" Michalus asked, eyebrows raised. "You really think so?"

"A mate?" Nia asked, looking up from sharpening her blades. The foxgirl had been quiet since he told her that only the two of them would be allowed to go see the dragon. She had a resigned look to her that he guessed meant she was prepared to die with him - if it came to that. But given how much effort she put into sharpening her scimitars, it didn't look like she was going to go down without a fight.

"Maybe." Ethan bit his lip again, not sure if he could voice his suspicion. After a moment, he sighed and continued. "Or its mate may have recently died."

Guinevere perked up. "If so, you think the dragon is taking out his grief on the surrounding countryside?"

Ethan shrugged. "It's an idea. But when it spoke of a mate, I thought I sensed sadness. So it's a possibility."

"It's a theory," Michalus admitted, rubbing his chin again. "And there's only one way to find out if it's true."

"Go up there and talk to it." Ethan nodded.

"Par'karr not want Ethan to get eaten by dragon," the kobold burst out.

"I think it knows where we are," Ethan told the kobold. "If it just wanted to eat us, it could have just flown down here and eaten us all."

"For all we know," Guinevere pointed out. "It could be on its way now."

Drorm shook his head. "Bal'Furtun is honorable. If the dragon gave its word, then it will keep it."

"The dragon gave no such word." The former queen rolled her eyes at the orc. "It basically said, come to me up in the mountain. There was no promise of anything. Or am I wrong?"

Shrugging, Ethan looked between Guinevere and Drorm. He thought back to the conversation he'd had with the dragon. "It didn't promise anything. It basically just said to come up and meet it."

"The question that concerns me a bit more than the dragon," Michalus said, "is what happens to the rest of us when you and Nia leave."

Ethan furrowed his brow. "What do you mean?"

"I mean," the wizard said, gesturing around. "If you leave, what will the orcs do? Didn't we establish earlier that they intend to kill us? Do we think they will try to kill the rest of us once you and Nia start towards the dragon?"

Everyone went quiet and exchanged looks. Then, all heads turned to Drorm with questioning looks.

Anger flashed across Drorm's features but then his shoulders slumped. "I don't know."

"So they could kill us as soon as Ethan and Nia leave," Guinevere said, throwing her hands up. "And I don't even have my armor. And you said you can't go get it before you go?"

Ethan shook his head. He'd actually tried creating two portals after his conversation with the dragon but once again it had fizzled out. "I tried. For some reason, it's not working."

"Oh my," Michalus said.

"So much for our escape plan," Guinevere growled.

"There must be some sort of magic preventing you from forming the portal," the wizard noted. "But I've never heard of an enchantment powerful enough to disrupt portals."

"Dragon magic," Par'karr breathed.

"You may be right, Par'karr," Michalus told the kobold.

"If anything was capable of creating that level of magic, it would have to be a dragon."

"You think the dragon has some sort of spell on the mountain to prevent portaling in or out of it?" Ethan asked, his mind completely blown by the concept of warding an entire mountain.

"Unless there is something inside the cabin to prevent us escaping," Guinevere pointed out, her gaze going around the room.

"Given that the dragon began scrying me as soon as I tried creating the portal," Ethan said, "I think it's a safe bet to say the dragon created it. Plus, I actually tried creating one as I walked over to your cabin - so it's not just the cabin."

"Which means we don't have our gear and we don't have any way to escape," Guinevere summarized.

"If you know any enemy will attack, you do not wait for it in the place of their choosing," Nia said.

Everyone turned to the foxgirl. Ethan cocked his head. "What do you mean?"

"They do not wait here for the orcs to attack," his wife told the group. "They come with us..."

"Nia..." he started to interrupt but she held up her hand.

"They come with us and then split away when we are out of view of the orcs," she continued. "We can meet up with them at the bridge - if the dragon does not eat us."

The group exchanged glances. Drorm tilted his head. "We would need to leave the horses. It would look suspicious if we take them onto the mountain."

"We must take only what we would normally take," Nia said. "Arouse no suspicion."

"Won't the orcs look for us?" Michalus asked.

Drorm shook his head. "Not if we go far enough to either side."

"What about when we don't come back?" the wizard asked.

"They will not come up the mountain," Drorm replied. "Only the shamans go up the mountain. No others are permitted."

"Except for us," Michalus pointed out.

Guinevere nodded. "If they don't come up the mountain, we should be able to sneak past them."

"Instead of meeting us at the bridge," Michalus said. "We could create a set of runes that we can carry with us so you can portal right to us if... er... when you leave the dragon and are free of the mountain's enchantment."

"Good idea," Ethan agreed. "Before we leave tomorrow, I'll create some runes and give them to you. Just make sure you keep them on the outside."

"Oh, right." The wizard nodded.

"It sounds like we have a plan," Ethan told the group.

"Good plan!" Par'karr grinned.

"If you call that a plan," Guinevere growled. "I don't like leaving the horses."

"It cannot be helped," Drorm said. "If we try to take them, it will make them suspicious."

"Then we're all clear on what we're going to do?" Ethan asked.

Everyone in the group nodded or made an affirmative

noise. Ethan nodded. "Ok, let's get some sleep and hope things go well tomorrow - for all of us."

Realizing their meeting was over, everyone got up and began heading to the door. Ethan said good night to them all as they left and then closed the door behind them.

When he turned around, he saw Nia had stripped off her clothes and was lying on the bed. He grinned but cocked an eyebrow.

"If things go poorly with the dragon tomorrow," the foxgirl said, giving him a "come hither" gesture, "then I will spend my last night loving my mate."

Unable to fault her logic, Ethan quickly stripped off his own clothes and joined her.

52

The next morning, the group assembled just outside of the village, dressed in their cold-weather gear. Ethan had taken a stone and used *Earth* magic to carve some runes into. He then hollowed out a hole on one end. Using a piece of leather, he made a loop so Michalus could strap it to his belt.

"Just remember not to put this in your pack," Ethan said, handing the rune stick to Michalus.

"Quite so," the wizard responded, taking the rune stick from him.

A few of the orcs had been milling around as Ethan's group finished getting ready. As Michalus looped the runestick onto his belt, Brodtha and a larger group of orcs came over to them. Stopping a few feet from his group, the female orc commander eyed them.

"The trail is marked with flags," Brodtha told them as she surveyed the group. "Follow it up and around the mountain to the cave entrance. Don't deviate from the trail. The slope is dangerous. More than one shaman has died on their way up."

The female commander looked up at the mountain, shielding her eyes with her hand. "The dragon will be inside the cave... if it doesn't fly out to meet you."

"Fly... out?" shivered Par'karr.

"Yes," the commander replied. "It hasn't happened while I've been here, but I have heard in times past that the dragon would fly out and snatch a trespasser right off the mountain."

The orcs near her snickered, looking over the group like one might look over some bugs that needed to be stepped on. Ethan guessed she had already filled in her troops on their orders.

"Good luck with the Bal'Furtun," Brodtha said. "I hope your mission succeeds. When you return, you are to report what the dragon says to me."

So you can kill us, Ethan thought. He saw a similar look on Nia's face but thankfully the foxgirl remained silent. Guinevere made a slightly sour face but turned away to look up the snow-covered mountain.

"Thank you," Ethan replied, trying to force some sincerity into his voice.

"We will be waiting for you to return," the commander told them and Ethan thought he saw a slight smile play across her lips.

"Come on," Ethan told his companions, motioning them towards the trail. "Let's get started."

～

THE GROUP FOLLOWED him out of the village and onto the only trail that led to the mountain. Within a few hundred yards, the ground became completely snow-covered. It was strange, but Ethan thought he remembered pictures of certain mountains in California that were similar. But if he remembered correctly, they were much warmer.

This mountain was not warm. Quite the opposite. The higher they hiked, the colder it became. Within an hour, he was seeing his breath. By the second hour mark, he was cursing the orcs, the dragon and everything else he could think of.

The wind seemed to rip right through his winter clothing, chilling him to the bone. And he wasn't alone. Everyone seemed affected by the cold, especially little Par'karr who struggled to keep up with them.

At the three-hour mark, they were far enough around the mountain that the orc village could no longer be seen. Ethan called them to a halt and looked around.

The area around them had a good amount of fir trees. If his friends used the trees for cover, they should stay out of eyesight of any scouts Brodtha might have set.

"This looks like a good spot for us to part ways," Ethan told the group.

Looking around, the others nodded their agreement.

"You're sure you'll be okay?" Guinevere asked.

"Whether we are or not is completely up to the drag-on," Ethan admitted. "Even if we were all there, it wouldn't make a difference if he wanted to kill us."

The warrior woman nodded. "True."

"Just keep heading down and try to get back to the

river, if you can," he told them. "I'll join you as soon as I can... if I can.

"If I don't show up in a day - two at the most - just assume the worst. If that happens, make your way back to the boulder to get your equipment."

"I won't have any way of opening it without a Chymera crystal," Michalus responded.

Ethan nodded. "It's hollow. A few decent whacks with a hard stone should break it."

"Hopefully, you will be there to open it for us," Guinevere told him.

Taking a deep breath, Ethan nodded. "Hopefully."

The group took turns clasping hands before Drorm, Guinevere, Michalus and Par'karr turned off the trail and began marching through the trees.

Ethan and Nia watched them navigating into the firs for a full minute before turning. Ethan looked at the foxgirl. "It's just you and me now."

"Just you and me," Nia repeated, glancing up at the mountain. "And a dragon."

"And a dragon," he chuckled.

He started up the trail but hadn't taken two steps before a squeal came from the direction the others had gone. It sounded like Par'karr!

Spinning, Ethan and Nia rushed into the woods, following the footstep in the snow. They got a few dozen yards before they saw the others. They were in a rough circle, looking down at something in the snow.

"You'll want to see this," Drorm told them as they came closer. Stepping into their circle, Ethan looked down at what had garnered their attention.

Half buried in the snow was the frozen corpse of an orc. Ethan had no idea how long ago the orc had died but he did know exactly how it had died. Staring down at the head, he saw a hole where the left eye should be. He swore.

"Doemenagg," Drorm growled. "They killed one of our shamans!"

"There's another over here," Guinevere said, bending down and brushing some snow away from what had appeared to be a drift. She gestured to another nearby drift. "Want to bet that's another one."

Drorm stalked over and, brushing some of the snow away, revealed another orc corpse. All three of the corpses had been killed the same way. They'd had their brains sucked out.

"The queen must have figured out the shamans were coming up the mountain and sent a few of her minions to get them," Ethan thought aloud.

"My people must be warned!" Drorm said. "No more shamans can make this journey if the Doemenagg are ambushing them!"

"How are you going to warn them?" Guinevere asked with a raised eyebrow.

Drorm stalked around. "They do not know I am helping you yet. I can return to the village and let them know. I will tell them the rest of you continued up the mountain."

Guinevere eyed him warily but then shrugged. "Up to you. Just be aware, it's possible those orders had your name on them too."

"I know. It would not surprise me." The big orc

nodded. "But my people need to know this."

Ethan looked to Nia. "Do you smell any Doemenagg around here?"

Nia shook her head. "I do not, but the wind is strong. Their scent might be carried away."

Drorm was still looking at Ethan and he realized that the orc was basically asking his permission to leave. "Drorm, do what you think is best. Just be careful."

"I will," Drorm said with a grin. "You be careful as well."

After saying their goodbyes again, Drorm hurried back to the trail and then headed back down the mountain.

"We should get moving too," Guinevere said. "I don't know this area like Drorm did and it may take me a while to find the river again."

Ethan looked back to the dwindling form of Drorm and, knowing he was out of earshot, bent down. "Help me uncover more of this orc."

Guinevere screwed up her face. "Why?"

He hadn't wanted to say anything when Drorm was with them because he wasn't sure what the orc would have thought about "borrowing" an item from a dead shaman. Looking up at Michalus, he grinned. "It's a shaman. It uses Chymera crystals too."

Michalus brightened. "Oh! Excellent point!"

The group quickly dug out the shaman and, searching him, found a brass amulet set with a Chymera stone. After a little prying and a bit of *Fire* magic, they managed to pull the amulet from the dead shaman. He found that the other two orcs had staves but realized they would be too recognizable.

He was about to leave them when an idea struck him. Taking out his knife, he pried the Chymera crystals from the staves and slipped them into his pouch. It was always nice to have some spares.

Turning, he handed the amulet to Michalus. "I'd keep this out of sight when you're near orcs."

"Indeed," the wizard said, shivering as he put the cold metal on and slid it beneath his shirt. "I feel better already knowing I can actually defend myself if we do run into a Doemenagg on the way down."

The group stood around awkwardly for a moment before Ethan cleared his throat. "It's not getting any warmer out here. We'd both better get moving."

"Good luck," Guinevere said and was quickly echoed by Par'karr and Michalus.

"You too," Ethan said.

"Stay safe," Nia admonished.

With their farewells spoken again, the two groups turned and headed their separate ways. All of them were extra wary, knowing that the dragon may not be the only predator on this mountain.

53

Three hours later, Ethan and Nia stood on a rock outcropping looking into a dark cave that led into the mountain. The cave opening was only twelve feet in height and nearly that wide. That meant, this wasn't the entrance the dragon used. It was probably meant for the shamans - or in this case, Ethan and Nia.

"Well," Ethan said, staring into the darkness, "I guess this is it."

"Yes, it is," Nia agreed. The foxgirl was staring into the cave as well, eyes darting around. With her night vision, she was seeing much more of the cave's interior than Ethan was. "The cave continues for ten or twelve yards and then turns to the left. I cannot see beyond that point."

"Last chance to turn back," Ethan told her. He'd tried opening a portal as soon as they reached the cave, to see if he would have any avenue of escape. Unfortunately, he'd run into the same problem he had down in the village. The portal just fizzled.

Nia looked at him and shook her head. "I am Tal'Cha. Where you go, I go."

Sighing, Ethan nodded. It was one thing to risk his own life, but he really wished Nia wouldn't have come. He appreciated her willingness to face the dragon with him, but if things turned out poorly, he had no way to protect her.

Summoning a globe of light, he started into the cave. "Let's not keep the dragon waiting."

The two of them followed the cave to where it turned and followed it through several other turns before it abruptly opened into a monstrous cavern that seemed to be the size of the mountain itself.

Glancing around the cave, Ethan could make out large outcroppings and stone ramps that led from one level of the outcroppings to levels that were higher or lower. It almost reminded him of a giant cat tree, but made inside of a mountain.

In fact, the center of the mountain was completely gone, except for a huge stone pillar that was carved to have ramps that led down into the mountain and up higher into places Ethan couldn't see.

The large cavern was lit by sunlight that filtered in from numerous, large caves that led outside. The openings were all different sizes. Several of them were large enough that the dragon could use them to enter or exit the enormous cavern.

Ethan recognized the cavern from his scrying. Somewhere in here is where he had seen the dragon and talked with it. No sooner than the thought popped into his head, when a voice popped in as well.

You came, a human and his foxling. The dragon echoed in his head, even louder than it had when he'd communicated with it through the scrying connection.

With a beating of wings and a loud thud, Firestorm landed on the outcropping nearest them, dropping down from someplace they hadn't seen above.

Forgive my use of mental magic, but my lips do not make the sounds of your kind. The dragon's head moved forward so it was a dozen yards away. It sniffed at the two of them and then raised a scaly eyebrow - or whatever passed for eyebrows on a dragon.

Without even thinking about it, Ethan checked out the dragon in his HUD.

```
Azzrrarr'Krritirr'Sshrratarr'Rritt'rr
    Dragon
    Level: 100
```

Ethan's eyes almost popped out of his head when he saw the dragon's level. Level 100! That was so much higher than anything else he'd met on this world. It was so far above him as to be nearly inconceivable.

How powerful was this creature? What special powers could it have? It was mind boggling to even think of it. But one thought that did solidify in his mind was: he did not want to fight it.

He also looked at the dragon's name and realized the dragon was right. It seemed full of way too many consonants to be pronounceable by humans. If he tried, he'd just butcher it and possibly insult the dragon.

I remember your scent. Both of your scents. You were at the ocean when I had to chase away some interloping fishmen, the dragon said as it tilted its head one way and then the other, presumably to get a better look at them.

Ethan and Nia exchanged looks. They hadn't realized the dragon had been aware of them. He realized they were lucky to be alive. He looked at the dragon in front of them. Hopefully his luck would hold out.

The dragon's long serpentine neck twisted so the dragon could get a better look at Nia. *And this must be your mate. What is your name?*

"Nia," the foxgirl said, standing proudly. "I am Tal'Cha!"

Tal'Cha? The dragon wrinkled its forehead. *What is Tal'Cha?*

"First wife!" she replied.

First wife? the dragon asked, head swiveling to Ethan. *You have more than one mate?*

"Uh... no," Ethan replied. The dragon had obviously understood Nia when she had spoken aloud, so he followed her example. Besides, there was no point in wasting *Mana* on mental communication. "She is my only mate."

The dragon looked from Ethan to Nia and then back at Ethan. *It is good to have only one mate.*

"I agree," Ethan said. Given his previous experience with women, he didn't think he could deal with two or more wives at once.

I am the one the orcs call Bal'Furtun, and others call Firestorm, the dragon said, inclining its head. *Though my true name is incomprehensible to your kind.*

"It is nice to meet you in person," Ethan said, inclining

his own head. He had no idea what protocol was when meeting a dragon but when in Rome.

"It is an honor," Nia said, also inclining her head.

The dragon's mood shifted and it moved its head to stare at Ethan. *The orcs want to know why I am attacking things in this area? Come, I will show you.*

Without any other words, the dragon twisted and began walking down the nearest ramp. Watching the dragon move close-up, Ethan couldn't imagine anyone fighting the creature - let alone winning. Not even the giant they had encountered would have stood a chance.

Nia gave him a questioning look and Ethan shrugged. "Let's follow him."

Ethan had said "him" because the impression he'd gotten was that Firestorm was a he. Not that he would be able to tell with a dragon, but he just felt the dragon was male.

Looking around, Ethan spotted a ramp that led down from the outcropping where he and Nia stood. Pointing it out, he motioned Nia to follow him.

Firestorm stopped and waited for them to catch up. The two of them hurried down the nearby ramp to where it intersected with the ramp that the dragon was on. As they moved along, Ethan realized something. "This cavern isn't natural, is it? You used earth magic to create it!"

The dragon twisted his head to look around the gigantic cavern. *The cavern was here, but yes, magic was used to mold it to better suit my kind.*

Looking around the cavern, Ethan realized most of the openings had probably been shaped too. Given the sheer amount of rock the dragon must have moved, he knew the

Mana requirements would have been enormous. He wondered just how powerful this dragon really was.

Then again, he was level 100. Who knew how much *Mana* the dragon had, let alone what other magic skills he might know. Obviously, that must be why the orcs sent their shamans to learn from the dragon.

"How long have you lived in this place?" Nia asked as they caught up to the dragon.

Once again, Firestorm twisted his head around to look at the cavern. He was silent for a moment, eyes filled with memories. *For too long to remember.*

The dragon turned his head back around and continued lumbering down the ramp. Ethan and Nia followed some distance behind, just out of reach of Firestorm's swishing tail.

As they walked, Ethan wondered what the dragon was leading them towards. He and his companions had briefly discussed it but hadn't come to any conclusions. Remembering that the dragon had used the words "our mountain" still led him to believe that Firestorm either had a mate or offspring - or eggs that would hatch into offspring.

Ethan tried to keep his attention in the present as they followed the dragon, realizing that speculation about Firestorm's reasons for attacking the area were about to become moot. That was, assuming that the dragon was about to show them the reason and not take them to the kitchen to start preparing them.

Firestorm continued to lead them down the ramps, deeper into the heart of the mountain. Looking over the edge of the ramp, Ethan could see that it extended hundreds of feet down. He wondered how far the dragon would take them.

As if in answer to his question, the dragon stepped off the ramps onto a platform that led from the ramp to another large chamber.

Ethan and Nia hurried after the dragon, only to stop in their footsteps as they took in what the dragon was walking towards.

There, on the far side of the cavern they'd just entered, was another dragon. It was curled up, like a cat, but it was the unmistakable form of a dragon. And unlike Firestorm, this dragon did not have red scales. Its scales were green. Just like the dragon they'd seen on their way to Castlehaven.

54

The green dragon was curled up like a cat, with its head resting on its foreclaws. Its eyes were closed but Ethan thought he saw the creature's huge chest moving as it breathed. He noticed that it didn't move as they came closer, despite not being able to miss the sound of Firestorm approaching.

Ethan could see bloodstains and remains of bones lying around the cavern and he swallowed. Hopefully those weren't human bones. And hopefully, they weren't the next course.

"Is that...?" Nia gasped as she took in the green dragon.

"The dragon we saw before," Ethan finished, taking in the dragon. It looked just like the one he'd seen before, only much larger up close. "I think so."

Ethan took the opportunity to bring up the green dragon in his HUD.

Nrrirrar'Sshaaaartar'Rrrarror'Grriirrara

Dragon
Level: 100

You have seen my mate? Firestorm asked, swiveling his head around to look at them. *When?*

"Uh," Ethan started, trying to play back the events of the last few months in his head. "A few months ago. Near Castlehaven."

Castlehaven? The human city to the north? the dragon asked. Ethan thought he felt a sense of urgency from the dragon, as he moved his head uncomfortably close to them. *What was my mate doing when you saw her?*

Ethan thought back to the first sighting they'd ever had of a dragon. It had been on their way to Castlehaven to re-start trade with Hawkshead after the kobold attack. It had been a while, but that was one encounter he wouldn't soon forget.

"She was chasing some pteranodons... uh... large reptilian bird creatures... near the ocean," he replied, remembering the incident in brilliant detail. "She was...um... eating them, I think."

The dragon made a rumbling sound in his chest and his head bobbed up and down as he turned to look at the green dragon. The sound might have passed for a chuckle to a dragon. *She always did have a sweet tooth for them.*

A sweet tooth? For pteranodons? That was news to him. Maybe their meat was sweet. Or maybe it was sweet to a dragon. Ethan didn't think he wanted to find out.

The dragon's head slumped as he looked at the green dragon, giving Ethan pause. He looked closer at the sleeping dragon to make sure his earlier assessment was correct and that the dragon was still alive.

The creature's chest was definitely moving and Ethan was quite certain he could feel her breath as she exhaled through its nose. If she were alive, then what was making Firestorm sad?

"Is something... wrong with her?" Ethan asked, gesturing to the green dragon.

The dragon growled. The sound reverberated through the cavern and Ethan physically felt the sound waves hitting him, like being too close to a subwoofer at a concert.

Firestorm swung his head at Ethan, suddenly looking much more menacing than he had just moments ago. The dragon's voice thundered inside his head, making him wince. *She does not wake! And when she does, she barely recognizes or responds to me!*

Ethan exchanged looks with Nia. Neither of them knew how to respond to that, so they both kept quiet.

Despite not saying anything, Ethan's mind immediately went to the Grail. If something was wrong with the dragon, maybe the magical goblet would heal it. But, he knew that even the Grail had limits.

He thought back to Michalus. The wizard had been gravely wounded and had, quite literally, been on his deathbed. The Grail had healed his body, but it hadn't restored his memory of what had attacked him. It wasn't until the Doemenaggs had attacked them, that he had finally remembered.

It was possible the Grail could cure physical maladies but not mental ones. Ethan was loath to offer the healing cup if the dragon's condition was a mental issue and not a physical one. Unfortunately, that meant he would need to learn more.

"Uh"—Ethan cleared his throat—"what... uh... happened to her that... um... made her this way?"

The dragon moved closer to Ethan and he felt Nia tense behind him. For a moment, he thought the dragon was going to eat them but then he stopped a few feet away. *I don't know for certain! She awoke before I did from our long sleep. When I awoke, she was as you see her now!*

The dragon shifted his gaze back to his mate. *She barely eats and only if I bring something here. She is wasting away!*

Something about her condition jogged something in the back of Ethan's mind, but he couldn't quite put his finger on it. He bit his lip, hating to pull the dragon's attention back to him, but knowing he needed to ask. "Do you know what caused it?"

Once again, the dragon moved his head so he was staring directly at Ethan. Reflexively, he swallowed. Once more, he hoped the dragon wasn't about to snap down on him and Nia.

I do not know for certain, the dragon replied, keeping his reptilian eyes on Ethan. *But I could smell something on her when I awoke. It was a foreign smell. Something I had not encountered before.*

The dragon sniffed them. *A scent that lingers on you, though it is old.*

Ethan's mind whirled as he wondered what it could be. Remembering their encounters with the fishmen, he thought back to the first time they'd encountered

Firestorm. He'd been going after fishmen then. Could that be it?

The fishmen were annoying, but he couldn't think of anything they could do to a dragon - especially a level 100 dragon. Unless it was some sort of magic Ethan hadn't seen.

I have been hunting them since I first caught their scent from my mate, the dragon continued. *Perhaps you are hunting them too.*

"The fishmen?" Ethan ventured. "You're hunting the fishmen?"

The dragon, who had started to turn back towards his mate, stopped and turned back to him. Firestorm shook his giant head slightly. *No, not the fishy ones. The prey I seek are like giant insects. They move quickly and wield magic, but they are no match for my own magic.*

Eyes going wide, understanding slammed into Ethan like a freight train. The dragon wasn't hunting fishmen, he was hunting Doemenagg!

The dragon nodded. *Yes. You know of what I speak.*

"The Doemenagg." Ethan nodded.

Is that what they are called? The Doemenagg? the dragon asked, mulling the word. *Doemenagg. Yes, I have been wreaking my revenge on them since I awoke - no matter where they are.*

Ethan groaned, slapping his palm against his forehead. Nia, who had been quiet the entire time, looked at him questioningly. He gave her a reassuring smile before turning back to the dragon.

"You haven't been attacking the villages and cities. At least, not directly. Have you?" Ethan asked.

Of course not, the dragon responded. *What do I care for the things of orc or man. I have been hunting the insect ones.... the Doemenagg, as you call them.*

"So the places you attacked..." Ethan started but the dragon nodded his massive head.

The places I attacked had the Doemenaggs, the dragon confirmed. *And I destroyed them with fire.*

```
Quest Complete.
   Fate of Excalibur - Part III
   Discover   why   the   dragon   is
attacking (1/1).
   Reward: 3000 experience
   You gain 3000 experience.
   You   have   received   a   new   quest
"Fate of Excalibur - Part IV"
   You   seek   the   legendary   sword,
Excalibur. You have learned that the
dragon  has  been  attacking  Doemenagg
after  his  mate  was  injured.  Report
your findings to the shamans.
   Tell   the   shamans   why   Bal'Furtun
has been attacking (0/1).
   Reward: 3000 experience.
   Accept quest (yes or no)?
```

Ethan accepted the quest. It seemed to indicate that the dragon was telling the truth. He had been hunting Doemenagg.

He remembered the burned-out villages they'd passed and cocked his head. "An entire village?"

The Doemenagg have been attacking men and orcs. They take them away. When I find them, I kill them, the dragon told them.

"Wait," Ethan said. "The Doemenagg are taking normal people? Where?"

South. They always go south but I cannot follow them, the dragon replied with a tone of sorrow. *I must stay near my mate. I dare not leave her alone for long. Without me, she does not drink or eat.*

That made sense. When Ethan had been in mental communication with what he thought was the Queen, he had sensed her to the south. Was that her nest? Or would it be a hive?

"So the orcs have it all wrong." Ethan snorted. "If anything, you have been helping them - keeping the Doemenagg from killing all of their shamans."

I do not know if I help them, nor do I care, the dragon said, anger seeping back into his tone. *I only want to destroy those who did this to my mate.*

Ethan understood the dragon's anger. Who knew how long these two dragons had been together. And now, they were separated by more than distance. Something was wrong with the green dragon. Something that the Doemenagg must have done to her. Something that had effectively made her an invalid.

The memory that had been escaping him suddenly snapped into focus. Odelina, the butcher in Hawkshead, had told him a story. She had said that her mother had been a wizard and that she had been killed by what Ethan now knew were the Doemenagg.

As tragic as that was, it was the rest of the story that

interested him. Odelina had said that her father had never been the same since that. She'd found him almost catatonic. He'd seen her father a time or two and he acted similar to Firestorm's mate.

But what had the Doemenagg done to her? And to Odelina's father? Some sort of magic? Another memory came slamming back to the forefront of his head.

When they were fighting the Doemenagg in Camelot, one of the creatures had sprayed some sort of green mist at Nia. It was the only nonmagical attack it had done - other than using its appendages.

Had the green mist been poison? Perhaps even a neurotoxin? Could that be what affected Firestorm's mate and Odelina's father? If it were some sort of physical damage, then perhaps the Grail might be able to help.

It was worth a shot. Ethan knew if it were Nia affected by that condition, he'd at least try the Grail on her.

He cleared his throat, causing the dragon to turn from his mate to look at Ethan. "I might have something that could... heal her."

The dragon's eyes widened in surprise and possibly hope. His huge head came within inches of Ethan. *Tell me more.*

55

"We have access to a magical cup that seems to be able to heal just about anything," Ethan blurted out as he stared at the dragon, only inches away. He felt Nia pressing up against him and thought he felt her trembling. Was she afraid?

Ethan was surprisingly calm, given how near Firestorm was to him. He was so close, he could both feel and smell the dragon's warm breath. He had to constantly resist the urge to gag.

Where is this cup? the dragon demanded. *Will it work on my mate?*

The dragon was so close, Ethan was having trouble deciding which eye to look at, since he couldn't look at both at the same time. He picked the right one and explained the Grail's location. "The Grail is in a tomb. It...uh... emits a high-pitch sound when removed from the tomb..."

Where is this tomb?! the dragon's voice thundered in his head, the creature's desperation evident in the mental tone. It was clear he cared deeply about his mate and Ethan prayed that the Grail would actually be able to help her.

"It's near Hawkshead," Ethan replied quickly, wishing the dragon would back away just a bit. "I have some runes that I can use to open a portal to it, but my portal magic isn't working."

At that, the dragon did back his head away from him, twisting his neck to look around the mountain. *The mountain is enchanted to not allow portal magic. A human wizard did this for us, since we dragons do not enchant items.*

"A wizard enchanted the entire mountain?" Ethan whistled, mind spinning from the sheer amount of *Mana* that would be involved, not to mention Chymera crystals.

The dragon looked over to his mate. *Yes, the wizard, Merlin, was a friend to both of us.*

Ethan's eyes went wide. "Merlin?! Merlin enchanted this?! THE Merlin?"

Twisting his serpentine neck back to look at Ethan, the dragon gave a nod. *You know of Merlin? Does he still live? He hasn't visited us in a hundred years.*

Mind still reeling from the unexpected news, Ethan wasn't sure what to make of the dragon's revelation. First, to find out that Merlin had somehow enchanted an entire mountain was completely mind blowing. But it was the second part of what the dragon had said that truly intrigued Ethan.

The dragon had said that Merlin hadn't visited him for a hundred years. Not a thousand years, or over a thousand years, which was about how old Ethan thought the journal was. Firestorm had said a "hundred" years. If that were true, it would be the most recent contact with the wizard yet. Could Merlin still be alive?

He'd gotten the impression from Guinevere that her father was dead. Plus, if Merlin was alive, he would have thought that the man would have either contacted his daughter or made himself known in the world.

Ethan suspected the Merlin that Michalus had known, and who had helped him build the portal detector, was the original Merlin. But that was still hundreds of years ago. If the dragon had actually met with him only a hundred years ago, the dragons might be the last ones to have seen Merlin.

You can open a portal to the cup of healing? the dragon asked in his mind, breaking him out of his thoughts.

"Yes," Ethan said. "But I would need..."

The dragon moved his head past him, lumbering closer to him. He felt Nia cling tighter to him, both of them unsure what the dragon was doing.

Stopping with his forearm near them, the dragon craned his neck so he was looking back at them. *Climb onto my back. I will fly you above the level of the enchantment's protection. Then you can create a portal to the cup.*

"Uh," Ethan stuttered, looking from the dragon's head to his back. The dragon had angled his forearm so he would be able to climb up the limb, onto the creature's back.

Yet, while it might sound fun in books and look exciting in movies and on TV, the prospect of riding a dragon in real life was much more intimidating.

For one, there was no saddle and the dragon's back was much too broad to wrap his legs around. Plus, the creature's scales would make holding on nearly impossible. As soon as the dragon took to flight, he'd slide off and probably fall to his death.

The dragon made a sound that Ethan had previously guessed was a chuckle. *Do not be afraid. I will hold you on with magic. You will not fall.*

Ethan looked at the dragon's head. He took great pains to suppress the "are you out of your mind" look that he knew must be on his face. After all, he knew that the dragon could just kill them both with one snap of his jaws. What reason would he have to go through an elaborate ruse to take him into the sky, only to drop him to his death?

He swallowed nervously and nodded. Steeling his resolve, Ethan took a step towards the dragon's forearm. At least, that's what he tried to do.

Finding himself unable to move, he looked back to Nia who was now holding onto him so tight that it was starting to hurt. Looking into her wide eyes, he saw the foxgirl was pale and was shaking her head.

"Nia?" he questioned. "You okay?"

Nia shook her head vigorously. "Don't go."

"It's okay," he reassured her, seeing something akin to terror in her eyes. "I'm just going to fly up with the dragon and retrieve the Grail."

"Flying is for birds..." The foxgirl shook her head again and then looked up at the dragon. Her voice came out quiet, barely a whisper. "And dragons."

Nia's fear was so uncharacteristic. The normally fierce

and fearless foxgirl was obviously terrified of the mere thought of flying on the dragon's back. Ethan realized it might be the cultural and technological differences in the worlds they came from.

Coming from Earth, the concept of flying was nothing new to Ethan. He'd flown in planes many times for work or vacation. Even the idea of riding a dragon had been explored in a number of books, movies and TV shows. There was even an animated film series about taming dragons and riding them.

Looking at his wife, he guessed their experience with flying came from what they observed in other animals. The very idea that beings other than avians - and in this world, dragons - might be able to fly was probably alien to Nia and the culture she had grown up in.

Gently disengaging himself from her clutching hands, he looked into her eyes and tried to project a confidence about riding the dragon he didn't fully possess. "It's okay. I'm a wizard. Even if I fall, I can catch myself with air magic."

The dragon, who had been patiently watching their exchange, nodded. *I will not let anything happen to your mate.*

Wide-eyed, Nia looked from Ethan to the dragon and then back to Ethan. Her brow furrowed in uncertainty, she gave him a small nod and slowly released her grip on him.

"I'll be fine," he said, focusing on the fact that he could actually use magic to slow his fall or even hover in the air. He'd actually levitated the entire party out of the tomb. Keeping himself from going splat should be easy - he hoped.

With a wink at his wife, he turned and carefully climbed up the dragon's forearm to his back. Once he was atop his shoulder, Ethan looked at the dragon's head. "Uh... where do you want me?"

Go to the center of my back. There are spikes there. Sit down between two spikes. You should be able to hold onto them as we go. I will hold you in place with magic, as well. The dragon's voice in his head was soothing, but still held an undertone of urgency. Clearly, the dragon was anxious to see if the Grail helped his mate.

Gingerly, Ethan climbed the dragon's back until he got to the spikes that protruded along his spine. Positioning himself just beyond the neck, even with the shoulders, he slid between two of the spikes, wrapping his legs and arms around one of them.

Good. I will hold you in place with air magic. Do not be alarmed if you feel it, the dragon explained. Almost immediately, Ethan sensed the *Air* magic being channeled and felt a pressure against his legs, pushing him down.

No sooner had he felt the magic, when the dragon began to lumber up the ramp. He just managed a feeble wave to Nia before Firestorm took them back up to the next level.

Climbing up the ramps much quicker than before, the dragon took only a few minutes to reach a level where there was an opening in the mountain large enough for him to fit through. Without warning, Ethan slammed back against the spike pressing against his back as the dragon darted forward with a speed that seemed in contradiction to the creature's large size. And then... Ethan was falling.

Unable to suppress a girl-like scream as he was

suddenly in freefall, Ethan was abruptly slammed back against the spike at his back as the dragon unfurled his wings and began flapping.

Ethan suppressed a shiver, once again exposed to cold air, but this time the air was not only freezing, it was buffeting his face and body, seeming to cut right through his clothes and chill him to the bone. He cursed with chattering teeth.

The dragon veered to the right and for a moment, Ethan thought he would slide off the dragon. Yet, the dragon's magic held and he didn't even budge an inch. Still hanging onto the spike in front of him like his life depended on it, he watched as the dragon circled around the mountain, slowly getting further and further away.

Finally, the dragon leveled off and began to hover. He flapped his wings rhythmically to keep them at a fairly consistent height. Ethan once again heard the dragon's voice in his head. *We are clear of the mountain's enchantment.*

"Okay!" Ethan yelled, shivering uncontrollably now. He breathed warm air between his cupped hands and then rubbed them together so that he had enough feeling in them to hold the Chymera crystal.

Once he was sure he could grasp the crystal, he pulled it out of his pouch and, with a force of will, opened a portal to the tomb. Reaching in quickly, he pulled the Grail from its resting place and allowed the portal to wink out. "Got it!"

He felt the dragon's rhythm falter for a moment as the Grail cleared the portal. The dragon snaked his head around to look at it. *The sound it makes is... annoying. Let us hope it works on my mate.*

With that, the dragon went into a dive and spiraled back down to the entrance to his mountain, all while Ethan clutched the dragon's spike and screamed like a 12-year-old girl.

56

The flight down was mercifully quick, with the dragon diving down and then unfurling his wings just as they reached the level of one of the large openings. Ethan's stomach lurched as the dragon's momentum was abruptly diverted. He and the dragon swooped into the opening so quickly that Ethan thought they would crash. Then, the dragon adjusted his wings again and they slid to a stop.

Breathing heavily, Ethan kept his mouth shut to prevent himself from losing his lunch. The dragon crouched down and the magic that had been binding him to the dragon dissipated. The dragon twisted his head to look at him. *You may get off now.*

Nodding, he slid down and then off the dragon. When he hit the ground, Ethan swayed slightly, feeling slightly lightheaded. Taking deep breaths, his sense of equilibrium quickly returned.

As he began to feel both better, and warmer, he saw

Nia running up the nearby ramp. The foxgirl raced the final few steps of the ramp and onto the platform where he stood. She threw herself into his arms, kissing him all over his face. "I was watching from the cave entrance! You flew like a bird!"

Chuckling despite himself, Ethan returned the embrace. "Piece of cake."

After a moment, Nia backed away and looked down at the Grail. "You were able to retrieve it."

"Yes," he replied and looked from Nia to the dragon. "Let's go try it."

Yes. Let us try this magic cup quickly, the dragon said, his face wincing. *The noise continues to get louder.*

Ethan knew from experience that Firestorm was correct. Merlin had enchanted the cup to emit the sound to keep it from his grandson, Mordred. Mordred had been a channeler who had completely given in to his transformation and become a demon.

In Mordred's hands, the Grail's healing properties would have given him virtual invulnerability. With its ability to heal, only a mortal wound would have brought down the channeler turned demon.

But the type of demon he had turned into had a weakness to high-pitched sound. By enchanting the Grail to emit the sound and have it grow steadily louder, Merlin had effectively put the Grail out of reach of the demon.

The only time the Grail didn't emit a sound was when it was resting on Arthur's tomb. Ethan wasn't sure if Merlin had done that purposefully so that if Mordred had found it, he would always have to visit the tomb and possibly face who he had been - Arthur's son.

Realizing the dragon was still looking at Ethan, he nodded. "Yes, the faster, the better."

They quickly followed the dragon down several ramps to the chamber where the green dragon lay curled up. If it had moved at all since they left, Ethan didn't notice. It appeared to be in exactly the same position. At least, until they got closer with the Grail.

The green dragon snapped open her eyes. Although the eyes looked somewhat vacant, they zeroed in on Ethan and the Grail almost instantly. Then the dragon began to stir.

She must think you are trying to hurt her, Firestorm told them. *Quickly, hand me the Grail and get behind me.*

The green dragon began growling at Ethan, looking menacing despite the full eyes. He swallowed. Having an angry dragon staring at him unnerved him a bit. He worried that at any moment, the formerly docile dragon would lash out and snap him in half with one bite.

Keeping his eyes on the green dragon, Ethan held up the Grail for the dragon to take. Briefly, he wondered how Firestorm would take it with his giant claws. Feeling *Air* magic being channeled, Ethan felt the Grail tugged from his grasp.

The cup floated up in the air. Then, Ethan felt *Water* magic being channeled and water filled the cup. Obviously able to discern the source of the sound, the green dragon's eyes left Ethan and followed the cup.

Whatever happens, Firestorm told them. *Stay behind me. She is not what she once was, but she could still harm you.*

Nia took Ethan's hand and tugged him back further. Nodding to her, he allowed himself to be pulled near the entrance as they waited to see how Firestorm would get his mate to drink water from the Grail.

"I can hear it now." The foxgirl grimaced. "It continues to get louder."

"Just hang in there," Ethan said, squeezing her hand. "We'll get rid of it as soon as the dragon makes her drink."

She nodded and they both turned to watch the two dragons.

Ethan turned just in time to feel a massive channeling of *Air*. He saw the green dragon stiffen and he guessed Firestorm had managed to wrap the entire dragon in shackles of *Air*. He whistled quietly at the display of power.

Nearly faster than Ethan could follow, the Grail shot to the green dragon's mouth. Then, much to his horror, the Grail shot into her open mouth. It appeared as if the green dragon tried to bite down but her mouth must have been held by *Air* because her jaws quivered but couldn't close.

Hovering inside the green dragon's jaws, the Grail tilted and dumped the contents into the creature's mouth. After it was done, the magic cup shot back out. Firestorm then levitated the cup over to Ethan and let it drop into his waiting hands.

Ethan was looking over the Grail to make sure it still seemed intact when Nia tapped him on the shoulder. She pointed at the green dragon.

Looking at the dragon, Ethan could see an immediate change in the dragon's expression. No longer did it look around dully. Instead, fierce eyes darted around the cave. The green's eyes fixed briefly on Ethan and Nia before turning to face Firestorm.

There was an exchange of rumbling growls that lasted several minutes as the two dragons seem to be having some sort of conversation. The exchange ended with Firestorm moving close to the green dragon and nuzzling her neck.

"I guess it worked," Ethan whispered.

"Yes," Nia breathed. "They seem happy now."

Ethan thought back to when he had almost lost Nia to a psionic fragment of a Cthulhu. The demon had left some part of its mind or spirit in the foxgirl and it had almost succeeded in crushing her mind and transforming her into a demon. He'd been able to use his *Mental* magic to destroy it. But the mental fight had cost him some of his *Stamina*. Despite the cost, he would gladly do it again.

Remembering how good he'd felt when he had gotten her back, Ethan looked out at the two dragons and smiled. He reached down and took Nia's hand and gave it a squeeze. She returned his smile and squeezed his hand back.

The dragon's affections were cut short as they both winced and looked over at Ethan. Knowing the Grail must be getting louder, he gave them a sheepish shrug. "Sorry."

Come, Firestorm said, the voice in his mind sounding pained. *Let us return the magic cup to where we cannot hear it.*

Firestorm came over and, crouching down, allowed Ethan to once again climb onto his back. No sooner had he managed to get into place than Ethan felt *Air* pushing him down into place. At the same time, he lurched backwards as the dragon shot up the ramp much more quickly than the last time.

Before he knew it, they were outside once more, with the wind howling around him as the dragon spiraled downward before unfurling his wings and beginning to gain altitude. Once they were several hundred feet up, Ethan heard the dragon in his head. *Quickly, send the cup back.*

Shivering and teeth chattering, Ethan managed to open a portal back to the tomb. He shoved the Grail through, being careful to make sure it was sitting upright on the tomb, before pulling his hand back through. "It's done!"

Ah, that is so much better, the dragon sighed mentally. *Let us return.*

Before he knew it, they were back inside the dragon's lair and Ethan was trying to get warm. Nia and the green dragon joined them on the platform they'd landed on, coming to greet them.

I understand I have the two of you to thank for my recovery, the green dragon said mentally. Although the dragons sounded similarly, there was definitely a feminine feel to the voice.

"We were happy to help," Ethan said. "I'm glad it worked."

As am I, the green dragon inclined her head. *I have no memory of the last few months, but my mate tells me I was... unwell.*

"I think you were attacked by a Doemenagg," Ethan said. "I think they have some venom or something that affects the victim's brain."

The green dragon cocked her head one way and then

another. *I do not remember this... Doemenagg. Who or what is it?*

There was some growling between the two dragons and Ethan guessed Firestorm was filling her in on the Doemenagg. At one point, the female dragon let loose a tremendous roar, slamming her tail against the floor. After a few minutes, the dragons turned to him.

I have explained to her about the scent I detected on her and my hunt for the creatures over the last few months, Firestorm said. *We have decided that after you leave, we will hunt them down to the south and find their lair. They will never do this to either of us again.*

Ethan nodded. "I think that would be a great service to the world if you wiped them out."

My mate is feeling like her old self. She is angry and wishes to seek revenge immediately, the red dragon told them. As if to emphasize the point, the female dragon slammed her tail into the side of the cavern. The blow caused rocks to fall from the cavern wall and ceiling. *Can you make your way down the mountain?*

"Yes," Ethan said and then remembered the orcs and their orders to kill him and his party. He smirked as an idea came to him. "I think the orcs want to kill us for learning about you. Do you think you could give me some sort of paper or stone tablet that would let them know... maybe... not to kill us?"

The two dragons exchanged looks and then did some more growling at each other before turning back to Ethan and Nia.

We will stop at the orc cities and make sure they know that you are under our protection, the dragon said. *If they harm you or your mate, we will visit them with destruction as they have never seen.*

Taken aback, Ethan quickly remembered his other friends. "Do you think you can include my friends too?"

Yes, the dragon replied. *For what you did to bring back my mate, your friends are our friends. We will not forget what you have done, and dragons have long memories.*

The dragon paused and then looked at Ethan. *There is one thing I can give you, that may help you.*

Ethan raised an eyebrow, thoughts of treasure or magical weapons coming to mind. After all, wasn't that what you got from a dragon's lair? Or perhaps that was just in the stories.

The dragon held up a claw and suddenly the skin on Ethan's chest burned briefly. Flinching, he pulled back his shirt to see a glowing dragon tattoo on his chest.

It is my sigil, Firestorm said. *It is magical and will not fade, nor will the magical cup erase it. It is something I give to the orcs who I have trained.*

You have gained Magical Sigil of Knowledge.
You have gained: Sigil magic.

"Woah! Did you just... teach me a skill?" Ethan asked, happy that the pain was already fading.

Yes, it is how I teach the orcs, Firestorm replied. *I imprint the knowledge of magical skills into the design of the sigil. As long as you have it, you will have the knowledge I have bound to it. Eventually, if you are wise enough, you will incorporate the knowledge into your own mind.*

Ethan opened his mouth to ask how it worked but the green dragon made a low growling sound, her head gesturing impatiently towards one of the large openings.

Alas, my mate hungers for revenge. She is anxious to destroy the Doemenagg. We thank you and bid you farewell. Both dragons inclined their heads at Ethan and Nia before lumbering over to the nearest cave entrance and then leaping into the air.

Watching them go, Ethan snapped his fingers. "Darn! We should have asked him how the sigil works and how I access the knowledge. We could also have probably got them to give us a ride and then created a portal to the others."

"No! No! No! We will walk!" Beside him, Nia shook her head vigorously. "Yes, walking is good."

57

The two of them managed to make it down the mountain. It took them until well after dark before they got beyond the protection enchantment that blocked portals. There was no sign of either the dragons, orcs and, thankfully, no sign of Doemenaggs either.

Outside of the enchanted area, Ethan summoned a portal to the runes that Michalus wore. The portal showed an open area, with a campfire. Sitting around the campfire were his companions. All save Drorm.

While the portal manifested as a shimmering doorway on his side, Ethan knew it was invisible at its destination. People and items appeared to materialize out of thin air. So, although he could see them, they would not be able to see him. It was almost like scrying.

Ethan paused as he considered the similarity between the two. He really hadn't been able to get scrying to work, but perhaps he'd been approaching it wrong. Maybe he should be treating it more like portal magic.

"Are you ready?" Nia asked, looking into the portal. "I, for one, would not mind a nice warm fire."

"Same here," Ethan said and took Nia's hand. "Let's go."

The two of them hopped into the portal and entered the strange kaleidoscope tunnel of the Bifrost. The colors swirled around them in intricate patterns. Beyond the colorful tunnel he was traveling through, Ethan did see what looked like planets, suns, maybe even entire galaxies. It really was spectacular. And then it was over.

Blinking, Ethan and Nia appeared near the fire, startling their companions. Guinevere started to reach for her short swords before recognizing them and relaxing. Michalus looked wide eyed at them as he fumbled for the amulet around his neck. Par'karr grinned and hopped to his feet.

"Ethan! Ethan and Nia back!" the little kobold squeaked. Par'karr looked them up and down. "Talk to dragon? Dragon no eat you?"

Ethan smiled. "Yes, we talked to the dragon. And no, he didn't eat us."

"Glad you're okay, my boy," Michalus said, getting to his feet much more slowly than Par'karr. "Did you actually find out what caused the dragon to start attacking?"

"Let's sit down near the fire and I'll tell you all about it," Ethan replied, already moving to the fire. "I'm freezing."

Once all of them were seated around the fire, Ethan related their encounter with the dragon. The others listened with rapt attention as he explained talking with the dragon, the dragon's mate and how he thought a Doemenagg had caused the female dragon's condition.

"So you actually rode a dragon?" Guinevere whistled. "I've never heard of anyone riding a dragon. That's something for the history books."

"Par'karr not want to ride dragon." The little kobold shivered. "Par'karr stay on ground."

"Very wise, Par'karr," Nia agreed.

"I find it interesting that a Doemenagg would actually attack a dragon," Michalus said, rubbing his chin. "It couldn't really have believed it had any chance of success."

Ethan bit his lip for a moment. "I'm not sure it did attack the dragon."

He had been thinking about the female dragon's story and her condition since they'd left the mountain. There was no way to know for certain, but he did have some theories. "I think it came across a Doemenagg while it was flying around."

"Really?" Michalus asked. "What makes you come to that conclusion?"

"Just a hunch really," Ethan said. "We saw the green dragon on the way to Castlehaven several months ago. Shortly before we met you, Michalus, on the way to the library."

The wizard inclined his head, indicating he remembered.

"I'm guessing, it woke up from hibernation, or dragon sleep, or whatever they call their long sleep," Ethan continued, "and it went out hunting - or maybe just to explore. Anyway, it happened across a Doemenagg, didn't know what it was and swooped down to either investigate or eat it."

"Eat it." Par'karr nodded, making a chomping motion with his teeth.

"Either way," Ethan went on. "I think the Doemenagg fought back with some sort of green mist neurotoxin that caused that condition."

"Neuro what?" Guinevere asked, brow wrinkled in confusion.

"I saw it try to spray Nia with some sort of green mist during our fight in Camelot," he said. "I thought it might be acid, but now I think it might be some sort of toxin that affects people's brains. I know a survivor of an attack who had a similar affliction."

"That's quite a stretch," Michalus commented. "After all, their purpose seems to be to... uh... collect the brains of wizards. Why use a toxin that effectively damages their brains?"

Ethan nodded, having thought of it himself. "I think it might be a weapon they use on non-wizards. And in this case, I don't think the Doemenagg knew the dragon was a wizard - if that's what they are."

Michalus looked skeptical but then Guinevere came to his defense. "You might be right. During the war, we occasionally came across people with the same symptoms you said the dragon had. Even my father never figured out exactly what had happened to them. But it did happen."

"If that's true," Michalus said with a frown. "It's disturbing to think that there is something that can do that to a person - or even a dragon."

Thinking back to Earth, Ethan knew there were all

sorts of biological weapons that had been created by the governments. Or rather, the rumors of biological weapons. Some of those could kill with only a few drops. If this green mist weapon was powerful enough, even a little bit might affect a large creature like the dragon.

"But you said the Grail cured it, right?" Guinevere asked. "That means we have a cure if one of us were to get affected by this green mist weapon."

"True," Ethan agreed. "But let's hope it doesn't come to that. After all, the dragons just waged war on the Doemenagg!"

Michalus wrinkled his forehead. "Couldn't the Doemenagg affect both of the dragons the same way?"

Ethan shook his head. "From what I saw, I think that's a close-up-type weapon. Somehow, I doubt the dragons are going to get anywhere near close enough for the Doemenagg to use that on them. Firestorm said he has been hunting them since he first smelled them on his mate - and he's been fine."

"Right," Michalus admitted. "And to believe, this entire time the dragon's actually been helping the people by killing the Doemenagg and not attacking them."

"That's the impression I got," Ethan told the group. "And I have a feeling that if the dragons wanted to destroy the orc cities, they could do it without breaking a sweat."

There was silence around the fire for a few minutes until it was broken by Guinevere. "What's the next step? Do you think the orcs will listen to the dragon?"

Ethan and Nia looked at each other and both nodded at the same time. "I think the dragon will be persuasive."

"Orcs not kill us now?" Par'karr asked.

"I don't think so," Ethan responded. "But I don't know if they will honor their agreement to show us the sword."

"So then all of this would have been for naught?" Michalus questioned.

"We did save a dragon who was gravely wounded," Nia pointed out.

Guinevere ran her hand through her hair. "And for that matter, with two dragons going after the Doemenagg, we may not have to worry about them either."

Michalus nodded thoughtfully. "A fair point."

"We may not even need the sword Excalibur," Nia added.

Ethan bit his lip again. Nia might be right, but he had his heart set on at least seeing the sword. "If the orcs will honor their word, I'd still like to see it."

"As would I," Michalus agreed. "An artifact of that significance would be fascinating to study."

"Then what's our next step?" Guinevere asked. "Return to the city? It will be a long walk without the horses."

"I can portal us back to the river," Ethan told her. "We have to get all of our stuff, anyway."

"Right," Guinevere acknowledged. "But from there, without horses, it's a good 3-4 days walk. Unless you can portal us back to the city."

Ethan frowned. Even if he could, he wasn't sure he would want to. He needed to see whether they were going to be killed on sight before he just waltzed into their city. "No, I guess we'll have to get our stuff and then walk back to the city."

"We will be exposed on the road," Nia pointed out, "if the orcs do not abide by their word."

"Let's hope it doesn't come to that," Ethan replied. "If we are attacked and it looks overwhelming, I can always open a portal for us to escape."

"And if they catch us by surprise?" Guinevere asked with a raised eyebrow.

"That's why we have my wife," Ethan said, putting his arm around Nia. "And her talented little nose. She should be able to smell any ambush and give us fair warning."

"Yes, I will be able to smell the orcs." Beside him, he felt the foxgirl sit up straighter. He caught her wrinkling her nose. "They really are not that difficult to smell."

Their plan in place, Ethan and his companions set up their bedrolls, picked watches and then turned in. Given what they'd been through over the last few days, Ethan hoped tomorrow would be a nice, peaceful day.

58

The next morning, they ate breakfast and quickly packed up their bedrolls. After so long, it felt strange to be missing the horses and Ethan wondered if it would be worth going back to the village for them.

Unfortunately, the dragons had only mentioned stopping in the major cities, not every little village on the way to do battle against the Doemenagg. There was no guarantee the orcs in the village wouldn't try to kill them on sight. It wasn't worth it. They could buy new horses.

Once they were packed, Ethan opened a portal back to the boulder they had secreted away all of their magic items. The two women went through first, weapons ready. Once they made sure it was clear, Par'karr and Michalus went. Ethan went last.

For the second time in as many days, Ethan was in the rainbow bridge that was the Bifrost. This time, he tried to look beyond the colorful tunnel and to the stars and galaxies that flashed by. That's when he caught sight of something that made him gasp.

Before he could fully register what he'd seen, Ethan stepped out onto the road with the others. He shook his head. His mind was reeling from what he'd just seen - or thought he'd seen.

"Are you okay?" Nia asked him, a look of concern on her face.

Ethan looked at her and cocked his head. "I'm not sure. I think... I just saw... my galaxy."

Nia cocked her head. "Galaxy?"

He nodded mutely, trying to wrap his head around it. What he'd seen in the Bifrost was almost a perfect picture representation of the Milky Way. At least, as close as he could remember from the various pictures he'd seen.

"What is Galaxy?" Par'karr asked, eyes wide with curiosity.

"Uh," Ethan started, trying to figure out how to explain it. "It's a collection of... um... stars... my galaxy is called the Milky Way...."

"Milky way?" Par'karr asked. "Many cows?"

"No," Ethan chuckled at the little kobold. "That's just the name. Although, my planet does have lots of cows. But I think I actually saw it."

"You saw your galaxy. What does that mean, my boy?" Michalus asked. The wizard didn't seem fazed at all by the mention of galaxies, so at least this world understood the concept of it. Perhaps some wizard, or even non-wizards, were astronomers.

"I'm not sure," Ethan said. Then he frowned. "Honestly,

I don't even know that it was my galaxy. I'm sure there are other galaxies that look like it."

Ethan couldn't remember any numbers of statistics off the top of his head, but he knew there had to be more than one spiral galaxy in the universe. There was no way to know if what he'd seen had been the Milky Way.

"Always nice to see home, though," Guinevere said with a smile that didn't reach her eyes.

Her mention of home suddenly caused Ethan to remember the other conversations he'd had with the dragon. His eyes went wide as he realized he'd completely forgotten to tell the warrior woman about Firestorm's mention of her father. He swore.

"I'm sorry," he blurted out. "With everything that went on yesterday, I totally forgot to mention: your father enchanted the mountain against scrying."

"He what?" Guinevere gasped, shocked. "When?"

"I don't know," Ethan told her excitedly, "but they said he visited a hundred or so years ago. He may still be alive."

As soon as he said it, Guinevere's face fell. She shook her head. "No, Ethan, my father died a while ago."

Feeling like a jerk, Ethan floundered for a moment. "Sorry, I thought... maybe..."

Guinevere waved him off as her eyes dropped to the ground. "It's okay. I never really speak of the details... but he died because of me."

"You?" Ethan gasped.

Sighing, the warrior woman gestured at the boulder. "How about you open this boulder up and I'll tell you while I put my armor on."

Nodding, Ethan gestured at the boulder and channeled *Earth*. As he did, the outside of the boulder peeled open, revealing their items inside. "There you go."

The group began pulling their items out as Guinevere began talking.

"A little over a hundred years ago, maybe more, a large group of channelers and warlocks broke away from the rest of civilization and formed their own city called Patheos in secret..."

"Patheos?!" Ethan interrupted. "Where the library of Daemonium is?"

"The same one." The woman grimaced. "I forgot you mentioned that you had been there."

"Oh yes." Nia nodded, pushing down some bad memories. "We were there."

"Par'karr get ambushed!" the kobold squeaked.

"If you have been there, then I'm sure you've seen the destruction," she said with a raised eyebrow.

"Yes, everything but the library was wiped out," Ethan said with a nod.

Guinevere sighed. "My father did that."

"Your father wiped out Patheos?" Ethan asked incredulously. He remembered the place looked like a bomb had gone off in the middle of it. He couldn't even imagine the amount of power it would take to do that.

The former queen nodded sadly. "I went there to investigate a rumor of a demon that resembled... Mordred. I was captured and held prisoner. They sent word to my father that they had me and to come to Patheos."

"Did he?" Michalus asked, seemingly fascinated by the story.

"He did," Guinevere replied, head downcast. "They kept me hidden away and forced him to create the library, linking it to another place so their precious books would be safe..."

"Ah," Michalus interrupted, bobbing his head. "That was back when warlocks and channelers were still banned in all civilized cities."

Guinevere nodded. "Exactly. He did as they asked and once it was completed - or nearly so - he demanded to see me before he put the final touches on it. He told them he wanted to make sure I was still alive."

"Did they let him see you?" Nia asked.

"They did," she replied. "They brought me up to the front of the library where he was about to put the final crystal into the doorway. He looked at me, told me he loved me and then... poof... he portaled me to the river nearby. The next thing I knew, I was blasted off my feet by an explosion from the city."

The warrior woman paused then, a single tear falling from her left eye. No one spoke and the silence stretched on until she finally broke it.

"When I picked myself up and looked towards the city," she said, a faraway look in her eyes. "There was a... cloud... shaped like a mushroom... rising above the city. I started back to the city right away and found it the way you saw it - devastation everywhere. Everywhere but the library."

"You believe he was killed in the explosion," Ethan said, more of a statement than a question.

Guinevere sniffed and wiped away the lone tear from her eye. "He's dead. If he wasn't, he would have found me.

He had plenty of time since then to find me... but he didn't. No, he's gone.

"That's when I sought out my son... Mordred," she told them. "He was the only family I had left."

Everyone was silent for another long moment until Guinevere chuckled mirthlessly at the pile of armor on the ground. "I haven't even started putting on my armor yet."

Reaching down, she began to strap on her armor, piece by piece. Ethan motioned the others to leave her in peace and gather their own things.

Ethan pulled his trident from the boulder, looking once more at the large Chymera crystal it held. He channeled some *Mana* into the crystal and sealed up the boulder after everyone had retrieved their items. After using his previous crystal the last few days, it felt good to have the larger crystal back. Whether it was the cut or size of the crystal, he didn't know, but it really did make a difference.

Only moments afterward, he felt the familiar sensation of the hairs standing up on the back of his neck. He sighed. Someone was Scrying them... again.

Skill increase: Scrying magic +1%.

For a moment, he thought it might be the dragons. Perhaps they were looking in on them, making sure they were okay. Maybe the dragon would speak with him again using telepathy.

He waited for a few moments but nothing happened. Frowning, Ethan began to "feel" around the area until he sensed the origin point of the Scrying. Now that he'd done it once, back with Firestorm, it was easier to find this time.

Pushing his consciousness through the "hole" that the Scrying was coming from, he immediately felt disoriented as his perceptions went through a radical shift.

No longer was he looking at things from land. Instead, he was looking through what appeared to be water. Yes! He was underwater. As soon as he realized it, he got a bad feeling in the pit of his stomach.

Turning around, he stared into the eyes of a very large fishman. Without a frame of reference, he only knew it was large because there were a dozen smaller ones nearby. The small ones didn't seem to notice him - they stared up at the big one.

The big fishman did seem to notice him. Ethan saw its eyes widen at him and then narrow as it seemed to take him in. Swearing soundlessly, Ethan willed himself back into his body and severed the connection.

Skill increase: Scrying magic +1%.

As he did so, there was a jerking sensation and he was suddenly back in his own body, gasping as pain lanced through his body. There was no sense of being watched any longer, just a pain inside him.

"Ethan!" Nia cried, seeing him double over.

"I'm okay." He grimaced, pushing himself to his feet. The pain was already fading and he looked around, expecting the Scrying to start up again. There was nothing. He swore loudly.

"What happened?" Michalus asked. "You seemed to be daydreaming and then you just doubled over."

Ethan frowned. "I felt scrying. This time, I was able to scry back."

"You scried back?" Michalus asked, eyes wide. "That's extraordinary!"

"Not really," Ethan growled, looking around at the group. "I think the ones who were scrying on us the whole time... were the fishpeople."

59

———

Everyone looked towards the water. The group looked on for several minutes, hands on weapons, expecting to see fishmen climbing out of the river. But there was nothing.

"I'm going to scout the river with an elemental," Ethan told them, glancing around at his companions. "It's the only way to know for certain."

He was about to summon his water elemental when Nia's ears twitched and she looked to the forest. She cocked her head, her fox-like ears rotating. She pointed into the trees where the path entered the woods. "Horses are coming. Several."

"Orcs?" Guinevere scowled. "From the village maybe?"

"It could be anyone," Michalus suggested. "Perhaps someone from the villages we passed."

Par'karr bobbed his head. "Villagers?"

Guinevere shook her head. "Coming from a fairy and troll-infested forest?"

Michalus scratched his chin thoughtfully but then shrugged. "Without magic, they wouldn't be bothered by the fairies and it took us most of the day before we ran into trolls."

Looking around at the boulders, Ethan pointed to several large ones. "Let's hide behind these rocks and wait to see who it is."

"If it is orcs?" Nia asked, her hands still on scimitars.

"Let's hope they pass us by," he said grimly. "If they attack... we kill them."

Nia nodded with satisfaction, as did Guinevere. Michalus and Par'karr didn't appear quite as comfortable but also nodded.

"Hurry," Nia said, gesturing to the forest. "They are almost upon us."

He and his companions quickly hid behind the two largest boulders. Ethan, Par'karr and Nia hid behind the one to the right of the trail, while Guinevere and Michalus hid on the left side. They stayed low and peeked around the corner of the large rocks as they waited.

Their wait wasn't long. As Nia had predicted, the riders broke through the cover of the forest within two minutes. Or should he say, the rider.

Leading nearly half a dozen empty horses was a single rider, an orc. As the orc got closer, he slowed down, looking around the area. That was when Ethan recognized both the rider and the horses. Standing up, Ethan waved and called out a greeting. "Drorm!"

The orc flinched in his saddle, his head snapping to where Ethan had just stepped out from behind the boulder. Drorm relaxed slightly when he saw Ethan, urging his horse towards the boulder.

"You must mount up!" Drorm called out as he got closer. "They are..."

"More horses!" Nia hissed, her ears twitching. "Many more! Coming quickly!"

"Brodtha and a dozen of her troops are right behind me!" Drorm yelled.

"Didn't the dragon tell them not to kill us?" Michalus asked.

Drorm's brow wrinkled in confusion as he looked at the wizard like he was crazy. "Bal'Furtun? Talk to us? No, the dragon did not say anything. Was it supposed to?"

Everyone looked at Ethan, who shrugged. "Firestorm did say cities. The village was probably too small for him to really think about."

Guinevere rolled her eyes. "So Brodtha still wants to kill us?"

"Does that mean you talked to the dragon?" Drorm asked quickly. He cast a worried glance over his shoulder towards the trees. "You know why the Bal'Furtun is attacking us?"

"It's a long story," Ethan said, walking towards his horse. "We can talk about it once we get someplace safe."

"They are almost here," Nia growled. "They are moving quickly."

Drorm growled. "They are pushing their horses too hard! They will kill them!"

"But they've managed to catch up to you," Guinevere snarled.

As the warrior woman spoke the words, over a dozen

orcs on horseback came thundering out of the forest. Ethan recognized the lead orc as Brodtha and saw that her eyes widened in recognition as she saw them. Yet oddly, she didn't slow.

Instead, the female commander spurred her horse faster and thundered past them. As she went by, Ethan thought he saw a wicked grin on her face. The faces of the other orcs who followed her looked fearful. He thought it was an odd combination until he heard Nia cry out. "Trolls!"

Spinning, Ethan saw that his wife was right. Emerging from the forest, galloping on all fours like beasts, were at least a dozen trolls. As they broke cover, the trolls skidded to a halt, standing up and howling as they looked from Brodtha and her fleeing horses to Ethan's smaller group.

Ethan cursed, glancing up at Drorm. "You'd better move the horses behind the boulder! Otherwise, they'll go for them first!"

"Maybe we should let them!" the big orc replied, his head turning to look at the trolls. The horses were whinnying and stomped nervously at the ground to get away from the trolls.

The creatures were breathing heavily and pounding their chests like apes. Ethan guessed that they must be out of breath from chasing the horses. It was probably the only reason they hadn't attacked yet. But that wouldn't last long.

"Move the horses slowly," Ethan told Drorm. "Try not to attract attention. If they think they're about to bolt, they may charge."

The big orc looked back at the trolls and nodded. Then, slowly, he walked his horse behind the boulder.

"Ethan!" Nia hissed. "Look!"

Looking away from the trolls, to his wife, he followed her outstretched finger to what she was pointing at.

A hundred yards or so down the road, Brodtha and her orcs had stopped. The group had turned their horses and were now facing Ethan and his group - as well as the trolls.

"Are they coming back to help?" he asked aloud, not really believing it.

From his side, he heard Drorm snort as he slipped off his horse and began tying them to a downed tree. "No, she's making sure they kill us before she kills them - or lets them run back into the forest."

Par'karr growled. "No help?! Bad orc!"

Guinevere and Michalus, crouched low, made their way to Ethan and the others. The warrior woman looked over Drorm. "I have to admit, I wasn't sure we'd see you again."

Drorm just scowled and looked over at the trolls. "You may not see me much longer. That is a lot of trolls."

Michalus looked from the trolls to the orcs. "Am I to understand that the orcs are going to stand back and let us fight the trolls on our own?"

"They are honorless curs!" Nia spat, keeping a wary eye on the trolls.

"If we start to win, can we expect them to stab us in the back - literally in this case - while we are fighting?" Guinevere asked Drorm.

Drorm's face flushed but his head swiveled to take in

the line of orcs on horses. He deflated slightly. "I don't know what their orders were, but I wouldn't put it past them."

"They will let the trolls weaken us." Ethan frowned. "Let us use up our mana on them, then they'll attack."

"It's what I'd do," Guinevere said, shrugging as Ethan frowned at her. "Hey, with two wizards in the party, they probably know they don't have a chance against us in a straight up fight. Maybe with the rest of them, they might have - just from sheer numbers."

"I think Brodtha suspected that I was going to meet you," Drorm said, looking back at the female commander. "But just in case, she left the rest of the troops at the village if you returned."

"And bring trolls," Par'karr pointed out.

"I'm sure that was more of an accident that anything else," Drorm said. "The trolls must have caught our scent and then followed us through the night. I was in the lead, so I never even noticed them."

"But Brodtha over there did," Guinevere snickered. "And decided to bring them along, rather than deal with them."

"It does appear that way," the big orc admitted.

"Too much talk," Nia growled. "How are we planning to deal with the trolls? And then the orcs?"

All eyes turned to Ethan and he tried to quickly formulate a plan that they would live through. As he did, Michalus cleared his throat.

"Not that I disagree with the upcoming battle," the wizard interjected, "but Ethan, you could just portal us all away. There's no need for us to fight either the trolls or the orcs."

The group looked at each other and then to Ethan. He shrugged. "I can do that..."

Ethan trailed off as things suddenly went quiet. "Did it just get real quiet?"

As one, the group turned towards the trolls. No longer were the creatures panting and banging their fists into their chest. Instead, they all stood, looking at Ethan's group. Then, with a blood-curling roar from the largest troll in the center, they all charged forward.

60

Thinking back to his days playing tabletop roleplaying games and given that the trolls were charging in an almost straight line, the words "Wall of Fire" popped into his head. Without a second thought, Ethan raised the trident in what he hoped was a dramatic gesture. He channeled fire at the same time.

With a whoosh, a wall of fire that spanned the length of the charging line of trolls suddenly sprang up directly in front of the running horde. A gasp went up from his companions, as well as the orcs behind them.

The trolls had been running full force. The sudden appearance of the wall just in front of them gave them no chance to change direction. Unable to stop in time, the trolls ran, stumbled or fell through the fiery wall.

You critically burn Forest Troll for 31 fire damage.

You critically burn Forest Troll for 28 fire damage.

You critically burn Forest Troll for 34 fire damage.

You critically burn Forest Troll for 33 fire damage.

You critically burn Forest Troll Alpha for 29 fire damage.

You critically burn Forest Troll for 30 fire damage.

You critically burn Forest Troll for 28 fire damage.

You critically burn Forest Troll for 33 fire damage.

You critically burn Forest Troll for 32 fire damage.

You critically burn Forest Troll for 29 fire damage.

You critically burn Forest Troll for 31 fire damage.

You critically burn Forest Troll for 33 fire damage.

At the same time the wall sprang into existence, Ethan felt a surge of *Mana* leave him. As the wall of fire winked out of existence, he quickly brought up his HUD.

Mana: 78

He grimaced as he did the mental math. The wall of fire had used nearly a third of his *Mana*! He needed to be careful since he knew he had to save some for the orcs, as well.

On the other hand, it might just have been worth it. Ethan stared out at the trolls howling as they tried to put out the flames that had ignited in their hair and leather loincloths.

"Quick! While they are distracted!" Nia yelled and charged forward.

"Stab them through the heart or the head, decapitate them or slash their throats!" Guinevere yelled as she joined the fray. "They heal quickly from anything else!"

Nia, Guinevere and Drorm all charged out at the trolls, but were quickly left behind by Par'karr's rabbits. The large red-eyed creatures raced forward with frightening speed and embedded their unicorn-like horns into the head of one of the rolling trolls. The creature stiffened and then went limp as the rabbits struggled to pull their horns out of its head.

At the same time, there was a double thud as the kobold let loose with a double shot from the magical shotgun. Unfortunately, the troll he'd been shooting at had been rolling and both shots missed. Par'karr growled and immediately began reloading the weapon with two more stones.

Michalus hadn't been idle either. The wizard was tossing balls of fire around at the wounded trolls. While not as spectacular as the wall of fire Ethan had conjured, they probably weren't using up a third of the elf's *Mana* either.

Ethan saw a few experience messages as the others began killing the recovering trolls, but ignored them for the moment. He followed Michalus's example and began flinging fiery darts at the trolls who were starting to rise.

> *You burn Forest Troll for 23 fire damage.*
> *You burn Forest Troll for 19 fire damage.*
> *You burn Forest Troll for 22 fire damage.*

The trolls hit by his flaming missiles squealed in pain but didn't stay down. As he looked around, he saw that four or five were unmoving. That left seven who were starting to get to their feet. And that included the big one Ethan guessed was the alpha of the pack.

"Focus on the big one!" Ethan yelled out and pointed his trident at the large troll. He sent another blast of fire just as Par'karr got off a single shot with his magical weapon. At the same time, Michalus hit the thing in the head with a fiery ball.

The troll bellowed in pain and anger but was momentarily blinded by Michalus's fireball to the head. The creature was forced to close its eyes as it swatted at its face with its huge hands, trying to extinguish its large, bushy eyebrows which had caught fire. That was all the distraction Par'karr's rabbits needed.

Racing in, the kobold's demon rabbits closed the distance and then leaped up and embedded their horns in the alpha's groin. The creature's closed eyes snapped open as its mouth opened in an "O" shape. A strangled gasp escaped the wounded creature, followed by a pitiful wail.

Ethan and Michalus both hit its face again with fireballs just as Nia danced between two other trolls. Dodging in, she spun her small body in a circle with both blades outstretched. The spinning foxgirl's scimitars sliced through the alpha's neck and its ugly head toppled to the ground.

There was a momentary break in the fighting as the trolls saw their alpha fall headlessly to the ground. There were now only six left and they seemed to realize that the tide had turned. Not only were half their number dead, but their leader was dead too.

The remaining trolls gave some angry howls and growls and then turned and fled into the forest. Ethan might have thrown some fireballs after them but he knew he needed to conserve his *Mana*. There were still the orcs to deal with.

"That was unexpected!" Brodtha's voice yelled out. "But I'm afraid..."

"That you have to kill us because we talked to the dragon... blah... blah... blah..." Ethan interrupted, causing the female orc's face to go crimson. "Don't you even want to know what the dragon said?"

Brodtha's angry glare faltered for a moment. He guessed her orders had been to get the information first, then kill them. Otherwise, what would be the point of even sending them to the mountain if they were going to kill them before they found out the answer.

The orc commander seemed to realize it too. "What did the dragon tell you?"

Ethan shook his head. "I'll tell the shamans when I see them."

"You will tell me now!" the commander ordered. "Or I will have my troops kill your companions."

"I don't think so," Ethan retorted. "You saw what we did to the trolls."

There was some grumbling from her troops. They'd seen what Ethan's group had done and despite their leader's bravado, they weren't in a hurry to go against two wizards and the rest of his group.

"You overestimate your abilities," Brodtha bellowed back at him. "We are not undisciplined animals like the trolls. We will not waver in our duty."

"Do not do this," Drorm yelled out. "They are our allies."

"I have my orders." Brodtha snorted. "You don't have to throw away everything you worked for. Leave the others to us and leave, Drorm. The orders don't apply to you. Just them."

Drorm looked from Brodtha to Ethan and the group. He seemed to be reconsidering his position but then shook his head. "Ethan and his friends have proven themselves true allies. Your orders are wrong and I will fight alongside them."

Brodtha seemed to give an uncharacteristic sigh, before a look of resignation came over her face. "You made your choice. You have betrayed your oath and sided with enemies of the orcs!"

"None of us are enemies..." Drorm shouted but the orc commander cut him off with a gesture.

"I gave you a chance!" Brodtha chuckled. "That's what I'll tell your mother when she asks how you died. It's on your head now!"

While they were talking, Ethan quickly looked at his stats.

Mana: 54

He was at 50% of his *Mana*. That didn't leave him much against so many orcs. Sadly, Brodtha was right. These were seasoned soldiers. And she was a commander. Chances are, she'd already given them orders to target Michalus and him first.

That was probably their plan. It certainly would be his plan, if he were the commander. Once the orcs managed to kill both of them, he doubted the others would last much longer with the superior numbers against them.

"I can create a portal out of here," Ethan said quietly.

"We should kill the honorless curs!" Nia spat.

"Ethan's right," Guinevere said. "These orcs are trained warriors. We might be able to take them, but I don't think all of us will make it out alive."

"She's right," Drorm said with resignation. "These are trained warriors. They will give us no quarter."

"Par'karr okay with portal," the kobold squeaked.

Ethan realized their time had run out with a single word that echoed across the distance between them.

"Charge!" screamed Brodtha and as one the orcs spurred their mounts into a charge.

Ethan cursed and was about to raise another wall of fire when the nearby water exploded and dozens of fishmen began springing out of the water.

61

The sudden appearance of the Akugyo startled the charging horses, who were galloping near the river. Their riders struggled to control the panicked mounts but the horses veered away from the fishmen. This caused them to slam into the horses nearby, which in turn caused them to crash into yet other riders.

In moments, the charging line dissolved into chaos as three horses and riders went down. Two of which were trampled by others, causing both of those horses to falter and send their riders flying.

Most of the other orcs, including Brodtha, managed to avoid the fallen horses and rein their mounts in. They had just come to a stop when Ethan felt a strong surge of *Water* magic. A ball of white crystal flew from somewhere in the river into the midst of the orcs and exploded into fragments of ice.

Once again, the orcs dissolved into chaos. Ethan saw splashes of blood as ice peppered the orcs and horses. The screams of orcs and the whinnies of the horses filled the air and several more horses and orcs fell. No sooner had the orcs began to recover from the exploding ice ball when the Akugyo managed to reach them.

Fighting a mounted opponent would normally be difficult. The height difference and the sheer weight of the horse gave the rider an advantage most times. But not this time.

The recovering orcs were in disarray and the long tridents of the fishmen were practically like spears and gave them the reach to impale the riders. A few orcs managed to spur their horses away from the melee but the others were cut down.

His group had been watching in stunned silence but Nia elbowed him. "What do we do? There are too many of them!"

Ethan looked at the river and saw that more fishmen were emerging from the water. With a quick glance he counted at least twenty of the fishmen that he could see. Plus, there was also a Akugyo wizard who was staying back in the water.

"That's a lot of fishmen," Guinevere agreed. "Discretion IS the better part of val..."

"Brodtha!" Drorm bellowed suddenly, interrupting the warrior woman.

They turned to see Brodtha, who had managed to escape the initial onslaughts, go down as one of the fishmen impaled her horse. Unfortunately for the attacker, the horse fell on top of it, crushing it.

Drorm started forward but Guinevere grabbed his arm, stopping him. "It's too late."

They saw she was right. At least three other fishmen moved in, stabbing the orc with their tridents until she stopped moving.

"Curse them!" Drorm spat.

Ethan wasn't really sure where his concern was coming from. Hadn't the female orc been about to kill them all? Why had he been about to rush to her defense?

The last of the orcs went down and was quickly killed, leaving twenty fishmen staring at Ethan and his group. He cursed. Guinevere and Nia were right. There were too many.

"Get ready! I'm opening a portal," he told his companions. The group nodded in relief, none of them liking the odds they now faced.

An idea came to him then and he spun towards Michalus. "The rune stick I gave you! Throw it over there!

"We can always return when they're gone." Ethan pointed to the area opposite from the river. Leaving the runestick would give him an anchor point to open a portal back here later. By then, hopefully the fishmen would be gone.

Nodding, Michalus began fumbling with his belt.

Focusing his will on the runes back in Arthur's tomb, Ethan began to open a portal. He felt it forming, but then something happened. He felt a surge of portal magic from the river. The magic intersected his own portal magic and he suddenly got a really bad feeling.

Boom! There was a magic detonation from the forming portal that sent everyone sprawling backwards.

You take 21 points of magic damage.

Painfully, Ethan pushed himself to his feet. His ears were ringing and he blinked his eyes to clear his vision. It took a moment for him to see. When he did finally look around, he saw a ten-foot crater where the portal had been about to open.

"Wha-? What happen?" Par'karr groaned.

"Did your portal do that?" Michalus asked, blinking his own eyes.

The voices were muffled to Ethan's ringing ears so he shouted back. "Something interfered with the portal. I think they tried to open a portal on top of my portal - or in it. I'm not really sure."

"Oh my," Michalus murmured. "Opening a portal within a portal could cause..."

"An explosion?" Drorm growled. "Yes. I figured that out."

"Then we are trapped here?" Nia said, her face dark as she looked at the incoming fishmen.

Ethan cursed. "Maybe not. If I can disable the fishman wizard, we can still get out of here."

"How?" Guinevere demanded, wiping blood from her eyes. The warrior woman had a gash in her forehead that must have come from hitting something when they were blown back.

He knew he couldn't use most of his spells since he couldn't actually see where the wizard was. The river was too far away now for a water elemental and other elementals would be ineffective in the water.

Yet, there was one thing he could use that didn't require line of sight. Something he'd used against the

Doemenagg in Camelot. It had worked then, if not exactly the way he had thought.

"Mental magic," Ethan replied, tapping the side of his head. "Just keep them busy."

"Sure," Guinevere said sourly. "We'll just keep them busy."

"We'll do what we can," Michalus said and raised his staff.

Ethan nodded and then quickly sent his consciousness out towards the river. As he did so, he picked up on the minds of the approaching Akugyo. Knowing none of them were his target, he raced past them at the speed of thought. Then, he came to the river.

While he couldn't "see" into the river, he did sense a multitude of minds in the river. Some were dim compared to the others. Given the way and the speed that the minds were moving, Ethan guessed those were sharks. Then there were a dozen more Akugyo, probably soldiers. But one of the minds burned much brighter than the others. The wizard.

Skill increase: Mental Magic +1%.

Launching himself at the brighter mind, Ethan clamped down his will on it. Or, at least, that's what he had intended to do. The will slithered away from him, like a fish or an eel, making it difficult to grasp. At the same time, Ethan knew that the wizard had become aware of him.

Skill increase: Mental Magic +1%.

"It knows what I'm doing," Ethan said through gritted teeth.

Sensing the wizard was about to cast something, Ethan mentally retreated from the creature and instead decided to distract it.

Launching his mind at one of the sharks, Ethan seized control of it with no problem at all. He sensed the creature's unrelenting hunger and stoked it to an unbearable level before pointing him at the fishmen.

Skill increase: Mental Magic +1%.
Skill increase: Mental Magic +1%.

The whole process had taken a second but in that time, the wizard had launched some sort of magic outside the water.

Ethan grunted as he felt something pierce his arm. Staying outside his body, he did manage to see the message in his HUD - which was somehow with him in his disembodied form.

King Quo'Plo'coo'Blup freezes you for 18 ice damage.

Reading the message a second time, Ethan felt his mind's eye grow wide. The wizard was a king?! A king of the fishpeople? Why the heck was it attacking them? Was this some sort of surface invasion?

Cursing to himself, Ethan sensed the confusion his rogue shark had created and quickly hopped from shark to shark, sending the ten huge sharks into a feeding frenzy. The manipulated creatures began attacking fishmen and shark alike. Ethan sensed magic from the king, but this time it was directed into the water. Most likely at the attacking sharks.

With the king distracted, Ethan once again launched himself at the king's mind. The king tried to slither away again but wasn't quite fast enough.

"Hurry, Ethan!" part of his mind heard Nia shout.

With a massive force of will, Ethan clamped down on the king's mind. He immediately felt the king resisting him but, unlike the Doemenagg queen, he guessed it didn't know *Mental* magic. At least, it hadn't tried any sort of counter attack.

"Ethan!" he heard Par'karr scream and knew he didn't have much time.

CALL OFF YOUR FORCES! Ethan mentally shouted into the creature's brain.

The king's mind stopped squirming and then Ethan heard a voice in his own mind. *Return what you have stolen.*

Ethan blinked. Or rather, he would have blinked if he had been in his body. *What are you talking about? We didn't steal anything.*

The trident! Give it back to me! the king demanded.

Confused, a bit angry, Ethan responded. *Wait?! All of these attacks have been about the stupid trident?!*

Yes! Return it! the king demanded again.

"Nia is down!" part of Ethan heard and his blood went cold. Concern and anger flooded into him and he poured it all into his mental attack against the king, raking his emotions across the king's mind like claws. He felt his enemy's mind stagger.

You hit King Quo'Plo'coo'Blup for 31 mental damage.

Release me and I will call off my soldiers, the king cried out.

He briefly considered continuing his attack but Nia could be dying - possibly even dead. He needed to check. He needed to check now!

Fine! Ethan bellowed mentally. *But if you try anything I will rip your mind to shreds in the most painful way I possibly can.*

I will call them off, the king said weakly.

Releasing the king, Ethan snapped himself back to his body and into the chaotic melee. His friends had been defending him and were all bloody. At least ten Akugyo lay dead at their feet, but more were pressing in.

On the ground, leaning against his leg was Nia. She was clutching a nasty-looking wound in her stomach with one hand, while still weakly fending off attacks with the scimitar in her other hand.

Feeling his anger boiling over at the sight of his injured wife, Ethan summoned the magic to burn these fishmen alive. He was about to release it when three blasts from a horn sounded from the river. The fishmen stopped attacking and took several steps back, glancing towards the river.

Not wasting the opportunity, Ethan let the magic he had been summoning fade and fumbled for the portal pouch that led to the Grail. "Hang in there, Nia!"

Pulling it free and summoning water into it at the same time, he bent down and put the cup to her lips.

Nia winced as the magic healed her and then blinked up at him and smiled.

"Why did they stop?" Guinevere asked, her eyes darting around at the fishmen.

Seeing Par'karr had a grave wound in his leg, Ethan handed the goblet to the kobold, who took it eagerly.

"I think I have a temporary truce with their king," Ethan replied.

"Their king?" Michalus asked. The wizard was bloody as well, but Ethan thought most of the blood wasn't his.

"Give me a second," Ethan replied. "I need to continue my conversation with him."

Reaching out again, Ethan easily found the king's mind. This time, instead of an attack, he just opened a channel for communication.

Thank you for calling off your soldiers, he told the king.

Will you return the trident? the king asked him. His tone was insistent but wary.

You have received a new quest "Trident of the Kings"

King Quo'Plo'coo'Blup has told you that the trident is the symbol of power for his people. He has asked you to return the trident to him. Alternatively, you could keep the powerful artifact for yourself.

Return Trident of the Kings to King Quo'Plo'coo'Blup.

Trident of the Kings returned (0/1).

> *Reward: 1000 experience, +1000 reputation with Reef Clan*
> *Keep Trident of the Kings.*
> *Reward: Trident, -1000 reputation with Reef Clan*
> *Accept quest (yes or no)?*

Ethan briefly read the quest and accepted it. It wasn't like he had much of a choice.

What is so special about this accursed trident that you keep attacking me and my friends? Ethan demanded.

It is the symbol of my power, the king replied. *It was taken by my, shall we say, wayward son.*

Ethan cursed inwardly. He'd killed the king's son. That wasn't good. *Uh... sorry for killing your son, but he started it.*

The king made a dismissive noise. *I have dozens more offspring. That son was a particular disappointment. He took the trident without permission and then lost it. In death he is even more of a disappointment than he was in life.*

Uh... okay, Ethan muttered mentally. He wasn't sure how to respond to that but he remembered that fish laid tons of eggs at a time; maybe fishmen reproduced the same way.

But the trident has been the symbol of our kings for generations, the king said more forcefully. *We must have it back.*

Ethan sighed inwardly. The Chymera crystal in the trident was the largest and most well cut Michalus had ever seen. Channeling magic through it was so much easier. He didn't really want to give it up.

At the same time, it was something important to an entire race of people. Was it really right to withhold from them - even if they had attacked him first? Then again, it had been a rogue fishman who had attacked them, not the fishpeople in general.

Remembering the Scrying, Ethan asked another question. *It was you who was scrying on us?*

Yes, the king admitted. *I was able to scry the trident and send my forces to intercept you. Unfortunately, you proved too much for them. I was forced to come myself.*

If I give you the trident, Ethan asked, *what then?*

Then my people and I will return to the depths, the king replied. He seemed to sense Ethan's unasked question. *We will not bother you or your people again.*

Very well, Ethan said. *I will return it.*

Thank you, the king said.

As an afterthought, Ethan added. *Next time, you might just want to ask first, before going to war over it.*

Hmm, was the king's only reply.

Cutting his mental link with the king, Ethan blinked his eyes back in his body. With a last look at the trident, Ethan channeled *Air* and sent the trident soaring over the heads of the fishmen, and into the river.

Just before the trident was about to hit the water, a watery hand formed from the river and caught it. The hand held it for a moment before disappearing with the trident beneath the surface.

```
Quest Complete.
    Trident of the Kings
    Return Trident of the Kings to
King Quo'Plo'coo'Blup.
```

Trident of the Kings returned (1/1).

Reward: 1000 experience, +1000 reputation with Reef Clan

You gain 1000 experience.

You gain +1000 reputation with Reef Clan.

You gain +1 Fame.

Ethan saw another Akugyo rise from the water with a conch shell and blow a long blast, followed by two short blasts. As the sound echoed through the area, the fishmen turned and began shambling back to the river.

The group watched them go. Within a few minutes, they had all disappeared back into the river. Another minute later, Ethan saw shark fins heading back out to sea.

"Fishmen gone?" Par'karr asked, wiping blood from his scaly head.

"I think so," Ethan replied.

"I think some explanation is in order," Guinevere said, turning to him and the others nodded their agreement.

Ethan realized all of his conversation had happened mentally. His companions hadn't heard any of it, nor seen the chaos he'd set into motion under the surface. With a mirthless chuckle, he began relating his conversation with the king of the fishpeople.

62

"So, all of the attacks from the Akugyo were because of the trident?" Michalus asked as the group rode towards the city.

At Drorm's insistence, they'd buried the orc bodies but left the fishmen and trolls to rot or, more likely, to be eaten by scavengers. They'd picked up a few supplies from the dead horses, but hadn't taken any other loot from the Akugyo or the orcs.

Once they were done with the burials and looting, they'd decided to head to the city and see if the dragon had kept his word and told the shamans not to kill them. If not, Ethan was ready to give up on seeing Excalibur.

At this point, the dragons were heading south to get their revenge on the Doemenagg. Given how powerful the dragons were, he didn't think the insect creatures stood a chance.

If that were the case, then having Excalibur to fight them seemed like a moot point. He still wanted to see the enchantments on the blade, if possible. But now it was mostly academic and certainly not worth risking his companions over again.

"Ethan?" Michalus prompted.

Realizing the wizard was still waiting for an answer, Ethan turned back towards Michalus. "It seems that way. The king really wanted that trident back."

"The Chymera crystal was certainly the largest and well cut I've seen, but how many lives did they throw away to get it back? I hardly think it's worth it," Michalus responded.

"I got the feeling that there was some sort of sentimental or perhaps official component to it," Ethan said. "I think it was more of a symbol of power than anything else."

"Like a human king's crown?" Drorm asked. "It has no power in itself, but it is a symbol of the power of the king. Losing it would make the king look weak."

"So all of those fishmen died because the king's bratty son decided to steal Daddy's trident and go kill some humans," Guinevere snickered.

"It was a matter of honor," Nia said, speaking for the first time since they'd left the scene of their battle. "They were honor bound to retrieve the trident."

"I've lived a long time, and it seems all honor is good for, is getting you into trouble," Guinevere said with a sigh. Her voice grew quiet and sad. "Or getting you killed."

The conversation stalled then and they continued towards the city. They stopped for lunch and Ethan used his water elemental to get some fish from the river. Nia cooked them over a campfire and then they all ate.

"After those rations," Michalus commented as he took a bite of his steaming fish, "a nice cooked meal really hits the spot."

"Fish good!" Par'karr agreed between chews.

"If the dragon has commanded that you should not be harmed," Drorm said, "you may enjoy a few meals in the city before you leave."

"I wouldn't mind a day or two of downtime," Guinevere said. "It's been a long, exhausting few days. Provided, of course, that the orcs aren't trying to kill us."

Drorm shook his head. "If the dragon - I guess I should say dragons - have spoken, no one will dare attack you."

Guinevere raised an eyebrow. "That didn't stop Brodtha."

A flicker of emotion played over Drorm's face and he let out a long breath. "I do not believe the dragon spoke to those in the village. Even if it did, they were chasing after me at the time."

"Why were they even chasing you?" Ethan asked. "I mean, the kill order didn't include you, right?"

Drorm was quiet for a moment, staring into the fire. Finally, he looked up. "Brodtha was my aunt."

Everyone looked at Drorm in stunned silence.

"Your aunt?" Ethan finally managed. "Brodtha was your aunt?"

Drorm nodded.

"And she was still going to kill you?" Guinevere asked.

Drorm nodded again and then sighed. "My mother and Brodtha had a falling out when my mother became a shaman. Brodtha had always been the better warrior and had been the favored daughter with a promising career in the military..."

"Until your mom became a shaman," Ethan guessed.

"Exactly," Drorm agreed. "Once my mother became a shaman, everything changed. In our culture, the shamans rule. In one swoop, my mother was elevated above her sister."

"And Brodtha resented her for it," Guinevere added with a knowing nod.

Drorm was quiet again, his eyes dropping back to the fire as emotions played across his face. "Brodtha and my mother grew further and further apart. At some point, my mother suspected Brodtha was starting rumors about her behind her back."

"Against her own sister?" Nia asked, disapproval showing on her face.

"That's what my mother said," Drorm answered, "but no one could ever prove anything. Eventually my mother had enough of it and assigned her to the mountain village."

"Out in the middle of nowhere, where she can't do any harm," Guinevere smirked. "That's what I would have done."

"She'd been there for over ten years," Drorm said. "Much longer than any other commander before her."

"So it was more like permanent exile," Ethan said. "No wonder she wanted to kill you."

Drorm shook his head. "No, you do not understand."

Everyone looked at Drorm again. Ethan shrugged. "She didn't try to kill you?"

"At the end, maybe," Drorm admitted. "But she gave me a chance to abandon you and save my honor."

"But her orders were not honorable," Nia pointed out.

Drorm sighed. "I know. That is why I couldn't let them carry them out. Even if it meant I was exiled from my people."

"So, wait," Ethan interrupted. "Are you saying Brodtha, your aunt, was trying to help you?"

"Yes," Drorm answered. "That's why she went after me. She knew I would help you and was trying to save me from throwing my career away."

"She was trying to stop you from dishonoring yourself," Nia noted with approval.

"Yes," Drorm acknowledged. "At least, dishonor myself from her point of view."

"But you were the honorable one," Nia told him with a nod.

Drorm snorted. "The others will not see it that way. I fought against orcs executing lawful orders. I am responsible for the death of a commander. I will face death or exile."

"Technically," Michalus broke in, holding up a finger. "You did not fight against them."

"What?" Drorm asked. "I sided with you..."

"But you did not fight them," Michalus continued. "Nor are you responsible for her or the others' deaths."

"But..." Drorm started but Ethan cut him off with a grin.

"Michalus is right!" Ethan said excitedly. "You didn't do anything. The fishmen killed them - through no fault of your own."

"But..." Drorm opened his mouth to rebut the argument but then closed it. He cocked his head, lost in thought for a moment. Finally, he nodded. "This is all true. But, I did defy the orders."

"Orders which the dragons themselves countermanded," Guinevere pointed out. "And assuming the shamans wish to stay in their good graces, then they would have countermanded them, as well."

Drorm nodded. "The shamans would never do anything to anger the dragon...uh... dragons."

"You keep saying 'dragon,' singular," Ethan said, noticing the slip. "Even before, it was all about Firestorm, I mean, Bal'Furtun. What about the other dragon? The green one? Why does no one mention that one?"

Ethan realized he'd never gotten a pronounceable name for the female dragon and Firestorm had never offered a human pronounceable name.

"Honestly," Drorm replied with a shrug. "I did not know there was a second dragon in the mountain. No one does - except perhaps the shamans who have visited Bal'Furtun."

"Wait." Ethan shook his head. "Your people have been going to the mountain for over a thousand years and in all that time, you never knew there was a second dragon?"

Drorm shrugged again. "We knew of a second dragon, a green dragon like you mentioned, but we did not know it was Bal'Furtun's mate. A green dragon has been spotted throughout the decades and many stories have arisen from the sightings."

"Stories?" Par'karr squeaked.

"Some believe the green dragon is actually Bal'Furtun,

others believe it was a rival dragon and Bal'Furtun keeps us safe from it... there are many stories," Drorm replied. He looked thoughtful. "I believe there is actually a story that the green dragon, sometimes called Nom'Chal'Mo, or Forestwing, is actually the mate of Bal'Furtun."

"I find that strange," Ethan said. "This entire time, no one really knew about the green dragon, uh... Forestwing."

"As I said," Drorm retorted. "The shamans may have known, and they keep their secrets."

"Indeed," Ethan agreed, thinking of the secret orders to kill them. "I think I will have a little chat with them when I see them again."

The conversation stalled again and they realized they were all done with their meal. By mutual consent, they began packing up their stuff and retrieved the horses. Within a few minutes, they were back on the road, headed towards the city.

63

Once they were back on the road that paralleled the river, the group picked up their pace. Ethan's goal was to make it to the city before nightfall. He wasn't sure whether the dragons had stopped at the city and what the orcs' reaction would be if they had.

His plan was to wait outside the city until nightfall and then send Drorm in to see what the state of affairs was. If they weren't kill on sight, they'd go ahead into the city. If they were? At this point, Ethan was ready to give up on Excalibur. He would portal them back to Hawkshead and be done with it.

~

THEY MADE good time on the road. In the late afternoon, the group arrived just outside the city. But, they were in for a surprise. Lined up across the road, several hundred yards in front of the gate, were a half dozen orcs on horseback.

Ethan signalled the group to halt and looked to Drorm. Before he could ask the orc about their welcoming party, Drorm spoke.

"It is the shamans," he started flatly.

Straining his eyes, Ethan couldn't make out any real details on the orcs. "Are you sure?"

Drorm snorted. "Of course. I recognize my mother."

Even as Drorm mentioned his mother, one of the figures spurred their horse forward slowly. Ethan frowned at the line of orc shamans.

"Be ready, Michalus," Ethan told the wizard. "If they attack, block everything you can while I open a portal."

The elf nodded. "I will do my best."

"My mother approaches," Drorm told them.

The figure continued to get closer and Ethan was in for a bit of a shock. Drorm's mother, Unandum Thunderflame, looked different in the daylight as she had in the dimly lit room he'd first met her. The resemblance between her and Brodtha was definitely more pronounced. It was easy to see now that they were sisters.

Ethan frowned as he thought of Brodtha. He wondered if there would be any repercussions to them for the commander's death. That was all they needed.

Unandum continued her horse's slow pace until they were about twenty feet apart, then came to a halt. Everyone was quiet for a long moment before the shaman finally spoke.

"You have succeeded in talking with the dragon," Unandum said. Ethan noticed it wasn't a question. She took a deep breath and let it out. "Bal'Furtun has named you Dragonfriend. No orc will dare harm you, lest we incur the dragon's wrath."

Ethan felt himself relax a bit but he suppressed the smile that wanted to come to his face. The dragon had stopped by the city and obviously told them not to harm Ethan and his friends. Hopefully, that meant there wouldn't be any trouble.

"So you've rescinded the order to have us killed?" Ethan growled.

Unandum gave Drorm an accusatory look and Ethan realized she believed that her son had betrayed them. Knowing Drorm, he'd probably confess to it too.

Drorm started to open his mouth but Ethan preempted him. "Brodtha tried to kill us after we spoke to the dragon. I got the strangest feeling that you ordered it."

Turning her attention back to Ethan, Drorm's mother didn't even try to deny it. "It is our way. The dragon and its teaching are for the orcs only."

Ethan gave the orc a sour look. "So you say. But the dragon doesn't feel the same way."

"The dragon has taught us for generations, and only us," Unandum retorted.

"You mean, like this," Ethan said, pulling his shirt open to reveal the glowing sigil on his chest.

Unandum gasped and from the corner of his eye, Ethan saw the other shamans shift uneasily. Petty as it was, he reveled in their discomfort.

"The dragon gave you the mark?" Drorm asked, eyes glued to the mark.

"Yes," Ethan replied, unsure of the significance.

Drorm spun towards his mother. "You know what this means!"

The female orc shook her head. "No, it cannot be!"

"It is the law!" Drorm growled, steel in his voice. "Even the shamans are not above the law."

"What law?" Ethan asked, looking from Drorm to his mother.

"He is not orc!" Unandum spat.

"Does the law specify he must be an orc?" his friend asked triumphantly.

Drorm's mother snapped her mouth shut as she seethed, eyes narrowed at Ethan. She looked like she wanted to attack Ethan and he wondered if the dragon's word would keep them safe.

Tired of not knowing what was going on, Ethan turned to Drorm. "What law? What is going on?"

"Tell him, Mother," the big orc demanded. "Tell him the law."

Unandum gave her son a nasty look but then sighed. Her shoulders drooped and shook her head. "The first in every generation to be given the mark... is given the office and title of High Shaman."

Ethan shrugged and gestured at Unandum and the other shamans. "I don't understand what you mean."

Obviously, these shamans had been here before him, so he wasn't sure what they were talking about. Had the dragon not given them the sigil for some reason? He thought Firestorm had said it was how he passed knowledge to the orcs - by giving them sigils.

"None of us have been taught by the dragon," Unandum growled in frustration. "The dragon has been asleep for a hundred years. I and the others were taught by the last generation, who were taught by the generation before that."

Ethan chuckled, causing Unandum to narrow her eyes again at him. "So what? I'm high shaman?"

"Yes," the shaman said between clenched teeth. "According to our law, you are high shaman."

"Cool." Ethan grinned. "So what does that mean?"

"It means, you lead the council of shamans," she growled.

He wasn't quite sure what to make of this new development. It was obvious that high shaman was an important position. Ethan just had absolutely no desire to have anything to do with the shamans. Not that he was one to hold a grudge, but they HAD ordered him and his friends to be murdered.

"I don't want to be high shaman," Ethan announced.

"Yes, you do," Drorm said, causing his mother to glare at the big orc. "The high shaman has control over who sees the artifact - Excalibur."

That got Ethan's attention. "So... I can, you know... let myself go see it? Just like that?"

Grinning, Drorm nodded. He turned to his mother. "Isn't that right, Mother?"

"It is," growled his mother, gritting her teeth together so hard, Ethan thought he could hear them grinding.

"Cool!" Ethan grinned. "Take me to Excalibur."

"We cannot," Unandum answered quickly.

"I thought you said..." Ethan started but Drorm's mother held up her hand.

"It is not here," the shaman told him. "It is two days' ride to the south."

Ethan looked at Drorm for confirmation and the big orc nodded. "It is in a mountain tomb, to the south."

"Fine," Ethan said, looking around at his companions. They seemed as confused as he was about the turn of events. "We can stay the night in the city and then head out first thing tomorrow morning."

Unandum was silent for a moment and Ethan thought she might be about to object. Finally, the shaman nodded. "I will arrange an escort for you."

"I don't need an..." Ethan started but Drorm's mother interrupted him.

"You are Dragonfriend," the shaman said. "If any harm befalls you while you are in our lands, I will not risk the dragon's wrath. I am sure the rest of the council will agree."

Ethan looked around at his companions questioningly.

"There is safety in numbers," Nia pointed out, though she kept a wary eye on Unandum and the other shamans.

"I agree with Nia," Michalus told him. "It would be nice to have an escort through unfamiliar lands."

Par'karr just shrugged. "Orcs. No orcs. Par'karr not care."

Guinevere scowled, glaring at the shaman. "I don't trust them. After all, they did make the orders to kill us."

Unandum's face flushed in anger but she seemed to get it under control. "We were... wrong."

Guinevere snorted but shrugged at Ethan. "Like I said, I don't trust them but it's up to you."

"The others will not harm you now," Drorm assured him. "You are high shaman and you are Dragonfriend. No orc will harm you."

"You sure?" Ethan asked.

"It is as my son says," Unandum answered before Drorm would reply. "No orc would harm you and risk the wrath of the dragon - dragons now, it seems - since Bal'-Furtun was accompanied by another dragon."

"Yes," Ethan said, "that's his mate."

"Bal'Furtun's mate?" the shaman gasped. "And we have not known about her until now?"

"Not sure why the dragon didn't tell you." Ethan shrugged. "But the green dragon is his mate and has been for quite a long time by the way he was talking."

Unandum shook her head but then suddenly seemed to remember something. She looked back at Ethan. "You spoke to Bal'Furtun. Did you find out why the dragon is attacking us?"

With everything that had happened, Ethan had nearly forgotten the reason why he'd gone to the dragon in the first place. He nodded but kept quiet.

Drorm's mother stared at him expectantly for almost a minute before finally letting out an exasperated breath. "And?!"

"And the dragon has not been attacking you," he told her. "He's been attacking Doemenagg. Apparently, one of them somehow injured his mate and he was hunting them down wherever he found them."

Quest Complete.
   Fate of Excalibur - Part IV

Tell the shamans why Bal'Furtun has been attacking (1/1).
Reward: 3000 experience
You gain 3000 experience.
You gain +3 Fame.

"You are sure?" the shaman asked.

"That's what he told me," Ethan said. "And I believe him, given the things I saw."

Unandum cocked her head and was quiet for a long time. It was obvious she was replaying the attacks back in her mind. Finally, she shrugged. "I must think on this and tell the others. Your escort will meet you tomorrow morning to take you to the sword."

You have received a new quest "Fate of Excalibur - Part V"
You seek the legendary sword, Excalibur. After performing their task, the shamans have agreed to take you to the sword.
Follow the orcs to the sword. Try to pull the sword from the stone (0/1).
Reward: 1000 experience.
Accept quest (yes or no)?

Ethan accepted the quest. It appeared the orcs would keep their word after all. He grinned. "I appreciate that, can we go to the inn? I'm starving."

64

The next two days went by quickly and without incident. Unandum and another of the shamans, Senamm Stonelash, escorted them, along with twenty orc warriors. Ethan wasn't sure if he should be honored or concerned.

At the end of the first day, they turned towards the mountains. Late afternoon of the second day, they reached a pass between two mountains that led to a hidden valley with a collection of stone mausoleums.

Unandum called them to a stop and pointed down into the valley. "The sword is in the tomb below."

Ethan looked around the small valley and back at the pass they'd come through. "How did you find this place?"

Senamm scowled but Drorm's mother's eyes darted to Ethan chest, where the sigil was hidden by his shirt. She sighed. "When we had taken the city, shamans began taking this route to Bal'Furtun. A group of shamans on their way to the dragon found it when they were looking for shelter from a great storm."

Ethan raised an eyebrow. "A mana storm?"

"Mana storm?" Senamm asked and then cocked his head. "That is an apt name for them. Yes, they found it when searching for shelter from a... mana storm."

"This is the tomb of Lord Bryan DeMarcus. I recognize the crest on the doors," Guinevere said, riding up alongside him and pointing to the larger, central mausoleum.

Nodding, Ethan looked around the area again, then turned to Unandum. "Where are the guards?"

He expected that, like the small village near the dragon, they'd have some sort of guard post nearby. But despite a second look, he spotted no village or outpost.

Drorm's mother shrugged. "Its protection is its secrecy. No one knows its location except for us shamans and those who have been deemed worthy to try to pull the sword from the stone."

Ethan turned around in his saddle and looked back at their orc escort. He shot the shaman a confused look. "All the shamans and now these 20 orcs."

Unandum shook her head. "Our escort is made up of those who have been given the opportunity to draw the sword. They already knew of the place and are sworn to secrecy."

Ethan nodded. He already knew what lengths the shamans went to protect their secrets. They'd been ready to have Ethan killed. Chances are, any orc who mentioned the location of the sword met a similar fate.

Senamm barked some orders to their escort and the

orcs dismounted and began setting up camp. "We will go alone. The others can set up camp."

"I go where Ethan goes," Nia stated, having quietly brought her horse close to them.

The two shamans exchanged looks and then nodded. "You are high shaman, you have the power to grant an audience with the sword to whomever you wish. If you wish your wife to come, she can come."

"Good," Ethan said. He had been about to insist anyway, so this made things easier. He looked back at the rest of his group. "Anyone else want to come with us?"

"I told you before," Guinevere said with a shake of her head. "I tried pulling the sword out already. It didn't work. Seeing it again would... just bring back painful memories."

"I'd like it if you came," Ethan told the woman. "Just to verify that it is the right sword."

"Fine," she retorted.

"Par'karr want to see sword," his kobold companion squeaked.

"Me too," Michalus said, spurring his horse forward.

Ethan grinned as he looked at the wizard. "I thought you might."

"Drorm?" Ethan glanced at the big orc.

"I will stay here," he answered with a glance at his mother.

Ethan opened his mouth to ask why but a slight shake of the orc's head made him pause and close his mouth. For some reason, Drorm didn't want to go with them, that was obvious. Also obvious was that the orc didn't want to discuss it. At least, not right now - or in front of his mother.

"That's fine," Ethan told him. "You can help get the camp ready."

Drorm grunted his acknowledgement and then he began pulling his pack off his horse.

"I guess this is everyone," Ethan said as he turned back to Unandum.

Without a word, the orc shamans dismounted their horses and handed the reins to a waiting orc soldier. Drorm's mother motioned to him. "We go on foot from here."

With a shrug, Ethan dismounted and signaled for the others to do so as well. Once they handed their own reins to Drorm, he and his companions turned back to Senamm and Unandum.

Seeing them ready, the two shamans led them down the slope and through the small collection of stone structures until they stopped in front of the largest, central mausoleum.

The mausoleum was made completely from white marble and must have been an amazing work at one time. Unfortunately, it appeared time and the elements had taken their toll. The marble was chipped and any luster it once had was gone to years of exposure.

Despite that, Ethan saw the crest carved into the double doors. It was a shield with a dragon on half and what appeared to be a sun with sunbeams on the other half. If it had been painted, the paint had long since been wiped away.

Senamm and Unandum each took a door and, with a heave, pulled them open. As the doors swung outward, sunlight bathed the interior of the mausoleum.

Looking closely, Ethan saw two large sarcophagi in the large room that was revealed. Both were crafted from the same white marble, though both looked in much better shape than the exterior. They reminded him of Arthur's tomb and he wondered if that was simply the way the tombs were made back then.

But as striking as the sarcophagi were, they were not the thing that captured his attention. Between the two tombs was a large marble statue of a regal-looking man with a long, well-kept beard.

The statue was nearly as tall as the eight-foot ceiling and he struck an imposing figure, dressed in full plate mail armor. Having seen the carved relief of King Arthur's face, Ethan knew this was not him. It must be Lord Bryan.

"Ha!" Guinevere snorted beside him. "Lord Bryan never looked like that - not even in his prime."

In front of the man was a circular piece of granite laid onto the floor. The rougher granite was a sharp contrast to the marble used in the rest of the mausoleum. Sticking out of the granite was a long, silver sword that reflected the light as if it had just been polished.

Ethan had no doubt, this was Excalibur. This was the mythical sword that Arthur had carried into battle countless times. A blade that was a legend, even back on Earth. And now, it was right here - in front of him.

"It looks more... ordinary than I expected," Michalus said. "I expected something more... grand."

"It is a beautiful weapon," Nia breathed. "It was made for war, not for show."

Cocking his head, Ethan stared at the weapon and realized they were both right. In the movies, Excalibur was this gorgeous sword with an ornate hilt and cross-guard and sometimes even runes on the blade itself. This weapon had none of that. It was a plain, unassuming sword. Was this even Excalibur?

Glancing over at Guinevere, he raised an eyebrow. "Is that Excalibur?"

The warrior woman stared at the sword and nodded slowly, emotions playing across her face.

Ethan's feet seemed to move on their own accord as he began to walk to the sword. As he got closer, he noticed something he hadn't before. Embedded in the middle of the crossguard was a large gem.

He froze a few feet from the blade. Looking closer at the gem, he realized it wasn't a gem at all. It was a crystal. It was a large Chymera crystal. "Michalus! Look!"

Michalus moved forward and looked where Ethan was pointing.

"A Chymera crystal!" the wizard exclaimed. "Even larger than the one in the trident."

"Do you think it's the focus crystal for the sword's enchantment?" Ethan asked.

The wizard peered at the sword and then pointed to the pommel and the crossguard. "There are more - smaller but you can see how the light hits them."

Ethan moved a step closer and looked where Michalus had mentioned. Sure enough, there were lines of crystals on the crossguard. He reached out with his magical sense and felt the *Mana* in the crystals. Lots of *Mana*.

"Go ahead," Guinevere said from behind him. "Try to pull it out."

Ethan glanced behind him at the warrior woman and

then to Nia, who nodded. He felt the excitement and anticipation surge through him as he looked back at the sword.

He nodded and took a step closer to the sword. This was it. The moment of truth. He knew he had been secretly hoping he could pull the sword free and now he finally had the chance.

Reaching out gingerly, he grasped the smooth, cold grip of Excalibur. With all of his strength, he pulled.

The sword didn't even budge.

```
Quest Complete.
   Fate of Excalibur - Part IV
   Follow the orcs to the sword. Try
to pull the sword from the stone
(1/1).
   Reward: 1000 experience
   You gain 1000 experience.
   Congratulations!
   You have reached level 8.
   +1 Attribute Point.
   New        ability:        Greater
Specialization.
```

Ethan was so disappointed from not being able to pull the sword, that he barely even noticed the new level.

65

Ethan tried twice more but the sword didn't budge. He sighed in disappointment and backed away. He'd really felt like he would be able to free the sword. Apparently, not.

"Don't look so down," Guinevere said. "I'm his own daughter, and I couldn't pull it out."

"Go ahead and try," Ethan told the others. "Maybe one of you will be able to pull it free."

Par'karr hurried over and grinned up at Ethan. "Par'karr try. Give Ethan sword!"

The kobold hopped up on the granite and grabbed the sword. With a groan of exertion, Par'karr tried to pull the sword out of the stone. Nothing happened. After a minute of trying, the kobold hopped down.

He looked almost as disappointed as Ethan. Par'karr looked up at Ethan with tearful eyes. "Par'karr sorry. Par'karr not able to get sword."

Ethan smiled down at his friend and rubbed his scaly head. "It's okay, buddy. I couldn't do it either."

Michalus and Nia also tried with the same result. None of them had been able to budge the sword.

"Just like my dad. He loved his impossible puzzles." Guinevere snorted. She lowered her voice so she sounded like a man. "You must think like a wizard, my dear." The warrior woman shook her head. "He was such an arse."

Ethan cocked his head at Guinevere as her words played though his head. Merlin had told her to think like a wizard. Was that the way to pull the sword out? Think like a wizard? Was magic the key?

Turning back to the sword, Ethan channelled *Air*. He intended to grab the hilt with *Air* and pull it free but as soon as his magic touched the sword, it dissipated. He was reminded of Arthur's tomb and the stone around it. There was also Guinevere's armor. All had been enchanted somehow to repel magic.

Unandum chuckled, probably sensing his use of magic. "You don't think we didn't try that? Neither the sword nor the stone can be touched by magic."

Frowning, he tried *Air*, *Earth*, *Fire* and even *Water* but the magic just disappeared as soon as it touched either the granite or the sword. Finally, he gave up and backed away.

"Nice try," Guinevere muttered. "But it's like my armor. Magic doesn't work on it."

Ethan nodded. It was as he thought earlier. Merlin had probably used the same enchantment on her armor as he had used on the sword. And all magic just seemed to melt away from her armor.

He blinked. That wasn't exactly true. One type of magic had worked on it - or worked on Guinevere while she was wearing the armor! Excitedly, he stepped towards the sword and grasped the grip of Excalibur again.

> **You have received a new quest "Fate of Excalibur - Part VI"**
>
> **You seek the legendary sword, Excalibur. After listening to Guinevere, you believe the sword may only be able to be removed through magic.**
>
> **Use magic to remove the sword from the stone (0/1).**
>
> **Reward: 5000 experience, +10 Fame.**
>
> **Accept quest (yes or no)?**

"Trying again?" Nia asked with a raised eyebrow.

"If you don't do it the first time," Drorm's mother told him, "it doesn't work the other times either. Many orcs have tried."

The way he'd first learned Aether, or portal, magic was back in a little town on the way to the library of Daemonium. His towel had slipped off and he'd been so embarrassed, he'd somehow teleported from where he had been, into a nearby tub.

It had been the first time he'd used portal magic and he'd done it without using a portal. He'd simply... teleported to where he wanted to be. Could he do the same thing while holding Excalibur? If so, would the sword come with him?

He'd created portals before and even in her armor, Guinevere had been able to go through them. It was possible - just possible - that the sword might do the same thing. He might be able to teleport the sword out of the stone.

Focusing on a spot by the door, Ethan pushed *Mana* into himself and willed himself to teleport. He felt a resistance - like the sword didn't want to come along. He channeled more *Mana* into the spell, willing himself and the sword to be at the other spot.

He could feel a portal wanting to open in front of him but he didn't let it. Instead, he thought only of moving from where he was to where he wanted to be.

There was more resistance from the sword and then... a tearing sensation and it felt like he was being stretched in impossible ways. And then... poof! He was in the swirling rainbow tunnel that was the Bifrost.

Ethan was spiraling through the Bifrost. He looked at his hand to see that Excalibur was grasped firmly in his grip. He wanted to scream a victory cry but something weird happened with the sword.

It almost looked like mist was coming from the sides of the rainbow tunnel and gathering around the sword. Ethan watched, fascinated as the mist seemed to solidify into a shape. Then he gasped as he recognized the shape as a head - a human head - made of mist.

The head turned and seemed to look right through him. Then a ghostly wail issued from it. "Find me! Find me!"

Unsure how to respond, Ethan stared at the misty face

for a second before asking the obvious question. "Who are you?"

The mist began to dissipate, moving back towards the sides of the Bifrost. Just before the head disappeared completely, Ethan thought he heard the wailing voice. "Merlin..."

Pop! Ethan was suddenly back in the mausoleum, at the spot near the door he'd been focusing on. In his hand, free from the granite... was Excalibur.

Unable to focus on the sword at the moment, Ethan spun towards Guinevere. The warrior woman was gawking at him. Actually, everyone was staring at him.

Quest Complete.
Fate of Excalibur - Part VI
Use magic to remove the sword from the stone (1/1).
Reward: 5000 experience, +10 Fame.
You gain 5000 experience.
You gain +10 Fame.

Before any of them could say anything, Ethan looked into the warrior woman's eyes. "Guinevere! I think I just saw your father!"

Guinevere blinked. "You... what?"

"I think I just saw your father... in the Bifrost. He said to find him," he told her excitedly.

The former queen looked at him in disbelief. "But my father is dead."

You have received a new quest "Legacy of Merlin - Part I"

The legendary wizard, Merlin, has spoken to you in the Bifrost and asked you to find him.

Find out where Merlin is trapped (0/1).

Reward: 5000 experience, Unknown.

Accept quest (yes or no)?

"I think he's alive," Ethan said. "And I think he just asked for my help!"

Without hesitation, Ethan chose Yes.

EPILOGUE

Pain! The pain of her children assaulted the Queen on all sides. Her children were dying everywhere and her link with them was flooding her with pain.

It was dragons, she knew. Dragons who had come from the north, raining down fire and acid onto her drones on the surface, killing them by the dozens. Perhaps even the hundreds.

The Queen felt her anger rising. She had spent hundreds of years cultivating this hive. She'd stealthily been building up her forces into the massive army that it was. Years and years of abducting the humans, elves, orcs and others and implanting her eggs into their bodies to incubate. And now it was all coming crashing down!

The dragons were already digging down into the hive, using vast amounts of magic to uncover even more layers of her lair. They were systematically wiping out her entire brood and the Queen didn't even know why.

She'd known of the dragons during her last war. The Queen had sensed how powerful they were and went to great lengths to avoid them. And it had worked. During the last conflict, they hadn't come out of their lairs.

In fact, had it not been for the Merlin and the Arthur, she would now be ruling this world and her own world too. But no, the Arthur had killed her - killed her with that awful sword. She shuddered at the memory.

The entire hive shuddered as the dragons used more *Earth* magic to burrow deeper. They were close now, very close. Her minions were not strong enough to overcome the dragons. As much as she despised admitting it, she was not strong enough either.

The Queen cursed in her own language and cursed in the languages of men, orcs and the other races whose memories she had absorbed. She had to flee. She had to abandon her lair and the hundreds of years it had taken her to build all of it.

She looked around at the birthing chambers and the ambrosia stores that could accelerate the growth of her offspring. So much would be lost - but not her. No, she was too valuable. She had to escape.

With a mental command, she ordered her elite guard to prepare the escape passage. As her guard scrambled away to fulfill her commands, the Queen reached out to her other servants. She would need them to buy her time to escape.

With a thought, she ordered her remaining drones to an all-out assault on the dragons. She knew they had no chance. The dragons were much too powerful. But their deaths would buy her life. And after all, they existed only to serve her. What greater joy and satisfaction could they have than to die for her?

The remaining drones around her shuffled out of her chamber. She mentally blocked off the messages of pain that were coming from the hundreds dying by the dragon's magic. Her drones had their orders and they would die happily for her. There was no need to continue the communication and suffer their pain. It could be their own.

Taking a last look around her once-grand chamber, the Queen hurried after her guards. So much work. So much time. All lost.

Her thoughts went to the human she'd made mental contact with. The one who knew the secrets of the portals she desperately needed. The Queen had seen the other world he'd traveled to during their brief contact. She needed that knowledge. Needed it to return to her own world.

She had to find the human. Had to drain all of the knowledge from his primitive brain herself. Absorb it. Only then would she gain the knowledge that she needed.

The Queen stopped in her tracks as a wave of power rippled through her. Above, she felt the dragons pause as well. They'd felt it. Strong Aether magic. Very strong. Instinctively, the Queen knew where it had happened - to the north.

The human! It had to be the human wizard whose mind she touched! He must be powerful indeed if she felt the ripples of the portal this far south.

Feeling the dragons resume their attacks on the hive, the Queen knew she had to go. Time was short and her prey was near. She would have to personally find him and devour his brain. Yes. That's what she had to do.

She came to the entrance of the escape tunnel and paused. Her triangular head rotated to look back at her hive.

If the dragons got this far and found the escape tunnel, they might guess that she had escaped. She couldn't risk that. Ordering six of her eight guards into the tunnel, she faced the remaining two.

When we are gone, enter the tunnel and collapse it onto yourself, she told her guards.

Yes, my Queen, their voices echoed in her mind as the guards responded as one. They would do what they were bred to do - follow orders.

Without another thought for the drones or the guards she left behind, the Queen ducked into the escape tunnel and began racing down it. She wanted to be far, far away before the dragons found her chamber.

She followed the tunnel for nearly an hour before emerging several miles away. Twisting her head and focusing her bulbous eyes, the Queen looked south.

Circling what used to be her hive were two dragons, a red and a green. They rained down destruction on her once-great hive but paid no attention to her. Turning her head back around, she issued mental orders to her remaining guards.

As one, they all moved to the north, keeping under cover of the trees so the dragons didn't spot them.

Soon. Very soon, she would have what she wanted. She would have the human wizard and she would suck every succulent morsel of its brain out.

END

JOIN THE ADVENTURE

Thank you for reading this book! If you enjoyed it, please consider leaving a review on Amazon or tagging me on social media.
Tag me @authorjohncres1 on Twitter and @authorjohncressman on Facebook and Instagram!
Reviews help readers like you find this book. More readers means more sales, and more sales help independent authors like me to be able to write more books!
To learn more about the author and his other books and projects, visit the author's website at:
https://www.johnecressman.com
Or visit him on Facebook
https://www.facebook.com/authorjohncressman/

LITRPG

To learn more about LitRPG, talk to authors including myself, and just have an awesome time, please join the <u>LitRPG Group</u>.

MORE LITRPG

For more information on this book and other exciting LitRPG/GameLit books, please visit the following Facebook groups:
LitRPG Books
https://www.facebook.com/groups/LitRPG.books/

and

GameLit Society
https://www.facebook.com/groups/LitRPGsociety/

ACKNOWLEDGMENTS

I'd like to acknowledge all the members of the LitRPG Authors' Guild who helped me in so many ways! Without your help, I could never have gotten this far!

I also want to acknowledge the 20Booksto50K Facebook group! I've received lots of help and inspiration from them and I recommend the group to new and experienced authors.

Also, a big thank you for everyone who had bought one of my books. Your support really means a lot to me.

ABOUT THE AUTHOR

John E. Cressman is an author, magician, mentalist, hypnotist, programmer, and longtime lover of roleplaying games and fantasy/sci-fi books.

As a teen, he wasted long hours creating D&D fantasy campaigns for his friends to play. He has tried several pen and paper roleplaying games from the original Dungeons and Dragons, Traveler and Star Frontiers to the new Pathfinder games.

He still enjoys computer RPGs and MMORPGs, with his current favorite being Elder Scrolls Online. He used to play Skyrim, but then he took an arrow to the knee.